W9-AXZ-710

"I'm going up to check on Allie."

Earl nodded, a faint crease between his brows the only indication he thought Meg was behaving strangely.

All she was going to do was peek in on her daughter, she told herself. Why did she suddenly feel so frightened?

She opened Allie's door quietly and peered into the dimly lit room.

For an instant she couldn't make sense of what she saw; then she realized the bed was empty and unmade. Opening the door farther, she stepped in and turned on the light. No sign of Allie.

Troubled, Meg started to turn to leave, but then caught sight of a piece of paper on Allie's pillow. Her heart climbed into her throat, blocking it.

On legs that shook, she walked over and lifted the piece of paper in a trembling hand.

*Mom, I know I make everybody unhappy,
so I figured it would be better if I went away.*

RACHEL LEE

Snow in September

ISBN 1-55166-554-9

SNOW IN SEPTEMBER

Visit us at www.mirabooks.com

Printed in U.S.A.

To my daughters, Heather and Holly,
for all the lessons in motherhood.

1

The small brown spider dangled by a slender thread of silk, blowing around in the dry Colorado breeze.

Meg Williams watched it with great sympathy. She figured they were both being buffeted by the wild winds of life, clinging by a slender thread, and hoping against hope that eventually they would bump into something strong and solid. Something stable. Something to carry them out of the dangerous winds.

It was a dry, cool mountain morning, and Meg had slipped out onto the weathered deck with her morning coffee, needing a few moments of peace before she faced the day. Before she faced her mother and her daughter, both of whom had become major sources of misery in her life.

But, of course, if that was the sum total of her misery, she had little to complain about. Right? Right.

Sighing, she sipped her coffee and watched the spider lengthen its thread. Now the careless breeze carried the little creature within inches of the deck railing. She wondered if the spider could see how close it was to security, or if it was going to have to bang against the wood to know it was there.

From inside the house, she heard the clatter of the frying pan on the stove. Her mother was up and about now, starting breakfast. It would be the kind of breakfast Meg had grown up eating: eggs, bacon, toast. Too heavy and too fattening, but Vivian Clede clung to habits she'd learned as a child and young woman on the farm in Nebraska. She served enough calories to satisfy a ravenous field hand, then complained that Meg never ate enough.

Meg smothered another sigh, contemplating fried eggs and bacon. Her stomach rolled over, and she thought wistfully of a piece of fresh fruit or a bran muffin. But Allie, her teenage daughter, would devour a healthy serving, she reminded herself. Allie had a supercharged metabolism that allowed her to eat anything and still look coltish and too thin. So, long ago, had Meg.

At last the spider knocked against the railing and clung, its wild ride over. Now it would probably set about weaving a web under the railing to catch itself a juicy dinner. If it survived that long. Vivian was apt to be after the thing with a broom long before dinnertime.

Meg took another sip of her coffee and tried to rustle up the energy to go back inside and start the day. It was Saturday, a day she would have liked to spend doing something with her daughter. If matters ran true to form, however, Allie would be on her way out the door to see her friends as soon as the breakfast table was cleared, Vivian would start housecleaning, and Meg would make the weekly grocery-store run.

The monotony of routine had advantages, but sometimes the sheer emptiness of it made Meg want to cry.

The sliding glass door behind her opened. "Breakfast is ready," Vivian said in a disapproving tone that implied Meg was slothful for not cooking it herself. Not that Meg could have. From the instant Vivian had moved herself in with them, she had commandeered the kitchen. For a while Meg had tried to help out but had quickly learned that nothing she did was quite up to her mother's standards. Finally she had given up.

"Thanks, Mom," she said without turning around. "I'll be there in a minute."

"You'll come right now before your egg gets cold." The sliding glass door closed with an emphasis that was rather surprising, given its heaviness. Great, Vivian was in a mood.

For an instant—just a fierce, blinding, horrifying instant—Meg hated her husband for dying and leaving her with all this mess. At least when he'd been around Allie had behaved and Vivian had kept herself in Nebraska.

With a violent movement she emptied her coffee cup over the edge of the deck, startling a chipmunk.

"Sorry, guy," Meg said when the chipmunk stood up on its hind legs and scolded her. "I didn't see you."

She took a couple of deep breaths of fresh morning air, squared her shoulders and went inside.

She could hear Vivian yelling up the stairs for Allie to get out of bed now and come eat this instant. Saturday mornings. God, they were glorious.

She was refilling her coffee cup when her mother came back into the room.

"You've got to do something about that child," Vivian said sternly. "Staying up until all hours talking to people on the Internet..."

"It's a children's chat room, Mom. It's supervised by adults. She can't get into too much trouble."

"She's getting into enough trouble if she doesn't get her sleep. She's a growing girl."

"She's also fourteen, and I seem to remember wanting to stay up all night myself at that age."

"I never let you."

"No, you didn't." *But that didn't mean you were right.*

"You're letting her run wild, Meg."

"No, I'm letting her find herself. She hurts, Mom. Her dad died eight months ago."

"And you lost a husband and I lost a son-in-law. Allie doesn't have any corner on the market for pain."

Meg turned to look at her mother, feeling a roiling anger that she didn't dare express. Instead, she tried to find some feeling of affection for the woman who had raised her.

Vivian was short and stout, with iron-gray hair and a nose that was reaching downward for her chin. All Meg could manage to feel this morning was gratitude that she hadn't inherited her mother's nose. She had, unfortunately, inherited her tendency toward plumpness. Each day was a battle to keep herself in a size ten, a battle that Vivian wasn't helping with bacon, eggs, biscuits and fried chicken.

"Sit down and eat," Vivian said sharply. "Allie will just have to eat hers cold."

At least Vivian wasn't demanding she go upstairs and drag her daughter out of bed. Meg sat and ate her egg and one strip of bacon, all she could swallow. Then she leaned back in her chair, sipping her coffee and gazing at her mother. She was truly glad she didn't look like Vivian but instead resembled her father, with an upward cast to her features, and his honey-blond hair and green eyes.

Every line in Vivian's face headed downward, as if life had dragged her toward the floor. She was a miserable-looking woman, and had looked miserable since the death of Meg's father. These days Meg couldn't remember if her mother had been happy even when her father was alive. Nor did it really matter, she supposed. They were all unhappy right *now*.

"Do you have a shopping list for me?" Meg asked.

"It's on the refrigerator, like always."

Irritation surged in Meg, filling her mouth with bitterness. It took effort to reply calmly. "I meant to ask if the list is complete, Mom. Anything you want to add to it?"

"I write everything down the minute I think of it."

Of course. Vivian was always on top of everything.

"Are you going to get that girl up?" Vivian demanded.

"Let her sleep, Mom. If she's not up when I get back from the store, I'll wake her."

"You let that child get away with far too much, if you ask me."

Meg rose and carried her dishes to the sink, where she started rinsing them for the dishwasher.

"Are you listening to me, Margaret Mary?"

Margaret Mary, her full given name, always a signal of her mother's displeasure.

"I'm listening, Mom." She turned to face the older woman. "I hear you. I'm not answering because it's too damn early in the morning to have a fight."

"Don't you swear at me."

Meg put her dishes in the dishwasher, rattling them expressively. "I'm a grown woman. I'll talk how I choose and raise my daughter as I see fit, and if you don't like it, you can always go back to Monroe Corners."

"Is that the thanks I get for coming here to take care of you after Bill died? Is that the way you treat me—"

"Enough, Mother!"

The sudden silence crackled with tension. Aware that if she said another word she might create an unmendable rift, Meg grabbed the shopping list from the refrigerator door, got her purse from the hall table and headed for the front door.

She flung it open and found herself face-to-face with Sheriff Earl Sanders, her late husband's best friend, her daughter's godfather. His hand was raised as if he was about to knock.

The first thing she noticed was that he wasn't in uniform, and a burst of sudden relief left her almost weak. He hadn't come officially to give her some awful news. She never saw Earl, though, without remembering the night that he had come to tell her Bill was dead, killed in a car accident on a snowy mountain road. Some part of her wanted to scream, *I can't take any more!*

Grabbing the doorjamb for support, she battled for calm even as an uneasy concern over her own emotional state wound its icy way into her mind. She was dangerously overreacting, she realized.

"Are you okay, Meg?" Earl asked.

He had a deep voice that always reminded her of the lazy purr of a large cat, a tiger or a leopard. She had heard that voice crack like a whip when someone gave him a hard time, but for her there was always that lazy, soothing rumble. He was a little taller than average, with dark brown hair and brilliant blue eyes, and fit from his passion for running, hiking and skiing through these mountains. He and Bill had often gone on weekend hiking trips throughout the Colorado Rockies.

He wasn't wearing his uniform today, she reminded herself, seeking some balance on the emotional pinnacle where she was precariously perched. He was wearing jeans and a lightweight flannel shirt against the morning chill, and there was nothing in his square, bronzed face except genuine concern.

"I'm fine," she managed to say levelly. "It's been a stressful morning, that's all. How are you, Earl?"

"Been better, been worse," he said, a smile creasing the corners of his eyes. "*You're* looking pretty rocky, though."

His gaze raked her face, trying to read what lay behind what she hoped was a pleasant smile. "Mom and I were just quarreling," she offered, hoping he would believe it was all as simple as that.

He nodded, his face revealing nothing. "Looks like you're getting ready to go out. I just stopped by to see how you were doing."

As he'd done once a week since Bill's death. "Thanks. We're fine, really. Managing." Managing was the best she could say about anything since Bill was taken. For her, managing seemed liked a major moral triumph sometimes. She ought to invite Earl in, but she couldn't make herself do it, not with her mother in a mood. Earl didn't need to see just how ragged all the emotions around here were.

"Good. Good." He nodded again, looked away toward the quiet pine forest and the snowcapped peaks beyond. "I love September. Well, if there's nothing you need, maybe I can persuade you to join me for a cup of coffee."

Having coffee with him would give her an excuse to be away from the house longer, and this morning that was exactly what she needed. She felt as if she were drowning in her mother's moods and her daughter's anger. She felt as if every single minute of the day when she wasn't working she was dealing with Allie's or Vivian's current emotional crisis. Sometimes she wondered if she was ever going to get a minute to have a crisis of her own.

Self-pity, Meg. Cut it out.

"Sure, that'd be great," she said, her smile becoming more genuine with relief. "Let's go."

"My car?" he suggested as they descended the railroad-tie steps that Bill and he had put in eight years ago to replace crumbling concrete.

"I'd better take mine. I need to go grocery shopping."

"I can bring you back up here after you shop if you like."

It was a kind offer. It was also an offer that could

cause talk in the small mining town of Whisper Creek. It hadn't taken long for Meg to figure out that, as a widow, she was prey for every male who figured she must be lonely for a man in her bed. She had to take great care because she had a young daughter. On the other hand...

"It's okay, Meg," Earl said quietly. "Everybody knows I was Bill's best friend."

She looked at him, surprised that he understood so much.

He shrugged a shoulder. "I know people. I hear all the gossip. Hard for them to say anything if we have coffee in broad daylight and I get you and the groceries home by noon."

She almost laughed, but the urge felt so strange and uncomfortable that she didn't give in to it. God, when was the last time she had laughed? No wonder Allie was growing so difficult. Not only was she fourteen, but she was living with a mother who never smiled and a grandmother who complained endlessly, in a house that was shrouded in emotional gloom.

"Thanks," she said. For once she wouldn't have to be behind the wheel on the curve that had killed Bill last winter.

The sun was still September-warm, but as she stepped off the porch into the rutted dirt driveway, she felt the cool breath of the mountains as it rustled the pines and aspens, and goose bumps prickled her neck. Winter was right around the corner now, and she wondered if the return of snow and ice would renew her mourning. Somehow she didn't think the sight of the first snowfall was going to put her in the Christmas spirit the way it used to.

It was still early in the autumn, though, and the aspens hadn't begun to turn yet, except for an occasional leaf. For now she didn't have to worry about winter, and for now she refused to do so.

Earl handled his sport-utility vehicle with the ease of someone who'd been driving narrow, curving mountain roads all his life. Despite his confidence, Meg didn't start to relax until they had rounded the fatal curve.

"You thought about moving into town for the winter?" Earl asked.

She'd had to last winter, after Bill's accident. She had simply not been able to make herself drive on the snow and ice, past that curve. But after two months, she had forced herself to return to the mountain eyrie they had built with so many hopes and dreams. "No, I'm going to stay at the house. Last winter was...different."

"Yeah." He fell silent and stepped on the accelerator. From here on out it was straight and level, just a couple of miles up the broad valley. "Well, you know you can always call me if you need anything."

"Thanks, Earl."

Earl had been part of her life since she'd become engaged to Bill, a friend who was always there for both of them, a good buddy at all times. He'd helped build the house with his own two hands, working right alongside Bill and Meg, and he'd even taken care of Allie when they'd needed a baby-sitter. Always there. Always ready to help. Always Earl.

She glanced over at him now, wondering how he was dealing with Bill's loss, and feeling suddenly awful that she'd never asked him. But now wasn't the time. She had a feeling he would prefer it if she never asked him questions like that.

But he must be hurting, too. When had she become so utterly selfish?

She opened her mouth, about to apologize for her self-involvement, but Earl spoke first.

"Is your mother going back to Nebraska any time? Or is she here permanently?"

"It's beginning to look permanent." Nearly eight months seemed like it.

He nodded once. "How do you feel about that?"

"Like I might kill her before Thanksgiving?"

He laughed. The sound was almost explosive, as if it had come out of him without warning. "Bill always said she was a piece of work."

"That's putting it mildly. My fault, I guess. I've kind of abdicated, letting her run everything. Now I'm going to have to fight tooth and nail to get any autonomy back." She'd been thinking about that a lot the last week. Probably a sign of healing. Whatever it was, it was the primary reason she was so angry and irritable. Her life had gone to hell, and then she had spinelessly turned over the reins to her mother so she could crawl into a cocoon of hurt and guilt and ignore everything else. She was getting exactly what she deserved, and it didn't make her proud.

Earl took them to the Korner Kafe, a run-down diner famed for its coffee and down-home cooking. It was late enough that they missed the breakfast crowd, and early enough that the lunch crowd hadn't started to collect. The only other people there were two elderly men, the waitress and the cook. Earl offered to buy her breakfast, but she declined.

"I just ate, Earl. Orange juice for me." It was as close as she could get to fresh fruit at the diner. Vivian, she thought, would probably be welcomed as a cook here with open arms. "So how are *you* doing?" she asked him.

He shrugged. "Same old, same old."

She doubted that assessment was even remotely accurate. At the very least, he'd missed a half-dozen weekend trips he would have taken with Bill this past summer. "Did you find someone to go hiking with you?"

"No. Somehow I don't feel much like doing it anymore."

"Oh, Earl." A wave of sadness washed through her.

"Hey, it's no big deal. Probably wouldn't have done it anyway."

The "anyway" being if Bill hadn't died. The lines were painfully easy to read between. "I've been so selfish," she said. "Thinking only of myself since…since…" She couldn't even make herself say the words aloud.

"Perfectly natural, Meg. You lost a huge chunk of your life."

"So did you."

"It's not the same. Not the same at all."

No, she thought grimly. For him it was probably worse. Bill had been a part of Earl's *entire* life, not just the past fifteen years. They'd been closer than brothers.

"How's Allie doing?" he asked, neatly changing the subject.

"I don't know. She won't talk about it. For a while

she was so depressed it was like having a ghost in the house, but lately—lately she's been so angry it's like living with a volcano.''

"Probably a good sign."

"I hope so. She's spending a lot of time with her friends, and I guess that's a good thing. But I'm worried about the way she tries to avoid me and her grandmother." She gave a bitter little laugh. "Not that I can blame her. The two of us are always rubbing each other the wrong way."

"Maybe you'd better suggest to Vivian that she go home."

"Maybe." But that Herculean feat seemed beyond her. Danger lurked in the dark wells of memory, and there were a whole lot of ugly things she didn't want to dredge up. And Vivian undoubtedly *would* dredge them up.

"Well, it's not my place to be giving you advice," Earl said after a few moments.

"Why not? You've been a good friend for a long time." Which was the proper thing to say, but not at all what she was feeling. He didn't answer, and she sighed and looked out the window at the sun-drenched street. There was a special clarity to the light in the mountains, and she felt an old, familiar urge to get out her paints. But there was no place for that in her life anymore.

The worst part of being with Earl, she thought, was that she couldn't be honest with him. She couldn't tell him the truth about Bill, or about their marriage, or about what had happened that last day. She had to keep silent, because Earl thought the world of Bill, and she couldn't bear to disillusion him.

And with each passing week, their conversation had become more limited and more stilted, because she couldn't speak truthfully about anything she was feeling in her heart or thinking in her mind. She couldn't bear to show Earl the ugliness inside her.

Without Bill to bind them, the gulf between them was growing, and she had the feeling she was losing something irreplaceable with each lengthening silence between them. But Earl wasn't *her* friend, she reminded herself. He was Bill's friend. His friendship with Meg had been based entirely on the fact that Meg had married Bill. Hardly surprising that, without Bill, they were beginning to become strangers.

But Earl didn't seem to want that to happen. He kept stopping by and trying to draw her out of her shell. Maybe he thought he owed it to Bill.

Or maybe he was concerned about Allie. Earl had been a second father to that child. The thought of Allie caused her heart to accelerate suddenly.

Allie. She couldn't let this mess with her daughter continue. She had to break through the girl's barriers somehow and get her to talk about what she was feeling. Find a way to mend the rift that seemed to be growing rapidly as the rift between her and Earl. Maybe more rapidly. Not all of this could be because Allie was fourteen.

Earl was nearly done with his coffee, she saw, so she drained her orange juice. "I'm sorry, Earl, but I really need to get on the stick. I need to get home...." She trailed off, not wanting to admit that she was suddenly panicky about her daughter. It was as if some awareness at the back of her mind about the seriousness of Allie's emotional state had suddenly burst to the forefront. Guilt for her lack of attention nearly choked her.

"Sure," said Earl, standing and throwing some change onto the table. "Let's go."

Meg hurried through the supermarket, filling Vivian's list mechanically and as quickly as she could. She departed from it only long enough to pick up a bag of Gummi Bears for Allie, ordinarily forbidden for the sake of the child's teeth. Bill had forbidden them, along with chewing gum and a number of other things. But Meg wasn't Bill, and she didn't think one little bag of candy was going to cause any permanent harm.

But it *could* open up an avenue of communication with Allie, and she was suddenly desperate to do that. Whatever it took.

For some reason, she remembered Allie's face last night just before she went to bed, remembered the sad, angry, yet almost wistful look on her daughter's face. God, why hadn't she followed Allie to her room and insisted they talk right then?

Because she was too wrapped up in herself. Another wave of guilt rose in her, tasting sour in her mouth.

Earl drove her straight home, saying not one word about her odd behavior. Nor did he try to engage her in conversation. The gulf between them was now so wide that Meg had the feeling they could barely see each other across it. Another loss. She didn't think she could stand it. Some part of her had been counting on Earl to always be there for her the way he had always been there for Bill. Maybe she had counted on too much.

At the house he climbed out to help carry the groceries in. She almost told him she could manage by herself but bit back the words. Maybe part of the gulf between them had to do with her refusal to accept any help. Maybe he needed to do little things for her and Allie. Maybe it was part of his healing.

The house seemed quiet despite the sound of the vacuum. Vivian, who was cleaning the rug in the living room, stopped long enough to give Earl a chilly greeting.

"Is Allie up yet?" Meg asked her mother.

"No." Vivian's lips pursed disapprovingly. "She must have been up all night in that chat room. She hasn't stirred a muscle. But you said to let her sleep...." She shook her head and turned the vacuum on again, silencing further discussion.

Meg carried the groceries into the kitchen and dropped them on the counter. Earl put his bags beside hers. She started to empty them, to put them away, but stopped.

"I'm going up to check on Allie," she said.

Earl nodded, a faint crease between his eyebrows the only indication he thought she was behaving strangely.

Meg stood at the foot of the stairs for a minute, looking up the polished redwood risers, hesitating. All she was going to do was peek in on her daughter, she told herself. Why did she suddenly feel so frightened?

Her legs felt like lead as she climbed the stairs. Behind her she heard the ceaseless groan of the vacuum, fading away as she rounded the corner into the hallway that led to Allie's room.

She opened the door quietly, in case Allie was still asleep, and peered into the dimly lit room.

For an instant she couldn't make sense of what she saw; then she realized the bed was empty and unmade. Opening the door farther, she stepped in and turned on the light. No sign of Allie.

She must have left early this morning, Meg thought, and hiked over to Kate Exline's place. The two of them were nearly inseparable. But why hadn't she so much as said goodbye or let anyone know where she was going?

Troubled, Meg started to turn to leave, but then caught sight of a piece of paper on Allie's pillow. Her heart climbed into her throat, blocking it.

On legs that shook, she walked over and lifted the piece of paper in a trembling hand:

Mom, I know I make everybody unhappy, so
I figured it would be better if I went away.

2

"She ran away." The words had to force themselves past a tongue that felt thick. Meg looked at Earl, standing frozen by the front door, as if he had merely been waiting to say his goodbye. At her mother, who stood like a statue, her hand gripping the vacuum-cleaner cord she'd been putting away.

The silence that answered her was profound, as profound as the silence that had fallen after Earl told her Bill was dead, as profound as the silence when Dr. Helm had pronounced her father dead. In such silences, death lurked.

Into the silence came a rustling, rattling sound. Meg looked down and saw that the paper she held was shaking like a leaf in a hurricane. "She ran away," she said again, feeling the funeral knell in her heart.

Earl crossed the foyer and took the paper from her quaking hand. "She probably went to a friend," he said. His voice no longer held that lazy purr he reserved for Meg. It had become firm, businesslike. Coplike.

Meg's legs gave way, and she sank onto the steps, gripping the banister as if it were a lifeline. "God..." It came out a whisper. "Not my baby...."

"I told you that girl was running wild," Vivian said. "I warned you you were giving her too much freedom."

Meg couldn't respond. She didn't care. All she could think of was Allie.

"That's not going to help anything, Vivian," Earl said flatly. "It's not unusual for kids this age to run away. The smart ones go stay with a friend. Meg? Meg, look at me."

She lifted her head, a head that felt as if it weighed a ton, and looked at him, listening to the ache in her heart that told her this was all her fault for being so selfish and self-absorbed.

"Meg, I'm going to need a list of Allie's friends. Can you do that for me?"

"Yes. Yes." The strength rushed back into her body as quickly as it had deserted it. "I can call them. I have their numbers."

"Let me do it," he said. "While I make these calls, I want you to think of anyplace else she might have gone. Friends who aren't so close. Places she might try to hide for a while. How much money did she have? Think about these things for me, Meggie."

She nodded and pushed herself up from the step. Without a glance at her mother, she went to the study to get the list of Allie's friends' phone numbers, a list she had gathered over the years because, in theory, Allie never went anywhere without leaving a number where she could be reached. There were nineteen names on the list.

Earl took it, sat down at the desk and reached for the phone. Meg expected him to call his office first, to tell his deputies to look for Allie, but he didn't. He called Kate Exline's parents.

She wasn't there. Call after call produced the same results, and Meg began to pace the study frantically, unable to hold still while her mind scrambled around trying to find some escape. She tried to think about the things Earl had asked her to consider, but her mind balked, refusing to focus on anything except the sound of Earl's voice as he spoke on the phone. Each time he dialed another number, painful hope gripped her. Each time he hung up, despair nearly drowned her.

Allie had run away. Her mind refused to accept it, but the alternatives were even worse.

Finally Earl reached the end of the list. Silence filled the study, broken only by the soft sound of Meg's rapid footfalls on the carpet as she paced.

"Oh, God," she whispered. "Oh, God, Allie..."

"No one's seen her today," Earl said. "They're going to ask their kids if Allie mentioned anything about going anywhere. Meg...Meg, when was the last time you saw her?"

Her heart squeezed until it hurt. "Last night," she said hoarsely. "Last night around ten. She said she was going to bed...."

"And you believed her," Vivian said harshly from the doorway. "You knew she was going to get on the Internet again. She probably ran off with some pervert—"

"Vivian," Earl said, "that's not helping. We need to think about ways to find Allie. Making accusations isn't going to get her home any sooner.'' He softened his words with a smile, as if he didn't want to alienate Vivian. ''Listen, I could really do with a cup of coffee. Is there some made?''

''I'll make it,'' Vivian said. With a disapproving shake of her head, she left.

Earl turned his attention back to Meg. ''Can you log on to Allie's computer and read her e-mail?''

She nodded, her heart skipping a beat. ''But I never do that. It would be...'' A betrayal? Could she really be thinking that *now?* Under these circumstances? Everything else was turned on its ear. Why not this? ''I'll go do it.''

He followed her, and Meg couldn't escape the feeling that this was a double betrayal of Allie. She would be justifiably furious to know that her mother had read her mail, and even more so when she learned that Earl had read it, too.

If Allie ever came home.

She drew a breath that sounded like a sob and climbed the stairs again. It was all Bill's fault, she found herself thinking. If he hadn't died... *No!* She couldn't allow herself to think that way. Bill's death had been an accident. And Allie hadn't run away because of it. She'd run away because her mother had abandoned her emotionally. Blame rested squarely on Meg's own shoulders and no one else's.

Allie's room looked empty in a way it never had before, as if by running away she had taken away some ineffable essence of herself. The computer whirred as it came on, beeping as usual, but it sounded somehow different this time.

Feeling like a trespasser, Meg sat in her daughter's

chair and clicked on the Internet icon. Moments later, Allie's mailbox was open to her. It was empty. She checked the Trash folder and found it, too, was empty.

"Nothing," she said to Earl, her voice breaking. She couldn't decide whether this was good or bad. It was simply another straw torn out of her grasp.

"Check her address book," Earl suggested. "See if she's got any e-mail addresses in there."

There were dozens of them, all identified by first names and screen names only. No help.

"E-mail them all," Earl said. "Ask them if Allie said anything to them about leaving home. I'll be downstairs."

Meg sat staring at the addresses for several minutes, unable to make herself do as he had asked. What if one of those names, looking so innocent on the screen right now, was the name of some pedophile who had lured her daughter away? He wouldn't answer an e-mail. Or, if he did, he would claim to know nothing. Nor was there any reason to assume that any of these children would answer her. They might feel they needed to protect Allie.

It was only another slender straw, and it offered little hope. But she clutched at it anyway, sending the same message to all those inscrutable names.

This is Allie's mom. She ran away from home early this morning. Did she say anything to you about it? I'm so worried. Please help me find her.

Downstairs, Earl went to the kitchen to get a cup of coffee from Vivian.

"Aren't you going to have your deputies look for Allie?" Vivian demanded.

Earl wasn't very fond of Meg's mother. A lot of that attitude probably came from Bill, who hadn't liked the woman at all. But a lot of it came from what he'd seen of her over the past eight months. Vivian Clede was a sour, bitter, unhappy and extremely critical woman.

"Not if I can avoid it," he told her. "It would be better for both Allie and Meg if we can keep this quiet."

Vivian's frown deepened. "Keeping it quiet is the last thing anyone should worry about right now! That child could be in serious trouble."

"Yes, she could be," Earl agreed. "But she probably isn't. She ran away, Vivian. She wasn't kidnapped. Now, I want you to go up to her room and see exactly what she took with her. You and Meg both. I want to know exactly what's missing."

With Vivian off his back, he went into the study again, closed the door and locked it. This time he called the sheriff's office and asked to be put through to Lydia Valdez, the juvenile officer. His palms were damp, he realized, and his heart was hammering like a horse's at the end of a stiff quarter-mile race.

"Lydia, it's Earl. We got a problem."

"Shoot," Lydia said.

"Allie Williams ran away sometime after 10:00 p.m. last night. She left a note saying she was going away because she makes everyone unhappy."

"Hell."

"Yeah. Right now what I've got is that none of her friends have seen her, and she wiped all the e-mail off her computer. Does that sound suicidal to you?''

"Did she give anything away to anyone?''

"I don't know yet. I'm going to give you the names and numbers of all her friends. I can't call and ask from here. I don't want Mrs. Williams to hear me.''

"Got you. The e-mail being erased doesn't sound good, but it might just be an attempt to cover her tracks. But I wouldn't treat it as an ordinary runaway, boss. I'd call out the dogs.''

"That's what I figured.'' He battled a rising sense of panic, reminding himself that he would do no good for Allie or Meg if he stopped thinking clearly. "Okay, I'll fax the phone numbers over to you. Get on it right away. Get help if you need it. I'm going to see if the mother and grandmother can figure out what's missing from the girl's room.''

"I'd check her computer for a journal, too. A lot of kids keep their diaries there these days.''

"Good thinking. The fax is on its way.''

When he hung up, he wasn't feeling any better. He slipped the sheet of paper on which Meg kept track of Allie's friends into the fax machine beside the desk and watched it feed its slow way through.

At this point he didn't know if he would have felt any better if they'd found a bunch of e-mail on Allie's computer. The girl might just be compulsively neat about such things. He had a habit of deleting all his e-mail at work as soon as he'd replied to it, unless there was a good reason to hang on to it. But there was something about the emptiness of her e-mail folder, and the emptiness of the Trash folder where deleted messages were sent until deleted a second time, that disturbed him. Too neat. Allie was leaving no traces.

The fax machine beeped, signaling that the transmission was complete. He removed the paper from it and put it back on the desk so Meg wouldn't know what he had just done.

God, this was a nightmare. He couldn't have loved Allie more if she were his own daughter. The possibility that she might have attempted suicide, or that she might be wandering out there all alone and unprotected, was almost more than he could bear.

But he couldn't afford to indulge his feelings right now. Right now the situation needed him to be a cop. Finding a ledge of calm within himself, he planted both mental feet firmly on it and refused to look over the edge into the abyss below.

Upstairs, he found the women were at opposite sides of Allie's bedroom, going through the girl's things. He stood in the doorway for a moment, watching them, wondering if the hostility that crackled between the two was what had driven Allie away. Kids had a tendency to see themselves as the center of the universe and to interpret adults' behavior in relation to themselves. Had Allie thought she was responsible for this anger?

"Find anything missing?" he asked.

"Some clothes," Meg said, her voice stretched tight. "She took clothes with her."

"That's good."

They both looked at him as if he was crazy, but he didn't explain. He didn't want to mention suicide to them. In his heart, however, relief was heavy. If she had taken clothes, she probably didn't intend to kill herself. Unless she had given the clothes away?

"What clothes are missing?"

"Her jacket," Meg said.

Hope died. Even a suicidal girl would want a jacket against the coolness of the mountain night air. "Anything else?"

"I'm not sure!" Meg said. "She does her own laundry and buys a lot of her own clothes with her allowance. I don't know how many pairs of jeans she has, or... I think her pink sweater is missing. And maybe one of her flannel shirts. I'll have to check the hamper...." Meg trailed off and dashed a hand over her eyes. "I can't be sure," she said hoarsely. "I can't be sure."

He nodded. "It's okay, Meg." He figured she was too upset to be thinking clearly right now.

"It's not okay! I ought to know what clothes my daughter has! What kind of mother am I?"

He wanted to reach out to her and offer comfort, but checked himself. Vivian was right there, and God knew what she would make of a simple hug. "It's okay," he said again. "If I asked you to make a list of everything in your own closet, could you?"

"I..." She shook her head. "I guess not."

"Neither could I. We know she took a jackct and maybe a sweater. That's good. What about underwear?" He needed some indication, *any* indication, that Allie intended to make a trip.

Meg shook her head. "She bought herself all kinds of underwear. She liked pretty things. She must have dozens of bras and panties that I wouldn't even recognize."

"So she has a lot of money?"

"She gets an allowance and makes extra by baby-sitting on weekends."

"Do you have any idea how much money she might have had with her?"

Meg stared hollowly at the floor. "Maybe two hundred dollars. She was saving for a leather jacket."

Two hundred dollars widened the search considerably, he thought unhappily. That was a bus ticket to Denver or beyond, and money for food for a few days. "Okay. I have to make a phone call. What I primarily need to know is if any of her favorite things are missing. Keep looking."

Vivian hardly spared him a glance as she worked her way through Allie's closet.

"Maybe she kept a diary on her computer," he suggested, before he turned away. "Check for that, Meg, okay?"

As he left, he saw her turn numbly to the computer.

Downstairs in the study he called the bus station. It was a small town, and it was rare when more than a half-dozen people caught any bus leaving from here. In just a few minutes he learned that none of the buses departing this morning had carried a girl matching Allie's description. That could be good news or bad, depending on how he viewed it. She could have thumbed a ride. Or she could have killed herself.

He had seen Allie just a week ago, and now, in hindsight, he tried to recall if there had been some warning sign that he had missed. She had seemed subdued, but she'd been subdued since her father's death. He was hurt to think that she hadn't confided in him if she was feeling this bad. But Allie had always been a reserved child, even as a tot. He had always had to ask her to share her thoughts and feelings, but even when asked, she rarely said much.

No, he hadn't noticed anything unusual about her last weekend. And maybe that was the problem. Maybe they'd all been wrong to ascribe her moodiness to Bill's death. Apparently something else had been going on in Allie's life, concealed by the camouflage of mourning.

He just hoped it hadn't driven her to do the unthinkable.

And he couldn't wait any longer. A glance at the clock told him it was after two. Soon the sun would pass behind the mountains, flattening the light and making it more difficult to search. By eight the impenetrable night would have fully settled in.

Reaching for the phone, he put the wheels in motion.

The command-post van was parked out front; the dogs were scouring the surrounding area looking for some scent of Allie. It wasn't easy—the girl's scent seemed to be everywhere. His deputies were searching for tracks on the ground and in the brush that might indicate what direction she'd taken off in. And slowly but surely, local people were gathering, wanting to help with the search.

When Lydia Valdez called Earl, though, she called on the house phone. He took the call in the study, closing the door behind him.

"I didn't want to put it on the radio," she told him. "Anyone could hear, and they still don't have the phones operating in the mobile command post."

"That's okay. We've got permission to use the home phones. They've got three lines, so let me give you the numbers in case this one is busy." He rattled them off, reading them from the multiline phone in front of him. "Now, what have you got for me?"

"She gave away her Spice Girls CDs to Julie Armistead and her rock collection to Sandy Miller." Lydia Valdez's voice was somber.

Earl's hand tightened on the phone. "Rock collection?"

"Yeah, apparently Allie Williams was a junior geologist or something. A regular rockhound, according to Sandy, at least until her father died. That's all I've managed to find out so far. Julie said she thought Allie was acting funny, but was just in some kind of mood, so she accepted the CDs and plans to give them back to Allie. Sandy thought Allie had just gotten bored with the rocks. According to her, boys are more interesting now, but apparently Sandy used to share Allie's interest in geology. All the other girls we spoke to say they didn't notice anything unusual, that Allie's been depressed since her dad died."

Earl's heart sank straight to the toes of his boots. "I don't like this."

"Me neither," Lydia agreed. "You find out any more?"

"She didn't take her bike, so she could have struck out in any direction. We're still trying to find some trace."

"I'm running out of ideas, boss."

He didn't want to admit that he was, too. He glanced toward the window and saw that the sun had passed behind the mountains. The light was dimmer now, and shadows had virtually vanished. With the sun gone behind the peaks, the temperature would be beginning its inexorable drop into the upper thirties later tonight. He didn't want to think about what that could mean for a girl with nothing but a jacket to protect her.

"Keep me posted," he said to Lydia.

"The same here."

He hung up the phone and felt helplessness wash over him in an overpowering wave. At his fingertips he had every possible resource of law enforcement, and none of it was going to do a damn bit of good for a little girl out there in the cold. God, he hoped she had found some safe shelter.

With little else to do, he decided to go back outside and check on the searchers.

But just as he rose from the desk, the study door burst open and Meg came running in, looking almost wild.

"I found something!" she said almost breathlessly. "I found something. She went to the attic and took some of the camping gear, Earl! She took a sleeping bag, a backpack and the little kerosene stove Bill got for hiking. And her hiking boots are gone!"

"Check the kitchen and see if she took any food."

Hope, he thought as he followed Meg to the kitchen, was almost as painful as despair. Allie probably hadn't taken these things if she meant to meet some pedophile, who was more likely to want to meet in the comfort of a motel. And she wouldn't have taken camping supplies if she meant to kill herself, would she? But why had she given her possessions away? Because she really intended to never come home? What was she thinking? And why?

He had seen the light of relief in Meg's eyes, though. Apparently she, too, had thought Allie was considering suicide. He didn't want to tell her that taking a few camping supplies might only mean that Allie wanted a little time to herself before she took the final step. Or that she only wanted to get far away before she did it. And he would never mention just how dangerous these mountains could be at any time of year for a hiker alone, even an experienced one.

Vivian had staked out the kitchen, making coffee and sandwiches for the people who were searching for some sign of Allie's passage. Her frown as they entered the room was a clear signal she didn't like their invasion, but Meg didn't even seem to see her.

Meg headed directly for the pantry. "We still have Bill's freeze-dried food for camping, don't we, Mom?"

"No."

Meg froze halfway to the pantry. After a moment, she turned to face her mother, the expression on her face cold as stone. "No? Why not? I told you that stuff keeps for ages and we might need it during a blizzard."

"I was going to replace it. Some of it was getting near its expiration, and Allie wanted things for a food drive at school, so I gave it to her."

Meg's mouth opened, then closed sharply. Earl hesitated to intervene, but he had a feeling that Meg was close to an explosion of volcanic proportions, one that might rupture her relationship with her mother forever. Neither woman needed that, especially not now, with Allie missing.

"When was this, Vivian?" he asked, stepping between her and Meg. "How long ago?"

Vivian shrugged. "A week. Two maybe. I don't exactly remember."

Meg's gaze leaped to Earl. He could feel its stinging hope.

"It's no big deal," Vivian said truculently. "She took some other stuff, too. Peanut butter, some canned food. We won't get a blizzard for at least another month. Plenty of time to replace it."

Earl nodded, glanced at Meg, then went to the wall phone beside the refrigerator. Lydia Valdez answered on the first ring. "Lydia, I need to know if there's been a food drive at the school in the last few weeks. I don't care if it's Saturday. Call the principal."

He hung up.

"She may have planned this for a while," Meg said from behind him. She sounded almost dazed, and ready to shatter. "She planned this!"

"We don't know that yet," he said without turning to look at her. All of a sudden he had the worst urge to turn Allie Williams over his knee and give her a spanking she would never forget. The urge shocked him, because he would never, ever, lay a finger on her or any other child. But right now, he could have whaled the tar out of her like his dad used to do to him.

"Why didn't she just talk to me?" Meg asked, her voice low and anguished. "Why didn't she just talk to me?"

For once Vivian didn't say a word.

Earl felt his heart breaking for Meg and for Allie. He loved them both, and they'd had more than their share of troubles this past year. God, he asked silently, why do you do this to people?

But God didn't answer, and Meg was standing behind him on the edge of despair. He made himself turn and look at her, made himself ignore the way his heart squeezed with pain for her.

"This is good," he said.

"Good? How can anything be good? My little girl is all alone out there in the mountains! It's getting colder by the minute, she could be hurt or frightened—" Her voice broke, and two huge tears rolled down her cheeks.

"She just wants attention," Vivian said. "Girls that age just want attention. Well, she's got it, and I hope she's enjoying it."

"Mother, will you just shut up!" Meg almost screamed the words, then ran from the room. Moments later, Earl heard a door slam somewhere in the house.

He looked at Vivian. "Mrs. Clede," he said coldly, "if you don't have something helpful to offer, I suggest you keep your damn mouth shut."

Vivian drew back. "Don't you dare talk to me that way, you…you…guttersnipe! Oh, I heard all about you from Bill. Nothing good can come out of an alcoholic and a whore."

Another man might have wanted to hit her, but not Earl. He'd been hearing these insults since long before he was old enough to understand what they meant. Despite where he'd come from, he'd made something of himself.

But he wondered how the hell Meg had managed to avoid killing this woman for the last eight months.

Another man might have said something cutting with words—God knew, the opportunity was staring him in the face—but he'd learned to keep silent a long time ago. He gave her one last look, and turned on his heel.

He had more important things to worry about.

Outside, the gathering had grown. Men had gotten off work at the mine and were beginning to show up, armed with flashlights, wrapped in jackets that would keep them warm later. The cooling air snaked through the weave of Earl's flannel shirt, but he hardly noticed it. He looked around at the faces that were waiting only for directions to begin combing the mountainsides.

Bill had been a manager at the mine, and these men had liked him. He'd stood up for them during a labor dispute a few years ago, and had kept management from shutting down the mine to break the back of the union. At the time Earl had thought Bill was committing career suicide, but he'd admired him for his stand. Nor had Bill's career seemed to suffer after the conflict was all over.

He had to say something to these men. They were all looking at him expectantly. He cleared his throat.

"Thanks for coming," he said. "We still don't know what direction she took off in, but we *do* know that she took camping gear with her. That means that if she doesn't get into trouble, she ought to make it through tonight okay."

A murmur passed through the gathered group, heads nodded.

"Maybe she went up to Caprock, Earl," one of the men said. "Bill used to hike up there with her all the time."

Earl hadn't known that, and he wondered why Bill had never mentioned it. "Good idea, Hal." He glanced at his watch. Four-fifteen. "Why don't a few of you head up that way? I'll get one of the dog handlers to go with you. It's three hours till sunset, so don't dawdle. I don't need to be looking for all of you."

There were some subdued chuckles, some uneasy glances, as if they felt awkward about laughing in these circumstances. Earl was a great believer in humor, especially black humor. He'd been a cop too long not to appreciate its usefulness.

Carl Rios brought one of the dogs back, and he and three of the miners set out in the direction of Caprock. If they moved steadily, they ought to get there in an hour. Earl felt a painful twinge of hope that Allie had gone to a place where she had spent time alone with her father. It would make sense, a lot of sense. *God, please let it be.*

Then he saw Matt Dawson hovering in the background, standing alone by a pine tree, his hands thrust into his pockets, his mouth set in its usual angry line.

Earl had mixed feelings about the sixteen-year-old. On the one hand, he'd come from the same kind of background himself, so he knew not to condemn the boy simply because his parents were trash. On the other, he recognized a troublemaker when he saw one. Matt was not only angry, he had a tendency to lash out. So far, other than some fighting, Matt had stayed out of serious trouble, but Earl had a feeling that could change at any moment.

But the boy might know something about Allie. They weren't all that far apart in age.

He walked over to the kid, nodded to him. "Matt. Why are you here?"

"I heard about Allie. I want to help with the search."

Earl nodded again. "You know her?"

"Nah. But I seen her around at school."

"You have any idea why she might have run away?"

Matt shook his head, his scowl deepening. "I never talked to her or anything. Why? You think I had something to do with it?"

That two-by-four on Matt's shoulder was going to make his life awfully difficult, Earl thought, stifling a sigh. "No. I'm just asking everybody if they heard anything at all. Anything that might help."

He looked at the boy again and saw a fresh bruise on his chin. "Somebody hit you?"

Matt shrugged. So, thought Earl, the kid's dad had been at him again. But Matt would never say so, and the rest of the world could only wonder about it until he did. "You know, Matt, if you ever want to tell me who keeps beating you up, I'll put his ass in jail for a long time."

Matt shrugged again, as if it didn't matter.

"Up to you. Well, listen, if you hear anything at all from anywhere about Allie, be sure you tell me, okay?"

"Sure. No kid ought to be out in these mountains alone."

He sounded so old sometimes, Earl thought. So very old. "Exactly. Thanks for coming."

Matt gave a jerky nod, as if it felt uncomfortable. He was probably more accustomed to shaking his head.

Earl walked away, looking up at the mountain that rose behind the Williams house, at the deepening darkness beneath the stands of fir and aspen, and started praying as hard as he'd ever prayed in his life.

3

Night was creeping up from the valley and out from beneath the trees, swallowing the last of the twilight glow. Earl felt it creeping into his bones, a cold dread that wouldn't let go.

He stood outside, waiting for the last of the searchers to return, unwilling to yield another soul to the dangerous whim of the mountains. Until the last man was back, he couldn't be sure that Allie's actions hadn't cost another life.

As they came back in, in twos and threes, the men looked dejected, but they hung around, reluctant to return to their homes until the last searcher returned and they could know whether the child was found. Meg, on the edge of hysteria, had still managed to dig out a forty-cup electric coffee urn and had set it on the porch with every mug and cup she had. Vivian made sandwiches and brought them out, until she had no bread left. The searchers were glad of the coffee, but no one seemed to want to eat, as if eating while the child was lost was somehow obscene.

Earl told them to eat, made it an order, reminded

them that they would be no good to anyone if they grew fatigued and cold. But never in all his life had he seen food disappear in a deeper silence. When anyone spoke, it was in the hushed tones of a funeral home.

Finally the last man was back. The group grew even more silent, and every eye fixed on Earl, as if he might have some idea how they could continue in the dark. But Earl knew the mountains too well and would brook no such foolishness. Life was hard enough in a mining town without someone breaking his neck in a night search. But even as he did the right thing, he hated himself for it, hated himself for the human limitations that meant a child would spend the night alone on the side of the unforgiving mountain.

"Go home," he said. "We'll start again in the morning, those of you who can come. At first light." It would be Sunday morning, and he had a feeling that most of them would be here, as well as some who were working the night shift at the mine right now. No one worked on Sunday.

Still they didn't move, and he realized he had to offer them some hope to take home with them and carry them through the chilly night. "Allie took camping supplies with her," he said. "She took a sleeping bag, a stove and food. The principal called earlier to say there was no food drive, so Allie must have taken the supplies for herself. She'll make it through the night."

One of the men spoke. "She went camping a lot with Bill. She knows how to take care of herself."

"That's right," Earl agreed. "She can make it tonight. And maybe a few more nights."

The oppression lifted, just a little, and the searchers straggled away to the cars that were parked all along the driveway and down the rutted road. One by one the cars roared to life, turned and directed the beams of their headlights down toward the valley. Finally the last of them was gone.

It was a moonless night, and the starshine was cold and weak, swallowed by the dark earth and the trees. A wind blew, moaning softly through the trees, but no other sound disturbed the silence. Earl thought of a fourteen-year-old girl up there in the mountains somewhere, all by herself, and wondered if the wind was unnerving her, and if the night seemed all the darker because she was alone. Then he had an idea.

As he passed the coffee urn, he reached over to pull the plug. Then, bypassing the front door and everything that lay inside the house, he went to the command post and stepped into the trailer. The two men there were packing up and getting ready to leave for the night.

"Get me a plane," he said without preamble. "A plane or a helicopter."

"How come?" asked George Murphy, his newest deputy. George had been a cop in Denver for a couple of years before he'd bailed out on city life and moved to Whisper Creek for the peace and quiet. So far, he hadn't gotten much of either.

"If she built a fire to keep warm, we'll be able to see it now that it's dark."

Midget Baldridge—known as Midget because he was the shortest guy on the force, maybe even the shortest guy in town—immediately picked up the phone and dialed. "How many planes you want?"

"How far can a fourteen-year-old girl walk in twelve or thirteen hours, and how many planes can we fit in that area without colliding?"

"I'll find out." Midget was a good cop as long as he didn't let his Napoleon complex get the upper hand. Earl often had to keep an eye on him.

Twenty minutes later, two rescue planes were in the air, flying a search grid centered over the Williams house. Midget volunteered to stay and keep in touch with the planes. Only then did Earl feel he could go inside and face Meg.

This wasn't the first time he had faced this. He'd lost count of the times over the last fifteen years that he'd had to mount a search party for a lost hiker, or for a plane that had gone down. He'd lost count of the times he'd had to look at worried friends or family and say they'd found nothing. But this time was different. This time it was the daughter of his heart who was out there alone on those rocky crags. This time it was his own dear friend he had to give the bad news to.

Vivian opened the front door just as he reached it. Her eyes lifted to his instantly, and he saw something wink out in them. As if they had gone dead. He felt a sudden surge of sympathy for her, but she didn't give him a chance to express it.

"Ate me out of house and home," she grumped, pushing past him to go collect the dishes.

"Let me help with that."

Then she said something unexpectedly generous.

"You go talk to Meg," she said. "Last thing she needs right now is to be alone. I'll deal with this."

"Sure I can't do anything?"

"Well, you could pick up some things at the market before you get started in the morning. These men are going to be hungry, and they about cleaned me out already."

"I'll take care of it."

Then there was no further excuse to avoid facing Meg. All his life, when he hurt, he wanted to be alone, and that was what he wanted right then. It didn't make him the best person to deal with people who needed support and comfort rather than solitude. Feeling utterly inadequate, he went inside.

The house was silent. Empty. He sensed that Meg was there somewhere, but he couldn't hear her. The downstairs rooms were empty, and dark except for the kitchen. On feet that felt like lead, he began to climb the stairs, following his instinct.

He was right. Meg was sitting on the edge of Allie's bed, holding her daughter's pillow tightly, as if she were trying to hug it to death. When he stepped into the room, she didn't even glance up.

But she knew he was there. "She's out there all alone," she said, her voice thick and flat.

"I know." He pulled the desk chair across the room until he could sit facing Meg. "I've got a couple of search planes up. If she lit a fire, they might see it."

For an instant a painful hope invaded Meg's face, then slipped away. "She won't. She doesn't want to be found."

"She might not think about that, Meg. It's cold out there."

"I know...." Her voice grew ragged. "Oh, God, I know."

He wanted to reach out and take her hand, but he didn't dare. She looked so fragile right now, as if the only thing that was holding her together was her will. The merest touch might shatter her. He tried to find something reassuring to say, but he couldn't think of anything she didn't already know. Repeating the obvious wouldn't help at all.

"I'm going out with the search parties tomorrow," she said presently.

"Meg..."

"I sat here all afternoon, hoping the phone would ring and it would be her. Hoping she'd suddenly walk in the back door and say she'd been mad but she was over it. It didn't happen. It's not going to happen. She ran away, Earl. She really ran away."

There was no answer to that. Feeling as useless as teats on a bull, he just sat there, his mind scrambling around for some way to help her, for some way to find Allie, for some way to deal with his own rising terror.

"So I've got to help look for her," she said. "I've got to."

"It would be best if you didn't, Meg. We need you here for when we find her, not off somewhere in the mountains." He didn't want to tell her that in her present emotional state she might be incautious and get herself or someone else into trouble. He was wearing two hats right now, and trying to balance his worries with the needs of being a good sheriff was tying him up in knots. In Meg's shoes, he would want to search, too. But, as sheriff, he knew that wasn't wise.

"Almost everyone who was here today is planning to come back, and we'll have the men from the night shift at the mine, too. They really admired Bill."

She didn't answer, but something passed over her face that left him feeling really uneasy, as if there was something he didn't know but needed to. And he didn't know how to ask.

He rose, pacing over to the window, looking out uselessly, only to see his own reflection in the glass against the pitch beyond.

"I did something wrong," Meg said.

He turned to look at her. "What?"

"Damned if I know." Her voice was bitter, harsh, a sound he wasn't used to hearing from her. It was an echo of her mother. "But I must've done something, Earl. Why else would I lose my husband and daughter within a few months?"

"Hold on there. You haven't lost your daughter. We'll find her."

"Maybe. But I've lost her anyway. Why else would she run away?"

He couldn't answer that. Not really. But he tried anyway. "Kids that age get strange ideas, Meg. Teen runaways are as common as fur on a goat."

She'd always liked his homespun similes, but this time she seemed deaf.

"I've been trying to think all day what I did wrong," she said. "There's got to be something. But all I can remember is that I tried to do everything right. Until Bill died. God, I've been a terrible mother these last eight months! Selfish. Allie was hurting, and I didn't even see it.''

"You saw it. We *all* saw it. We all just thought it was because of Bill.''

"Yeah.'' She shook her head, then bowed it and buried her face in the pillow. "But it couldn't be, could it?'' she said, her voice broken and muffled. "Not after eight months.''

He returned to her side, reluctant to sit on the bed beside her, so he laid his hand on her shoulder, hoping the touch comforted. "Kids this age get all kinds of cockamamy ideas,'' he repeated. "They do dramatic things to get attention. It doesn't mean the parents have failed. God knows I've seen enough runaways in fifteen years on the force. You'd be surprised how often it's over some stupid thing that could have been resolved if the kid had just spoken up.''

She lifted her face and looked at him. Her eyes were swollen but dry. "That's the whole point, Earl. Even if she had spoken up, I probably wouldn't have heard her. I've been so damn self-absorbed since Bill died.''

He could tell her that was understandable, that they'd all been wading in grief and loss for the last eight months, but he realized nothing he could say was going to make her stop beating herself up. At least not until Allie was safely home. Then she would get pissed at someone besides herself—most likely Allie. For now, though, there wasn't a damn thing he could do or say to ease either her fear or her self-recrimination.

For that matter, there wasn't much he could do to ease his own. He was more wounded than he could say that Allie hadn't come to him with her problem, whatever it was. God knew he'd done his level best to be a stand-in for Bill these past months.

"Come on," he said finally. "You can't sit here all night staring at this empty room and worrying yourself sick."

"No?" She gave a short, broken laugh. "What else can I do except worry?"

"Get busy. Watch a television show, mop a floor. Anything. After the search planes come in, if they haven't spotted anything, we'll go to town. Vivian wants food to feed the searchers tomorrow."

"At least she has something useful to do."

He reached for her hand and tugged her to her feet. "So do you. You don't have to let Vivian do it all by herself."

"Right. Like she'll even let me into the kitchen."

"Like she has any right to keep you out. It's *your* kitchen, Meg."

For an instant he thought she was going to refuse to come with him. But then she sighed and led the way. Vivian was in the kitchen, loading cups into the dishwasher. Earl went out to retrieve the coffee urn and carried it into the kitchen. When he set it on the counter, Meg took over, emptying it and washing it. Vivian didn't object.

Which was good. Except now *he* didn't have a damn thing to do, and he was staring into the maw of the longest night of his life.

The search planes were back on the ground by nine, with no news. The grocery store closed at ten, but it was a small town, and Earl knew if he and Meg showed up before closing to buy food for the searchers, the place would stay open until they got what they needed. He insisted that Meg join him, making her pull on a jacket and run a brush through her tousled hair. Vivian watched them, and something about the look in the woman's eyes disturbed him. Well, hell, it didn't mean anything. Vivian disturbed him even when she was in a good mood.

Meg asked Vivian if she wanted to go along. Vivian just handed her a list. "*Somebody's* got to be here in case that child shows up."

Meg's face turned white. Earl had to battle down an urge to wipe the floor with Vivian. God, what an unforgivably cruel thing to say.

"I'll stay," Meg said. "You go, Mother. You know what you want better than I do." She reached for the buttons of her jacket, but Earl stopped her.

"You're coming with me," he said flatly. "The only way you're going to get through this is to keep moving." Then he turned to Vivian. "Apologize to Meg." He expected her to refuse.

Vivian surprised him, though. "I didn't mean anything by what I said. I just meant one of us should be here, not that there's anything wrong with Meg going. We've got to feed the searchers. It's only right." She reached out as if she would have touched Meg, but Meg pulled away and started for the door.

Earl looked at Vivian, thinking he ought to say something, but the woman's expression forbade it. "I'll have her back by eleven."

Vivian just nodded and returned to her pointless cleaning of an already clean kitchen counter.

The ride to town was silent. Earl figured Meg's

thoughts were lost somewhere up on the mountain, and his own weren't far behind. He kept trying to think of something to say that might distract her, but he kept coming up empty, mainly because he couldn't distract himself, either. Worry gripped him like a fist in his stomach and wouldn't let go.

But as they approached the outskirts of town, Meg suddenly said, "What if she didn't go up into the mountains?"

"Meaning?"

"What if she hiked down to the highway and hitch-hiked out of here? We might be looking in the wrong place."

"It's not likely, Meg. She wouldn't have taken the camp stove if she wasn't intending to camp out. But I already thought of that, anyway. I've got a bulletin out on her. If it hasn't already turned up on the news, it'll be on the ten-o'clock report, along with her picture."

"Oh."

"I'm sorry I didn't think to tell you."

"It's okay. I just thought of it now. I've been so focused on her being up in the mountains."

"Me, too. But I followed all the standard missing-person procedures. It's pretty much automatic." All he'd had to do was set the ball rolling. "Lydia Valdez, my juvenile officer, is good at this kind of thing. She has a whole list of procedures she follows."

"That's good."

Silence built again, heavy and cold. And he still couldn't think of a single useful thing to say.

"I keep thinking about yesterday," Meg said as they drove along the town streets to the supermarket.

"Yeah? Did something happen?"

"Not a thing. At least, nothing I can point to and say that's what went wrong. It seemed like every other day. Not one single thing was different. And no matter how many times I go over what Allie and I talked about, I can't find anything that would explain her running away. But she must have been planning this, Earl. She didn't just go off on a whim."

"Probably not. Usually when that happens, there's been a fight or something."

"Well, we didn't fight about anything. And, as far as I know, she didn't fight with Vivian, either. Usually, when the two of them get into it, I can tell even if I wasn't around when it happened. Neither of them is very good at hiding their feelings." Suddenly she barked a harsh laugh. "Listen to me. Not good at hiding her feelings? Allie must be a far better dissembler than I'd have ever believed."

"It's probably just the result of how she's been feeling all along. My guess is that nothing really changed. She probably just decided that she couldn't handle it anymore."

"Couldn't handle what? That's what really worries me, Earl. What is so awful that she felt she had to run away?"

He didn't have any answers for her. If they were ever going to get any answers, they would have to get them from Allie.

Miles away in the mountains, Allie Williams crawled into her sleeping bag. She was sheltered by an old miner's cabin, a rough-hewn creation of logs with a dirt floor, unoccupied for nearly a century except by bugs and mice.

She thought about those bugs as she lay in the dark, with her mummy bag zipped up tightly so nothing could crawl inside. Her nose ached with the cold, and she was sure she had never felt as lonely as she did right now.

In the daytime the mountains seemed friendly, but at night they were full of threat. She thought of bobcats and bears and tried to be very silent and very still.

It really shouldn't matter if a bobcat or bear found her, she told herself. It would be over that much quicker. She wouldn't have to get up the courage to do it herself, and besides, if a bear ate her, her mom would never know that Allie had wanted to kill herself.

So it would be better for her mom if a bear found her. And probably easier for Allie than having to jump off a cliff somewhere.

She wanted it to look like an accident. After all, she'd already ruined her mother's life once. She didn't want to do it again.

That was why she was going to wait a few days before she did it. So it would look like an accident. She figured Uncle Earl wouldn't be easy to fool. He'd probably already started wondering if she was suicidal. He knew her too well.

So she was going to spend a few days collecting new rock samples and then find a convenient place to slip off a sharp drop. Falling, she had heard, was the easiest way to die. It felt like flying, she'd read somewhere.

Tears tried to seep from beneath her eyelids, but she wouldn't let them. They would only make her colder, and they wouldn't do any good, anyway. But holding them in made it hard to breathe, and made her throat so tight it hurt.

She was doing the right thing, she reminded herself. It didn't matter if she was scared and cold. It was exactly what she deserved. If not for her, her father wouldn't be dead, and her mother wouldn't be so unhappy. She should never have been born.

But thinking about that only made her want to cry more, so she forced herself to think about the rocks she was going to collect tomorrow, and how much warmer it would be when the sun came up. She wondered if her friends on the Internet and at school would miss her, and decided they probably would, but only a little. She felt sorry for making them feel bad, but she couldn't keep on ruining her mother's life.

As sleep finally started to steal over her, she found her thoughts drifting to her grandmother. Grandma Vivian wouldn't miss her, she decided. Not at all. Grandma never had anything to say to her except criticism. But given what Allie had heard the day her father died, she could understand that. Allie had ruined Meg's life, and Grandma knew it, too.

Yes, it would definitely be better for everyone when she was gone.

4

Day was little more than a pale glow in the east when the searchers returned to the Williams house. They gathered in an ever-growing crowd equipped with flashlights, ropes and first-aid kits, and gratefully drank the hot coffee and ate the hot buttered biscuits and sausage that Vivian and Meg brought out by the trayload.

Vivian might have slept last night. No one knew. She had vanished into her bedroom the instant Meg and Earl returned from the store.

Neither Meg nor Earl had slept much. They'd sat up all night together, sometimes talking, sometimes silent. Meg had paced until there was a visible path in the living-room rug. Once or twice she had nodded off in the easy chair, and Earl had watched over her sleep. It had been disturbed sleep, full of nightmares. His own, such as it was, hadn't been any better.

Meg watched as Earl spread out maps and divided the searchers into three groups, directing two of them to drive to more distant points and begin their search there. He was expanding the search area, she saw, and building a cordon around the area that might possibly contain Allie, working its way back toward the house. A group of dogs left with each search party.

Then, except for the crackle of radios from the command-post trailer, the woods were quiet again. Pink light was radiating across the sky now, and high clouds were visible. Day had come.

Earl took Meg's arm and led her back inside. The air was so chilly this morning that his earlobes were aching, and Meg's face had a red, raw look to it. When he touched her, he felt her shivering.

"You've got to get some sleep," he said as they stepped inside. "You've got to lie down and sleep."

"I can't."

"You should try anyway. I'll wake you up if anyone finds anything, but you're not going to be any good to anyone if you don't sleep."

"What about you?"

"I'm fine for now. I've had more practice with this. Just go curl up on the couch under that little blanket you made."

"Afghan," she said automatically. She shivered again and looked around the house, seeing it with the eyes of a stranger. It didn't look like home anymore, as if the events of the past day had deprived these walls of any comfort and familiarity. The house, which had once seemed just right for their small family, now seemed huge, empty and echoing with loss.

"I'm going to sell this place," she said to Earl. "Whatever happens, I'm getting rid of this cursed house."

Then she thought how that might sound to him. He had labored right alongside her and Bill to build this place from the ground up. The three of them had done every bit of it except pouring the slab and footers, and the wiring. Countless weekends and evenings had gone into this structure. It had been an exciting, happy time, and the three of them had savored every minute of the adventure.

Meg's throat tightened, and she swallowed hard, missing those times even more than she missed her husband. Allie had been a baby then, a cooing, gurgling little bundle of happiness. Where had Allie's happiness fled?

Instead of following Earl's direction to take a nap, she went into the kitchen. Vivian was there, scrubbing the dishes left behind by the searchers. Scrubbing them instead of putting them into the dishwasher. Needing to keep busy.

Meg felt a flicker of concern for her mother, a flicker that had survived all the years of anger between them. Crossing the kitchen, she laid a hand on Vivian's shoulder. Her mother stiffened. Meg drew her hand back as if burned.

"There's food for you in the microwave," Vivian said woodenly. "You'd best eat something. Earl, too."

Food was her mother's answer to every crisis, Meg found herself thinking. No matter what in the world happened, Vivian could be found cooking a meal. There were, she supposed, worse ways to deal with catastrophe. "Can I help?"

"No...no...I need to keep busy."

So did Meg, but her mother wouldn't think of that. "Okay." She went to the microwave and pulled out the plate of biscuits and sausage. She could probably swallow a biscuit and a glass of milk, but the sausage made her stomach turn over.

Earl was there, watching her from the doorway. She wondered why he kept watching her so intently. Was he afraid she was going to fall apart? She wouldn't. Not while Allie was still missing. Later might be a different matter, but she didn't want to think about any *later* that didn't involve a happy ending. She refused to think about anything at all except getting out a couple of plates for herself and Earl, some flatware, and two mugs of coffee. Vivian always kept a fresh pot of coffee on hand.

"Eat," she told Earl, pointing to a seat. It wasn't the most gracious invitation, but she couldn't force herself to say much more. He sat and waited for her to serve herself before he filled his own plate.

Vivian finished washing the dishes. When she set the last cup in the drying rack, she announced, "I'm going to lie down. I didn't get any sleep last night." Without even so much as a glance at them, she walked out of the kitchen.

Earl spoke. "What is her major malfunction?"

"What do you mean?"

"The way she reacted when you touched her."

"Oh." Meg was past feeling any concern for old grievances, or any interest in them. "She's been angry with me for years over something I did."

"Well, it's high time she forgave you."

Meg shrugged. "She never will."

Earl didn't say any more, and she was grateful. Her mind felt like a dark, dead place, and her thoughts didn't want to focus on anything at all. Not even on whether they would find Allie. It was almost as if someone had thrown a switch, making it impossible for her to think. As if she had burned out a fuse and nothing was left except dark numbness.

She moved, she spoke, but it was as if she were a robot. She'd felt this way once before, she realized. Years ago, when her father had died. She'd reached a point where she just couldn't feel anything at all.

And that was where she was at right now. With almost clinical detachment, she asked, "Do you think she's okay?"

"Allie? Or your mother?"

"Allie."

"Yes, Meg, I think she's okay. I think she's hiding somewhere out there trying to work through some problems. I think, if we don't find her first, that she'll come home in a day or two."

She nodded, but nothing inside her changed. Probably because she didn't believe him. Life had taken everything from her. Why should she believe that it would treat her daughter any differently? Prickles of grief and fear were trying to break through the black cotton wool that protected her, but she refused to let them. Something inside her had died, and she wanted it to stay dead.

Earl spoke. "What's Vivian mad at you about?"

"You don't want to know. Believe me, you *don't* want to know."

He nodded and let it go. She was willing to bet, though, that he would come back to it at some future date. Right now that didn't matter. All that mattered was that he not wake her up from the numbness.

The numbness lasted for a while. It got her through cleaning up after the meal, got her through going to the living room and lying down on the couch. It even got her to the edge of sleep. Or maybe exhaustion did that.

But fear found her in her dreams, and she wandered down long, empty corridors calling Allie's name.

Allie could hardly move when she woke in the morning. The cold had seeped into her sleeping bag enough to stiffen her. But still, it was warmer inside than out, and she didn't want to crawl out of her cocoon. But she had to. She had to find a place to hide. She knew they would be searching for her, and even though she had gotten a head start on them yesterday, today they might catch up.

She thought she remembered a small cave not too far from the cabin, little more than a hole in the mountain, just enough room to crawl into and cover herself with brush. It would do, because nobody else was likely to even know it was there.

Finally, facing necessity, she crawled out of the mummy bag. The air in the cabin was icy, and her nose was numb. She took her little kerosene stove outside, into a patch of warmer morning sunlight, filled an aluminum pan from the creek and began to boil some water.

It suddenly struck her as stupid that she was boiling her drinking water. After all, she fully intended to be dead in a day or two. Why was she concerned about not getting sick from the water? But her dad had taught her well, and had managed in the process to scare her enough that she couldn't make herself drink the water until it was boiled. She might be dead in a few days, but she didn't want those yucky amoebas crawling around inside her even that long.

Her breakfast consisted of peanut butter scooped out of a plastic jar with her finger, and some dried soup made with the boiled water. They didn't go well together, but after the cold night she was ravenous.

She cleaned up carefully after herself, taking care to brush the ground with a pine bough to remove her footprints. Then she hiked farther up the mountain, seeking the cave.

It was exactly where she remembered it, and she dragged some brush up to it, to cover the entrance in case she heard anybody approach. For now, though, she could sit in the warm sunshine and let it bake the chill out of her. And she could look for some interesting rocks.

Loving rocks was one of the things that made Allie weird, and she knew it. Long ago, like most kids, she'd saved pretty pebbles in her pocket. But at some point she'd gone far beyond pretty pebbles, and now she could read the stories in the rocks she studied. She knew everything about the local geology, even the amazing fact that this high point in the Rockies had once been a seabed. She loved hammering her way through the limestone deposits and finding seashells.

But other kids thought she was strange to be interested in something so boring. They called her a nerd and a geek, and she supposed she was. It didn't hurt her too much, though, because she happened to prefer the company of other nerds and geeks. And besides, her mom had always told her that she should never be ashamed of being smart, and that her interest in rocks was a wonderful gift.

Allie thought so, too. She could sit up here all alone on the side of a mountain and read stories that other people didn't even know were there. And now that she was warming up, she didn't even feel as lonely and lost as she'd been feeling last night.

In fact, she decided that being out here in the woods made her feel closer to her dad. She'd loved going camping with him, and even knowing that he hadn't wanted her to be born didn't diminish the pleasure she felt in those memories. Of course, it was all her fault he was dead, and she felt guilty for remembering anything pleasurable at all, but there was nothing else to do here except think and remember, and it seemed appropriate to her to remember, seeing that she was going to die soon. It seemed like the right thing to do with her last hours.

There was a nice limestone outcropping a few yards away, and she thought about taking some samples. After all, taking samples was going to be her cover for what she was doing out here. But then she thought of the searchers and realized they might hear her hammer. Sounds carried a long distance in the clear cold air, though not as well as they did at lower altitudes. She'd learned something about that in science last year.

Anyway, using her hammer would probably draw the searchers right to her, so she contented herself with picking up loose stones and examining them.

Finally it was nearly noon, and she was beginning to feel both sleepy and hungry. Sitting in the sun did that to her. She pulled out a granola bar and a strip of beef jerky, and ate. Still no sign of the searchers. Not a sound except the breeze and the birds and the burbling of the brook down by the cabin.

After a while, it seemed silly to keep sitting. The ground was hard beneath her bottom, and cold. It wouldn't hurt to lie down for while, she thought. The sun felt warm on her skin, and her muscles still felt stiff from last night. It would feel so good to just lie down.

She closed her eyes to block out the sun, until at some point she drifted off to sleep.

Matt Dawson found her there. He hadn't joined the other searchers this morning because they made him feel uncomfortable. They looked on him as a kid, a troublesome one, and didn't seem to feel very happy about having him with them. He figured it was better to search alone.

He couldn't really articulate why it was he felt the need to search for Allie Williams. He'd never said more than two words to her. Except he was suddenly remembering the time in elementary school when she'd shared her sandwich with him because he didn't have any lunch.

But other than that, she might as well have lived on a different planet. She was one of the kids he watched from afar, wondering what it was like to have nice parents who joined the PTA, a mother who brought cupcakes to school on your birthday, and nice clothes to wear.

Those had been childish concerns, and he thought he'd outgrown them. In fact, he'd pretty much stopped thinking about Allie and all the kids like her.

He'd left envy behind somewhere in his twelfth year, when he'd realized it was a waste of energy. He had what he had, and thinking about what other people had wasn't making him feel any better about his lot.

He'd thought about Allie a little last year when her father died. He might have felt sorry for her, except that it had made him feel good, in a bad sort of way, to know that even the golden kids with perfect lives didn't always have it easy.

That had shamed him in some way he couldn't define, and he figured it was shame that had dragged him out here to look for her. Besides, he still owed her something for that sandwich.

He avoided the other searchers and their carefully laid-out search areas and followed his instinct. He remembered the old miner's cabin up the mountain, an isolated, ramshackle log structure in the middle of nowhere. Almost nobody knew it was there; it had long since been forgotten, and nearly swallowed by a hundred years of forest growth. He'd hidden out there himself a couple of times over the years, when staying at home with his dad had just seemed impossible.

But Allie had hiked all over these mountains looking for her stupid rocks—he'd heard her talking about it with that geeky friend of hers—and he figured she'd come across the cabin.

And if he were a girl planning to spend the night alone on the side of a mountain, he would want walls and a roof around him. Something that would make him feel safe from animals.

When he got to the cabin in the early afternoon, he was at first dismayed that she wasn't there. But when he looked closer, he recognized the signs that someone had been smoothing the pine needles. Little bits of fresh dirt were stirred up. And inside the cabin, the hard dirt floor showed signs of some recent scuffing.

She'd been there for sure. He felt pretty good that his intuition was right. And the girl wasn't as smart as she probably thought she was. What's more, as of this morning, she had still been well within the search area. They were going to find her.

Matt wanted to find her first. Nobody in town had much good to say about him, and he told himself he didn't care, but he sure wouldn't mind being a hero for just one day. Just one lousy day was all he wanted.

But Allie had already moved on. Looking around, he tried to figure out which way she would go. It depended on what she was hoping to accomplish. If she wanted to be found eventually—and he considered that a distinct possibility—then she wouldn't wander much farther than this, because the search area would get so large that they just wouldn't be able to look everywhere. He remembered that much from math.

So he figured she was probably hanging around here somewhere, hoping to be found. But where?

He wandered up and down the mountain for a few hundred yards in every direction, and when he finally found her, fast asleep on a rock in the sun, he almost didn't believe his eyes.

She looked, he thought, like Sleeping Beauty in a movie he'd seen years ago, when one of his teachers took pity on him because he never got to go to the movies like other kids. She looked almost magical, yet so small and defenseless that, for the first time in his life, Matt Dawson felt a protective urge so strong it swelled his chest unbearably.

He knew there wasn't much time to get her back down the mountain before dark, but he didn't wake her. Instead he sat nearby and watched her sleep, and wondered how her life could have become so bad that she had run away. It just boggled his mind.

The sun crept closer to the mountain peak, and still she slept. But clouds were beginning to boil up, too, promising an afternoon rain or something worse. When at last they swallowed the sun, he knew he couldn't wait any longer. He couldn't risk her getting wet.

"Allie. Allie, wake up."

She jolted upright, looking panic-stricken. Then she saw him. "What are you doing here?" Her voice was cracked and dry from sleep.

"I was looking for you. Most of the town is looking for you. We need to get back."

"No!"

"Come on. Give it up. They're going to find you."

Her chin thrust out. "No, they won't."

He hesitated. For some stupid reason, he'd thought that she would just come with him once she knew the game was up. And he wasn't stupid enough to think he could carry a screaming, kicking girl down the mountain. Stymied, he said, "Why not?"

"Because I won't. Because I'm never going home. Never."

Impatience bubbled up in him. "Why?" he asked harshly. "What's so fucking awful in your life that you can't handle it? Christ almighty, you're a wimp. You don't know how easy you have it."

She jerked her head backward, as if he'd hit her. "You don't know," she said, her voice quivering.

"Well, whatever the hell is going on, it can't be as bad as what I've been putting up with. And you don't see me running away."

"Maybe you should."

"Yeah, right. And wind up in juvenile detention. No thanks. Life sucks enough without being in jail."

"You don't understand."

"Yeah. Sure. I don't understand that your mom's so worried about you she looks like she's gonna collapse. If I ran away, my mom wouldn't even notice."

"So run away."

"No."

"Why not? Are you a coward?"

He could almost have hit her, except that he had vowed he was never, ever going to use his fists on anybody who didn't hit him first. He was never going to be like his dad. And he sure as hell couldn't tell her that the whole reason he stayed put was because if his dad didn't have him to knock around, he would beat up his mother. He *had* to stay.

"I'm not a coward," he said finally. "But *you* are."

"No, I'm not. I've ruined everybody's life, and I'm not going back."

"Oh, come off it, you twit. You couldn't have done anything *that* bad. What did you do? Collect too many rocks? Get an F in math?"

She shook her head, and her chin trembled. "I was born," she said almost inaudibly. "I was born."

Now he knew she was crazy. He might have regretted being born himself a lot of times, but he'd never blamed himself for being born. He hadn't had anything at all to do with that. No, that one was his dad's fault, for not keeping his pants zipped. "Come on," he said. "It's not like you were born on purpose."

She lowered her head, and her long, dark hair shadowed her face. He sat looking at her, waiting, but she didn't say anything. Finally he looked up at the sky, and what he saw galvanized him.

"Come on, we gotta go. It's gonna rain in a minute."

She stood up, reaching for her huge backpack. "To the cabin," she said. "I'm not going any farther."

He let it go for now. Once it started raining, neither one of them was going anywhere else. Rain could kill you in these mountains. You could get hypothermic in no time at all.

"Okay," he said, letting her think she'd won.

The first big, fat drops started falling just as they reached the cabin. The first one caught him on the nose, and it felt like ice. They hurried inside, standing in the darkness for a minute while their eyes adjusted.

"I've got a camp stove," Allie said as cold wind whipped through the glassless window and doorless door. "Want something hot?"

"Sure." Why not? They were stuck until the rain passed, anyway.

They hunkered down in a corner as far from the drafts as they could get, and Allie unpacked her stove and another package of dried soup mix.

"I forgot," she said suddenly. "We need water for this."

Stifling a sigh, Matt rose and went to look out the

window. The rain was still falling in isolated drops. If he hurried, he might make it before he got drenched.

"Give me something to get it in," he said.

She handed him a large, lightweight aluminum pot with a flat, loose lid and a handle looping across the top. It would work even if he had to run, provided he held the top on. "Man, you sure know how to camp."

"Daddy taught me."

He hurried out of the cabin, toward the stream. The raindrops were still few and big, but when they struck him, they stung, as if they were ice. He found himself wondering if the snow line had descended this far. God, he hoped not.

He slid down the rough bank to the stream, filled the pot quickly and clambered his way back up, barking his shin in the process. The wind was getting even colder now, cutting through his shabby jacket and the old flannel shirt beneath it. And the raindrops were falling harder and faster, too. He felt his shoulders get damp in the time it took him to sprint to the cabin.

When he stepped back inside, he found that Allie had already lit the stove. The blue light of the flame drew him, and he hurried toward it, setting the pot beside her. The warmth was welcome, and he hunkered down, holding his hands out.

"Christ, it's getting cold out there," he said.

"You shouldn't use that word."

"Yeah? Wanna make something of it?"

She didn't answer, just put the pot on the stove.

"Sure you got enough propane to heat that? Maybe I should make a fire."

"I've got another bottle with me."

But he was already thinking about a fire, about how much warmer it would be, and how impossible it was going to be to build one after it rained. Without another word, he jumped up and hurried back out into the blustery day, gathering everything he could find that might make a decent fire. The way he figured it, he could build one in the cabin, near the window, as long as he didn't make it too big. It was practically like a wind tunnel in there, so the smoke wouldn't kill them. Maybe.

But it was the best he could think of. He carried a couple of armloads of dead wood into the cabin, then sought out some dry pine needles under one of the trees. The rain was getting steady now, steady and icy, and he was getting wetter, too. Finally he faced the fact that if he stayed out here much longer he was going to get himself in trouble.

Inside the cabin he dumped his handfuls of pine needles near the wood, then returned to the stove. The water wasn't even steaming yet, and he held his fingers as close as he could get them to the burner. They felt almost numb, and he wished he'd brought his mittens with him today.

Allie reached out and touched his shoulder. "You're wet."

"I'll be okay," he said gruffly. "I'm not soaked."

But she didn't listen to him. She pulled her rolled-up sleeping bag off her pack and handed it to him. "Wrap this around yourself. It'll keep you warm until you have some soup."

He didn't argue. He was all too aware that he was on the edge of shivering. Shaking out the bag, he draped it over his shoulders, then sat cross-legged in front of the stove. The sleeping bag would catch whatever heat came his way and keep him warmer. "You okay?" he asked her.

"I'm still dry, and my parka's a good one."

Sitting there, waiting for that damn water to boil, he wondered which of them was crazier. He knew better than to come up here with nothing but the clothes on his back, especially at this time of year. And he'd been even stupider to sit there watching her sleep while the clouds built up. Maybe the truth of it was that he didn't want to go home any more than she did.

"It feels like it's going to snow," he remarked along about the time the water got around to steaming a little.

"Yeah. I think it might."

"You don't sound worried."

"Why should I? I'm never coming down off this mountain."

"What are you going to do? Stay up here and be a hermit for the rest of your life?"

"I guess you might say that."

But he had a feeling she meant something else, and it unnerved him. He didn't know how to phrase his suspicion, though, so he decided to wait.

When the water boiled, she insisted on letting it boil a while. She told him all about the parasites in the water, and how you had to boil it so you wouldn't get sick. He decided she wasn't suicidal, because if she was, she wouldn't be worrying about bugs in the water.

When she was satisfied all the invisible bugs were dead, she scooped out a cup of boiling water and dumped a pouch of dried soup in it. "Let it sit a couple of minutes," she told him. At this altitude, water boiled at a much lower temperature, so it took longer for the noodles to soften than the package said. But he already knew that. He'd been living here his whole life.

"What about you?" he asked.

"I only brought one cup. I'll have mine after you're done."

"You're sure?"

"You're the one who's wet."

She let the water keep on boiling while he drank his soup, and while it was a waste of her propane, he didn't say so, because the heat from the stove and steaming water felt so good as it curled around him under the sleeping bag. The soup felt even better, going down just hot enough to drink without burning his tongue. And it was just enough to make him realize how hungry he was.

"More?" she asked when he passed the cup back.

"You first." Besides, he didn't figure she had all that much food with her, and if it snowed, life was going to get hairy for them both.

She drank her own soup, then split a granola bar with him. He felt a lot better now. But he wished she didn't have to turn off that stove.

It was getting darker inside the cabin. Pushing himself to his feet, keeping the sleeping bag over his damp shoulders, he went to the door and looked out. Late afternoon. Maybe five o'clock already. The rain was falling faster now, a steady drumbeat on the roof, which, amazingly enough, wasn't leaking yet. They weren't going anywhere tonight.

He looked at the heap of dead wood he'd brought into the cabin. It wouldn't be nearly enough for the whole night. It suddenly struck him how well prepared she seemed to be, so he took a flyer, asking, "You got a poncho?"

"Sure. I always carry one."

"Why didn't you say that when I was out getting the water and wood?"

"Because I didn't know if you were coming back."

He couldn't argue with that. "I want to get some more wood in here. What I got isn't enough for the whole night."

"Okay." She pawed through her pack again and came out with a small, neatly folded vinyl square. "Be careful. It'll tear easily."

He gave her back her sleeping bag, wrapping it around her shoulders, then pulled the poncho over his head. It was big enough for a grown man, and had a hood. The rain tapped on it like fingers as he went under the trees to find more fallen limbs that hadn't gotten too wet yet.

Half an hour later, he had enough wood to satisfy himself. He gave Allie her poncho back, watching the care with which she folded it. Then he set about digging a fire pit in the dirt floor.

"You shouldn't build a fire inside," Allie said.

"This isn't inside. This place has got more holes in it than Swiss cheese. The smoke won't be bad."

"But what if the cabin catches fire?"

"It won't. I'm gonna build a *small* fire."

At least the work was warming him up. When he was satisfied that the pit was deep enough, he began to lay the fire.

"Did you ever go to the ruins at Mesa Verde?" she asked him.

"Nah. I heard of 'em, though."

"Well, before the Anasazi started building their cliff dwellings, they used to live in pits in the ground that were covered over with wood."

"Yeah? So?"

"An awful lot of those places burned down because the roofs caught fire."

"Well, I ain't going out to dig a cliff dwelling right now, so we're just gonna have to risk it. I'll be careful."

He was, too. He resisted the urge to make the fire big enough to really warm them and settled for one that they could hold their hands and feet over. Every little bit would help.

When he finally had the small fire burning, he noticed she wasn't at all hesitant about coming over to sit beside it.

She spoke. "We should take turns staying up to watch the fire tonight. In case."

"Fine by me." All he knew was that she had a sleeping bag and would probably be fine, but without the fire he would be frozen to death by morning. "This was a stupid idea, Allie."

"What?"

"Running away to the mountains. You know how many people are out here risking their necks to find you? And now I'm stranded, too, and I don't have a sleeping bag. Promise you'll bury me if I'm an icicle in the morning?"

"You didn't have to come for me."

"You ought to be damn glad someone did."

She didn't answer, just bowed her head again. He had a feeling she was just beginning to realize the seriousness of what she had done.

Which was a good thing, he told himself. But it didn't keep him from feeling sorry for her.

5

From the minute the clouds started to gather, Mcg began to panic. She'd lived in these mountains long enough to know what this could mean, to know that getting wet up there could be a death sentence.

"She probably took rain gear," Earl said. "She knows how to camp and hike, Meg. And there are plenty of places to stay out of the worst of it."

But every time he went out to the command post to get an update, the news got worse. Searchers were straggling in, wet and tired, unable to continue. And finally one of the returning parties reported seeing snow. The highest peaks had been white for weeks, but now the snow line was descending.

Meg stood at the sliding glass doors that opened off the breakfast area and stared up at the forbidding, unforgiving mountains, lost now in dark clouds. Her face was pale, and she was hugging herself with desperation, as if the cold outside was creeping into her bones. It was warm inside; as the temperature had fallen, Earl had built fires in the two woodstoves that heated the house. But Meg didn't feel the heat at all.

All she could feel was the cold that held Allie in its grip.

"My baby's going to die," she said, her voice stretched to breaking.

"She knows how to take care of herself, Meg," Earl said firmly.

"Not when winter comes," she said. "Not in the cold and rain. Not for long. She couldn't have that much food. What happens when the wood gets too wet to burn? She couldn't have all that much propane for the stove...." Some part of her was giving up hope, preparing for death. All she could think of as the hours crept by was the bad things that could happen to Allie. In her world, those bad things didn't just happen to other people. They happened to *her*. They happened to the people she loved. They were real. First her father, then Bill, and now Allie. It should have been too much to grasp, but somehow it was all she could believe.

Bad things happened to her and the people she loved, and it was all her fault.

"We'll search again tomorrow."

She hardly heard him. Tomorrow most of the men would need to go back to work. Tomorrow was too far away anyway. Allie's sleeping bag was some protection, but it might not be enough. Try as she might, she couldn't remember what temperature that bag was supposed to be good down to. Freezing? It wouldn't be enough. God, she hoped Bill had bought bags that were good down to zero. But she didn't know. That had been Bill's department, and for the first time in months, she honestly wished Bill was still there.

The thought made her feel guilty. Guilty for how

little she had really missed Bill. Guilty for the fight that had caused his death, even though she hadn't started it. Guilt was her constant companion. And now she had Allie to feel guilty about, too.

But guilt was nothing compared to fear and a sense of impending loss that tightened her throat and made her chest ache until she couldn't breathe.

Earl took her arm, dragging her away from the window and into the study, away from Vivian. Vivian had settled down in the living room with her Bible and was reading it out loud, as if reading the verses would somehow make this nightmare go away. Meg was past that. Her only prayer was a constant, "God, please, God, please, God, please..." The litany ran ceaselessly in her mind, framing every other thought she had.

"Talk to me," Earl said when they were sitting on the love seat. "Talk to me."

"About what?"

"It doesn't matter. Just anything that crosses your mind."

But there was nothing she was willing to say out loud. Everything in her mind was surrounded by dark secrets that couldn't bear the light of day. Secrets that would make Earl turn from her in disgust, and she didn't think she could handle that loss on top of everything else.

She looked at Earl, at his rugged square face, and thought how kind he looked. He'd always been a kind man. She couldn't remember any time when he hadn't been. But kind or not, Earl wouldn't understand the ugly things in her life. And all those ugly things made her feel that she was deserving of every bad thing that came her way.

She wished she could cry. It might ease the unbearable pressure in her chest and the ache in her throat, but the tears weren't there. She'd cried them all out last night. There wasn't a single tear left in her anywhere.

And there was nothing to say. What could she possibly say? Allie was missing, and the next time she saw her daughter it might very well be in a coffin. Those things didn't bear talking about, either.

"Look," Earl said after a few moments, "I can't make any promises, but I *believe* we're going to find Allie, and that she's going to be okay."

"Don't lie to me. You know there's less hope with every passing hour, especially now that it's snowing up there."

"Why are you so determined to believe the worst?"

"Because I don't deserve any better." The ugly, harsh statement came out before she could stop it, and she saw the shock on his face. Oh, God, why had she said that? Even if it was true, she should never have said it to him.

"That's not true, Meg. I don't believe that, and neither should you. But, true or not, *Allie* doesn't deserve this."

He was angry with her, she realized. For an instant she didn't understand why. Then she did. He was angry because she was giving up on Allie. Angry because she was acting self-centered, as if she was all that mattered in this. And he was right. She might deserve to lose everything that mattered to her, but

Allie didn't deserve to die. "I'm sorry," she said through lips that felt stiff. "I'm sorry. You're right."

"It's okay." As if regretting his anger, he reached out and touched her shoulder. "You're just all mixed up from the stress."

He might make excuses for her, but she never could. This was more proof she was an awful person. It ought to be her out there freezing on that mountain and not Allie.

"Just what do you think you've done that's so bad?" he asked.

The question shook her. It was her fault he was asking, and because of that she owed him an answer. But there was no way she could tell him. She was saved by a knock on the front door. Earl went to answer it.

She could hear him talking to Midget Baldridge in the foyer, and she leaped up to go hear what he was saying.

When he saw her, Midget nodded. "Ms. Williams. Sorry, no news. I was just telling the boss here that the last of the searchers are coming in. It's getting wicked up there."

Meg's hand flew to her mouth, trying to hold in the scream that wanted to rise from the pit of her stomach. She didn't want to hear from anyone that it was getting wicked up there, and certainly not from someone who'd lived all his life around here. What she could see from her windows scared her enough. She didn't want to know how much worse it really was.

"We'll get back on it first thing in the morning,"

Midget said to her, as if he understood her reaction. "We surely will."

But at what point were they going to give up? Meg wondered. At some point they were going to decide they didn't have a hope of finding Allie. She'd seen it happen before, with other searches. Tomorrow might be the last day of hope they would give her.

Turning, she ran upstairs to her bedroom and fell facedown on the bed she had once shared with Bill. When she started screaming, the pillow muffled the sounds.

Downstairs, Vivian, who had listened from the living room, looked at Earl. "It's *her* fault, you know. Letting that child run wild. It's all her fault."

Something snapped inside Earl. He'd spent the last thirty-four hours as upset and worried about Allie as any of them, but he hadn't been allowed to show it because he was the sheriff. The strain had gotten to him.

"What the hell is the matter with you?" he snapped. "What kind of mother are you?"

Vivian's face turned white, and her lips compressed into a tight line. "You don't know what Meg's done."

But Earl was having none of it. He took a menacing step toward Vivian. "You listen to me, and you listen good, woman. You shut your yap and stop making Meg feel worse, or you pack your bags and go back to whatever hellhole you crawled out of."

Two bright spots of red appeared on Vivian's cheeks. "You can't make me."

"Don't test me."

Vivian turned sharply on her heel and disappeared.

Midget cleared his throat. "Christ, boss, what's the matter with that bitch?"

"Damned if I know. But I'm not going to stand for it."

"I wouldn't, either. Things are bad enough without that."

Earl nodded, and turned his attention back to the matter of the search. He asked Midget for the latest weather report, which didn't sound promising, but at the back of his mind he was wondering what could have happened to make Vivian Clede so hateful toward Meg.

Then he went to look for Meg. He found her still lying on her bed, her face buried in a pillow. Without asking if it was okay, he sat beside her and began to rub her back. Tomorrow, he decided, he was going to join the searchers and to hell with protocol. One of his deputies could oversee things, but he couldn't sit on his hands any longer.

Meg didn't move, but he could feel tremors in her back, as if she was weeping. It didn't get much worse than this, he thought. A child missing in the mountains... At this point he was beginning to wonder if it wouldn't be better if Allie had tried to hitchhike to Denver. But no one had reported seeing her, or a child like her, and the camping supplies pretty much indicated she'd gone into the mountains.

Which was better than falling in with a pedophile, but not completely. Not with winter deciding to settle in early, from the looks of it.

He found himself praying that she was safe and sheltered, that she'd found an overhang to protect her from the wind and snow. That she had enough food, and that she'd found enough dry wood to make herself a fire. He hoped she wasn't too frightened, but he feared she was. Hiking alone in the mountains could sound like a really great thing until you were lost alone in the dark, cold and snow.

And he found himself thinking that God couldn't do this to him, couldn't take both his best friend and his best friend's daughter from him. God couldn't possibly be that cruel.

Even though he knew God probably had nothing to do with it, and that life could indeed be that cruel. Only last year he'd seen a fire take a man's wife and children from him. It could happen. It happened all the time. And there was no reason why he should be any safer from that than the rest of the world.

But scared as he was, as much as his heart was threatening to break, he was starting to feel the first flickers of anger. Anger at Vivian for her treatment of Meg. And anger at Allie for doing something so stupid. It didn't matter that she was only fourteen. She should have known better than this. With all the times that Bill had taken her camping, she should have known how dangerous a stunt this was.

And maybe she did know. Maybe that was why she'd done it. Maybe Allie didn't mean to come down from the mountain at all.

There was a blizzard blowing outside. Matt Dawson sat beside the fire, wearing Allie's parka. She'd insisted he take it, because she had the mummy bag to curl up in. The jacket was too small, too short in the sleeves, and it wouldn't zip around him, but where it covered him, he felt a whole lot warmer. She'd also given him her mittens.

She was sound asleep now, and even though he was growing tired, he didn't want to wake her. He was so cold that he feared falling asleep. Shivers kept running through him, and he kept edging closer to the fire. Desperate, he put a couple of extra pieces of wood on it, risking setting the roof on fire. He watched the embers fly upward and saw that they winked out before they reached the roof. It was okay.

The wind was whipping through the cabin, but they were out of the worst of it. From time to time, though, he saw a snowflake whiz by, reddened by the fireglow. The world outside the cabin, strangely enough, seemed to be growing brighter. Probably because of all the snow blowing around.

If it was as bad out there as it looked, they were in deep shit. A heavy snowfall would make it impossible to get down from the mountain. They wouldn't be able to tell where the obstacles were, and they would probably break bones. Worse, they would be cold and wet, a dangerous thing to be.

He was only sixteen, but life had made him a man in some ways, and it was the man in him now that considered the stupidity of his own actions. Where did he get off thinking he ought to come up here by himself? Without any supplies? Without decent gear? It was one thing to do this in July when he was all alone, and another to do it in late September when winter was inching its way down from the peaks.

Now he was stuck here along with Allie, and supplies she'd brought only for herself were being stretched to feed him. A little while ago he'd looked in her backpack, and what he found didn't make him happy. Whatever Allie was doing up here, she hadn't expected it to take more than a couple of days. She hadn't brought that much food. Which meant they were both going to be pretty hungry by tomorrow night if they couldn't get home.

Shivering, he held his hands closer to the flames and tried not to think about how it was so cold that the heat from the fire didn't seem to reach more than a few inches. Allie looked cozy enough in her mummy bag, but she was beginning to get restless, and he suspected the cold was getting to her, too. He wished he'd been able to think of some way of covering the cabin door. It would have cut down on the wind and kept it just a little warmer in here, even with the window.

He wondered how people had ever managed to survive in places like this, even with doors and glass in the windows. His feet were beginning to feel like blocks of ice, and he stuck his boots out toward the fire. In a minute the soles would get hot and nearly burn his feet, but the heat they retained would keep him from getting frostbite for a little longer.

Allie moaned. At first he wasn't sure it was her and not the wind, but then she moaned again. A couple of seconds later, he saw her eyes open.

"I'm cold," she said.

"Me, too."

"Is it time to trade?"

"Nah," he said, lying. "You've only been asleep a few minutes."

"Oh. It feels like longer."

"Probably because you're so cold."

"Yeah."

He waited for her to go back to sleep, but she didn't close her eyes. She stared at the fire. He wondered what she was thinking about, but when he caught the gleam of a tear running down her cheek, he nearly panicked.

"What's wrong?"

"Nothing. I'm just sad."

He reached out and wiped the tear away with his mitten. "You don't want to get your face wet," he reminded her.

"Thanks."

"Listen," he said after a minute. "We've got to get down this mountain tomorrow."

"Maybe you do. I'm staying."

"Why the hell do you want to do that? Are you crazy? You're gonna die up here."

When she didn't answer, he understood the truth. He'd thought about killing himself a few times and had even come close, once or twice, so he wasn't chock-full of arguments against it. Sometimes he even thought that he'd backed off only because he was too chicken to do it. And now that he thought of it, if it had occurred to him to come up here and just stay until he froze to death, he might have actually done it.

"I think about killing myself sometimes," he said.

Her head lifted, and she looked at him. "You do? Why?"

"Because I get sick of everything, you know? Sometimes I think I can't handle another day."

She nodded and wiggled until she was on her side facing him. "Does your dad hit you?"

He stiffened. "I didn't say that."

"I know. But I always wondered. You get an awful lot of black eyes and bloody lips."

He squirmed. It wasn't something he wanted to admit to anyone, because he felt guilty about it somehow. Dirty. Like it was all his fault. And maybe it was.

When he didn't answer, she said, "I thought so. Why didn't you kill yourself?"

"You want the truth?"

"Sure."

So he told her the truth he'd believed when he decided not to do it, not the part about feeling like a chicken later because he hadn't. For some reason, he felt a moral obligation to keep Allie from doing something crazy. "Because I'm too damn ornery."

For an instant she didn't make a sound, then a little giggle escaped her. "Ornery? Really?"

"It's God's truth. I figure killing myself would just make it too damn easy on the rest of the world. I didn't ask to be born, so why should I get out of *their* way?"

She nodded slowly, as if she was thinking about what he said. Encouraged, he continued.

"Besides, only chickens kill themselves. It's the coward's way out."

"I don't know. I think actually doing it takes a lot of courage."

He kind of agreed with her, after his own experience, but he wasn't going to say that. "It takes more courage not to do it."

She didn't answer, just closed her eyes, and after a bit he thought she'd gone back to sleep. He envied her. Right now he would have done just about anything to feel warm again. He eased closer to the fire, thinking he was cold enough right now that if his mittens caught fire he wouldn't even notice it.

The howling wind was one of the loneliest sounds he'd ever heard. When he finally got up to stretch his cold-stiffened muscles and looked out the window, he saw that the snow was still blowing around, and drifting a little beneath the trees. It wasn't that deep yet, he assured himself, so maybe they weren't getting all that much new stuff. He hoped not.

He paced around the small cabin, trying to be quiet about it so as not to disturb Allie. Little by little his muscles relaxed and he began to feel a bit warmer. He was also getting hungrier by the minute. Soup and a granola bar hadn't been enough supper, not when he was so cold and morning was a long way away.

Allie surprised him, sitting up suddenly. "I'm hungry," she announced.

"Me, too," he admitted.

"There's some more jerky in my backpack. And we can boil some water and make soup."

"I'll make it for you. But you don't have a whole lot of food, Allie."

"I won't need much."

That made his heart feel heavy, but he didn't say anything. Instead he got the water they still had left and put it next to the fire to heat.

"We gotta get home tomorrow," he said again.

"You can go. I'm staying."

"Don't be silly. You don't want to die."

"You don't know what I want."

"Yes, I do, and I think you're crazy. Whatever's

got you so upset right now will seem silly in a few weeks.''

"You don't know. Besides, I've been upset about this for eight months now. It's not getting any better.''

"Well, my life's not getting any better, either, but I'm sure it will once I'm old enough to be on my own.''

She appeared to think about that, watching the flames dance. He put a couple more branches on the fire and watched the embers fly upward, then wink out.

It seemed to take forever for the water to heat, but at least it was something he could do that had a finite limit on it, unlike this endless night. It was something to focus on, something to look forward to in the next few minutes. It seemed to help.

She spoke. "Why don't we trade now? You can warm up in the sleeping bag for a little while.''

But he knew if he got in that sleeping bag, he would fall asleep. And he didn't trust Allie not to walk out into the snow while he was snoring and disappear forever. "I'm fine," he said. "Really.''

"You sure?''

"Positive.'' He stopped pacing and settled down by the fire again, soaking up its warmth. He wished he had a watch so he would have some idea how much longer this was going to last.

"I really only slept a short time?'' she asked.

"You hardly conked out before you woke up again.'' It was a lie, but he said it remorselessly, because he didn't want to argue with her about taking turns.

"Okay." She seemed to accept that. "I just feel so awake."

"It's the cold. Better to feel awake, anyway."

She didn't answer, but squirmed around inside her sleeping bag, trying to get into a more comfortable sitting position.

"Look," he said after a minute. "Whatever you're planning to do, promise me you'll take a couple of days to think about it."

"Why?"

"Because I need to be sure you're sure about this. I couldn't live with myself if you went off and did some harebrained thing."

"That's not fair! I'm not your responsibility."

"Sorry, Allie, but it feels like you are, since I found you."

"Nobody asked you to find me. I sure didn't."

"Don't act like a kid. Try being grown-up about this."

"Listen to you. Like you're an old man."

"I'm two years older." Which wasn't a whole lot, and even he knew it. "At least talk to me about what's bothering you. Maybe it's not as bad as you think."

"Right." She made a disgusted sound and looked down. This time her hair didn't cover her face, because she had the hood of the mummy bag zipped tightly. All he could see was the oval from her eyebrows to her chin.

"Look," he said. "I'll make you a deal. If you promise not to do something stupid tomorrow, I'll go down the mountain and get you some more food."

"How do I know you won't tell everybody where I am?"

"I'll make you a promise. I never broke a promise yet."

"You don't have any money."

"I got some." About twenty bucks he'd collected from weeding Mrs. Beaudry's stupid garden.

"I've got money," she said after a minute. "Plenty of money. I'll give you some."

"Fair enough. But you have to promise you won't pull anything while I'm gone. Give it at least another day to think this through."

It wasn't so very different from what she'd originally intended anyway, so she nodded. "Okay."

"You promise?"

"I promise. And you have to promise, too."

"I promise I won't tell anyone where you are."

She seemed satisfied with that. When the water was heated, he filled a cup and mixed soup in it for her. Then he passed her a strip of jerky. She unzipped her bag just enough to poke one hand out.

"You have to eat, too," she told him.

He didn't feel bad about doing so, now that he knew he was going to get her more food tomorrow. But he didn't want to eat too much, because she would need it while she waited for him to return.

It helped, though. A cup of soup warmed him on the inside, where he was getting dangerously cold. He just hoped he could get down this damn mountain in one piece, then back up with the food.

Well, he would do it because he had to. It was the only way he could be sure to keep Allie alive. And he had a lot of practice doing what he had to.

6

The night was endless. Earl dozed in a chair near Meg, who was still lying on her bed, still fully clothed. She'd refused his insistence that she eat something. She did sleep, though. Exhaustion made her do it, even though it was restless sleep.

Just before first light, Midget and George returned to open the command post. Midget brought him a change of clothes, and he risked taking a shower and changing into a fresh uniform. God knew, after two days he smelled like a barn animal.

Meg was just waking when he returned to the bedroom. The leaden dawn barely penetrated the windows, but he saw her sit up and push her hair out of her eyes.

"Take a shower," he suggested. "I'll make us some breakfast. Then we'll join the search."

His words galvanized her. She was up and off the bed like a shot, disappearing into the bathroom.

Good. He'd said the right thing. Not that he had a hope in hell that the two of them would be able to do anything the other searchers hadn't, but he knew he couldn't wait around another minute. And Meg probably felt the same way.

He went downstairs and gave thanks to God that Vivian was nowhere about. He was in a mean, ornery mood, and one wrong word from that woman would have put him through the roof.

He found bacon and eggs and coffee, and started them. He made toast in the toaster oven, and buttered it thickly. They had to eat well if they were going to spend time out in the cold.

The day lightened a little more, and what he saw out the window did not please him. White snow powdered the world. It wasn't thick down here, but he was sure it was a lot deeper up above.

Midget came in through the front and joined him in the kitchen. "They're gathering again," he told Earl. "Not as many as yesterday, but that's hardly surprising. They got families to feed."

And it was a workday. Earl had expected this. "How's the weather?"

"Clearing. Ceiling's at ten thousand feet and lifting."

"Can the search planes go up again?"

Midget shrugged. "I'll check it out." He turned to leave, and paused as Meg came into the room. "Morning, Ms. Williams. We're getting ready to search again."

"Thank you." But her tone was flat and her eyes were hollow, and Earl wondered if he was making a mistake letting her come with him. In her condition she would probably hamper him. But he didn't have the heart to stop her.

Earl scooped the bacon out of the pan and let it

drain on a paper towel. He cracked a couple of eggs for her and three for himself, and turned down the heat on the pan a little.

"You're going to eat," he said to her. "Either you eat, or you don't come with me."

She nodded. He wondered what the dark secrets were behind her hollow eyes. And he was afraid to ask, because he had the feeling that if he knew the truth, his life would change forever.

She spoke. "I need to make coffee for the searchers."

"I'll do it," Vivian said, coming into the kitchen. She headed straight for the coffee urn without once glancing at her daughter. Earl managed to keep his mouth shut.

It occurred to him that the tension in this household was almost enough to make *him* run away. And the silences...the silences were getting longer and deeper. There was something seriously wrong here in addition to a runaway child.

After breakfast, he sent Meg to dress for the trek and went out himself to review the maps. The searchers had been pretty good about reporting how far they'd gotten, and he was disappointed to see that none of them had gone as far as he'd hoped yesterday. Even if Allie had hiked only half the day yesterday, until the clouds moved in, she had enlarged the search area enough that it was almost hopeless. There just weren't enough bodies to cover all that ground. If the child decided not to answer when someone called her name, they could walk right by her. And if she was hurt and unconscious...

Well, he couldn't let himself think about that. No way. That kind of thinking was self-defeating.

The morning air stayed icy, even as the day lightened. If the clouds didn't dissipate, he had very little hope that any of the snow would melt. Every breath he was expelling blew a cloud of steam, and his ears and nose were already aching. When Meg joined him, he pulled on a ski mask. "Let's go."

"Where to?"

"I've been looking at the maps. There's an area straight up the mountain that wouldn't be too hard to get at from here that hasn't been searched."

"Sounds good to me."

He looked at her. "Are you sure about this, Meg? It's not going to help anyone if you can't make this climb. We'll be ascending for the next couple of hours."

"I'll make it."

He figured she probably would, on sheer determination alone.

He gave directions to the other searchers—there were only a handful of them today—and sent them on their way. Midget reported that the planes couldn't go up until the ceiling reached at least twelve thousand feet, which it probably would around noon. On the other hand, the pilots were hopeful that they would be able to spot Allie if she moved at all, because she would leave a visible trail in the snow anywhere the trees broke.

That information seemed to hearten Meg. She stood a little straighter, and her chin poked out a bit. Neither of them mentioned the possibility that Allie could have frozen to death overnight, but he knew they were both thinking about it.

The first part of the climb wasn't that difficult, but it wasn't long before they were on rough ground, having to climb up and down through narrow gorges and over rocks. The snow made it even more difficult. Nearly every surface was slippery, increasing the amount of work they had to do.

After about forty-five minutes, Meg was panting heavily and beginning to lose her coordination. Earl called a halt and offered her a granola bar. She took it as if it were medicine.

"You were right," she said finally.

"About what?"

"I was stupid to come out here." She waved her arm at the surrounding woods. "It's a big mountain. We could walk right past her and never see her. Somehow…"

Somehow she hadn't wanted to believe that. He could understand. "I'm here, aren't I?"

"It's impossible, isn't it? If she doesn't want to be found, or if… Well, it's just about impossible."

"Hey, look. The searchers have been over this area. She's not right around here. In another hour, we'll get to an area that hasn't been checked yet, and we'll do a search grid. You'll feel a whole lot better then."

The wind gusted suddenly, blowing up a cloud of snow that stung their faces. Meg wiped the melting crystals off her face and bit into her granola bar with determination.

After she swallowed, she said, "I can't give up hope."

"Of course you can't. It's too damn soon, anyway."

"Is it?" She sounded almost listless. "It's so cold...."

He watched her turn her head and look up at the mountain through the trees, as if she hoped her eyes could pick out something hopeful. Or as if she was measuring the mountain as an opponent.

He ate his own granola bar, keeping himself warm by shifting from one foot to the other. He knew they would find Allie. The only question was whether they would find her in time. He was trying not to remember all the times they hadn't discovered a missing hiker until spring, when the snow melted.

A few minutes later they started climbing again. Meg seemed better for a while, but after about twenty minutes her coordination began to suffer again. He watched her make three attempts to climb over a slippery rock that she should have been able to take in one. He shouldn't have brought her up here.

The thought filled him with dread. He cared about Meg. Just how much he cared was something he refused to look at. She'd been his best friend's wife, for crying out loud, and he was both a loyal and honorable man. All these years he'd had a special feeling toward her, but he'd always categorized it as a friendship.

But as he climbed, he found himself remembering the first time they'd met. It was better than thinking about Allie and where she might be. It was an escape, for just a few minutes, and while he felt guilty about it, he was eager to take the relief the memory offered.

Meg had been a brand-new bride then, just showing

the first signs of Allie's impending arrival. She'd been shy, almost reluctant to speak to him, seeming almost intimidated by both Earl and her husband, as if they were too loud and too big. And she had looked so delicate, so fragile. Just like Allie.

But right there and then he'd felt a protective urge fill him, and it had never gone away. It had extended to Allie, when she was born, but for Meg it had always been especially strong.

There had been times over the years when he'd wondered if Bill and Meg were as happy together as they should be, but he'd always dismissed the questions as coming from a green-eyed monster in the animal part of his brain. It was no secret to him that he'd always wanted that kind of special relationship.

And it was no secret that the closest he'd ever managed to come to it had been with Meg. His best friend's wife. Just a friend.

Meg slipped again, and this time she fell, crying out as she hit the ground. He was at her side instantly.

"Are you hurt?"

"No. I'm fine." She gave him a wan smile. "Just...frustrated."

He helped her up, and this time when they resumed their climb, he stayed tacked to her side. A fall would be especially dangerous in these cold wet conditions. A broken leg would create problems he didn't want to think about. He should have insisted she stay at home.

But he hadn't. And now he had to make certain he got her back down safely, even if they didn't come across Allie. Did he need a head doctor or what?

"Who's that?" Meg asked suddenly.

He lifted his head and looked in the direction she was pointing. A dark figure was coming down the slope toward him.

"Allie?" Meg said, just a whisper, her voice breaking.

"No." It wasn't Allie.

"No," she agreed, her tone forlorn.

As the figure drew closer, Earl recognized it. "Matt Dawson. What the hell is he doing up here alone?" He called out, "Hey, Matt!"

The figure stopped moving. Then, with what seemed like reluctance, Matt began coming their way. When he got within fifteen feet, Earl said, "What are you doing up here alone?"

"Looking for Allie," the youth said, his expression closed. He looked down at his feet.

"Alone? Do you know how dangerous that is?"

The boy shrugged. "The men didn't want me around. They don't like me. So I came by myself."

Earl looked him over. "You're not even dressed right."

"I noticed." Matt's tone was truculent. "I'm going to get warmer clothes."

"Good idea. But don't come up here alone again. I don't need to be searching for two people."

"Sure." Matt shrugged, as if it didn't matter.

"Did you see anything?" Meg asked him, her voice tight with hope. "Anything at all?"

"Nah."

Earl saw Meg's face crumple, and he instinctively reached for her hand. "It doesn't mean anything, Meg." Then he turned to the boy. "Where were you looking?"

"Up around that old miner's cabin up there." He jerked his head. "I figured she might have gone there for shelter."

That was exactly where Earl had been planning to look, and he felt his heart sink. "You checked out everything up there?"

"All over," the youth said. He still wouldn't look at Earl. "Just like you said. In a grid."

Earl's heart suddenly felt like lead, and he realized his strongest hope was dying. He didn't dare look at Meg for fear she would read death in his eyes.

"We'd better head back down, Meg," Earl said.

She nodded, her head hanging.

"The planes will start searching soon. They can do more than we can. She must have built a fire by now."

But Meg didn't say a word. She just turned and started stumbling down the mountain.

Matt felt like an absolute shit as he followed them. When he'd promised Allie not to tell anyone where she was, he'd imagined that he just wouldn't volunteer the information. He'd never imagined that he would have to lie to Allie's mom.

It was the first time in his life when he'd been in a situation where every choice was wrong. He simply couldn't break a promise, though. It seemed funny in a kid whose dad had been breaking promises his whole life—or maybe not funny. All he knew was that it was wrong to break a promise, and he'd extracted a promise from Allie in return for his. He couldn't betray that trust. And he couldn't risk doing something that might make Allie break her promise to him.

So, to assuage his conscience, he promised himself something. He promised himself that once he got back up that mountain with supplies, he would find a way to talk Allie into coming down.

When they got back to the house nearly two hours later, Matt was feeling about two inches tall. Mrs. Williams wanted him to come inside and have something to eat, but he refused. He couldn't be near her another minute, because his promise was getting weaker by the minute. He dashed straight to his beat-up old car—bought with money from doing odd jobs since he was twelve—and roared down the road toward town. It was only then that he realized the sheriff hadn't even asked him why he wasn't in school with all the other kids today.

Earl had radar. Intuition, ESP, whatever, he always thought of it as radar. And something about Matt Dawson had his alarms going off like mad. He didn't follow Meg into the house right away. Instead he went to the command post and spoke to George, who said Midget had gone for a lunch break.

"No news," George said. "The planes think they'll be going up soon, though."

Earl looked out the door of the command post and decided that was wishful thinking. If anything, the clouds seemed to be lower now. And darker. "Listen," he said to George. "Get on the radio. I want somebody to follow Matt Dawson. He's on his way back to town right now. Tail him, find out what he does and get back to me. And don't stop watching him until I say so.''

George nodded. "Okay. Anything else?"

"Yeah, don't let him know he's got a tail."

Every kind of crazy thought was filling Earl's head now, from some misguided Romeo and Juliet thing, to rape and murder. If anybody had asked him, he would have said Matt Dawson wasn't capable of rape or murder, but with a girl missing and Matt acting strangely, he wasn't betting on anything right now.

His stomach turned over a couple of times, but it wasn't from hunger. The things he was thinking right now were dark and ugly, and they sickened him.

He went up to the house to check on Meg, but she'd locked herself in the bedroom. Vivian was again in the living room, reading the Bible out loud in a monotonous drone.

Something was so wrong in this house it angered him. What kind of mother offered no comfort to her daughter in circumstances like these? Why was Vivian so cold, and why did Meg act as though she deserved it? He didn't know which of the women he wanted to shake more, but he would settle for whichever of them would talk the fastest.

And what had Vivian meant when she said he didn't know Meg? That was horseshit.

Back out in the command post, he listened to the reports as they came in. The searchers were finding nothing; the planes still hadn't gone up. It wouldn't be long before the search parties would have to give up because of the cold. He knew it was inevitable, but he didn't like it.

Matt Dawson went to the store when he got to

town, according to the report the deputy radioed in. Bought a lot of lightweight food. Dried soup, beef jerky, some candy and granola bars. A couple of bottles of propane.

At that, the hair on the back of Earl's neck stood on end.

Then the kid went to Goodwill and bought himself a new winter jacket. Seemed normal. After all, the rag that Matt was wearing couldn't be keeping him very warm. Some mittens. A ski mask.

Then the hardware store for a backpack and an ax.

That was when Earl's alarms became deafening.

"He's heading back out of town," reported the cop who was following him. "Back up toward the Williams place."

"Let me know where he stops."

George spoke. "Where the fuck did he get all that money?"

Earl didn't answer, but he was thinking about the two hundred dollars Allie had saved. It must've seemed like an awful lot of money to Matt. Maybe too much.

And he didn't want to believe what he was thinking, for Allie's sake and Matt's both.

"He's pulling off the road," the deputy reported. "About a half mile east of the Williams place."

A good place to start hiking from, Earl thought. Almost as good as the Williams place itself—if you were headed for that abandoned miner's cabin.

He thought quickly, deciding the best way to handle the situation. If they simply followed the kid, he might catch on and mislead them. If they confronted him, he might deny all knowledge and refuse to take them to Allie. He decided on following.

"Pass by him and come up to the house," he told the deputy. "Pick me up. We're going to follow the kid."

Twenty minutes later, he and Sam Canfield were following Matt Dawson's tracks into the snowy woods.

Meg had cried herself dry again by the time she came out of her bedroom. Hope was withering with each passing minute, but neither the death of hope nor the tears she had cried could ease the pressure in her chest or the tightness in her throat. Dry-eyed, she went to her daughter's room and sat on the bed, hugging Allie's pillow.

She could still smell Allie there, and the scent clawed at her soul. Allie, her baby. Looking around the room, she studied the posters and the dolls and the stack of teen magazines. There was a little stuffed green alien doll with big black eyes sitting on the computer. Allie had named him Herm, and for a time had slept with him every night. There was the science-fair award for a geology presentation hanging on the wall over the computer, and Meg remembered how proud she had been that night when Allie took second place.

The rock collections, all carefully labeled and glued to sheets of poster board, were missing now. As were the Spice Girls CDs that Allie listened to endlessly. The gaps mirrored the growing hole in Meg's heart.

She didn't think she could bear this loss. She really didn't think she could survive it. Anything else she could handle, but not this. Oh, God, not this. If anything happened to her daughter, there would be no reason left to live. Fear and grief warred in her, holding her almost paralyzed.

She should never have let Earl bring her down the mountain so soon, she thought now. Never mind that Matt Dawson had already searched the area they'd been heading for, never mind that she'd been growing so cold and fatigued that she kept tripping. There must have been some other place they could have searched. And if she hadn't been so cold and tired that she wasn't thinking clearly, she would have realized that.

And where was Earl, anyway? Why hadn't he come to tell her the search planes had gone up? A glance out Allie's window told her why. How had she failed to notice that the day had darkened again, and that the clouds were sweeping low, concealing the peaks?

Even if Allie had managed to survive last night, how could she possibly survive another one like it?

Jumping up from the bed, she went downstairs. She ignored her mother's droning voice from the living room and looked everywhere for Earl. When she didn't find him, she pulled on her jacket and went out to the command post.

George Murphy jumped when she opened the door. "Oh. Hi, Ms. Williams. No news, I'm afraid. The searchers are coming in now."

"What about the planes?"

He hesitated, then shook his head. "They never got off the ground. We're socked in."

As if she hadn't noticed. "Where's Earl?"

"He went back up the mountain. To search."

For an instant Meg thought her knees were going to buckle. Now she had two people up on that mountain to worry about.

The higher they climbed, the worse the weather got. Earl and Sam exchanged looks but kept forging forward. The clouds were surrounding them now, but at least it hadn't started snowing. Matt's trail was easy enough to follow, and by this point Earl had a pretty good idea they were heading straight for the abandoned miner's shack.

The day was getting dark, even though they had a few hours before sunset yet, and Earl began to worry whether they would be able to see their way back down.

It was getting so that they had to pause frequently, too, to catch their wind, but they couldn't halt too long, because the cold started to get to them. From Matt's tracks, though, it appeared the boy was pausing often, too.

"What do you think he's up to?" Sam asked finally.

"I don't want to think about it," Earl said flatly. "But I think he knows where Allie is."

"Well, yeah, that would make sense. Can't imagine any other reason the stupid kid would hike into a brewing snowstorm."

"Me neither." He and Sam went back a long way, and their minds tended to run on similar paths.

"I mean," said Sam, his tone growing wry, "look at us two idiots. Would we be out here otherwise?"

"Nope."

"On the other hand, maybe the kid just got fed up with his old man and decided to run away himself."

Earl shook his head. "There was something funny about the way he was acting when Meg and I caught up with him on the mountain earlier."

"Well, I hope to God you're right. I know Meg can't handle much more of this, and I'm starting to feel *I* can't, either. What the hell made that girl do something so foolish?"

"I wish I knew. But I mean to find out." And he was damn well going to, he promised himself. No more of Meg's evasions. He was going to demand she explain a bunch of things to him, because whatever was wrong in that house had caused his godchild to run away.

And whether she liked it or not, that made it his business.

They were close to the cabin now. Earl signed to Sam to slow down, so they wouldn't startle the boy, and received a nod in return. Moving as stealthily as they could, they followed Matt's tracks through the trees until they could just barely make out the cabin. Earl was thinking about the best way to approach it when he heard a bloodcurdling sound.

"No!"

Matt Dawson's scream tore through the air, then was swallowed by freshly falling snow.

7

Earl charged forward, caution forgotten. He could hear Sam hard on his heels. They burst into the clearing, but Matt was nowhere in sight.

"No!" This time the scream was quieter, more anguished, but it gave Earl direction. He headed uphill toward a rocky gorge, slipping in the snow, nearly spraining his ankle on a rock. He found Matt standing at the edge of the gorge, looking downward.

Matt heard their pounding feet and turned to face them, his expression so stricken that Earl felt his heart stop.

"She promised," Matt cried. "She promised me she wouldn't!"

All of a sudden Earl couldn't breathe. All of a sudden he felt as if his shoulders were melting, running downward into a puddle of weakness. Hot and cold washed through him in shocked waves.

At the bottom of the gorge, Allie lay like a broken rag doll.

"She promised me," Matt said again, crying now. "She promised me!"

Earl ignored him. "Sam, see if you can raise any-body on the radio. We need help *now*."

Sam probably nodded, but Earl never looked at him. He couldn't take his eyes off Allie's small body at the bottom of the ravine. Without a single thought for his own safety, he began to make his way down to her, sliding at times, nearly falling at others. Behind him he heard Sam talking into the radio. The snow was falling faster now, like the wildly whirling flakes in a snow globe.

He reached the bottom and found himself standing in a couple of inches of icy water. Some of it made it through the waterproofing on his boots, but he hardly noticed. Stumbling to Allie's side, he squatted and put his hand inside the throat of her parka, feeling for a pulse. Her lips were blue, but her cheeks were still pink, a good sign.

There was a pulse. For an instant, relief washed through him in a surge so strong he couldn't move. Then he yelled up the slope, "She's alive!"

Training took over. He forced himself to forget that this was Allie lying here so still and silent and began to check for broken bones. When he touched her left femur, he felt a break. At his touch, she moaned without regaining consciousness, flailing and tossing her head. It was a good sign, he told himself. She probably hadn't broken her neck or back.

He looked up and through the snow saw both Sam and Matt looking down anxiously.

"We've got to get her out of here somehow. Matt, do you have a tarp? A sleeping bag? A blanket?"

"She has a mummy bag, Sheriff."

"Get it, will you? And bring your ax down here when you come. Sam? You raise anyone?"

"All I'm getting is static. I'll keep trying."

"When Matt gets back with the bag, bring the rope down, will you?"

"Sure thing."

While he waited, he talked to Allie, trying to wake her up, but she remained unresponsive. Pulling off his own jacket, he laid it over her legs, which were covered only by jeans. Then he prayed as hard as he had ever prayed in his life.

Ten minutes later, Sam and Matt joined him. Together they chopped some saplings to make a splint for her leg. Allie groaned as they tied it to her but still didn't wake. When Earl's gaze met Sam's, he saw the same fear he felt reflected there. It didn't look good.

They chopped down a couple more saplings, cut some holes in Allie's sleeping bag, then carefully lifted her into it, putting the saplings on either side of her. When they zipped her in, they had a jury-rigged stretcher with the saplings poking out either end.

Getting her up the side of the ravine was difficult, but they managed it at the cost of some bruises to their shins and knees. At the top, they stopped long enough for Sam to try the radio again. Still nothing but static. Snow was falling heavily, and the world was a dark gray.

It didn't look good at all, Earl thought as he lifted his end of the stretcher. It didn't look good at all. And he still hadn't asked Matt Dawson what the hell was going on here.

Allie didn't weigh much, but the ground was rough

and the snow was slippery, which made the going tough. From time to time, Sam tried the radio again. Matt took turns, spelling Sam and Earl when they needed it, but the kid was already tired and fatigued. More fatigued than he should have been, Earl thought, considering he hadn't done any more climbing in the cold today than Earl had.

"What the hell is going on?" he asked Matt on puffs of air. "What were you and Allie doing up here?"

"Nothing! I mean, I found her yesterday, and we got snowed in."

"So why didn't you tell her mother and me where she was when we asked you earlier?"

"Allie made me promise not to tell anyone. I was afraid if I broke my promise—"

Matt broke off, making Earl even more suspicious. "Afraid of what?" he demanded.

But Matt merely shook his head.

"And what were you screaming about, that she promised you?"

Again Matt shook his head. "She'll have to tell you, Sheriff."

"Look, the kid's at death's door and I have a right to know why. She's my goddaughter, for Chrissake!"

Matt took over, spelling him, giving him a chance to get his breath back and work up a good head of anger.

"Look, Dawson, the situation is suspicious as hell. The girl disappears, and three days later we find you standing over her broken body. I could make a case for locking you up for a good long time. So maybe you better tell me what's going on."

"I told you! I found her yesterday, we got snowed in, and she made me promise not to tell anybody where she was! And that's all there is to it."

"And just what did *she* promise *you?*"

Matt walked in silence for a while, hardly seeming to notice when he nearly lost his footing. His jaw was working tensely. When Matt slipped again, Earl nudged him aside, once again taking hold of the makeshift stretcher. His arms were aching now, and even the break hadn't helped all that much.

Then Matt startled him by speaking. "She promised she wouldn't kill herself if I promised not to tell where she was."

Shock left Earl cold, colder than the snowy day could have done. Cold all the way to the roots of his very soul.

Sam spoke. "Take over for me, kid."

Matt obediently changed places with him, and Sam keyed on his radio.

"I don't believe him," Sam said to Earl. "The kid screamed no, then we find Allie at the foot of the ravine. Maybe they had a fight and he's covering the fact that he pushed her."

It was easier to believe than Allie wanting to kill herself, but not by much. Not when Allie had left that note.

"I don't think so," Earl said reluctantly. "I don't think so."

Twenty minutes later, Sam was able to raise George on the radio. Help was on the way.

Meg was standing at the glass doors at the back of the house, looking out at the falling snow. The clouds seemed to be brushing the tops of the trees now, and the day had darkened so much it looked like late evening.

Her back and legs were stiff from standing for so long without moving, but she didn't notice. It was a kind of suspended animation, as if everything inside her had gone still and silent. She wasn't even thinking. She was past thinking about anything. All she could do was feel, and feeling swamped her with terror, dread and anxiety.

Allie, come home. God, please, let Allie come home. The words had been running through her mind so long that she hardly heard them. Every muscle in her body was tense, but she didn't notice. *Allie...*

"Something's going on," Vivian's voice called from the front of the house.

Meg jerked out of her stasis in an instant, and she hurried on stiff legs to where Vivian was looking out the window.

"What?" she asked.

"Lotsa cars. An ambulance."

Meg tugged the curtain out of her mother's hand and looked herself. What she saw brought her back to painful life. Three sheriff's cars. The search and rescue ambulance...

Oh, God, someone was hurt. Grabbing her jacket from the bench by the front door, she tugged it on and hurried outside.

"What's going on?" she called to the men who were unloading a basket stretcher from the back of the ambulance.

They exchanged looks, then one of them said, "Injury on the mountain."

"Who? Who's hurt?" Her heart was hammering so hard now that it hurt, and when nobody answered her, she wanted to scream. She ran down the steps, then raced across to the command post and threw the door open.

"George, what's going on? I want to know *now!*"

He pulled his headphones off and looked at her. "They found Allie," he said. "She's alive, but she has a broken leg. Sam and Earl are bringing her down now."

Meg's legs started to buckle, and she grabbed the door frame. "You're sure? How bad? Is she really okay?"

"All I know is she has a broken leg. Yes, she's really okay."

Meg sagged down onto the step, too weak to stand, too exhausted to cry. She sat there, watching as the rescue team gathered its supplies and started up the mountain with a couple of deputies. A broken leg. Thank God it was only a broken leg. That would heal.

But the rest of it would probably be harder to heal. Only, she couldn't think of that right now. All she could think of was that her daughter was coming down that mountain, and in a little while she could put her arms around her and tell her how much she loved her. Just a little while longer.

After a bit, as her strength returned, she realized she needed to make food and coffee. Those men were going to be cold when they brought Allie down, especially Earl and Sam. And Allie would need a hot drink, too....

She ran back to the house, where she found Vivian

in the kitchen, making sandwiches, heating a huge pot of soup on the stove.

"Allie's okay!"

"I heard."

"A broken leg, but that'll mend."

"Unlike some things," said Vivian.

Meg turned on her mother. "Just what do you mean by that?"

"You let that child run wild. This never would have happened if you'd listened to me!"

God, thought Meg. Her mother couldn't even soften enough to feel joy that Allie was okay. She felt a burst of anger so hot that it blinded her for a moment. And, as if from a distance, she heard her own voice say, "None of this would ever have happened if I hadn't listened to you years ago."

She heard Vivian's gasp, but she didn't care. She was past caring about anything at all except that Allie was okay.

The searchers emerged from the woods an hour later with Allie in the basket stretcher. Meg ran to her daughter's side and felt her breath catch as she saw how pale and cold her child looked.

"Allie...Allie?"

The rescuers kept moving toward the ambulance, and Meg stumbled as she tried to keep pace. "Allie, sweetie?"

An arm suddenly closed around her shoulders, and she was drawn into Earl's big, comforting embrace for the first time since Bill's funeral.

"Meg," he said.

She looked up at him, free enough of fear to notice

how exhausted he looked, how sunken his eyes seemed. How blue his lips were.

"Are you okay?" she asked him, finding room to care about something in addition to Allie. Caring more than she probably should have.

"I'm fine. Listen, about Allie..."

Her heart stopped. "What? *What?*"

His mouth tightened, and so did his arms, as if he was afraid she would slip away. "She's been unconscious since we found her."

The world tipped and reeled, and Meg closed her eyes. "Oh, God," she whispered. "Oh, God..."

"It's probably going to be all right," he said. "But she took a pretty bad fall. You ride with her in the ambulance, okay? I'll catch up later."

She wanted his strength then as she had never wanted it before, but he helped her up into the ambulance and then turned away, saying to Sam, "Take the Dawson kid in for questioning."

The ambulance doors closed with a thud, and moments later it started bouncing down the rutted driveway, while the medical technician began to work on Allie.

Meg was alone, without any support in the world, and nothing but memories of everything she had ever done wrong.

Earl joined Meg in the emergency waiting room at the hospital nearly an hour later. He'd taken time to change into some dry clothes, and had left Matt Dawson in Sam's care, hoping Sam could pry more information out of the boy.

Meg was staring blindly at a blank wall, her fingers

twisting constantly around each other. She looked like a woman who'd just been promised that everything was fine, only to find out it was as bad as it always had been.

"What did they say?" he asked as he slipped into a plastic chair beside her.

"She's still unconscious. They set her leg, now they're getting ready to do some more tests."

"Does she have to go to Denver?" This was a small town, with only minor medical facilities. If Allie needed a brain scan, they would have to send her out.

"Not yet. The doctor said her reflexes are fine, and he wants to do some more tests before he decides to send her to Denver."

"Well, that's good news."

She nodded, but the corners of her mouth were trembling visibly. "What happened to her, Earl?"

He couldn't answer that question, and this was absolutely *not* the time to tell her what Matt had said about Allie wanting to kill herself. "We're trying to find out, Meggie. But it looks as if she just took a fall."

"What about Matt Dawson? Why'd you take him in for questioning?"

He cursed himself for letting her overhear that. He should have waited a couple of minutes more before telling Sam what he wanted.

"He found her," he said, hoping she would leave it there for now.

She did. She nodded slowly, jerkily, as if her body were an unfamiliar machine she wasn't quite sure how to operate. "I seem," she said slowly, "to be having trouble absorbing all this."

"I know. I am, too." He slipped his arm around her shoulders and was relieved when she leaned into him. He couldn't remember how many times he'd wanted to comfort her that way but hadn't dared, for fear she wouldn't like it.

"It's not possible, is it?"

"What isn't?"

"That God would give me Allie back and then take her away again?"

He was inclined to believe that God was capable of just about anything, but he would have cheerfully died before telling her that right now. "I don't think so, Meggie."

"Me either." She drew a shaky breath. "I can't believe that's going to happen. She *has* to be all right."

"I'm sure she will be." He wished he felt as positive as he sounded, but Allie had been unconscious for hours now, and that wasn't a good sign.

Meg reached out and took his hand in hers, clinging to it. "It can't happen. I won't let it happen."

He nodded, battling the sense of hopelessness that was darkening the edges of his mind. He didn't believe in happy endings. He'd seen too many bad endings in his life, had experienced too many of them himself. But this time he was determined not to give in to the sense of doom that was haunting him. This time he desperately needed to believe in a happy ending.

"Mrs. Williams?"

She jumped and pulled away from Earl, looking up.

Dr. Dekker stood a few feet away, his hands stuffed into his white coat. He was a young doctor, new to Whisper Creek, but by virtue of his job familiar to most everyone in town.

"Good news," the doctor said. "Allie's awake."

"Oh, thank God!" Meg started to cry. She turned instinctively toward Earl, and he opened his arms to her, letting her cling to him and press her face to his shoulder. Allie was awake. The unbearable tension in him let go, and he bent his head, pressing his face to Meg's soft hair.

Dr. Dekker gave them a minute, then spoke again. "You can go in and see her. She's a little confused, but she knows who she is, and she's asking for you."

Meg pulled out of Earl's arms instantly and jumped to her feet. Earl rose, too, ready to follow, then realized that it might not be his place. Maybe he wasn't wanted. Maybe he wasn't allowed.

It wasn't a new feeling to him, being on the outside, being the one who didn't belong. He'd spent his whole life feeling that way. But this time, familiarity didn't make it any easier to take. He needed to see Allie.

Meg turned and took his hand. "She'll want to see you, too."

"Family only," Dekker said.

"Earl *is* family," Meg said firmly. "He's Allie's godfather."

Dekker shrugged. "Okay. She's in the last cubicle on the end," he added, pointing through a door and down a hallway. "We're setting up a room for her right now. She'll need to stay at least overnight, but you can probably take her home in the morning."

Meg was already racing down the hallway, and Earl hurried to catch up with her. He needed to see with his own two eyes that Allie was awake and making at least some sense. Then he promised himself he would withdraw and leave Meg and Allie alone together.

Allie was indeed awake, and as soon as she saw her mother, she burst into tears and cried, "Mommy…"

Earl stayed back near the doorway, allowing the privacy curtain to screen him from Allie and Meg for now. He could hear the two of them crying, could hear Meg saying over and over, "Oh, Allie…oh, Allie, I've been so worried. Oh, sweetie…"

And Allie sobbing violently, "I'm sorry…I'm sorry…."

That sounded good, he told himself. Especially Allie saying she was sorry. Whatever crazy notion she'd taken to make her run away must have vanished. At least for now.

But that didn't mean *he* was going to forget about it.

Eventually the crying quieted. Then Meg poked her head around the curtain. Her green eyes were red and puffy, but she was smiling. "Earl, what are you doing hiding over there? Allie wants to see you, too."

So Earl entered the cubicle and found his goddaughter lying back against a big pillow, looking smaller than she had in years. Her eyes were blackened from the concussion she'd suffered, and her broken leg, in a huge cast, was lying on top of the blankets.

Allie gave him a watery, wavery smile. "Hi, Uncle Earl."

"Don't you look just jim-dandy," he said with forced cheer. "I suppose black circles under the eyes are all the rage these days?"

She hiccuped a laugh; then more huge tears ran down her face. "I'm sorry," she said to him. "I'm sorry."

"What the hell happened, Chipmunk?" It was a pet name for her that he hadn't used in years, because along about the time she turned nine, she decided it was a baby name.

"I was stupid," she said, her voice breaking.

"Well, that goes without saying. Falling off a cliff is usually a stupid thing to do."

Again that hiccuping laugh that was on the edge of a sob. He wondered if he was overdoing the jocularity under the circumstances, but he wasn't ready to edge close to what was really going on here, because he suspected she wasn't ready yet, either. Besides, he didn't want to say something that might upset Meg all over again. Now that they had Allie back, there was plenty of time to deal with what had happened and why.

He approached Allie on the opposite side of the bed from Meg and took her hand. Then, overwhelmed by the love he felt for the child, he brushed her tangled brown hair back from her forehead and pressed a kiss there.

"You scared us to death," he told her, his voice a rough murmur. "Thank God you're alive."

They sat talking for a little while, telling Allie all about the search over the last three days. Earl noticed that Allie avoided mentioning why she'd gone up the mountain or anything about what she'd been doing there. And Meg just as scrupulously avoided asking her.

But after a bit Allie started to look really tired. Meg decided she was going to stay the night at the hospital, getting a cot in Allie's room. Earl took that as his cue to vanish.

"I'll see you tomorrow, Chipmunk."

She smiled wanly and squeezed his hand. "I guess I'll be here."

And she didn't sound at all happy about that, Earl thought with trepidation.

While it had snowed up on the mountains for the last two days, it hadn't snowed here in the valley. The streets were damp from rain showers, and the air was cold, but winter hadn't quite reached the town of Whisper Creek yet. Headlights glistened on the pavement as Earl negotiated the hill down from the hospital and turned onto Main Street to drive to the sheriff's office.

The sidewalks along Main had been paved with brick and lighted with Victorian-style streetlamps in an attempt to draw tourists. The attempt had so far failed miserably—mainly, Earl thought, because the town didn't have a whole lot to offer. Most of the buildings along Main were left from the days of gold and silver mining and were considered historic landmarks. Those that were open to the public, however, contained modern businesses—a variety store, a pharmacy, hardware store, bookstore, restaurants and even a real estate office. The truly interesting buildings, the ones that might draw crowds if they were restored, were closed. Over the years, various investors had attempted to resurrect the opera house, the old grand hotel and a few other of the more famous structures, but they'd run out of money almost before they'd embarked on restoration.

Which left a bar that had been in continuous operation since 1884. The Gold Nugget Saloon was still a thriving business, still boasting the original bar and tarnished mirrors, and the original oak-plank flooring. Unfortunately, it also provided Earl with some of his greatest headaches.

But a saloon wasn't enough of a draw for the kind of tourist traffic this mining town needed, so Main Street continued to look like a woman all dressed up with no place to go.

If you drove out west of town, in the general direction that Allie had taken, although ten miles south of where Allie had been, you could find a moonscape left behind more than a hundred years ago. In all the narrow gorges, huge heaps of slag dotted the landscape. Almost nothing grew in these gorges, even after all this time, because the slag was toxic. Here and there, as the dirt roads wound along the gorges, you would see the occasional bush that had managed to find a toehold but little else, except boarded-up mine entrances, some even bearing the trefoil that warned of radiation hazard. Thanks to the miners who'd built this town and pockmarked the landscape with their tunnels and slag heaps, Whisper Creek was an EPA Superfund site. When it rained, toxic chemicals ran off those slag piles and worked their way into the water. So far nobody had gotten sick. So far.

And Earl decided he was thinking all these gloomy thoughts about Whisper Creek in an attempt to avoid the real issue: Allie. Since this whole mess had started, his questions had been growing by leaps and bounds, and after watching Meg and her mother, he had loads of them. And none of them were going to get answered tonight. He had to let the trauma pass a little before he started poking his nose in and trying to find out exactly what Allie had intended to do when she ran away, why Meg felt so guilty about everything, and why Vivian acted as if her daughter were some kind of criminal.

At the station he went in and found Matt Dawson in the interrogation room, looking sullen and exhausted. Apparently Sam hadn't been very gentle. Not that Sam ever was. He preferred to come on like gangbusters and intimidate people into talking, but this time his method apparently hadn't worked. His notes said Matt had added nothing to what he'd said on the mountain.

Earl had a different method. He got the boy a soft drink from the machine and gave it to him. Matt downed it as if he hadn't eaten or drunk all day.

"You hungry?" he asked the boy.

"Starved. All I had today was some jerky and peanut butter."

"Great diet. You ought to see old age. Hang on a minute."

Out front, he told one of the deputies to run to the diner across the street to pick the kid up a meal.

"One or two burgers?" Nancy Ramirez asked.

"Make it two. He's a growing sixteen-year-old. And double the fries. Two milks."

She almost grinned. "You gonna make him drink the milk?"

"If I have to."

He went back to the interrogation room. Matt was still looking sullen, but not quite so tired with the sugar in him.

"So," Earl said, sitting across from the boy, "what really happened up there?"

Matt scowled at him. "I don't have to tell you anything. I didn't do anything wrong."

"Depends on how you look at it. Considering that girl was lost and you were running back up the mountain with food and an ax, I could probably make a case that you were holding her prisoner, maybe with intent to kill her, and she got hurt trying to run away."

Matt's face whitened. "She didn't tell you that. Because it's a lie."

"She hasn't told me anything yet, but if you don't start talking, it's going to be a long night."

"You can't keep me. I didn't do anything."

"I can keep you for seventy-two hours. A cell can get awfully small in seventy-two hours."

He watched the boy digest this, then said, "Look, Matt, I don't want to play the heavy here. I want to find out what happened, then let you go. But I've got to know what happened. Because right now, I can think of at least one cop who's convinced you were up to no good. And it isn't me."

Matt scuffed his feet on the tile floor and drummed his fingers on the tabletop, looking angry and trapped. "I told you everything there is to tell."

"So tell me one more time."

"I found her yesterday afternoon. She was sleeping on a rock in the sun, and I didn't want to wake her up." He shrugged, looking embarrassed. "It was stupid. I didn't even pay attention to the clouds coming in. She just looked so tired."

Earl nodded. "Then?"

"She woke up. I told her everyone was looking for her and she had to come with me. She said she wouldn't go anywhere with me, and I didn't see how I could drag her kicking and screaming down the mountain, especially since it had started snowing. I figured the smart thing to do was wait until morning in the old miner's shack."

"Okay." Earl doodled on the pad in front of him. "Then?"

"I got us some water, and she heated it on her little stove. Then I brought in some wood, because it was getting really cold and I figured I'd freeze before morning. She was worried I was going to set the roof on fire, but I kept it small. We talked...."

"About what?"

"I wanted to know why she was doing such a stupid thing. She wouldn't tell me. She just kept saying something about ruining everybody's life. And I got the feeling—" He broke off.

"What feeling?" Earl prompted.

Matt shook his head. "She wanted to kill herself, you know."

Earl's heart slammed. In that instant he faced a fear he'd been trying to ignore for three days. Every time it had crossed his mind, he found a way to dismiss it. Kids ran away all the time. They took crazy notions and skipped out. And yes, kids tried to kill themselves all the time, but not Allie. Nothing could be that bad in Allie's life. "How do you know?" he demanded, his voice cracking.

Matt looked at him uncertainly. "She kind of admitted it, finally. I told her killing herself was a lousy idea. That she ought to hang around and get even. That's what *I* do."

Earl nodded, feeling concerned for the boy. "All you have to do is tell me who keeps hitting you, son."

But Matt's face closed. "I thought we were talking about Allie?"

"All right. Let's talk about her. Did she listen to you?"

"I don't know. But in the morning she still wouldn't come off the mountain. She was almost out of food, and I knew I couldn't drag her down in the snow without getting us both into trouble. So I made her a deal. I promised I'd go and get food, and not tell anybody where she was, if she promised me she wouldn't kill herself while I was gone. She promised. I guess she doesn't believe in keeping her promises."

Earl's mouth tasted metallic. Fear. Fear of a kind he hadn't felt in a long time, and it was for Allie. And Meg. The two people he loved most in the whole world. "You think she jumped?"

Matt shrugged. "Hell, I don't know. I wasn't there. But people who are talking about killing themselves don't usually slip, do they?"

8

Meg's joy had considerably dimmed by the time she took Allie home in the morning. Not because she wasn't grateful that her daughter was alive and basically well, but because she could see that something was seriously wrong. She tried to tell herself it was only that Allie hadn't been allowed to sleep all night because of her concussion, but she knew she was lying to herself.

Allie was tired, yes, and grumpy, which was to be expected. But she was also withdrawn and sullen, and the shadows around her eyes were from far more than bruising from concussion.

Vivian greeted them at the door, but without much warmth. "I set up the living room as a bedroom for Allie," she told Meg in a tone that brooked no argument. "The child needs a few days to get used to crutches."

Allie looked at her mother. "I can do the stairs. And I want my own bedroom."

Meg nodded. "I understand that, sweetie. Why don't you take a nap on the couch for now, and later, after you've had some sleep, we'll move you up-stairs."

Vivian scowled. "I won't be running up and down them stairs to take her food and drink."

"I didn't ask you to, Mother. I'll do it." For now, at any rate. She was missing work, and while her bosses were understanding, she didn't know how many more days she could stay out without losing her job at the credit union. "And after a day or two, Allie will be handling those stairs like a pro anyway."

Vivian harrumphed. "You let that child get away with too much."

"That," said Allie, "is because she feels guilty."

Leaving the two women stunned behind her, Allie crutched her way into the living room and collapsed on the couch. Fifteen seconds later she was soundly asleep.

Meg stood in the living-room doorway for consid-erably longer, her legs trembling and weak. What was Allie talking about? She had never told her daughter about the argument she and Bill had had before his death. And no one else could have told her, because no one else knew. It was a guilty secret Meg had every intention of carrying to her grave.

Vivian had stomped off to her natural domain, the kitchen, and was banging pots around disapprovingly. Meg resisted the urge to let out a primal scream of frustration. Everything was back to normal, all right. Allie was being difficult, and Vivian was raging at the universe. And Meg, as always, was somehow caught in the middle.

Not knowing what else to do at the moment, Meg

went upstairs to shower and brush her teeth, two lux-
uries she had missed at the hospital.

It was while she was dressing in jeans and a flannel
shirt that she had a horrible thought. She paused only
long enough to pull on some socks to keep her feet
warm, then dashed down the stairs to confront her
mother.

Vivian was still in the kitchen. She'd moved past
banging pots, but when she saw Meg, she glared.
"The least you could have done was show some gratitude for me making a comfortable place for Allie to
stay until she can handle the stairs. But no, you've
never been grateful for a damn thing in your entire
life."

Meg froze, startled. Then anger at the injustice of
the accusation filled her. "That's not true, Mother.
I'm grateful for everything you've done for me."

"You have some way of showing it."

"Well, you know, maybe I'm sick of having it held
over my head all the time, sick of having it thrown
in my face. I didn't *ask* you to spend the last eight
months here, and I didn't *ask* you to take over this
household. You *chose* to do that, Mother. If you don't
want to do it anymore, don't. I certainly did it all
before you got here."

"That's what I mean about you! Ungrateful."

"I am not ungrateful." Meg drew a deep breath
and fought for control. This was *not* what she had
come in here to discuss. "But enough of this. We're
never going to see eye-to-eye on anything. But I do
want to know something."

It was a minute before Vivian calmed herself
enough to answer. "What?"

"Did you ever mention anything to Allie about Daddy?"

There was no mistaking Vivian's shock. "Of course I didn't! I've never mentioned that to a soul, and I certainly would *never* mention it to a child of such tender years. What kind of woman do you think I am?"

Meg, who had long ago decided that she would never understand her mother, didn't know how to answer that. "I'm sorry. But what she said—"

"What she *said*," Vivian interrupted harshly, "was that you feel guilty. And so you ought to. But the child thinks you feel guilty because she's fatherless, which is hardly surprising, considering how self-centered children are. She thinks you indulge her because her father died."

"Maybe I do, a little," Meg admitted.

"Let her run wild is what you do. And I can't think of a stupider reason to do it. Children need the security of knowing there are limits. They need to know their parents care enough to impose them."

Which was a surprisingly intelligent statement from Vivian, who generally criticized everything, agreed with nothing, and rarely needed a good reason for either.

Thinking about what her mother had said, Meg returned to the living room and sat in a chair watching Allie sleep. Her eyes looked so awful, she thought, hating to think about the kind of concussion that would cause so much bruising. Maybe that was the only reason Allie was acting the way she was. She'd had a terrible trauma and probably wouldn't be fully normal again for a long time.

But that didn't answer the question of why her daughter had run away in the first place. And that was the question that was piercing Meg's heart.

Earl didn't make it to see Allie and Meg until nearly three in the afternoon. He'd been shanghaied by a truck accident on the mountain highway that had spilled concrete road dividers across the pavement and led to four more accidents before all was said and done. Three people had been critically injured, and four more were in serious condition. It wasn't pretty at all.

By the time he got to the Williams place, he was rumpled, tired and cold, but he figured he could put all of that on hold until he found out how Allie was doing.

Meg let him in, looking at his uniform with the same flicker of discomfort he'd been seeing there since Bill's accident. He understood it, but it made him feel like a leper anyway.

"Allie's still sleeping," she said, "but you're welcome to join my vigil in the living room."

"Actually, if it wouldn't be too much trouble, I'd do just about anything for a cup of coffee right now. And a bite of anything to eat. Crackers. Chips. Whatever you can pull out of the cupboard."

She looked up at him, noticing for the first time how tired and drawn he looked. "Bad day?"

"I've had better."

With a sense of trepidation, she took him to the kitchen and was relieved to see that Vivian had apparently retired for her afternoon nap. At least she wouldn't have to deal with that. As always, there was a pot of coffee on the warming plate, and she poured a mugful for Earl, passing it to him as he sat with a sigh at the table.

"I've got loads of junk food," she told him. "Teenager in the house. What's your fancy?"

"The first thing you can grab."

"What about a sandwich?"

He waved the offer away. "It won't be long before I'm looking for dinner. Just a snack."

She passed him a fresh bag of chips and got herself a cup of coffee before joining him. "What happened?"

He didn't want to tell her, didn't want her to start thinking about Bill. In fact, in his present mood, having to think about her loss and her marriage would be an intrusion. For just a couple of minutes he wanted to pretend they didn't have Bill between them. It was selfish, and he knew it. But sometimes he was selfish.

"A truck dumped some concrete dividers on the road," he said, leaving out the gory details.

"How many people got hurt?"

Trust Meg to know there was more. "Seven went to the hospital."

"That's terrible. I'm sorry."

He waited for mention of Bill, but it didn't come. "How's Allie?" he asked finally.

"She's been sleeping since we got home. But I'm worried about her. She's acting...strangely. Withdrawn. Angry."

"Well, she's been through a lot." Then he wanted to kick himself for not telling her the truth. If Allie was suicidal, Meg needed to know that as much as anyone. But he didn't have the heart to tell her. Not yet.

"That's true. I think maybe it's the concussion."

"It wouldn't be the first time a head trauma has made someone act strange."

"I guess not."

He resisted the urge to get up from the chair and butt his stupid head on the wall. He shouldn't be minimizing this. But he wanted to talk to Allie privately first. He wanted to be sure Matt Dawson hadn't just concocted some youthful tragedy out of Allie's burst of anger over something. Kids had a way of dramatizing even minor things.

"Anyway," he said finally, "we'll keep an eye on her."

She gave him a smile then, a warm smile that seemed to say she appreciated his offer to be part of looking after Allie. It made him feel a whole lot better. "But we need to look after you, too," he said. "You look exhausted."

"I am. I didn't sleep much more than Allie last night. I was trying to keep her entertained so it would be easier for her to stay awake."

"And what about today?"

"I've been dozing in the armchair, keeping an eye on her. I'll make it until bedtime. What about you?"

"Oh, I got some sleep last night. Until I was called at five about the accident. I'm okay."

"Do you have to go back to work? If not, stay for dinner."

There was a time when he would have leaped at that invitation with joy, but after the last few days, he regarded it with trepidation. Dinner in this house, with all the tensions he'd been feeling, promised to be an uncomfortable experience. On the other hand, he wanted to spend some time with Allie. And with Meg. "I signed myself out before I came up here. As long as there's not another catastrophe, I'd like to stay."

"Good." The smile she gave him was almost grateful, as if she was relieved to know she wouldn't have to face the evening alone. Not that he could blame her. She couldn't be any more immune to the tension than he was.

"Mom? Mom?"

Meg jumped up from the table at the sound of Allie's voice and hurried to the living room. Earl hesitated, not sure he would be welcome, then followed at a slower pace. He could hear Allie whining, "I hurt all over. I can hardly move, and I need to go to the bathroom."

"Oh, boy," he heard Meg say, with a shimmer of sympathetic amusement in her voice. "'Houston, we have a problem.'"

Allie's whine changed almost reluctantly into a weary giggle.

"Well, is there anywhere safe for me to grab you?" Meg asked.

Good question, Earl thought. The child was covered with bruises from her fall.

"Um..." Allie sounded thoughtful, but in an almost playful way that did Earl's heart good to hear. "Maybe over here?"

"That'll never do," Meg said. "I'd have to try to lift you with two fingers."

At that point, Earl entered the room. "How's it going, Chipmunk? Need a lift to the john?"

"Uncle Earl?" Allie smiled widely when she saw him, and if it hadn't been for the bruising around her eyes, she would have looked as beautiful to him as any model who'd ever graced a magazine cover. "I just need to get up. If I don't move, it's only going to get worse."

"Smart thinking," he agreed. "So bite your lip and let me lift you."

She must have weighed all of ninety-five pounds, and he lifted her without the least trouble, setting her gently on her feet. He noticed her grimaces as he touched her bruises, but she never made a sound. Meg handed her her crutches.

"Liftoff," Meg said, smiling a smile that didn't quite reach her eyes. "Sea of Tranquillity, here we come."

"Moon rocks," said Allie as she adjusted her crutches. "That's what I want for Christmas."

"Good luck."

Allie's cast ran from her toes to her knee, and she wasn't yet allowed to walk on it. Earl gave her a little coaching on using the crutches—something he'd learned to do after a skiing accident—and she began to swing her way to the hall bath. Both Earl and Meg followed, hovering nervously. By the time she reached the bathroom door, Allie's face was flushed from exertion, but she looked proud of herself.

"I'll be right outside if you need any help," Meg told her.

Allie gave her a disgusted look. "I've been doing this by myself since I was two."

"I'll still be here. You haven't had to do it after a concussion and a broken leg."

"I did it in the hospital this morning."

"They have a bigger bathroom."

Earl had the worst urge to step in on what promised to be an argument, to tell Meg to lay off the kid and to tell Allie to stop treating her mother's natural concern as an insult, but Allie ended it by scowling at her mother and crutching into the bathroom. A moment later, the door closed. Emphatically.

"Oh, dear," said Meg. "I guess I did it all wrong."

"You didn't do anything wrong." He was troubled to see the shimmer of tears in her eyes.

"She seems to be fine now, though. Back to her old self."

Earl wasn't sure that was a good thing, not considering what Allie's old self had done on Saturday—and what she might have done yesterday.

"You know," Meg said, "I haven't thanked you properly for rescuing Allie."

"If there's one thing you never need to thank me for, Meggie, it's helping you and Allie out."

This time her mouth quivered and she closed her eyes. "Of course I need to thank you. From the bottom of my heart. For everything. I owe you."

Earl figured that maybe she did owe him—an explanation for what was going on around here. But just as he was thinking about blurting out the question, Vivian decided to appear at the top of the stairway. She looked down at Earl, her face registering the disapproval he'd come to expect from her.

"Where's Allie?" she asked without greeting Earl.

"In the bathroom," Meg answered.

To Earl, it seemed as if the tension between the two had ratcheted even higher than it was before.

"Mother," Meg said, "Earl's joining us for dinner. I'll cook."

"Have it your way." Vivian came down the stairs and disappeared into the living room.

"Great," said Meg. "Just great."

"Do you ever get tired of her?"

Meg's expression was almost wry. "All the time. But she's my mother."

"It might be easier for you if she treated you like a daughter."

"The thought has crossed my mind."

Allie opened the bathroom door just then. "What are you two talking about?"

"Not you," Meg answered promptly. "That's all you need to know."

Allie rolled her eyes and began to crutch her way into the hall. "Can I go up to my room now?"

Meg's eyes leaped to Earl. He shrugged. Meg returned her gaze to Allie.

"How about waiting until after dinner?" she suggested. "You don't want to do too much your first day. Remember what the doctor said? But after dinner we can get you all settled in up there, all right?"

"Okay. But I'm sick of the couch. I want to sit up for a while. In the kitchen, okay?"

"If we can figure out how to prop your leg up, that's fine by me. You can kibitz while I cook."

Allie was also hungry. As soon as they had her sitting on one chair, with her leg propped on another, she asked for a soft drink and some chips. Meg gave them to her without any argument about how it was getting close to suppertime. The girl dug in with enthusiasm.

"Allie?" Earl said. "Do you remember how you fell?"

"Sure." She shrugged. "I got too close to the edge. I forgot how snow can hang out in a ledge so you can't see exactly where the edge is."

It was reasonable, but Earl didn't feel it was likely. Why had the girl been walking so close to the edge to begin with? "Why did you go out there?"

"I was bored, okay? I'd been stuck in that stupid cabin for two days, and I was bored. So I took a walk."

Meg pulled a steak out of the freezer and put it in the microwave to defrost. "Why did you run away, Allie?"

The girl hunched her shoulder. "I don't want to talk about it, okay?"

"Okay. For now. But we're going to talk about it eventually."

"Why? It doesn't matter anymore. I'm here now."

"It matters to me that you were so upset about something that you ran away. We need to talk about it so we can fix it."

"You can't fix it," Allie said, her chin thrusting forward. "You can't do anything about it." She shoved the bag of chips away and inadvertently knocked them to the floor. She hadn't meant to do it; that was obvious to Earl, and apparently to Meg, too, because she didn't say anything about it. She just started sweeping the mess up.

But Allie didn't apologize, either. And that wasn't like Allie. Earl could see the strain on Meg's face as she realized that her daughter wasn't back to normal at all. As she realized that it was possible nothing would ever be normal again.

Dinner was a strained affair, with Allie sullen and Vivian reeking of disapproval. Earl gave up trying to make pleasant conversation, and Meg surrendered, too, a few minutes later.

After dinner, he and Meg helped Allie up the stairs, and Meg got her settled comfortably in her bed. They even moved the desk so that she could hold her computer keyboard on her lap and see the monitor, all so she could chat with her on-line friends. As they were leaving Allie's room, Vivian passed them in the hallway without a word and went to her own room, closing the door firmly.

Which left Earl and Meg alone. Downstairs, he helped her fold the blankets and sheets that were still on the couch.

Meg looked at him. "You must be sick of us, Earl." And she couldn't have said why that concerned her so. He was a friend. If he was tired of being treated rudely by her mother and her child, he could leave without wounding her, and she knew he would be back. But she didn't want him to go. She didn't want to spend the next three or four hours trying not to think about what was wrong with her child and what she was going to do about her mother.

"I'm not sick of you," he said, "but I'd like to give that mother of yours a good shake."

"Me, too."

They left the blankets and sheets stacked on the

end of the couch. Earl took the easy chair, and Meg curled up at the other end of the sofa.

"What's eating her?" Earl asked. "You can tell me, Meg. You know you can tell me anything."

Could she? She doubted it. Some things just didn't bear telling. "It's an old problem. I really don't want to get into it."

"Maybe you ought to get into it. I don't know how you can live like this."

"Sometimes I don't, either." She wanted to cry again, and she was getting awfully tired of wanting to weep. She would have loved to confide in someone, but she couldn't take the risk with Earl. Couldn't risk that the friendly way he looked at her would change forever.

"Well," he said finally, "that kind of leaves us with nowhere to go, doesn't it?"

"I'm sorry."

"Don't be sorry. Just understand that I don't like feeling helpless, and I'm feeling helpless right now. It's obvious you aren't happy. It's obvious that Allie isn't happy. And the tension in this house is thick enough to cut with a knife. If you won't let me help, you've got to do something about it yourself, Meg. Neither you nor Allie can keep this up."

"I know." And she *did* know. She just felt so guilty all the time that she hardly knew what to do.

"You might also consider that I'm a cop. I seriously doubt there's anything you could tell me that I haven't heard before. I'm pretty much unshockable."

But there were things she could tell him about his dear friend Bill that would probably shock him. They were things he might never forgive her for saying.

Bill was out of it now, but she couldn't do that to Earl, and she couldn't do that to herself. "It was a long time ago," she said again. "Vivian just bears grudges."

"You know, Meggie, you make it damn hard for a man to take care of you."

"I don't need anyone to take care of me. I can take care of myself." It wasn't true, and she knew it. She would have desperately liked someone to take care of her, but she wasn't going to admit it, and she certainly wasn't going to give him the knowledge that might help him pry the story from her.

"Look around you," he said almost impatiently. "I never saw anybody more in need of someone to look after her. Your mother needs a good talking to, your daughter—" He broke off.

"That's right," she said. "Leave Allie out of this, Earl. And quit badgering me. You're a good friend, but this isn't helping anything."

He subsided, but she could tell he wasn't happy about it. Earl was a fixer by nature. After fifteen years, she knew just how much he needed to help people make things right. It was one of the reasons he was such a popular sheriff.

But then he said something that left her thunderstruck. He said, "Matt Dawson says Allie was thinking about killing herself. This isn't something you can sweep under the carpet and ignore, Meg."

She was hot and cold by turns, frozen rigid by shock. Allie had wanted to kill herself? Running away was bad enough, but suicide? She couldn't move or speak as her mind tried frantically to find some way to deny it. But deep within her heart, she felt the hidden knowledge that it was true.

"She..." Her voice broke, her words wanted to stumble. "He can't...be sure." Her tone strengthened. "If Allie really wanted to do that, she would have done it right away."

He didn't say anything.

"She *would,* Earl. What the hell would be the point of wandering around on the mountain for a couple of days first?" She was practically screaming at him now. At another time the sound might have shocked her back to calm; she wasn't a screamer. But not now. Now screaming was *all* she could do.

The pain that was gripping her now was so tight and deep that it hurt to breathe. She doubled over. "She slipped," Meg said, squeezing the words out. "She slipped...."

Earl came to her side, wrapping his arms around her and pulling her into a tight embrace, holding her stiff body as close as he could. "She slipped, Meggie," he murmured. "She slipped. She said so, and it's probably true, because she promised Matt she wouldn't kill herself while he came down the mountain to get her some food. He made her promise that, Meggie, and Allie always keeps her promises."

She was gasping now, fighting for air, but she managed to say, "That's right. Allie always keeps a promise."

"But," Earl said relentlessly, "you can't ignore this. For Allie's sake, you have to pay attention. She was thinking about killing herself."

"You're right. You're right...." She was getting a grip on herself, and some of the tension was easing out of her muscles. She softened, just a little bit, but it was enough that she turned to him and buried her face in his shoulder. Long minutes later, her arms wrapped around him and clung as if he were a lifeline.

"I was going to wait to tell you that," he said presently, rubbing her back soothingly. "I was going to talk to Allie first. But...I'm sorry. You need to know. No matter how unpleasant it is."

He wouldn't have blamed her if she had run screaming out into the night. There was just so much one person could bear, and Meg had had more than her share of blows lately. But she didn't run. She clung to him for a long time, letting him rock her gently, letting him stroke her back. When she finally spoke, it was to ask one question.

"Why?"

"That's what we have to find out. Somehow we've got to get her to talk."

She turned her face up and looked at him. "Don't you have any ideas?"

He shook his head. "There's no way to tell. Kids get crazy ideas like this all the time. If they're still alive a few days later, their entire attitude could have changed. Allie might not be suicidal anymore. But we can't take the risk."

It felt good—too damn good, actually—to be holding Meg, but he forced himself to let go of her. This was neither the time nor the place to give in to feelings he'd been burying for years.

She sat back on the couch, looking as if she'd been horsewhipped. At some point, he vowed, he was going to find a way to make her smile again. She used to have such a beautiful smile, but it had been in evidence very little since Bill's death.

Which was to be expected, he reminded himself. She and Bill had had a wonderful marriage, and Meg had to still be seriously hurting.

And every time she looked at him, he thought, she must remember Bill. If the marriage had stood between him and what he wanted before, he figured that the *memory* of it must be an even bigger barrier. But he was used to not having what he wanted, and he barely noticed the dissatisfaction anymore.

He spoke, trying to corral his thoughts before they wandered to places that would make him feel guilty. "We've got to find some way to cheer Allie up. Some way to make her feel good about herself."

"What?" She looked at him hopefully. "A trip?"

He shook his head. "Not with her leg in a cast." Then he had a brainstorm. "You know Matt Dawson?"

"That troubled kid we met on the mountain? What about him?"

"I've got an idea. But let me talk to Allie first, okay?"

Five minutes later he was knocking on Allie's door. She called for him to come in, and he entered her teenager's den. She was still on the computer, tapping busily away.

"Good chat?" he asked.

"It's okay." She sounded indifferent, but judging by the way her fingers were flying over the keys, that wasn't exactly the case.

"Got a minute?"

"Sure." But she kept on typing.

He pulled a chair over near the bed, positioning it so that he could see her face but not her monitor screen. He didn't want her to feel that he was invading her privacy, although right now he was sorely tempted to take a look and see what she was discussing with all those faceless friends who so absorbed her. Was she telling them how she had gone up onto the mountain to kill herself? And why? Or was she just talking about it as though it was a crazy adventure, reaping all the excited interest and sympathy from those other teens locked to their glowing screens in darkened bedrooms? Was she making herself feel important? Did Allie feel she had been lost and forgotten in the grief that had occupied this house for the last eight months?

They were all questions he was dying to ask, but he knew if he did, he would never get a straight answer.

"I need a favor," he said.

"Sure. I promise not to run away again."

That didn't console him. She wouldn't have to run away to kill herself. "Thanks, but that wasn't what I was going to ask. I know you're too intelligent to make the same mistake twice."

That grabbed her attention for an instant, and her gaze flickered from the monitor to him. Then indifference masked her face again, and she returned her attention to the screen. "What favor?"

"Matt Dawson."

She appeared to go still for a moment; then her fingers began to strike the keys rapidly. He found himself having the errant wish that he could type half so well.

"What about him?" she asked finally.

"Well, I kinda owe him for finding you up on the mountain, and he could use some help."

"Not from me."

"Why not?"

"Because he broke his promise."

"Ah. You mean his promise not to tell where you were? He didn't break it, Allie. I followed him. But he keeps saying *you* broke *your* promise."

She looked up then and gave him her full attention. But her expression was sullen. "I don't ever break my promises."

"I know you don't, Chipmunk." The relief that filled him was overwhelming. So she *had* slipped. He wanted to grab her and hug her, but he wasn't ready to let on that he knew why she'd gone up the mountain. For now, he wanted her to think her secret was safe, because he didn't want her feeling cornered. "But Matt didn't break his, either. And he needs some help."

"Yeah?" She lowered her gaze to her screen again, but he noticed she didn't start typing.

"Somebody's beating him up, Allie."

"I know."

"But he won't say who. I think it's his father. The school thinks it's his father. But every time we try to do something about it, Matt just insists that he got into a fight with another guy."

She nodded slowly.

"I can't do anything unless I have the truth. And to get it, I need Matt to talk to me. Maybe you can help convince him to do that."

She lifted her eyes. "What makes you think I can do that?"

"Because you're closer to his age. I don't think Matt trusts any adults right now."

"He won't trust me if he thinks I broke my promise."

"So tell him you didn't. But he needs help, Allie. He needs help before someone kills him."

She shrugged, but he could tell she wasn't as indifferent as she was trying to appear. "Sure. I'll see what I can do."

"Great. I'll bring him up to visit you tomorrow." He patted her leg gently. "I really appreciate your help. You might be able to do something no one else can."

"Maybe."

"So, it's a good chat?" He indicated the monitor, deliberately changing the subject.

"I guess. Just a bunch of kids talking about music."

"Not my kind, I expect." He made a face at her, and when he left, he could have sworn he saw a faint smile tugging at the corners of her mouth.

9

While Earl went upstairs to talk to Allie, Meg went to the kitchen to make some mocha decaf and a light snack. None of them had eaten much at dinner, and she suspected Earl must be famished. She also laid out a snack to take up to Allie, knowing her daughter's teenage appetite.

She carried hers and Earl's coffee and snacks into the living room and set them on the coffee table. When she heard his step on the stairs, she hurried out to discover what he'd said to Allie. He was smiling faintly, and relief filled her.

"What happened?" she asked.

"I had a talk with her about Matt Dawson. She's going to help me get through to him."

Meg didn't know if she liked that idea. "Get through to him about what? And I don't know if I want Allie hanging out with a boy like that. Isn't he in trouble all the time?"

"Actually, he's never been in any serious trouble. Minor stuff."

"Still…"

"Basically he's a good kid, Meg. But he's angry. He's angry because his parents are abusing him and neglecting him."

"So take him out of the home!"

"We've tried. But he always denies anyone is hurting him. Always insists he got into a fight or took a fall. So far his injuries have been limited to bruises and one broken arm that *could* have happened the way he said it did. But as he's getting older, the beatings are getting worse. He's started missing school instead of just turning up with a split lip or a bunch of bruises. But he doesn't trust adults, Meg. None of us. So I'm hoping he'll trust Allie enough to tell her what's going on."

"I still don't think he's the kind of boy I want her associating with."

Earl shook his head. "Pull in your horns, Meg. Allie's actually looking forward to being Matt's saving angel. It'll do her a world of good to think about someone else's problems, make her feel better about herself to help someone else. And that's exactly what she needs."

Meg couldn't deny it. As she carried Allie's snack tray up to her—hot cocoa and two of the pecan sandies she loved so much—she thought about what Earl had said. She really didn't know of anything terrible that Matt Dawson might have done, and in a town this size, if Matt had done anything really bad, she would have heard about it. But she knew the type of family the boy came from, and she didn't want Allie getting close to that kind of trash.

But when she entered Allie's room, she discovered that her daughter liked Earl's idea.

"Uncle Earl wants me to help Matt Dawson," Allie said as her mother put the tray on her lap. "Yummy. Cocoa and cookies. Thanks, Mom." She looked up and smiled genuinely for the first time since she'd run away. Maybe for the first time in months.

"How do you feel about that?" Meg asked.

"Matt needs someone to help him," the girl said seriously. "He's got an awful life. He hardly ever has lunch, you know."

"No, I didn't."

"He sits around and watches the rest of us eat. Even when he was little. Sometimes I shared my lunch with him."

"Good for you. I'm proud of you." Meg felt her own mouth curving into a smile. This child couldn't possibly be suicidal. Matt had to be wrong.

But then Allie looked down at the tray. "Mom?"

"Yes?"

"How come Grandma is so angry at you all the time?"

Meg's heart skipped a beat. "Why do you ask?"

"Because I think she hates you. Do mothers hate their daughters?"

"Oh, God," Meg said, and sank into the chair at Allie's desk. It had never occurred to her that her daughter would extrapolate Vivian's attitude this way. "No," she said as firmly as she could manage. "At least, not all mothers hate their daughters. I certainly don't hate you. I love you, Allie. You're the best thing that ever happened to me. Ever."

"Really?" Allie looked doubtful. "So why doesn't Grandma feel the same way about you?"

Allie could feel her nails digging into her palms as she wondered about the best way to address this. She couldn't dismiss it—even Earl was commenting on the tension between her and her mother. "Well..." she said slowly. "I did something bad a long time ago. And she's still angry about it."

"What did you do?"

Meg shook her head. "Never mind. It isn't important now." *Bold-faced liar,* she accused herself. "But Grandma carries grudges. It's just the way she is."

"I can't imagine anything that awful."

"Well, I didn't go to jail or anything, if that's what you're trying to find out." She was relieved when Allie smiled faintly.

"So it wasn't that bad. She should just get over it."

"I agree. But this is the way your grandmother is."

"Are you like her?"

"What do you think?"

Allie shook her head. "You never stay mad at me for very long."

"You see? That's one thing I learned from her. Not to stay mad forever. Anyway, it isn't anything you need to worry about."

Allie seemed content with that, and after a bit, Meg went back downstairs. Earl was sitting on the couch, drinking his coffee. He'd already eaten the cookies she'd put out.

"Everything okay?" he asked.

"She seems to be doing better. I guess you were right about her helping Matt. It perked her up."

"It always helps to worry about something besides your own problems."

"A gem of true wisdom." She sat next to him and reached for her own coffee. "You're a good man, Earl Sanders."

She glanced at him in time to see his cheeks grow ruddy. She had to smother a smile. Earl had always been embarrassed by compliments.

"Just trying to mend things as best I can," he said, quickly hiding behind his coffee mug.

Later, when he left for the night, he astonished her by stopping at the door and bending to brush a kiss on her cheek. In all their years of friendship, he'd never done that before.

And she was even more astonished to realize how much she liked it.

Then, squaring her shoulders, she faced the fact that she was going to have to deal with her mother. She couldn't remain silent after what Allie had said, which would probably lead to having her heart ripped out yet again by Vivian. But for Allie's sake, she had to try to do something.

She found Allie sound asleep, with her light still on, the bed tray beside the bed and the keyboard in her lap. She moved the keyboard, turned off the computer and the lights, and left the room with the tray.

Instead of taking it down to the kitchen, however, she left it on the hall table and knocked on her mother's door.

"Mom? I need to talk to you."

"Come in."

She entered what had once been the guest room but was now distinctly Vivian's room. Vivian had even changed the curtains, using the sewing machine to run up some gingham ones she liked better than the woven ones Meg had hung there. On her bed was a quilt she had brought with her from home. Right now she was sitting in the wooden rocking chair for which she had made cushions that matched the blue and white curtains.

Meg perched on the edge of her mother's bed. "I want to talk about Allie."

Vivian closed her Bible and put it on the nightstand. "Okay."

"Mother, Earl said Allie was thinking about suicide when she ran away."

Vivian clucked her tongue and shook her head. "No. I can't believe that. That child is shamelessly indulged. There is nothing in her life that would make her feel that way."

"I wouldn't be so sure about that. She lost her father less than a year ago. And tonight she was asking me why you hate me."

Vivian's eyebrows rose. "I don't hate you. I'm your mother."

"That doesn't mean you don't hate me."

"This is ridiculous! Are you trying to say that I drove that child to suicide?"

"I'm saying nothing of the sort. But when a child Allie's age runs away from home and perhaps considers suicide, it seems to me that the people who are taking care of her need to take a good long look at themselves. That's you and me, Mother."

Vivian shook her head again but didn't say anything.

"Allie loves us both, Mother. It has to be very hard on her to feel the tension between us all the time. And she's wondering why you hate me. Why you're so angry with me. I'm not going to discuss the issue with her, but I have a strong feeling that Allie's unhappy because you and I are so unhappy with each other. At the very least, we ought to declare a truce.''

Vivian still didn't say anything, and Meg felt the worst urge to shake her.

"Look," she said finally, "what happened was over and done with fifteen years ago. It's time to forgive me. And you would, if you heeded your Bible better.''

Vivian gasped. "I'm a good Christian woman.''

"Until it comes to forgiveness. That's when you fall down." Meg rose. "I'm not going to argue with you about this. But for Allie's sake, maybe we'd better bury the hatchet.''

When she got out into the hallway and closed the door behind herself, she realized that her legs were shaking and her heart was hammering. Referring to that incident from fifteen years ago was never easy. Never. But telling her mother it was time to forgive her had been the hardest thing of all.

Because, deep in her heart, Meg didn't believe she deserved forgiveness. She'd come to terms with what had happened. She had even nearly come to accept that she had done nothing wrong. But even now, after forgiving herself, she still didn't feel she deserved anyone else's forgiveness.

Morning brought more snow. Looking out her bedroom window, Meg grew cold at the mere sight of it falling from leaden skies. Winter was a month early, and she found herself dreading it.

She checked on Allie and found that her daughter

wasn't in her room. Then she heard the most surprising sound: laughter. Allie was laughing somewhere downstairs. The sound lifted her spirits and made her realize that it had been entirely too long since anyone in this house had laughed.

Allie was sitting at the kitchen table, still in her nightshirt and robe, making biscuits with a doughnut cutter and using the hole pieces to make ears on the biscuits. And, wonder of wonders, Vivian wasn't objecting to the silliness but instead was suggesting Allie use little pieces of dough to make mouths and eyes.

Not once in the last eight months had she seen Vivian interact this way with Allie. The sight of it warmed her heart, and she stood in the doorway, reluctant to enter and damage the spell.

But then Allie saw her. "Mom! Look what I'm doing. Isn't it silly?"

Meg stepped close to the table. "I think it's kind of artistic, myself."

Allie made a face. "You always say nice things about anything I do. It's silly, and I know it. But it's fun."

Vivian was smiling, too, as she looked at Allie, but her face tightened as her gaze shifted to Meg. "Are you going to work today?"

"I'm thinking about asking for one more day off."

Allie spoke. "You don't have to do that, Mom. I'll be okay with Grandma. My head doesn't even ache anymore."

"But your eyes are becoming an interesting number of shades of green."

"Camouflage," Allie said, unconcerned. "That's

what it looks like. But it's a good sign, Grandma Viv said.''

"She's right.'' Meg rarely used those words when referring to her mother, but she made herself say them this time. If they were going to bury the hatchet, both of them would have to work at it. "I'll be back in a minute. I just want to call Joan.''

Joan Fenton was her boss at the credit union. Between the two of them, they pretty much ran the show, but even after fifteen years, Meg didn't feel comfortable trading on their friendship. Joan was her boss and, as such, deserved to be treated as one.

"Of course you can have another day, Meg,'' Joan said warmly. "Take the rest of the week if you need it. Payroll's not until next week, so we won't be that busy. How's Allie doing?''

"Well, her eyes are about nineteen shades of green, but she says the headache is gone, and she seems to be getting around on the crutches okay.''

"I'm so glad to hear that! Mind if I share the news? Everyone who's come in has asked about you and Allie.''

"No, go right ahead. I'm so grateful to all the people who helped search for her. I need some way to thank them.''

"A full-page ad in the local news rag will probably do it. Want me to arrange it? I'd be glad to.''

"Thanks, Joan. You're wonderful.''

"Of course.'' Joan laughed. "I'll remind you of that when the board turns down your raise this year.''

"Are they going to do that?''

"Hell, I don't know. But they do it most of the time, don't they? I keep telling them we're not keeping pace with inflation, but then, neither are their salaries at the mine.''

After Meg hung up, she went back to the kitchen. The biscuit mess had been cleaned up, and Allie was washing her hands and face with a damp paper towel.

''Be about fifteen minutes,'' Vivian said as she forked bacon out of the pan.

''Thanks, Mom.'' Meg poured herself some coffee and joined her daughter at the table. ''You sure look better this morning, sweetie.''

''I feel better.'' Twisting, Allie pitched the wadded wet towel into the wastebasket across the kitchen.

Meg longed to ask her if she was feeling better about the things that had made her run away, but she didn't want to do it with Vivian listening. Later, she promised herself, she and Allie were going to have a heart-to-heart.

After breakfast, Vivian announced her intention to clean upstairs, then disappeared. Meg cleared the dishes, while Allie sat drinking the last of her milk and staring out the window at the falling snow.

''Early winter,'' Allie remarked.

''Yes, it does look like it.''

''I wish we lived in Florida.''

The remark surprised Meg. She hadn't thought Allie ever considered such things. ''Why?''

''Because it doesn't snow. It's warm all the time.''

Thinking about the ordeal her daughter had probably suffered on the mountain in the cold, Meg felt her heart squeeze. ''Cold can be…uncomfortable.''

''It can kill you,'' Allie said.

The words disturbed Meg more than she could say. Was Allie still dealing with death? But she couldn't think how to phrase a question that her daughter wouldn't just dismiss as crazy. She needed a way to keep the girl talking.

She put the last plate in the dishwasher and turned to Allie. "Why don't you come into the living room with me? It's warmer, and I want to clean the wood-stove before I load it with more wood."

"Sure." Allie reached for her crutches, pushed herself up onto her good leg and swung out of the kitchen as if she'd been doing this her entire life.

Meg followed a minute later, carrying the ash bucket and shovel. She hated cleaning the stove, but it was a necessary evil. Allie had already settled onto the couch, and had turned the TV to a movie channel. A dinosaur was roaring through the streets of New York, pursued by helicopters. An effective barrier to communication, Meg thought, and one she was sure was deliberate.

There were still some large remnants of logs left from last night's stoking, and Meg pushed them to the side with her shovel before beginning to scoop out the ash. It was still hot, and so fine that it puffed out the stove door and coated the outside of the stove and the area around it. She could even taste it in her mouth.

The ash filled the bucket, even though she left a layer on the floor of the stove to make a bed for the burning wood. The remaining logs, with the added air, burst into flame again. She tucked in a few more and closed the door, waiting to see if they would ignite. They did.

"There," she said to Allie. "You'll be toasty in no time."

Allie nodded but didn't look at her, keeping her eyes on the TV.

So, thought Meg, this wasn't going to be easy at all. Allie's mood seemed to be roller-coastering. Great.

She carried the ash out onto the porch, leaving it to cool. Though feeling the icy bite of the wind through her flannel shirt, she didn't go back inside, just went to get another armload of wood. The cold, much as it hurt, also felt good. It was dry and biting, and so very different from the atmosphere in the house. Cleaner.

The wood was covered with snow, and her shirt-front and sleeves were wet by the time she got it to the wood box in the living room. Allie was still absorbed in her movie and didn't seem to see Meg. Oh well.

She went to get another armload and carry it to the wood box at the back of the house. When she and Bill had built this house, they'd hoped that one stove downstairs would do the whole job, but it hadn't. The house was just too big, so they had put another stove at the back of the house, to light on cold nights. With heat rising from both ends of the house, moving by way of the two stairways to the upstairs, all the bedrooms stayed warm.

At this time of year she usually only needed one stove at night, but this year was different. Everything was different.

She was washing up at the kitchen sink when someone knocked on the front door. Hoping it was Earl, she hurried to answer it. Instead she found the boy she had met on the mountain. Matt Dawson.

"Hi, Mrs. Williams," he said uneasily. "I just came to check on Allie."

Meg wondered why he wasn't in school, then noticed the ugly bruise on his jaw near his ear. Any resistance she might have felt toward him vanished the moment she saw the bruise.

"Come in, Matt. I'm sure Allie will be happy to see you."

He appeared surprised at the invitation, as if he wasn't used to being invited inside. He stepped in cautiously, taking great care to knock the snow off his boots first.

"She's in the living room," Meg said, pointing. "Go on in. Would you like a hot drink? Cocoa maybe?"

His dark eyes brightened. "That'd be great."

"I'll bring it in."

Too thin, Meg thought as she watched him disappear into the living room. That child was entirely too thin and gaunt. And that bruise... Shaking her head, she went to make the cocoa.

Earl was having a slow day at the office, which was a good thing. Days like the last few weren't something he exactly relished. On the other hand, searching for lost people and dealing with car accidents kept him from having to cope with paperwork, a huge mound of which was sitting on his desk still, even after hours of plowing through it.

Sighing, he leaned back in his chair and looked out at the gray day. His thoughts kept straying back to Meg and Allie, and finally he quit trying to rein them in. The paperwork could wait while he thought things through.

He was worried about them. Worried that they had no emotional ballast in that house. They'd all suffered a serious loss with Bill's death, but it was more than that. It was the animosity he felt between Vivian and Meg, an animosity he couldn't understand. It was the feeling he'd gotten lately that Meg had just given up somehow. And now there was Allie, a runaway, and possibly suicidal.

He'd always thought of Meg as strong. She'd worked hard right beside him and Bill to build the house, keeping up with them nail for nail and board for board, even though she was raising a child in addition to working. A couple of times when Bill and Allie had come down with the flu, Meg had cared for them both, even though she'd been sick herself. She'd always seemed both strong and serene.

But, of course, he didn't live with them. He only saw her when she and Bill were socializing or invited him over. He was beginning to wonder if that strength he'd seen in her had been real, or born of necessity. Because right now she seemed to be overwhelmed.

He supposed he couldn't blame her for that. Losing a dearly loved husband had to be far worse than losing a friend. For him, missing Bill was missing someone he'd seen a couple of times a week, gone hiking and camping with on the weekend occasionally. For her, losing Bill was losing a major part of her daily life. And everywhere she turned, she had to be seeing reminders of him.

Maybe she should move out of that house. Perhaps, however, severing her last tie to Bill, other than Allie, would be worse for her than facing the reminders every day. Maybe staying there reminded her of him in ways that made her feel good.

Maybe she was just clinging to her memories. Nothing wrong with that. But living in a monument to the past wouldn't necessarily leave room for anyone else. Maybe that was why Vivian was so hostile. Maybe she felt she was being excluded. Maybe Allie felt the same.

And if he didn't go up there more than once a week, he was never going to figure out what was going on. He could use Allie as an excuse to visit for the next couple of days, but then what? Meg might start to feel crowded if he began to show up every day on a regular basis.

Then there was Vivian, who had never liked him. He would be willing to bet she would kick up a fuss if he started showing up too often, and Meg didn't need that.

As his gaze wandered over the people passing on the cold streets below, bundled against the wind's bite, he found his thoughts straying to how good it had felt to hold Meg last night. And what a fool he'd been to kiss her, even on the cheek.

There were some things you were better off not knowing. And now he knew.

All these years, he'd been aware that he found Meg attractive, but she'd been his best friend's wife, so he'd ignored the feeling. Now she wasn't anybody's wife, and the feeling wouldn't leave him alone. Last night it had blossomed into something he couldn't ignore anymore, with a strength that almost unnerved him.

It made him feel guilty, somehow, as if he were doing something wrong. What would Meg say if she even guessed? He hoped she didn't, but her not knowing didn't mean he didn't know. He knew, all right. And going to her as a friend, knowing how much he wanted her, would be to become a wolf in sheep's clothing.

The thought startled him out of his reverie. Talk about overdramatizing. He felt what he felt, but he didn't have to act on it. And as long as he didn't act on it, he was no wolf.

It never occurred to him that his feelings might cloud his judgment about what was happening up there. Shaking his head, he went back to his paperwork, telling himself to bury all this nonsense.

He managed to do just that until the school called around three to tell him that Matt Dawson had been truant for the last three days and that his father said he didn't know where the boy was.

"Well," Earl told the assistant principal, Veronica Moyers, "I know where he was on Monday. He was instrumental in saving Allie Williams."

"I heard something about that. But he wasn't in school yesterday, or today, either, and I'm worried about him, Earl," Veronica said. "What if his fa—I mean, what if somebody really hurt him this time?"

He understood Veronica's circumspection. "I'll have my people keep an eye out for him."

"Thanks."

After he hung up, he found himself staring out the window again, thinking about Matt Dawson. He feared that boy was going to get himself killed if he didn't speak up. Worse, he feared that he might already have done so.

He called Lydia Valdez into his office and explained the situation. She promised to get right on it. "If he's been hit again, Lydia, bring him in on truancy charges."

"I thought you didn't want me to do that, boss?"

"I've changed my mind. It'll give me an excuse to put the fear of God into someone in that house."

"Good idea. When you do, let me go along. I've got a few words to say, too, and they've been burning a hole in my stomach for months."

"You got it."

After she left, he thought that he might have been wrong to cut Matt so much slack over the years. He'd done it because he knew how hard life was for a kid from a bad home, and racking up juvenile charges would only make Matt's future more difficult. But maybe he'd been wrong. Maybe it was time to let the law start slamming down on him, because through that, the law could slam down on his parents.

God, he hated domestic violence. Time and again he knew what was going on but had his hands tied because somebody wouldn't tell the truth about what was being done to them. He wished the Dawsons didn't live in such an isolated spot, because if they'd had neighbors, someone before now could have provided the evidence that would get that kid yanked out of that house.

But all the years when Matt was small, the evidence had been rare. An occasional bruise that *might* have come from an accident while playing. The serious abuse had only begun a year or so ago, and Matt was lying through his teeth about it.

No kid, no matter how angry, got into that many fights, and even if he had, somebody else would have been sporting bruises, too. Nobody else had any.

The more he thought about it, the unhappier Earl got. It occurred to him that during all those childhood years, when Matt had only an occasional bruise, he might have been abused in other ways. Ways that didn't leave marks.

Christ, he had to figure out what to do about that kid.

Which led him right back to Allie. Glancing at the clock, he saw it was nearly four. Time to quit for the day. Time to head up to Meg's place and see how his girls were doing.

It was the first time he'd thought of them that way. *His girls.* The possessive words passed through his thoughts, leaving only a minor ripple in their wake. It was a major shift, and he didn't even notice it.

Matt Dawson spent the day at the Williams house, and Meg found she didn't mind at all. The boy was surprisingly courteous for a young man she'd never heard a good word about, and surprisingly grateful for the food she made a point of shoveling in his direction. He and Allie played board games and cards, and watched *E.T.,* a movie that always made Allie cry, and that seemed to touch Matt, too. Of course, he didn't cry. Instead, he developed that particular form of uneasiness common to males when faced with strong emotion.

Vivian stayed out of the way most of the day,

cleaning upstairs. For once she even let Meg make lunch, and when Meg called her down for it, she even managed to say thank-you.

Life, Meg thought, was looking up. She was even able to smile warmly at Earl when he showed up unannounced.

His blue eyes reflected her warmth back at her. "Just thought I'd check up on my ladies," he said.

"We're doing really well. Matt Dawson came over today and is playing games with Allie in the living room."

"Then let's just go straight to the kitchen."

She lifted her eyebrows at that, but he put a finger over his lips. She nodded and led the way. The children didn't look up from their game as Earl and Meg passed the living-room doorway.

"Coffee?" she asked as he settled at the table.

"No, thanks. I've drunk enough today to float a battleship."

She sat across from him. "What's this all about?"

"The school called me. Matt's been truant for the last three days. I've got my juvenile officer looking for him right now. I suppose I ought to tell her to call off the dogs. But I'm thinking about arresting him for truancy."

Three days ago Meg might have told him to go right ahead and do it. After today, she was surprised to find she felt protective of Matt. "Do you have to? He's been just wonderful with Allie today."

"I don't want to get the kid in trouble, Meg. But an arrest might get my foot in the door with his parents. Give me a chance to say something to them about the way they're treating him."

Meg nodded. "It also might just make his parents angrier with him."

"That's a possibility." He sighed and rubbed his chin. "Okay," he said, with a smile in his blue eyes. "What would *you* do?"

She thought about it for a moment, then laughed. "Darned if I know."

The phone rang, and she went to answer it. One of Allie's friends. Now that she thought about it, she was rather surprised that Allie hadn't gotten a whole bunch of calls yesterday. She'd turned off the phone while Allie was missing, because they were getting too many calls from reporters, but she'd turned it on again as soon as they got home yesterday. Her puzzlement was answered almost immediately by Sandy Miller.

"I wanted to call yesterday, Mrs. Williams, but Mom thought it was too soon. I hope Allie isn't wondering why I didn't call."

"Your mom was probably right, Sandy, but Allie's feeling a whole lot better today. Let me put her on."

She went out in the hall and called to Allie to pick up the phone. Then she hung up the kitchen extension and rejoined Earl.

"Back to Matt," he said. "So you don't think I should arrest him?"

"I'm not sure it would do him any good, Earl. He's sixteen, anyway. Couldn't he just drop out of school if he wanted to? And he might, if he starts getting arrested for missing days."

"I hadn't thought about that." He sat back in his chair. "Hell. And here I thought I'd finally had a great brainstorm."

She had to laugh. Earl was good at that, she realized. For all the pain of the last eight months, he'd still managed to make her laugh.

"So how's it going with the battle-ax?" he asked.

"My mother, you mean? Actually, it's been pretty good today. We sort of had it out last night. Or rather, I had it out, and she's been making an effort today."

"That's good. Nice if it lasts."

"Yeah."

He hesitated, and even Meg couldn't miss that he wanted to press her about the root of the problem. Her heart was climbing into her throat in expectation of the question when Allie suddenly crutched her way into the kitchen.

"Hi, Uncle Earl," she said breezily. "Mom, can Matt stay for dinner?"

"Sure. That would be nice."

"Thanks." Allie crutched away, smiling.

"She seems a whole lot better," Earl remarked.

"Yes, she does. But I'm still worried."

"Suicidal thoughts shouldn't be ignored. Maybe you need to get her into counseling. You could go with her."

But the thought of visiting a counselor made Meg's heart jam in her throat. It would be useless if she didn't tell the truth, and she didn't think she could bring herself to do that.

And that was when Earl sideswiped her, catching her unprepared. "What exactly is your mother so angry about?"

And before Meg could stop herself, she blurted out the truth. "I killed my father."

10

Earl was stunned. For a minute he couldn't even breathe. Meg, a killer? He couldn't imagine it.

Before he could think of a thing to say, Vivian entered the kitchen. If she'd been more pleasant throughout the day than she usually was, nobody could tell it now. A scowl rode firmly on her face as she snapped, "Just how many am I supposed to cook for? Allie informed me that boy is staying. I suppose *you* are, too," she said accusingly to Earl.

Earl couldn't answer, and didn't have time anyway. Meg, looking pale and shaken, announced, "Earl is always welcome at my table, Mother."

Mother. Earl noticed that, something he could focus on as shock roiled inside him. Meg had always called her mother Mom. When had that changed? And why did the word seem to bring crackling tension into the room?

Meg spoke again, refusing to look at Earl. "However, I'm sure Earl doesn't want to stay."

He knew what she meant and felt loathsome because she was right. So he said the only thing he could. "I'd like to stay."

"Fine," Vivian said irritably. She stomped across the kitchen. "That means I need to thaw another chicken. Look at the time!"

"I'm sure you'll manage, Mother," Meg said. "The microwave still works."

Vivian snorted.

Earl shoved his chair back from the table, unable to take any more. "I need some fresh air." He was turned half away from the table when he realized he couldn't do this, either. Not without making a break he wasn't sure he was ready to make. He glanced back at Meg. "Come with me? Just a short walk."

She looked as if she wanted to refuse. He saw her hunch inward on herself, and he hated himself for making her feel that way. He'd asked for her trust and confidence, and he'd gotten it. What was he going to do now? Turn on her? He thought he was a better man than that. "Meggie," he said, forcing his voice to be gentle, "join me. Please."

They got their jackets and went out the front door, to walk along the driveway. Snow had been falling all day, but it was little more than isolated flakes, adding almost nothing to the thin white blanket. The wind was frigid, though, holding the moisture that was making the snow, and it seemed to cut right through Earl's jacket.

Without saying a word, they walked down the driveway slowly, taking care not to slip. Finally Earl found a way to speak.

"You're not a murderer, Meg."

"I didn't say I was." Her breath broke, and she

started to stumble. Reaching out with a large hand, Earl caught her under the elbow and steadied her. He felt better, suddenly. She wasn't a murderer. Not that he could have believed she was. But it helped to hear her say he wasn't wrong.

"So what really happened?" he asked.

"I don't want to talk about it, Earl." Her voice was tight, stretched to breaking. "With all I've got on my plate right now…" She trailed off.

His inclination was to be sympathetic, to let her off the hook. But the bottom line was, whatever had happened was affecting the situation now. His chest ached with sorrow and apprehension, though, and they walked a while longer before he took the risk of being both blunt and honest. "Meg, whatever is going on between you and your mother is affecting Allie. Whatever happened in the past is apparently having a big effect on right now. If you don't owe it to yourself to lance this boil, you owe it to Allie."

She caught her breath sharply, and when he looked down at her, he could see that she was battling tears. "I…can't," she said breathlessly.

"Sure you can. You *have* to," he said. "Have you ever considered that talking it over might make it seem like a smaller problem? That someone else might be able to give you an insight that will help you deal with this? Meg, it's not only that your mother is angry with you. It's the way you respond to it. The combination is what's making it so difficult to live in that house."

She drew a ragged breath. "Are you saying I drove my daughter to suicide?"

Christ! He'd known she was going to get defensive.

Why the hell hadn't he just kept his mouth shut? But he couldn't, for Allie's sake. For Meg's sake. And even, damn it, for his own sake. There was a festering sore that was making them all sick to varying degrees, and ignoring it wasn't going to cure it.

"No, I'm not saying that at all," he said firmly.

"Why not? I seem to kill everyone I love."

The statement rocked him to his core, and he stopped walking, turning her to face him. "Don't," he said, spacing his words for emphasis, "ever let yourself believe such a thing."

"Why not? It's true." A sob escaped her, and she tried to turn away, but he wouldn't let her. "Everyone I love…" The words trailed away on another gasping sob.

He couldn't stand it anymore. Reaching out, he enveloped her in a hug, as if he could surround her with his strength and keep away all the pain, all the fear, all the nastiness of life. He held her close because he needed to hold her close, needed to assure himself that she wasn't going to vanish like a candle flame in the wind, smothered by burdens too big to bear.

She was crying; he could feel the sobs wracking her frame and hoped that her face was pressed into the shoulder of his wool jacket so the tears wouldn't freeze as they fell. He felt the ache in his earlobes, and a very similar ache somewhere in his soul, as if they were both being frozen by troubled winds.

"Meggie," he murmured, and rubbed her back. "Meggie, it's okay. We'll work it out somehow. All of it. I swear."

Hasty words. He knew it even as he spoke them. He didn't know what he was promising, didn't know how he could make it happen, and didn't know if he could really handle it. But he had to believe that the friendship he felt for Meg could withstand anything. Nothing else was thinkable.

"I'm sorry," she said finally, trying to pull away and dashing the tears from her eyes. "I'm sorry. I'm being a big baby."

"It's okay. We all need to cry sometimes." He let her go reluctantly, surprised to realize he'd needed those moments of physical closeness as much as she had. That unnerved him. "I wasn't kidding, Meg. We'll get through this."

"Sure." But she stuffed her hands into her pockets and started walking again. Down the driveway, not toward the house, which relieved him considerably, because it meant she wasn't in a hurry to end the conversation. He decided to take that as a positive sign.

"So what happened?" he asked again, aware that he was taking a huge chance. "Just sketch it for me."

She didn't say anything for a while. She kept her head down, watching her footing, but from time to time a heavy sigh escaped her. A couple of times she looked up at the sky as if she might find an answer there.

"My dad," she said finally, her voice cracking. She paused, drew a breath, and tried again. "My dad saw... Bill and I were... Hell!"

"Having sex?" he suggested, knowing full well that Meg had been pregnant with Allie before the wedding.

"Uh, yes," she managed to say. But something in the way she said it led him to believe that wasn't the whole story, that there was something she was concealing behind that clinical description.

"And?"

"He was so shocked he had a heart attack. He died two days later without ever waking up."

"And Vivian blames you for this?"

Meg gave a jerky nod.

"That woman is nuts! Plenty of parents have walked in on their kids having sex without suffering heart attacks. If he was in such bad condition, any little thing could have caused the attack. Getting angry at Vivian might have done it."

She looked at him then, her eyes watery with tears. "You don't understand them. They're such good Christians. What Dad saw...well, it was a terrible, terrible...thing."

He noticed she didn't say "sin." And he thought that was significant, though he wasn't sure why. His cop instincts were kicking into overdrive, but he didn't know how to press her. He felt she'd confided enough for one session, to judge by the wild, despairing look in her eyes.

"Well," he said firmly, "you didn't kill your father. The next day he could have gone out to mow the hay, overexerted himself and dropped dead in the field. What happened would have happened anyway, sooner or later."

"That's easy to say," she said almost bitterly. "Don't you think I've told myself that a million times? But I was still the immediate cause of his death."

He stifled a sigh, feeling as if he were whaling against a brick wall and not even making a dent. People believed what they wanted to believe. He ought to know that by now.

But it hurt him to think she was in so much pain, and he cast about for something to say that might actually get through to her. When she turned and started trudging toward the house, he'd gotten nowhere.

Of course, nothing he said would probably matter a hill of beans when her own mother believed she was responsible for her father's death. Why should his opinion matter more than Vivian's? Hell, it couldn't matter even as much.

So what now, genius? he asked himself. Where do you go from here?

The snow-muffled world didn't offer any answers.

Vivian didn't exactly say anything to make anyone feel unwelcome during dinner that night, but she managed to do it anyway. Right after dinner, as soon as he had offered to help with the dishes and been refused—by Vivian, who made it quite apparent that she wouldn't trust him even with the chipped crockery—Matt excused himself, saying he needed to go home.

Earl was pretty sure he didn't, but he waited until the boy was outside before following him. "Matt?"

The youth hesitated, then faced him, his expression already stubborn.

"Where'd you get that fresh bruise by your ear?"

"I banged into a door."

"Yeah, right. I suppose it came looking for you."

Matt remained stubbornly silent.

"Look, son, I know what's going on, even if you

won't say it. If you ever need a place to stay, knock on my door. You don't need to hide out. Okay?''

After a moment Matt gave a short nod, then turned to walk to his car. Earl stood in the cold, watching him drive away, wishing the kid didn't have the temperament of a mule. On the other hand, he realized sadly, that stubbornness might have been all that kept Matt alive these many years.

It sure as hell had been all that kept *him* going sometimes.

Earl played a couple of games of backgammon with Allie in the living room, before the girl excused herself to go upstairs and chat on-line. He watched her crutch her way up the stairs, part of him wanting to race up and help her, part of him admiring how quickly she'd become adept at using the crutches. He applauded from the foot of the stairs when she reached the top, and she glanced back just long enough to grin at him. She was feeling better, he thought. Maybe he didn't need to worry quite so much about her.

Vivian had already disappeared to her room, making it clear she didn't wish to associate with Earl. He couldn't make up his mind whether that was a good thing or a bad one. He didn't especially want to hang around with Vivian. On the other hand, he couldn't be sure Meg was indifferent to her mother's disapproval of him.

But now there was just him and Meg, and that wasn't a good thing. Most definitely not. Because all he had to do was look at her to realize how tense and unhappy she was, and that didn't mesh with his own reaction when his gaze happened to fall to her breasts or hips.

She was a beautiful woman at thirty-four. More beautiful than she'd been the day she married Bill. The years had chiseled away some of her youth, but they'd left graceful lines in the place of softness. Her cheekbones were exquisitely etched, her chin a delicate line that flowed smoothly into her long neck. And her breasts...time had only made them fuller. Not huge, just...well, perfect.

But he didn't need to be noticing these things right now, not with Meg so upset. In fact, his sexual response to her, always a problem, seemed an even bigger one now. What she needed from him had nothing to do with the way he would like to bear her down on a soft bed and worship her with his body.

Nope. Bad place to go. It made him feel guilty. Even though he was no longer betraying Bill by having these feelings, he now felt as if he was betraying Meg.

So he would have left without touching her at all, but as they reached the front door, she reached out and caught his hand. "Thanks, Earl," she said. "Thanks for *everything*."

He should have let it go at that. But some impulse both deeper and stronger than thought took over, and he drew her to him, wrapping her in his arms and kissing her on the mouth.

As soon as he did it, he knew it was a mistake. He felt her stiffen, felt the hot rush of response in his own body. Now he would go back to his lonely house remembering exactly how she had felt against him, exactly how her mouth had tasted. And now she would probably never trust him again.

It was only an instant, but he felt it all the way to the depths of his soul. Shaken, he let go of her and stepped back. What he saw in her eyes was confusion and fear.

"I'm a shit," he said to her. "Ignore that." Then he walked out into the dark, cold night, knowing that neither of them was going to be able to do that.

Meg closed the door behind him, shaking from head to toe. Earl had unleashed a surge of violent emotion in her, an emotion she couldn't name. It terrified her. She stood with her forehead pressed to the door, closing her eyes and wishing she could lean on something as strong as that door forever.

"Well, wasn't that pretty?" Vivian's acid tone startled Meg and caused her to spin around in shock. Vivian was standing at the top of the stairs, looking down at her with disgust. "Up to your old tricks, I see. You always were a slut."

Hot and cold waves washed through Meg, making her feel weak, as if she was ready to pass out. "Let's not go there, Mother."

"Why not? Poor Bill isn't even in his grave a year, and you're already carrying on!"

"You don't know what you're talking about!"

"I know what I saw with my own eyes. The same kind of thing your father saw that killed him."

"It's not at all what my father saw."

"It just didn't get as far, is all."

"Mother, what my father saw was Bill raping me!" The words Meg had never spoken out loud had leaped out of her without warning, as if something inside had snapped and catapulted them into the open. Shock froze her as the ugly accusation hung in the air.

Vivian whitened, scarily so. She reached out and grabbed the stair railing for support, sagging dangerously. Suddenly worried that she'd killed another person she loved, Meg ran up the stairs and tried to help her, but Vivian waved her away.

"Don't touch me! How can you say such a vile thing?"

"Because it's true," Meg said, her voice breaking as tears started to flow. "Because it's true, Mother...."

Vivian straightened and looked at her. "I can't believe it."

"It's true...."

The two women stood looking at each other, one crying and silently begging for belief, the other looking wary, frightened and wounded.

"I can't," said Vivian. "I can't..."

"Listen to me. Please. Just listen to me."

After an endless moment, Vivian nodded.

"Not here," Meg said, wiping her tears with the back of her hand. "Not here. Allie..."

Vivian nodded again and led the way down the hall to her bedroom. Once there, she closed the door behind them. Meg sat on the edge of her mother's bed; Vivian took the rocker.

"If it's true," Vivian said finally, "why didn't you tell me when it happened?"

"Because I didn't know that's what had happened."

Vivian's face hardened. "You can't expect me to believe that foolishness."

"I know it's difficult. It took me years to understand what really happened, and I never wanted to say it, because it's so hard to believe. But it was *rape,* Mother."

Vivian averted her face, rocking rapidly. The creak of the chair sounded loud in the silent room. "You weren't hurt," she said finally.

"Not every rape involves getting bludgeoned and stabbed." Now that the subject was out in the open, she found she couldn't bear to discuss it. Couldn't bear to expose herself this way. It was an episode she'd done her best to bury, because thinking about it would only have hurt her marriage, and hurting her marriage would have hurt her child.

But she knew how difficult it was going to be for her mother to accept this. It had taken her nearly ten years to finally admit what had really happened that day in the barn. To admit that she hadn't given in to Bill because she wanted to. To finally accept the fact that the episode had been completely against her will. If it had taken her ten years, she couldn't expect Vivian to accept it in a matter of minutes.

And even accepting that the event hadn't been her doing, she found herself unable to fully forgive herself for her role in her father's death. Once she had decided what had really happened, she had begun to castigate herself for not fighting harder, for not screaming. She had *let* herself be intimidated, had allowed herself to be overwhelmed by greater strength. She had even allowed Bill to make her believe that there was something wrong with her for refusing.

Vivian looked at her. "You're making this up to excuse what you did. You ought to be ashamed of yourself."

Meg opened her mouth to argue but found her voice locked in her throat. Snakes of self-doubt began to wind their way through her, throwing her off balance. It had taken her ten years to decide she had been raped. Maybe she had reconstructed the memory. You read all the time about how some memory wasn't real, how people reconstruct it moment by moment and believe it fully. Oh, God, had some twisted portion of her done that?

She squeezed her eyes closed, and suddenly, just as vividly as if it were happening now, she remembered the way she had felt pinned beneath Bill. Remembered how hurtful his hands had been as he held her down. Remembered the way the hay had smelled, and how it had stung her bare body. She could even smell his sweat as he collapsed on her.

What if that memory wasn't real?

But all those years, she had felt something was wrong about what had happened. Right from the very moment itself. She had tried to ignore the feeling, reminding herself that she had owed the sex to Bill because they were engaged. Telling herself that he'd just gotten carried away because she'd let the petting go too far. Believing that he had been right when he said she would be just a tease if she didn't give in. Trying to forget how many times she had said no, how many ways she had begged him to stop, how she had tried to tell him it was wrong when they weren't married. And how he had laughed at her objections and then had grown irritated, until finally…

No, she told herself, it had been date rape. But the niggling doubts wouldn't go away.

"I told him no," she said to Vivian, measuring her words. "I told him to stop over and over again. And I never said yes."

Vivian shrugged. "Women don't always mean it when they say no."

Hearing those words from her mother was a betrayal that wounded her in ways she couldn't name. She felt something inside herself disintegrating, breaking into a thousand small pieces. And when the shattering stopped, she felt numb and cold inside, as if an arctic wind blew through her heart. With the numbness came a shattering certainty about what had happened.

"I meant it when I said no," she said quietly. "And I didn't kill my father. He heard me crying and asking Bill why he hadn't stopped. And if Daddy had lived, that's exactly what he would have told you. He had a heart attack because he saw that his daughter had been raped."

She headed for the door, deciding that tomorrow she was going to drive Vivian to the bus station and tell her to get lost forever. She didn't need to wear this hair shirt for the rest of her life. She had enough problems right now without this. She needed to get rid of Vivian so she could focus on Allie.

"If that's true," Vivian said from behind her, "then why did you marry Bill?"

Meg didn't answer. She couldn't answer. Her mother knew why she'd married Bill. Because in the aftermath of her father's death, the shock of Meg's pregnancy had been too much. Because Vivian had insisted it was the only right way to deal with it. Because Bill was Allie's father. And because, despite what had happened, Meg had loved Bill. Because it had taken her ten years to realize that her husband had not been entitled to take what he had stolen from her.

God, Vivian saw the world in such simple terms.

She closed the door behind her, then stood in the hallway, testing the numbness that filled her. It was good, she realized. She felt calm. Utterly and completely calm, as if her emotions had moved behind a glass wall. She could tell they were still there, but she couldn't feel them or hear them. They were mute.

If it was some kind of psychological break, it hadn't come a moment too soon. She needed the peace it brought her.

Calm, she was able to walk down the hall and check on Allie. Her daughter was sitting on her bed, absorbed in the glowing computer screen. For the first time Meg felt a serious qualm about her daughter's fascination with on-line chat. Maybe it wasn't just a harmless amusement. Maybe it was an escape, a way not to deal with reality.

"How's it going, Allie?"

"Okay."

No excitement, no smile. No shared tidbit about something she'd just read on the screen.

"Good chat?"

"Oh, it's okay. Some dweeb is dissing the Boptown Boys."

"Who are they?"

She got the expected eye roll. "They're a really great band."

"Oh, I thought everyone was hot on the Taffytown Train."

"They are so out."

"Oh." At sea again. Having a fourteen-year-old often made her feel like a Philistine. "So why is this dweeb dissing the—who were they?"

"The BB. That's what everyone calls them. Just because he's a jerk. He's trying to make everyone mad at him."

"Doesn't sound like much fun."

Allie shrugged. "Gloria's dealing with him. He'll shut up soon."

Meg didn't know if that was good or bad, or what it might mean about this Gloria. But she let it go for now. "Hungry? You didn't eat a whole lot at dinner."

"Like anyone can eat when Grandma's glaring. What *is* her issue? So she's mad at you. Does she have to be mad at everyone else, too? I felt sorry for Matt."

"I did, too. Matt seems like a nice enough..." She stumbled over the word *kid,* sensing that Allie would take it amiss if her mother referred to someone two years older than Allie as a kid. She struggled for a better term. "He seems like a nice enough young man."

"He is. Really nice. I don't know why everybody is so down on him."

Meg wasn't quite ready to credit her daughter with better judgment than most of the adults in town. "He seems...well, I think he's angry. And angry boys his age tend to frighten and irritate adults."

Allie shrugged. "Then they're stupid. He's got a lot to be angry about."

"Yes?"

But Allie didn't answer. Her face closed, signaling that this was something she didn't want to discuss with her mother. There were more and more things like that in life this past year.

"So," Meg repeated after a moment, "are you hungry? I can make you a snack. I'm thinking about one myself."

Allie's interest perked up. "Chicken sandwich? We sure had enough left."

"Sounds good. That's what I'll do."

"And can I have some more pecan sandies?"

"Absolutely."

Nothing, Meg thought, could be all that bad when Allie's appetite was good. At the back of her mind, she knew she was creating a fool's paradise, but right now she was ready to cling to any straw she could find.

She also knew, deep in her gut, that whatever Allie's problem was, it hadn't been a passing mood.

And suddenly she didn't feel quite so numb.

11

Earl forced himself to stay away from the Williams house for the next two days. It was better, he told himself, to get a little distance. To give Meg time to recover from her confession. To give himself time to get over that kiss.

Because he knew he was in trouble. He suddenly found himself unable to close his eyes without remembering Meg's face. Because the mere thought of her made his groin ache. He wasn't a man who was ashamed of his needs, but when it came to Meg, the feelings struck him as sacrilegious. As if he were betraying her.

Hell, she thought of him as a friend. He couldn't imagine that his place in her life would ever change. He couldn't dare to think such things, and he didn't know if he could live with himself if it happened anyway. Man, even thinking about it felt incestuous, because for so long, Bill's place in his life had been as a brother, and Meg—well, Meg had taken the place of a sister. Or at least he had tried to convince himself that was the case.

But he was discovering that he was pretty good at lying to himself. Oh, yes. And it shamed him.

And of course there was Allie. He had a feeling the girl would resent the hell out of it if she ever so much as suspected he might be taking her father's place with her mother. Not that Meg would ever be interested in a man like him, who'd come out of a bad home and had never been to college. He wasn't in her class. Vivian was right about him. He was a guttersnipe.

So what was the point in letting himself think about it? Time to dig a mental hole and bury the entire thing, time to get back to comfortable and normal, the way things had been before. He was good at burying things.

And so, apparently, was Meg. The thought took him sideways, making him forget his resolution not to think about her for a few days. He never would have imagined she was carrying so much guilt inside her. And he suspected, unhappily, that he'd merely seen the tip of the iceberg.

Which was why he didn't keep his vow to stay away until his usual Saturday visit. Allie gave him a good excuse to go up there on Friday afternoon, and Matt made an even better one.

As he was leaving the office to drive there, he encountered Matt. The boy was sullenly leaning against a lamppost on Main, not too far from the entrance to the office. Seeing him, Earl decided he could kill two birds with one stone.

"Hey, Matt," he called. "Wanna go see Allie? I'm heading up that way."

The boy slouched toward him, looking even angrier than usual. What had happened now?

"Nah," said Matt when he drew closer. "The old witch hates me."

"Who? Allie's grandmother?"

"Yeah."

Naturally Matt would be sensitive to that. He felt that most everyone hated him, and his way of dealing with it was to stay out of the way.

Earl looked him up and down, noting that the bruise near his ear was fading a little. And, thank God, there didn't seem to be any new ones. "Well," he said, "I never let that stop me from going anywhere. Allie likes you, and so does her mother. So screw the old dragon."

The remark surprised a laugh out of Matt, who suddenly looked his age, instead of like a frail old man. "Yeah," the boy said. "Screw her. I'll go."

"Well, come on, then." Earl felt he was making great strides to get the kid to ride along with him. He kept waiting for Matt to insist on taking his own car, but he didn't. He just climbed right into Earl's official Explorer.

"So," said Matt when they were on the highway just outside town, "you sweet on Allie's mom?"

The question, paralleling Earl's thoughts so closely, shocked him more than it would have otherwise. His denial probably came too quickly. "No. I was friends with her late husband."

"Oh."

The young man seemed to accept the explanation, much to Earl's relief. There were places he definitely didn't want to go, especially with a wet-behind-the-ears kid. "I'm also Allie's godfather."

"Oh. I don't have a godfather."

That hardly surprised Earl. He didn't think the Dawson family had ever set foot in church in anyone's memory—which probably had more to do with them being unable to get up early enough on Sunday after a hard night drinking than with what they believed. Or maybe not. That was something he didn't feel any particular curiosity about. "Your dad got a new job yet?"

From the corner of his eye, he saw Matt shrug. "I don't ask."

"What about you, son? You looking for steady work?"

"I can't get it. No one trusts me."

Earl wanted to swear. How was this kid ever supposed to make a life for himself if nobody would give him a chance? Anger made his hands tighten on the steering wheel. "You *want* a steady job?"

"Yeah, sure. I need the money."

Of course he did. The kid would probably use it to move out the first chance he could. "Well, maybe I can rustle up something. Let me think on it a while."

"Sure," Matt said, clearly not believing him.

But there had to be something, and Earl figured if he couldn't find a job, he would damn well invent one somehow. The kid wouldn't need a whole lot of work, not if he stayed in school, but he needed something regular. "I'll find something if you promise me you'll stay in school, Matt. You need that diploma."

Matt didn't answer, which convinced Earl that he'd better be very careful about the kind of job he found for this boy. No way was he going to help this kid drop out of school.

Vivian answered the door at the Williams house. "Meg's at work," she said shortly, as if that settled the issue.

"We came to see Allie," Earl said firmly. With a cop's practiced attitude, he stepped forward, and Vivian naturally stepped back. He was inside.

Vivian didn't look happy about it, but she said, "Allie's in the living room. Trying to catch up on homework."

"Great." Earl glanced at Matt. "You go on ahead. I want a word with Vivian first."

Matt nodded, giving Vivian a wary look, then eased past them and disappeared into the living room. A second later they heard Allie say happily, "Matt!"

Earl looked down at Vivian. "In the study or in the kitchen, but away from the kids."

Vivian hesitated, then nodded and led the way to her sanctum sanctorum, the kitchen. She even unbent enough to give Earl a cup of coffee, most likely because she wanted one herself and couldn't make herself be *that* rude. Earl began to feel amused by her.

And then he wondered what the hell he was doing. He hadn't thought this through, hadn't formulated a plan, didn't have an idea in hell if he was about to make things worse. All he knew was that he felt compelled to say something about the situation. He needed to open his yap or he plain wasn't going to be able to live with himself.

This time, he decided not to beat around the bush. "Meg didn't kill her father."

Vivian's face puckered up with anger. Considering

the way she usually looked, Earl wouldn't have believed it was possible for her to look any angrier and more disapproving than she ordinarily did. He was wrong.

"I suppose she told you that," Vivian said. "I got a different opinion."

"Actually, she told me she killed her father. When I heard the whole story, I told her she was wrong. And I'm telling *you* she was wrong. So are you. Your husband had to have had a weak heart to begin with, or a little shock wouldn't have killed him. If it hadn't been what he saw, it would have been something else, and probably before too much time passed. Meg needs to understand that, and so do you."

Vivian's eyes were dark with anger. "That girl has *always* blamed everyone else for things that happen because of what she did."

"No, she's actually accepting too much responsibility for things beyond her control. And I have a strong feeling you're to blame for that, Vivian. Any mother who can claim her daughter was responsible for a man's death by heart attack needs to take a serious look at how *she's* laying blame."

Vivian's face closed as if she had shut a door. Earl saw it and realized he might have made a big mistake by bringing this up. What if he had only made the situation worse for Meg? That hadn't been what he wanted to do at all.

Getting involved with this family was like stepping in horse manure, he thought. No matter how hard you tried, you couldn't shake the stuff off your shoes.

The thought disturbed him, because he hadn't used to feel that way. Back before Bill's death, spending time with him, Meg and Allie had often been the highlight of his week. They'd gone skiing together, hiking together, had barbecues on warm summer evenings, and had sometimes spent rainy or snowy Sunday afternoons playing cards. It had been as if they were all a family, including him.

But Bill's death had changed that. There had, of course, been his acute awareness of Meg's grief, which he was sure must exceed his own a thousand-fold. There had been the awareness that she was now a woman alone and his attentions could be misunderstood, both by the local gossips and by Meg herself. And there had been Vivian, who, now that he thought about it, had seemed to want to drive a wedge between Meg and the rest of the world. One by one, Meg's friends seemed to have fallen away, and he was sure that wasn't because Meg was widowed.

He looked at Vivian, looked at her miserably closed face, and wondered why this woman had become so bitter that she would willingly be a thundercloud in her only child's life.

Just because Meg's father had had a heart attack after finding Meg making love with Bill? He found that hard to believe. There had to be more eating Vivian than that.

"Have you always felt this way about Meg?"

Vivian looked startled. Then she turned her face away. "Who made this your business?"

"Nobody. But Meg happens to be a good friend of mine. And Bill was my best friend. So I care about what happens to her. Can you say the same?"

Vivian turned on him. "Of course I care!"

"You have a funny way of showing it."

"I'm angry at her. She took my husband away from me."

"That was an accident!"

"Oh, it started long before Hiram died."

Earl's heart seemed to slam, then skitter to a dead halt. He must have been a cop too long, he thought crazily. Because he could only think of one thing that might mean, and it made his stomach turn over. "Are you saying your husband...sexually abused Meg?"

Vivian gasped and paled. "What kind of pervert are you? I'll have you know he was a good man and never did anything of the sort!"

Earl felt a wave of relief nearly as great as what he had felt when he knew Allie was all right. He also wasn't about to be cowed by this shrew. "Then what did you mean?"

Vivian looked as if she wanted to tell him to get lost, but after the suggestion he'd just made, she had to defend her husband. She was incapable of leaving him to wonder now, and that was fine by him.

"He doted on that girl. She couldn't do wrong, no matter what."

And Vivian, thought Earl, had begun to feel lost in the shuffle. He'd never been married or had kids, but he'd seen similar situations among his friends, where one parent doted so much on a child that the other started to feel shut out. It could create a lot of resentment in the parent who felt he or she was taking last place to the child. Still...

"That's not Meg's fault," he said. "She isn't responsible for what her father did."

"That's what I used to think, until I realized that Meg was involved in everything bad in my life."

Earl couldn't believe he was hearing this. He simply could not believe that this woman was so twisted that she could believe such a thing. Then he reminded himself that she wasn't being rational; she was speaking from emotion, and emotions were rarely logical. But he didn't know what to say.

Vivian spoke. "She destroys everyone who loves her."

Earl was suddenly blind with anger. Nobody deserved that, certainly not Meg, whose losses had been every bit as great at her mother's, perhaps even greater. Certainly not a woman like Meg who, as far as he could tell, had always tried to do the right thing. "You're sick," he said to Vivian. "But if that's what you think, why don't you just get the hell out of here and go home?"

Vivian pushed her chair back from the table and stood, looking down at him. "I didn't mean she does it on purpose." Then she walked out of the kitchen.

God! Earl felt nauseated by what he'd just heard. No wonder Allie was freaking out, living with a woman like that. Even if Vivian didn't say these things out loud, her attitude was poisonous. And now he knew why Meg felt that everyone who loved her died. Vivian had probably planted that seed sometime in the last eight months.

From a distance, as if from another planet, he could hear the laughter of Allie and Matt from the living room. It did him good to hear those children laugh, especially Matt, who never laughed at all.

But it would take more than laughter to mend what was wrong in this house, and the more he thought about it, the more overwhelming it seemed.

But never, not once in his life, had Earl been a quitter, and he wasn't about to begin now. Not when the two people he cared about most in the world were in trouble.

Still, he could identify with the legendary Sisyphus. This boulder was big, and he feared that no matter how hard he pushed it uphill, it was still going to roll back down.

Meg wasn't happy to see the sheriff's vehicle in front of her house when she got home from the credit union. Not because she expected any more bad news—she was sure Vivian would have called her at work if anything had happened to Allie—but because she didn't want to see Earl. She'd exposed herself too much the last time she talked to him, and she didn't want to see knowledge of her secrets in his eyes.

But even worse than that was the tendril of anticipation she felt. She *wanted* to see him. She had always been glad to see him, but this was something more. She kept remembering the way he had held her, and she wanted him to do it again. More than ever, she wanted to crawl into the strength of his arms and curl up safely.

And that was ridiculous. He was a friend. *Bill's* friend. And because of what she had done, he could never be anything more.

She was surprised to see Matt in the living room with Allie, the two of them talking over her homework. But Allie looked so pleased, she decided she was glad Matt was there. She found Earl in the kitchen, staring rather soberly into a murky cup of coffee.

"I'm surprised Vivian let you in," she said as she dropped her purse on the table and hung her jacket over the back of the chair.

He gave her a crooked smile. "She didn't want to. You could say I just walked right past her."

"Good for you." She got herself a cup of coffee and freshened his. "So what's up?"

"Oh, I thought I'd bring Matt up for a couple of hours to see Allie. I wanted to know how you're both doing."

"Just fine, actually." Far from the truth, but it was a hope she refused to relinquish.

"Allie hasn't said anything about why she ran away?"

"Not a word."

He tilted his head to one side. "That's not good, Meg."

"I know. I called her school today. She's going to start seeing a counselor on Monday when she goes back."

"Good. But what about you?"

"I'll be just fine. I'm always fine." It was a litany she must have said a million times since her dad's death, a mantra she repeated ceaselessly in the back of her mind, trying to hypnotize herself into believing it. Sometimes she almost did.

She looked past Earl, out the sliding glass door to the deck, and found herself remembering the brown spider she'd seen there less than a week ago. God, it seemed like a lifetime. And what had happened to the spider? Had Vivian swept it away? Had it survived? What did spiders do in the cold?

"It's going to snow again," she heard herself say. It was safe to talk about snow.

"I heard. Winter's coming early."

Winter was already here, Meg thought. Settled in for the duration, inside these walls. "Fifteen inches."

"That's what they're predicting. Won't be long before it's ski season."

"Yeah. This'll make the ski resorts happy."

Earl shifted in his chair, and she sensed his impatience with her diversion. Too bad. She didn't want to discuss any sensitive topics with him. He was too good at getting her to spill her guts. She did, however, dart a glance his way, and found him looking thoroughly disgusted. She couldn't blame him.

"I spoke with Vivian," he said.

Meg's heart began to thud. Oh, God, had Vivian told him what she'd said about Bill raping her? Because if she had—but no. She couldn't have. If she had told Earl, he wouldn't be sitting across from her right now. He would have been long gone.

"That woman is poison," he said. "Why don't you send her back home, Meg? She's not good for you or Allie."

Meg didn't answer immediately. She stared out the door at the snow-frosted woods, the day's failing light and the shadows beneath the pines, and wished she could just run out there and disappear the way Allie had tried to do.

How could she explain the guilt that made her let Vivian stay, no matter how many times she vowed to send her away? How could she make him understand that every time she thought of sending her mother back to Monroe Corners, she remembered that there was no one there for her. That Vivian would be all alone. And that it was her fault, not her mother's. He would disagree with her. She knew he would. He would tell her it wasn't her problem. But it was. Everything was her problem.

Finally she said, "She doesn't have any place to go back to."

"Oh, come on!"

"She doesn't, Earl. She let her apartment go when she came to help out after Bill died. Monroe Corners is a small place. She might not be able to find anywhere to live."

"There's always somewhere to live. Give me a better excuse, Meg."

She turned and glared at him. "Then how about this? She's my mother, and I couldn't do that to her."

"Why not? She's abandoned you emotionally. What do you owe her?"

Too much, Meg thought. She owed her mother too much. "I don't want to discuss this. We'll work it out somehow."

"You haven't worked it out in eight months. And it's bad for Allie."

"Quit dragging Allie into this! Mother loves her as much as I do. She wouldn't harm a hair on that child's head."

"Maybe not. But maybe you ought to consider how it makes a child feel to see how much her grandmother hates her mother. And what it's like to have to live with that tension."

Meg suddenly felt like wilting. Too much had happened in the past week, and worries were stalking her mind endlessly, even when she tried to pretend that everything was okay. She was certainly scared to death for her daughter and hoping against hope that the school psychologist could get Allie to talk about what had sent her up into the mountains. She didn't need Earl badgering her on top of everything else.

She looked at him. "I thought you were my friend."

His face darkened. "Low blow," he said. "Friends don't stand idly by while friends destroy their lives."

"I'm not destroying my life."

"Maybe not. But you're sure as hell not doing anything to fix it."

"Just what am I supposed to do? Spill my guts so you can feel like you've done a good deed by listening? Then you walk away into your life, and I'm left alone in mine, with nothing changed except that now *you* know all the awful stuff inside me. Big help, Earl."

She could see he was struggling to maintain his patience, but she didn't care. He was badgering her, and she couldn't take it. Fond as she was of Earl, there were places in her life she couldn't take him into. Couldn't allow him into. Because if she did, there would be nothing left at all.

"You know," he said finally, "sometimes it helps to spill your guts, because you discover that what you're thinking is so awful isn't really that awful at all. You can discover that people who love you keep right on loving you anyway. And sometimes an objective ear can help you sort things out."

"How objective can you be, Earl? Bill was your best friend."

This was not the first time she'd said something

that had given him the feeling that Bill was involved in this misery in a way he wouldn't like. He didn't think she was doing it on purpose, but it gave him pause. There might, he thought, be things he didn't want to know about Bill. Things that would forever change how he felt about him. Did he really want to open that Pandora's box?

But Bill was gone, he reminded himself, and Meg was here. Whatever Bill might have done, or failed to do, his own primary obligation was to the living. To Meg. To Allie.

"That's right," Meg said, correctly interpreting his expression. "Some things are better left hidden."

"Not when they're eating people alive."

"What makes you so damn sure you can fix anything?"

"Maybe I can't. But maybe all you need is to know that people won't hate you for the truth."

If only she could have believed that. But she'd been living with the ugliness inside her too long to trust anyone else with it. Look what had happened when she'd tried to tell her own mother the truth. She hadn't been believed.

And maybe she was wrong about it all, anyway. Maybe she'd reconfigured her memory to suit herself and Bill had never really raped her. It was all so confusing now, and doubts were eating at her like maggots.

She thought she'd sorted out what had been bothering her all those years about what had happened in the barn. She thought she'd found out why she could never forget it, and why every time it crossed her mind she felt vaguely ill. She thought she had discovered why it was that, ever afterward, some part of her had been locked away from Bill, keeping a distance.

And now she wasn't sure at all. Maybe her mother was right. Maybe if Bill had really forced her, she would have struggled harder. Maybe she would have told the whole story right after it happened, instead of feeling ashamed and dirty, so ashamed and dirty she had never once been able to bring herself to talk about it.

If she had really been raped, she never would have married Bill, would she?

But none of this, *none* of this, seemed important beside what was troubling Allie. She'd been living with what had happened that day in the barn for fifteen years, and she could live with it for the rest of her life. What she couldn't live with was the idea that something terrible was bothering Allie. *That* was the issue that needed to be dealt with.

Earl spoke. "You used to paint, didn't you?"

The change of subject threw her off balance for a few seconds, but she welcomed it. Anything was better than Earl pressuring her to tell him her secrets. "Yes," she said finally. "I was an art major. I never thought I had the talent to support myself with it, but I figured I could teach."

"What happened?"

She shrugged. "Old story. I married Bill and dropped out to raise Allie. We moved up here, and there wasn't any way I could continue with college."

"Not even at the community college?"

"I was past that."

He nodded slowly. "So why'd you give up painting?"

"There was never any time for it. Always something else that needed doing."

"There's time for it now. Why don't you get some supplies and teach Allie? It'd be good for her."

That was the first thing he'd said that actually appealed to her. "Maybe I will. But I'll need to go to Denver to buy the equipment." With fifteen inches of snow coming, it wasn't something she was likely to do soon.

"We'll go tomorrow," he said. "I'll drive, we'll take Allie, make a day of it. If the roads get too bad, we'll spend the night."

"Earl..."

He leaned forward, his eyes fixing her. "You need something constructive and fun to do. We're going to have fun, Meg. The three of us. Whether you like it or not."

12

They left the following morning in Earl's Explorer. Snow had started falling before sunrise, and by the time they departed, several fresh inches covered the ground, and the flakes were whirling wildly.

This was insane, Meg thought. Driving out into an early blizzard was nuts. It was way too early in the season for this, and all the more dangerous because the ground beneath the snow was still warm, still wet. The highways were apt to ice over.

But Allie wanted to go. She was excited at the idea of spending a day in Denver, and had been thrilled when her mother suggested teaching her to paint.

Driving over the first pass was scary—for Meg, at least. The wind-whipped snow was nearly blinding, and only the tall reflectors, catching the Blazer's headlights, let them know where the road was. She consoled herself with the knowledge that on this stretch of road, at least, if they skidded off, there was no place to fall. Earl had chosen the safer way out, along the road the ore trucks followed. The other route to I-70 would have been foolhardy, full of twisting turns that hung over sheer drops.

Earl's grip on the steering wheel was relaxed, though, as was his posture. He didn't seem to think the driving was particularly difficult, but Meg found herself watching him constantly, looking for some sign that they might get into trouble.

And trying not to think how Bill had died. He'd driven out into a snowstorm like this after their last argument and had never come home. For herself, Meg didn't care. But Allie was in the car with them.

For all her excitement, though, Allie was quiet. Finally Meg twisted in her seat to look back at her. "Are you okay, honey? Are you hurting?"

"I'm fine," Allie said. "Just sleepy. Uncle Earl's just like dad, starting out at the crack of dawn."

"Hey, Chipmunk," said Earl, "we didn't start at the crack of dawn. The sun was fully awake."

"But I wasn't," Allie groused, though playfully.

"You just need to get to bed at a decent hour," Earl told her. "If you went to bed at ten, like I do, you'd be bright-eyed and bushy-tailed at 6:00 a.m."

Allie groaned. "That's uncivilized."

"Maybe, but I'm not the one who's sleepy this morning."

Allie laughed and told him he was a know-it-all. He assured her that that was exactly what a sheriff needed to be. Then he suggested that since they had a three-hour trip ahead of them, she could catch some shut-eye. A little while later, Allie was dozing, with a blanket to cushion her head.

Earl put some quiet music on the tape player, and soon Meg was dozing, too. She was vaguely aware that conditions must have cleared, because Earl speeded up for a long while. Then she felt the car slow down to a crawl, and concern jerked her out of sleep. When she opened her eyes, it was as if they were wrapped in a cocoon of white.

"Oh, God," she said. "Where are we?"

"Past Copper Mountain on the interstate."

"We shouldn't be driving in this."

"It's okay, Meg," he said, his voice a soothing rumble. "We've got the whole damn road to ourselves, and as long as I can see the reflectors, we're not going off it."

She glanced at the speedometer and saw he was doing about thirty-five. Little by little she forced herself to relax her muscles. "We should have waited until next weekend."

"Once winter arrives, there's no predicting when we'll have a good weekend. Besides, this'll probably almost disappear once we get past the Eisenhower Tunnel. It's not snowing at the lower elevations."

She found her hands knotting into fists anyway.

"You know, Meg," he said after a bit, "Bill went off the road because he took the curve too fast. He always drove too fast."

And that time, she thought, he'd driven even faster than usual because he'd been angry with her. Except for that argument, he might have been driving more cautiously. The thought didn't comfort her at all.

He spoke again. "Did I ever tell you about the time I almost went off a cliff?"

She looked at him, knowing he was trying to distract her and willing to let him. "No. What happened?"

"I'd been down in Glenwood Springs on business, and as I was coming up the back way, I got caught in snow. It wasn't much of a storm, the kind of thing we drive through all the time without thinking about it. But under the snow there was nothing but ice. I was coming around this tight curve on a steep upgrade when all of a sudden my tires lost their grip and I started to slide straight backward. I thought I was a goner for sure."

"My God!"

"I said something like that, too." He flashed her a quick grin, then returned his attention to the road. "Anyway, there was nothing behind me but a thousand-foot drop. And I knew it. I decided I'd have to throw the door open and try to jump out. But suddenly the tires caught and the car stopped."

"You must have been so relieved."

"Yeah. For a minute. I was almost afraid to move for fear the car would start sliding again. But finally I made myself get out and take a look. Meg, I was exactly one foot from the cliff edge. One miserable, lousy foot."

"What did you do?"

"Well, I thought about radioing for help, then I figured I didn't want to drag anybody else out on that road. I mean, if my studded snow tires hadn't kept me from slipping, it was pretty bad. I had visions of me and a tow truck both going over the edge. So I walked very carefully behind the car, almost positive that at any instant the sucker would start slipping again, and got my chains out. Picture me lying on that icy road putting chains on my car, twelve inches from a cliff. Not fun."

"How'd you do it?"

"I put the chains in front of the tires and worked them under as far as I could get them. The tough part was when I had to get back in the car and try to drive onto the chains. I was scared spitless. But it worked. I got the chains on and got home without any more trouble."

"I stay off the back way in the winter."

"Smart thing to do. I tend to avoid it myself as much as possible when the weather's bad. But it's not always possible. Of course, you can get yourself killed even on a clear summer day. I was driving up the canyon into Glenwood Springs one time, in the fallen-rock zone. Doing thirty-five. Came around a blind curve and found an oncoming semi in the next lane and a boulder right in front of me. I decided the boulder was the better choice. It ripped out the bottom of my car, though."

"Were you hurt?"

"Nah. The guy behind me hadn't been tailgating, thank God."

"I take it you're telling me this snow is nothing to worry about?"

He laughed. "Ask me again when we hit the tunnel approach."

But by the time they were on the climb to the Eisenhower Tunnel, the snow was no longer falling. Meg could look out the back window and see that the storm still had the mountains socked in to the west, but here, while snow had fallen, traffic had cleared the pavement so that it was just wet. On the other side of the tunnel it was the same, and as they began to descend toward Denver, the day grew brighter and the roads drier.

Allie woke up as they were approaching Westminster and began to chatter about all the things she hoped they could do that day. Earl agreed to visit one of the malls after they bought the painting supplies Meg wanted. He'd apparently done his research, because he drove them directly to a little store on a side street downtown that catered to serious artists.

Meg's initial feeling was one of sheer delight. It had been so long since she'd browsed tubes of oil paints and tested brushes that she felt like a kid in a candy store. A kid with a limited budget. Her heart began to sink as she looked at how much prices had gone up in fifteen years.

"I don't know if I can afford this," she finally said to Earl.

"Sure you can, Mom," Allie interjected. "We'll give up going out for dinner on Friday nights. Anyway, you don't have to buy *everything* at once."

"Wise child," said Earl. "You need this, Meg."

Maybe she did. But she'd been following a very tight, very strict budget since Bill's death so she could keep the house without demolishing her savings or the life insurance money that she was saving for Allie's college expenses. She hated to dip into savings for something as frivolous as this.

But Allie's face was a study in eager hope, and she knew her daughter wanted to do this as much as she did. And for Allie, painting might be very good therapy.

"Okay," she said. "But we start small." She chose a dozen tubes of paint, basic colors she could work with to create more colors, a handful of essential brushes, turpentine, palettes, two inexpensive easels and a couple of medium-size canvases. "Too bad I don't do watercolors," she remarked. "I could have saved some money."

Allie wrinkled her nose. "I don't like watercolors. Too pale."

"That depends on how they're done. But it's a lot more difficult technically. At least for me."

She blanched when the clerk totaled the bill but handed over her credit card without a whimper. She could stretch out the payments, she told herself, and maybe manage this without dipping into savings.

She and Earl carried the purchases out to the car, with Allie crutching behind.

"Lunch first," Earl announced as he closed the Explorer's tailgate. "What sounds good, Allie?"

"Hamburgers?"

"How did I guess?" He flashed a grin. "Meg?"

"Hamburgers are fine by me."

So they stopped at a popular fast-food place and ate inside. Allie looked so longingly at the toys that were being offered with the children's meals that Earl bought her two of them. She flushed, but the first things she pulled out of the bags were the toys.

Meg watched with aching pleasure. Allie was still a little girl sometimes, although she showed signs of growing up now. But she was glad her daughter could still take pleasure in some silly plastic dolls, as if part of her were still only five or six. Maybe she needed to remember how to do that, too. Maybe Earl was right about the oil painting.

After lunch they went to the mall, moving slowly

and sitting often to give Allie a chance to rest. Meg sprang for an outfit that Allie just had to have, and then for a couple of CDs she wanted. So much for her budget.

Then Allie turned to look at her. "What about *you*, Mom? Why don't you get something you want?"

"I did. The painting equipment."

For a second she thought Allie would accept the answer, but then the girl said, "It's not the same. You'll stress over the painting, because you used to be a good painter. I'm talking about something fun."

Meg looked at her. "How did you know I used to paint?"

"Dad told me."

But there was something in the way Allie's eyes slid away that told Meg that wasn't the whole truth. She glanced at Earl and saw that his face had grown thoughtful, too, as if he'd picked up on the same thing she had.

"Well, it was a long time ago," Meg said. "If I start painting again, it's going to be purely for fun."

Allie smiled. "That's okay, too. But you still need to get something just for you."

Earl agreed. "Go ahead, Meg. Just for you. Allie's right."

Meg pretended to glare at her daughter, expecting the usual laugh she got when she did that. Instead Allie seemed to shrink. Then she shrugged. "Whatever," she said, and moved away to sit on a bench.

"What was that?" Meg asked Earl, feeling almost dazed by the unexpectedness of Allie's response. "I was just kidding."

"I know you were. Allie's apparently not doing as well as she's been pretending."

Meg left Earl and went to sit on the bench beside her daughter. Allie seemed to be fascinated by the sight of her toes wiggling in the sock that covered her cast.

"Allie," Meg said, "I was kidding. I wasn't really mad at you."

"I know."

"Then why did you get so…depressed all of a sudden?"

Allie shrugged. "Just a mood."

It was possible, Meg thought. She didn't have a whole lot of experience with teenagers, but she seemed to remember that this was an age at which she had been extremely moody herself. "That's okay," she said presently. "You're allowed to have moods. But if something's bothering you…well, I hope you know that I'm willing to listen and try to help. Because I love you more than anyone or anything on this entire planet, Allie."

Allie lifted her head briefly and looked at her mother. For an instant, just an instant, Meg thought she saw Allie's chin quiver. But then the girl looked down at her cast again.

"I'll be fine," Allie said, unconsciously echoing her mother. "I'm just tired."

"Well, let's see if it's time to head home, or if we need to find a room for the night."

"I don't want to go home."

There was an underlying vehemence in that statement that shook Meg. "Why not?"

"I just don't want to. That's all."

"Okay. Let me check with Earl. He's driving. But if it's okay by him, we'll stay overnight."

"Fine by me," Earl said when Meg asked him. "I've got nothing pressing waiting for me."

He brought the car around to the nearest mall entrance, and Meg helped Allie in. A little while later they checked into a motel, getting adjoining rooms, one for Meg and Allie, and one for Earl. Allie professed herself to be exhausted and lay down to take a nap. Meg went over to sit in Earl's room with him, so as not to disturb her daughter.

"We couldn't have gone home anyway," said Earl, who was watching the weather channel. "It's getting worse up there."

Meg sat blindly staring at weather maps while Earl picked up the phone and called the office. For days now, part of her had been furtively hoping that whatever had made Allie run away had resolved itself. That Allie would go to the school psychologist on Monday and they would learn that she'd been upset about some stupid thing but had gotten over it. But what had just happened at the mall had shown her that the problem wasn't over with. Whatever had been eating Allie was still eating her.

And the realization made Meg feel panicky. If the problem wasn't gone, there was no telling what Allie might yet do. But she had nothing to go on, no inkling of what the real problem might be.

All she had were a few straws. Why had Allie reacted so oddly when Meg had glared at her? And why didn't Allie want to go home? Because of Vivian? If that was the case, Meg's mother was going to be leaving on the first bus out of town Monday morning, and no amount of guilt would make her change her mind. Allie came first.

But how was she going to find out? Did she have time to find out?

Earl hung up the phone. "Yep, it's bad up there," he said. "Fifteen inches already, and more on the way. It's supposed to clear out tonight, though, so the roads should be okay in the morning."

"Good." But she was hardly paying attention, so focused was she on her concern for Allie.

"Meg, what's wrong?"

She shook herself and looked at him. "I'm worrying about Allie. She was acting so strangely."

He nodded. "She *was* tired."

"I know." She looked past him out at the sunny fall day and found herself thinking about the snow at home. She was going to have to get out the snowblower to clear the driveway, and she hated doing that. They probably wouldn't even be able to get Allie up to the house until she did. Worse, she hadn't had the driveway graded this summer, so it was full of ruts that would become a real problem now.

It was as if she suddenly stood outside herself and saw herself as someone else would see her. And she didn't like what she saw. She'd let virtually every part of her life go to hell since Bill's death—including Allie. The driveway was just emblematic of all she'd let slide.

"Meg?"

"I was just thinking that I never got the driveway graded this year. It's going to be a pain to clear the snow off it."

"I guess so. Don't worry about it. I'll do what I

can to clear it, and I'll see that Dave Anson gets up there Monday to grade it."

She looked at him. "You can't keep bailing me out of my own stupidity."

"Why not? I wish I could bail you out of all your problems, but I guess I'll have to settle for dealing with the driveway."

"I need to be self-sufficient."

"You're already self-sufficient. But no one makes it in this world without an occasional helping hand from a friend."

"What have I ever done to help you?"

"You've given me a home away from home. How many nights did you cook me a decent meal, Meg? Or just invite me over to spend an evening? You've done plenty for me. Now let me do a little for you."

She couldn't argue with him, although if there were a balance scale for such things, she figured Earl had done her all the favors he ever needed to when he'd helped her and Bill build the house. And if that were in doubt, how about last weekend, when he'd found Allie? She was in his debt so deep she wished she could do something in return.

"Tell you what," he said. "I'll take care of your driveway if you'll have me over for Sunday dinner tomorrow."

Her mouth twisted wryly. "Even with Vivian?"

"Hell, I can take Vivian. If she barks too much, I'll bite."

She laughed—quietly, so she wouldn't disturb Allie—and felt a little better. Well, as much better as she could feel with worry about Allie still haunting her. "Speaking of the devil, I'd better call my mother and let her know we're staying the night."

He rolled his eyes. "I can hardly wait to hear what interpretation she puts on *this*."

"What can she think? Allie's with us."

"Mmm."

She knew what he meant, though. Given Vivian's hostility toward both Meg and Earl, she was apt to interpret this in the worst possible light, Allie or no Allie. For a minute she felt almost too weary to deal with it, but she wasn't inconsiderate enough to leave her mother in the dark.

So she picked up Earl's phone and called. Vivian answered on the second ring.

"Mother, we're going to stay in Denver overnight and come home in the morning."

"Good," was Vivian's surprising response. "It's blowing a real blizzard out there. I can't hardly see the trees from the house."

"Are you going to be all right?"

"I'm fine," Vivian sniffed. "Been dealing with blizzards my whole life long. How's Allie?"

"Sleeping. I think we wore her out. After we went to the art store, we did the mall."

"That would tucker her, on them crutches." Vivian was silent a moment. Then she said, "Be careful, Meg. Call to see how the roads are before you leave in the morning."

Meg hung up in amazement. She simply could not remember the last time her mother had told her to be careful. Or seemed to care if she was. But maybe she was just worrying about Allie. Yes, that had to be it.

"Everything okay?" Earl asked.

"Yes."

"No hassles?" He lifted his eyebrows.

"Not a one."

"Can I be surprised?"

"Why not? I am."

A little while later, he suggested that he go out and pick up something for dinner and bring it back to the room. "It's been a long day for Allie," he said. "She needs her rest."

"That's fine by me." And it was. A day outing to Denver had sounded like fun, and initially it had been. Except that she was discovering that after the past year of being mostly alone, except when she was at work, the crowds and shopping fatigued her more than they interested her. She'd become a hermit.

Which gave her something else to think about while Earl perused the phone book, looking for their dinner options.

Whatever had happened to make her prefer spending an evening in a motel room watching television over going out for dinner and perhaps a movie?

She'd always been a homebody to some extent. She couldn't have survived fifteen years in Whisper Creek otherwise. The only nightlife in the town was a couple of bars and a so-called nightclub at one of the motels, where a pianist played dance music six nights a week and anonymous small musical groups occasionally appeared for variety.

But when Bill had been alive, at least in the early years, she had wanted to do those things. They'd often gone out on Friday night to dance, even though the music was tenth-rate and the ambience consisted mostly of dim lighting. And she'd frequently insisted they go to Denver for the weekend to shop and see the sights.

But at some point she'd begun to lose interest in those things. Bill had never been very keen on them, so that might have been part of it. Yes, she had to go to Denver to shop, because there was really no place to get decent, reasonably priced clothing in town. So two, or at most three, times a year they'd made the trek. But they'd stopped going just to have fun.

Since Bill's death, she hadn't once left town. She'd even ordered Allie's school clothes from the Penney's catalog. She would have ascribed the change to grief, except that she could so clearly see that it had begun much earlier. As if at some level she had been bailing out of life.

She got up from her chair, leaving Earl with the phone book to occupy him, and went to her room, where she looked down on her sleeping daughter. She wasn't being fair to Allie, she realized. Because when she'd started bailing out of life, the things she had abandoned hadn't been only trips to Denver and Friday-night dancing. She'd been withdrawing from her daughter, too.

She sat on her own bed and closed her eyes, looking backward over the years, and realized when her problem had begun. It had begun the instant she realized that Bill had raped her. Instead of living in a fool's paradise, where their first mating had merely been passionately forceful, she had understood the uneasiness that always filled her, had understood that she had never really trusted her husband. That, in some deep part of her, she had always feared him.

Because he had violated her. He hadn't physically

hurt her, except for a few small bruises, but he had treated her as if her wishes and needs didn't matter, as if she were a thing to be used for his pleasure. As if *he* were all that mattered.

And somewhere deep inside her, something had been broken in those moments. Her father's death had clouded her feelings, muddying them so that she didn't know what hurt and why. She had blamed all her unhappiness on that, and on her mother's reaction to her, and hadn't realized for ten long years that there was another component to it.

She had buried it all. Her shame over the rape, and most of her guilt. She had focused all those bad feelings on her part in her father's death and had plunged into her marriage believing in her love for Bill. And she *had* loved him. Truly she had. And when their daughter came, she had felt nothing but joy. She had honestly convinced herself that her marriage was as good as anyone else's.

But when she had faced what really happened the afternoon Allie was conceived, she had uncovered what was broken inside her. She couldn't really trust Bill. Not even after all those years. And she had looked at herself and realized just how much of a sham a huge part of her marriage had been. She had always been trying to be perfect, for fear that if she was less than that Bill might—might what? What had she really thought he would do? Use his strength to overpower her?

But the inchoate fear had always been there, whether she had known it or not. And though she hadn't admitted it to herself back then in so many words, it remained that once she had recognized that something inside her was broken, she had begun to withdraw.

Bill hadn't really noticed it. They might have squabbled a little more often, but their squabbles were usually civilized, because she was afraid to wake the sleeping tiger. Until that last day. Until all of it had burst out of her in that terrible, terrible argument.

Which had killed him.

Now Earl wanted her to throw her mother out. He didn't understand why she was afraid of doing that. Did she want her mother's life on her conscience, too?

No, not unless it was the only way to help Allie. For Allie, she would do anything.

Allie rolled over on the bed, groaning as her cast banged her other ankle. "Darn it," she said sleepily, and her eyes fluttered open. Moments later she looked at her mother. "They need to put bumper guards on these things."

Meg smiled, and her heart lifted. This was *her* Allie. "Might be a good idea for sleeping. Not so good for hobbling around."

"When did the doctor say I get the walking cast?"

"I can't remember. I've got it on a piece of paper at home. Remind me tomorrow and I'll check."

"My arms hurt from the crutches," Allie told her.

"We shouldn't have spent so much time at the mall."

"That's okay. It was fun." Allie pushed herself up on the pillow. "What's for dinner?"

"We were thinking about picking up something. Uncle Earl's looking into it right now."

"Can we try painting tonight?"

"I don't think so, honey. It's messy. We don't have old clothes to wear, and if we get any oil paint on the rug or furniture, I'll have to pay for it. But we'll do it tomorrow as soon as we get home."

"Okay."

"Honey?"

"Mmm?"

"Why don't you want to go home?"

Allie hunched one shoulder. "I'm just sick of sitting around the house. At least here I get to sit around someplace different."

It could have been true, but Meg didn't believe it. "Is Grandma Vivian getting to you?"

"She always gets to me. I don't know why you let her stay when she treats you like that."

"Me neither. But she *is* my mother."

Allie surprised her with a sudden, impish look. "Does that mean I have to put up with you when *you* get old and miserable and nasty?"

"Sweetie, if I ever get miserable, old and nasty, I hope you'll throw me out on my butt."

"I think Grandma likes making you miserable," Allie said with surprising perspicacity. "I think she gets a charge out of being a hair shirt for you."

Meg felt her eyebrows lift and her mouth fall open.

"What?" said Allie. "What did I say?"

"I was just wondering when you suddenly grew up."

Allie half smiled. "I'm right, aren't I? About Grandma Vivian."

"You might be. I'll think about it."

"And then what? What are you going to do about it?"

Good question, thought Meg, looking down at her feet. Maybe her entire problem was that she felt she *needed* a hair shirt. Maybe keeping Vivian around had become some twisted penance for what had happened with Bill. Maybe she thought she was expiating her guilt.

She looked at Allie again and found her daughter watching her from wide, childlike eyes that couldn't possibly hold as much adult knowledge as they seemed to.

"Allie?"

"Yeah?"

"Did you run away because of Vivian?"

Allie looked surprised. Then she shook her head. "No. She pisses me off—"

"Language, honey."

Allie sighed heavily. "Okay, okay. She makes me mad sometimes, but mostly because of how she treats you. Why would I run away because of that?"

"Then why *did* you run away?"

Allie looked down, refusing to meet her mother's eyes. "I don't want to talk about that, okay?"

"You're going to have to talk about it sometime. I can't help you if you won't."

"Maybe I don't want any help."

That was one of the most frightening things she'd ever heard come out of her daughter's mouth. Meg felt anxiety close around her like a steel trap. "Allie…"

"Look, it's okay. I'm not going to do anything stupid."

But Allie's definition of stupid was open to question after last weekend. Meg didn't know how to explain that to her daughter without causing an argument or causing Allie to close up even more.

So she fell back on, "I love you, Allie. I'm always here for you."

And when her daughter didn't answer, she felt her heart crack.

13

Earl knocked on the adjoining door, which was ajar, and poked his head in. "Hey, ladies," he said. "I've got a list of wild, exotic places I can get some takeout. Ready to consider our menu?"

Allie sat up immediately. "Pizza!"

"Where's your sense of adventure?" Earl asked her. "I was thinking along the lines of roasted brains and pickled liver."

"Ewwwww!" Allie made a face. "Pizza's exotic enough for me."

Earl shook his head. "I am *so* disappointed in you. All of these delectable treats." He stepped into the room and looked down at the list in his hand. "I've got Moroccan, I've got Japanese, I've got Ma's Good Eats—which I presume is home cooking—I've got Chinese, I've got a deli, I've got...never mind. She wants pizza!"

Allie giggled.

Earl looked at Meg. "I am not, however, averse to hitting more than one restaurant. So if you want to be adventurous with me, Meg, we can get something else."

Meg, who didn't feel at all like eating, accepted the list from him and looked it over. "I don't know," she said finally. "I can't make up my mind."

"Well," said Earl, "I'm going to have sushi. The only time I ever get it is when I come down here, and I never pass up the chance."

"That'll work for me, too. With tempura vegetables."

"Consider it done." He vanished back into his room to call ahead and order.

An hour later, he returned with the food. He set up the spread on the table in his room, because for some reason it was larger than the one in theirs. He dragged some chairs from their room into his so that Allie could sit at the table with her injured leg propped up on one of them. With a flourish, he presented her with her small pizza and some packets of Parmesan cheese and crushed red pepper. He'd also gotten her a large bottle of her favorite soft drink.

Then he opened the three foam cartons containing the sushi. Meg looked at them. "My word, Earl! That's a lot of sushi."

"Hey, it's my dinner, not just an appetizer." He passed her another carton. "Eat your tempura before the batter gets soggy."

Allie turned out to be more adventurous than Earl had claimed, though, maybe just to spite him, Meg thought, because the girl tried the tempura and some of the sushi.

"Not too bad," Allie decided. "But I like pizza better."

"Good," said Earl. "More for me."

Allie laughed, and for a little while Meg enjoyed the illusion that they were a family having a good time. The thought gave her a pang, and she found herself looking at Earl and trying to ignore the unwelcome thought that she wished she had met him first rather than Bill.

But then she wouldn't have Allie, and Allie was the best reason in the world not to have any regrets about anything.

After dinner they found a bad pay-per-view movie to watch, which turned out to be a rollicking good time as they traded pithy comments on everything from the direction to the plot. Allie complained that it was impossible to watch the movie while she was sharing a room with a couple of film critics.

Allie turned in at ten. Meg was still wide-awake, so Earl suggested they watch the news in his room. They sat on his fully made bed, propped against pillows. It seemed innocent enough to Meg, especially with the adjoining door open several inches. Besides, she trusted Earl. He was her friend.

But somewhere between the weather—improving—and the sports the Broncos were the favorites in tomorrow's game—the entire atmosphere changed.

Meg couldn't have said what happened if her life had depended on it. All she knew was that she was suddenly, acutely aware of Earl. Her gaze kept straying to his long legs, stretched out on the bed beside hers, crossed at the ankles. He was wearing jeans, and the denim cased his thighs like a second skin, looking soft from repeated washings. Begging for her touch.

When her gaze strayed higher, she couldn't help noticing the bulge at the top of his thighs.

She snapped her gaze back to the TV, trying to concentrate on what the sports announcer was saying even though she didn't give a damn. She told herself she was just having normal sexual feelings, heightened by the fact that it had been nearly a year since she'd made love. It was just a normal, healthy female response, a sign that she was recovering from her grief.

But her heart started a deep, slow rhythm, and she found herself breathing shallowly, as a weight seemed to grow in her center, drawing her attention to the place between her thighs. A place that seemed to be growing heavier, warmer and more sensitive with each breath she took.

She wanted Earl, and some part of her realized that she had always wanted Earl. But she didn't dare move a muscle. This was wrong. He was Bill's best friend. He would hate her if he knew the truth about her. And there was Allie to consider....

He shifted, rocking the bed a little, and used the remote to change the channel. *An Affair to Remember* was playing.

"I love this movie," he remarked.

That surprised her. Bill had hated it. Too emotionally gooey and trite, he'd said. She would have thought that Earl felt the same. She watched Cary Grant and found herself seeing Earl.

When he lifted his arm and put it around her shoulders, she stopped breathing entirely. It felt so good and so scary all at once, and it was all she could do not to turn into him and put her head on his shoulder.

It had been so long since anyone had held her. Too long.

Little by little she relaxed, allowing herself to feel safe rather than threatened. It was okay. This was just a hug between friends, she told herself. He didn't mean anything by it. And little by little she was drawn into the movie.

Until she made the mistake of looking up at him to share her amusement. He wasn't watching the movie at all, she realized. He was watching her.

And suddenly her mouth was only inches from his. His gaze grew heavy-lidded, and his lips parted just a little.

Yes! shouted some voice in her head, even as her heart skipped a beat and her mouth went dry from both fear and anticipation. She shouldn't do this. She *knew* she *shouldn't* do this. But she couldn't stop herself, because she needed this more than she could remember ever having needed anything.

She became aware of small things. Of the weight of his arm around her shoulders, of the way his side felt pressed against her arm. She could feel his warmth. His strength. She could see the beard shadow on his cheeks, individual hairs. She could feel herself being drawn to him as if he were a magnet.

And then he kissed her. Rational thought disappeared in an instant. His mouth was on hers, his tongue foraging deeply, as if he needed to drink something from her and couldn't quite find it. She welcomed him, needing him to take whatever he wanted. Needing to give of herself for the first time in years.

He took the kiss deeper, until she was pressed back

against the pillows. He turned a little, and his body half covered hers. Joyous exultation filled her as she felt his weight on her. Reaching up, she wrapped her arms around him, trying to draw him closer.

The pressure of his hard chest against her breasts was exquisite. She felt her body arching toward him as desire became a drumbeat in her blood. She forgot that becoming lovers could kill their friendship, forgot that Allie was in the next room. Forgot everything except Earl and how much she wanted him.

His hand found her breast, squeezing gently, and shimmering waves of hunger passed through her to pool at her center. Soft...she grew soft for him even as she felt him growing hard against her. His thumb circled her nipple, bringing it to aching life and causing her to throb deep within. Her moan was swallowed by his mouth.

But as soon as she moaned, he seemed to come to his senses. He tore his mouth from hers and gasped for breath.

"Oh, God," he said, "this isn't the time."

It was as if someone had dumped cold water on her. *Allie.* Allie was in the next room. What if she'd seen or heard...?

She pushed herself away from Earl and levered herself off the bed. Hurrying quietly, she went to the door and peered in at Allie. Her daughter was soundly asleep, her back to the door. Relief flooded Meg, so strong that her knees felt momentarily weak.

"Is she asleep?" she heard Earl whisper.

She nodded, then reluctantly faced him. "That was stupid."

"I couldn't agree more."

But when he held out his hand, she did what she knew she shouldn't do. Instead of going to her own bed, she went to sit beside him again. The movie was still on.

"It's okay," he said. "I'll behave."

For a while she lay stiffly beside him. But little by little she began to grow sleepy. And somehow, hardly aware of it, her head came to rest on his shoulder, and his arms closed around her, holding her snugly.

She needed this, she thought dimly as sleep claimed her. She needed this, and there was nothing wrong with it.

Holding Meg while she slept was so close to a dream come true that Earl was almost afraid to enjoy the sensation. But he couldn't help himself. Meg was in his arms, sleeping on his shoulder, and the preciousness of her trust, of this moment, was overwhelming him.

He knew all the reasons he shouldn't let himself feel this. He knew all the reasons he should never have kissed her and discovered that kissing her was better than his wildest, most secret fantasies. He should never have let himself get this close to something he wanted but could never have.

He'd been a fool.

Well, it wasn't the first time he'd been a fool and probably wouldn't be the last. Now he had plenty of fodder for fevered fantasies when he was alone at night and wishing his life didn't have to be so solitary.

Which, of course, it didn't. Loneliness was a defense he'd learned in childhood, one he could have given up anytime over the last twenty years. Plenty of women had been drawn to his gun and badge, to his perceived power in town. He could have taken his pick.

He'd chosen not to, and he knew it. He was not the kind of guy who was ever willing to settle for second best. Solitude was preferable to a marriage made simply to avoid it.

But now his solitude was going to be plagued by memories of what he could not have. It had been one thing to admire Meg from afar and to think Bill was a lucky so-and-so to have found her first. It was another to have actually held her and felt her body against his, to have felt her response to his heat.

And he had no one to blame but himself for what that was going to do to his heart and his psyche.

Even so, he wasn't prepared to ease away from her and spare himself the pleasure-pain of holding her like this. He couldn't make himself do it. He needed her closeness, needed the feelings it was stirring in him. He needed the contact, even though it made him long to hold her closer still, made him long to bury himself deep inside her.

She had awakened desire in him so easily, and now it wouldn't go away. His limbs felt heavy; his groin felt heavy and subtly irritated, his every nerve ending seemed to be magnifying even the slightest sensation.

Closing his eyes, he gave up the battle and imagined that she woke and turned to him with a sleepy smile, offering herself in ways he knew damn well she would never do. Imagined her turning into him, clinging to him, demanding with her body that he come to her and take her.

His breathing grew heavier, and the ache in his body became almost painful. But he didn't fight the feelings. He let them fill him and assured himself they would eventually ebb, and once they ebbed, he would never get himself into this position again with Meg.

She deserved better of him. She deserved to be able to trust him as a friend. And he didn't want to blow their friendship out of the water by trying to take it to a different height. Nothing could kill a good friendship faster than becoming lovers.

He couldn't risk that.

He thought he heard a sound from the vicinity of the adjoining door. His eyes popped open, but he saw nothing. He thought about checking on Allie, but moving would probably wake Meg, and he didn't want to do that, not in his current state.

But there was no further sound, so he let his eyes droop closed again and lay there, aching more than he had ever ached in his life, until at last sleep claimed him.

Allie crawled silently back into her bed, turning her back to the door in case someone came to check on her. She didn't want anyone to see the tears on her face.

Uncle Earl was holding Mom. She was a big enough girl now to realize that was okay, but it hurt anyway. It hurt because it should have been her dad holding her mom, but her dad was dead. It hurt because her dad hadn't held her mom like that since Allie was much younger.

Along about the time she'd turned ten, she had sensed a change in the relationship between her parents. It had made her nervous for a long time, and she'd started to wonder if they were going to get divorced like everyone else's parents seemed to. They didn't laugh as much, and her mom had seemed sad and distant sometimes. Eventually, though, she'd gotten used to it, probably because that seemed the way things were going to be. Her parents didn't fight a whole lot or anything, they were just distant. To each other. But never to her.

But seeing Uncle Earl hold her mom that way reminded her of how it used to be. It reminded her that her dad could never give her a hug again.

And it worried her a little that Uncle Earl might take her mom away. It could happen, especially since her mom had never wanted her in the first place. Then what would happen to her? Would Mom leave her to Grandma Vivian?

She should have just died on that mountain last week. Why couldn't she have died when she fell? It would have made everything so easy for everyone.

Instead, she was still here, still a major problem for her mom. And she knew she was. Even though Mom was being so nice to her and planning to teach her to paint, she knew better. She'd ruined everybody's life. And she had no idea how to fix anything.

She was still lying awake a long time later when she heard her mother come into the room, change into her nightshirt and climb into the other bed. She was still awake a long time after her mother fell asleep.

Maybe if she talked to Uncle Earl, he could help her figure out what was the best thing to do. He always seemed to have the answers.

Promising herself that she would do that just as

soon as she could get him alone, Allie was at last able to sleep.

The weather had cleared up in the mountains by the time they set out for home in the morning. Nobody seemed to have much to say, though, and the silence was heavy in the car.

Earl noticed the silence and kept glancing in the rearview mirror at Allie, trying to read something on her face. Had she somehow come into his room last night and seen him holding her mother? Or had she perhaps seen them kissing? He felt guilty awareness that she might have, and if so, it was all his fault for not closing that door.

She wouldn't meet his eyes this morning. But she wouldn't meet her mother's, either. He had to find a way to discover what was bothering her before she went and did something stupid again. Christ, how was he going to get that little clam to open up and trust him, especially if she'd seen him with her mother last night? If she had, she probably hated him, thinking he was betraying her father.

Why had he been such a damn fool? He wanted to pound the steering wheel in frustration.

Then he looked at Meg and saw she wasn't looking at him, either. She must be feeling she'd betrayed Bill, too.

And he didn't know what he was going to do about it. Right now he wanted Meg with a craving that was driving him nuts, and he didn't see how he could slip back into his old roles with both of them. But he was going to have to try. For their sakes.

He chewed it over all the way to the Eisenhower

Tunnel, while the silence in the car kept getting heavier. Well, he finally decided, he couldn't undo his stupidity. So he had to find a way to make things better for both Meg and Allie. Somehow, some way, he had to do something for them that would make them both feel better about him.

So maybe, he thought as they were descending from the tunnel on the far side, maybe he could do something about Vivian. Maybe he could get that old crow to see some sense so life would be easier for everyone. Maybe he should work on lightening her up a bit.

He couldn't figure out how he might do that, but he had to believe that something would come to him. Because Meg and Allie meant more to him than anything else in the world. It didn't matter if they wanted him to disappear from the face of the earth. All that mattered was that he find some way to make things better for them.

And, by God, he was going to.

When Meg finally asked her daughter if something was wrong, Allie replied that she was just tired.

Meg wondered if that was the truth. Allie *did* look exhausted, though, too pale, with shadows under her eyes, visible despite the fading bruises from her concussion last week.

"Did your leg bother you last night?" she asked.

"I kept banging myself with the cast."

"I'm sorry."

Allie shrugged.

"You don't look well, though. Maybe I should take you back to the doctor."

"I'm *fine,* Mom," Allie said impatiently. "I'm just sleepy." As if to prove it, she closed her eyes.

Still concerned, Meg faced front. If a nap didn't make Allie look better, she promised herself, she was definitely going to make her see the doctor tomorrow. Maybe that concussion had been worse than anyone thought.

She would have liked to talk to Earl, but his face was set like granite this morning. Apparently he was regretting kissing her, and she could understand that. The feelings must have been uncomfortable for both of them.

But worse was the feeling that she'd somehow lowered herself in Earl's estimation. Why not? He thought of her as his best friend's wife. He probably didn't even think of her as a sexual being. And after the way she had responded to his kiss, he was probably thinking she was cheap and easy.

Maybe she was. Maybe that was what had really happened in the barn with Bill. Maybe she had been giving too much, until there simply was no turning back for Bill. Maybe she should never have let him give her those passionate kisses or let him touch her breasts, even though he'd sworn that was all he would do. She had behaved cheaply; why shouldn't he treat her as if she was?

And now she had behaved the same way with Earl. Of course he didn't want to look at her. She had probably disgusted him.

She pressed her temple to the icy window and stared out at the passing snowdrifts. Maybe her mother had been right about her all along. Maybe she *was* a floozy. Maybe she lacked the self-control that other women had. Maybe she had urges that were wrong. It was entirely possible.

They had certainly screwed up her life once. She couldn't let that happen again. And most especially not with Earl, who was more important to her than anyone else in her life except Allie.

So what if he was disgusted with her sexual response last night? He would get over that. That was a little thing compared to the secrets she harbored, the secrets that stood between them like a brick wall.

She couldn't afford to forget those secrets, even for a minute, because if she did, she might let Earl get too close. And if he got close, he would discover them sooner or later, and she would lose him completely. Forever. Because he would never be able to forgive her.

She glanced back over the seat at Allie and found her daughter still had her eyes closed. She didn't think Allie was sleeping, though. No, she felt her daughter was hiding secrets of her own.

And for the first time it occurred to her that secrets, far from protecting everyone, might be what was tearing them all apart.

14

When they arrived home, the driveway had already been plowed. Even more surprising was that Vivian seemed to be in a mellow mood. She greeted them at the door with a smile, and the house was full of the delicious aromas of roasting meat.

"It's about an hour till dinner," Vivian said, then reached out to hug Allie, who looked as if she would rather have been embraced by a grizzly.

"You two go sit in the living room and make yourselves comfortable," Vivian said to Meg and Allie. "You've had a long drive."

Meg looked at Earl, as if he might know what was going on with Vivian, but he just shrugged. She turned to her mother. "How in the world did you get the driveway cleared?"

"I didn't," Vivian said. "One of the men from the mine came up early this morning and plowed it. Said he was in the search party last week and got to thinking about three women having to deal with the driveway."

"That was awfully nice. Who was it?"

"Stan Gruber."

Meg remembered Stan only vaguely. She seemed to remember an older man, maybe fifty-five, who worked at the mine and had spoken to her a few times in town, asking how she was doing after Bill's death.

"I made breakfast for him after he finished," Vivian said. "Poor man doesn't have any family since his wife died and his kids moved away."

"That is sad," Meg agreed, trying to read her mother's expression. For once Vivian didn't look even slightly annoyed or particularly unhappy, but beyond that, she couldn't tell anything at all.

Vivian shooed her and Earl into the living room. Allie announced that she was tired and was going up to her room.

"Something's eating Allie," Earl said as he and Meg sat on the couch. Moments later they could hear loud music from Allie's room, loud enough to make the pictures on the walls vibrate.

Meg looked up at the ceiling. "She knows she's not supposed to play her stereo that loud." But she didn't move to go tell her daughter to turn it down. For now she was just going to endure it.

"And what got into Vivian?" Earl asked.

"Damned if I know."

"She usually treats me like a leper she'd as soon see the last of."

"She treats most people that way, Earl. Don't take it personally."

"Well, I do. Speaking of which, I'll be right back."

Since he had decided in the car that he needed to get on Vivian's good side in order to be able to take care of Meg and Allie, he figured now was as good a time as any, while the woman was in an uncharacteristically mellow mood toward him.

In the kitchen, he found her peeling potatoes at the sink. "Can I help with something, Vivian?"

"Not much left to do. What's wrong with Allie?"

"I don't know. She was fine yesterday, but she woke up this morning in a strange mood." He would jump off a cliff, though, before he would tell Vivian what he suspected the girl was upset about.

"Teenagers," said Vivian, as if that explained it all. And maybe it did. Earl pulled out a chair and sat at the table, watching her, trying to find some way to draw a conversation out of the woman. "It was nice of Stan to come plow the driveway."

"That's what I thought." Vivian kept peeling.

"Stan's a good man. He's always been a good man. Deacon in his church."

Vivian's interest sparked. "He is?"

"You bet. He's been a deacon at Calvary for more than twenty years now. I've worked with him quite a bit, because he's always one of the first people to offer to help when something bad happens around here. He's the main reason we had so much help searching for Allie. He got on the phone and started calling everybody he knew."

Vivian nodded. "What happened to his wife?"

"She had a brain tumor."

"Sad."

"It really was. He loved that woman."

Vivian finished peeling the potatoes and started slicing them into a pot of water that was heating on the stove. "You like mashed potatoes?"

"Love them."

"I'll make extra, then."

Earl felt almost welcome for the first time since Vivian had arrived in this house.

Vivian spoke. "So Allie had fun yesterday?"

"She sure did. Meg bought them oil paints so they can paint together, and she got Allie a new outfit and some new CDs. I'd bet one of those CDs is the one that's blasting right now."

Vivian actually laughed. "Meg used to do that, too. No matter how many times I told her she was going to ruin her ears."

"I'd probably have done the same thing if I'd had a stereo."

Vivian glanced at him. "You had a hard time growing up." It wasn't a question.

"Not as hard as some," Earl answered. The subject always made him feel uncomfortable.

Just then Allie appeared in the doorway. The music was still blasting upstairs. "Uncle Earl? Can I talk to you?"

He could tell she meant in private, but he was reluctant to break off his conversation with Vivian just as he felt they might actually be reaching a state of truce. "Not right now. In a couple of minutes, Allie, okay?"

She looked down. "Sure," she said. "In a couple of minutes."

Earl watched her hobble away, then asked Vivian, "Do you have any idea at all why she might have run away?"

Vivian shook her head. "She's been unhappy since her dad died. I didn't see anything else. She doesn't talk to me much. She doesn't really talk to anyone much.''

She astonished Earl then, by facing him. ''I've been thinking about what you said the other day, and you're right. I can't keep bearing grudges. It's not good for Allie.''

He felt himself smiling at her. ''I'm glad to hear that.''

''Now, you go talk to that child,'' Vivian said. ''Dinner's in forty minutes.''

Earl was just rising from the table when the phone rang. Vivian answered it, then handed the receiver to him. ''It's for you.''

He took the phone. ''Sanders here.''

''Boss? Boss, they want you at the hospital. Matt Dawson's had the shit beat out of him.''

His heart lurched, and the taste of bile filled his mouth. ''I'm on my way.''

He hung up. ''Sorry, Vivian. Emergency. I'll have to miss dinner.''

He was passing the living room, grabbing his jacket from the coat tree in the foyer, when Allie, who was sitting at the foot of the stairs said, ''Uncle Earl?''

''Not right now, Allie. I've got to go. Tell your mom.'' Then he was out the door and gone.

The bright Colorado sun was glaring off the snow, giving Earl an excuse to hide his eyes behind his sunglasses, at least from the half-dozen people he ran into in the parking lot. All the way into town he'd been berating himself for not intervening in Matt's life sooner. All that crap about not being able to act if Matt wouldn't tell them who was beating him? That might have been true legally, but sometimes in life you had to skirt the law.

What he should have done was drive out to the Dawson place and tell that asshole to keep his fucking hands to himself or he was going to be dead meat. He didn't need *proof* to put that pig of a man on notice. That was what he should have done.

But he hadn't done it. He'd spent so much time and effort trying to escape his own past and family background, trying to make people trust him, trying to prove that he was a solid, trustworthy, law-abiding man, that he'd forgotten there were times when the law failed.

But even as he was having those thoughts, he knew he was being a little too hard on himself. Going out and putting the fear of God in Ben Dawson didn't necessarily mean Ben would have listened or that Matt would have been safe. In fact, it might have made it worse for the kid, especially since they couldn't yank him out of that home without some proof that he was being mistreated.

Proof. God, there were times when he hated that word.

Mel Burch was the doctor on duty, a man who'd been practicing in this little town for a quarter century. He drew Earl into an empty cubicle.

"How bad is it?" Earl demanded.

"It's pretty bad. Somebody beat the kid with a baseball bat or something like it. He's got a skull fracture, three broken ribs, a broken arm and enough serious contusions to worry me."

"Is he conscious?"

"Yeah. Groggy and confused, but awake."

"How'd he get here?"

"His mother called the ambulance. She said he'd fallen in the ravine behind their house."

"Was that where they found him?"

Mel shook his head. "No, he was in the house. His mother said she and his dad dragged him out of the ravine so he wouldn't freeze. But the dad was nowhere around."

"Jesus Christ!"

"I'm reporting this as suspected abuse," Mel said. "But if the kid denies it..."

Earl nodded. "Can I see him?"

"Two cubicles down."

With a heavy heart, he walked down the corridor and into Matt's room. The boy lay on the bed, his head swathed in bandages, his eyes sunken and black. His arm was in a cast, and bandages enveloped him from his armpits down to where they disappeared under the sheets. Where he wasn't bandaged, big ugly bruises were visible. There was murder in Earl's heart right then.

"Matt?"

The boy's eyes fluttered open. "Sheriff," he said, his voice thick.

"Who did this to you?"

Matt's eyes closed.

"Son, you can't let this go on. Next time he'll kill you."

But the boy's eyes remained stubbornly closed. "Fight," he said.

"Yeah? Well, it sure wasn't a fair fight. Who was it?"

Matt said nothing, and Earl felt his frustration rise

until it was ready to spill over his internal dam. "Good Lord, boy, I don't know why you're protecting him. You ought to be protecting yourself. Nobody deserves this kind of treatment. Nobody."

But Matt still refused to speak. Earl let out a frustrated sigh. "I'll check on you again in the morning, Matt," he finally said. "Maybe by then you'll have grown some sense. But there's not a whole hell of a lot I can do to protect you if you won't talk to me."

Five minutes later he was back out in the blinding winter sunshine, putting on his sunglasses and wondering why the hell it was that kids refused to trust the very people who could help them. Like Allie. She wouldn't talk about what was troubling her. How could anyone help her when she insisted on keeping the problem to herself?

Did these kids really think that all adults would betray them?

That was when he remembered that Allie had wanted to talk to him, and that he'd put her off, telling her "not right now."

Lead suddenly settled in his stomach, and he swore under his breath. Maybe kids were right not to trust adults after all.

As he drove away from the hospital, he was torn about where to go first. Finally he decided that he *had* to talk to Matt Dawson's father first. Matt's life was at risk. Allie was with her mother and grandmother, and they could help her if she was having a problem. But he couldn't risk Ben Dawson going anywhere near Matt.

The Dawsons lived about five miles out of town, on a piece of property that had first been a mining claim. The property had stayed in the family ever since, though the mineral rights had long ago been severed, the way they had been to every piece of property hereabouts.

It was in a small valley, surrounded by mountains, a piece of land that had never been any good for farming, not that you could grow a whole hell of a lot at this altitude, anyway. Millie Dawson worked in town at the hardware store, bringing in all the money the family ever had. Ben hunted and fished, when he wasn't too drunk. It was a hard life.

The road back to the house from the highway hadn't been plowed. Tire tracks crisscrossed it and in places showed where someone had skidded out. He drove carefully and finally reached the house—such as it was, little more than a three-room shack. The Dawsons' old Chevy pickup was in the yard, but Matt's car was nowhere to be seen.

Getting out, Earl looked around, checking his surroundings with the uneasy scalp-crawling feeling of a lawman who knew he was in dangerous territory.

Nothing moved.

The door didn't open until he hammered on it the third time. Then Millie Dawson opened it just a crack, one frightened eye peering out at him.

"Miz Dawson, I'm looking for Ben."

Her eye widened. "He's gone."

"His car's here."

"No...the truck wouldn't start. He took Matt's car."

Which probably explained what had brought on Matt's beating, Earl thought. The boy wouldn't have given his drunken father the car willingly. "Where'd Ben go?"

"I don't know. He didn't say."

Earl stood there for a minute, considering giving her a message for that son of a bitch, then realized that if she delivered it, she would probably wind up in the hospital, too.

"Thanks, Miz Dawson. Sorry to bother you."

The door closed behind him before he'd turned fully away. That was when he realized that she hadn't even asked him what he wanted Ben for.

She knew.

Meg knocked on her daughter's door and called that dinner was ready. Apparently Allie didn't hear her over the music, so she tried to open the door— and found it locked.

In that instant she catapulted from the constant level of anxiety that had been plaguing her since Allie came home to a full-blown state of fear. Allie never locked her door.

She knocked again, this time with the heel of her fist, hammering hard and loudly.

And this time Allie answered. "Go away!"

"Dinner's ready." Meg shouted to be heard.

"I'm not hungry. Just leave me alone."

"Allie…"

The music turned up even louder, drowning her out.

Meg stood staring at the door, fear creeping into every cranny of her being. Allie had never done this to her before. Never. And she didn't know whether to walk away and let her daughter calm down, or to panic.

God. She thought it had been tough when Allie hit the terrible twos. She'd thought nothing could be quite as scary as facing down a two-year-old with the sense that if she lost this battle, she was going to lose every battle of wills for the rest of her daughter's life. Knowing she was on the brink of losing all control.

Now here she was in the terrible teens, with no road map to guide her, no idea whether she should be terrified or patient. With memories that her daughter had been contemplating suicide only a week ago.

And suddenly everything became significant. The way Allie hadn't wanted to see her friends or even talk to them much on the telephone for the last week. The way she had seemed to turn to that troubled boy, Matt Dawson, while holding everyone else at a distance.

The smell of incense was seeping out from under the door. Was Allie doing drugs? The incense was a new thing, something Allie had gotten from a friend just a couple of weeks ago. Something she had burned only once before and then wrinkled her nose, claiming the smell was too heavy. She was burning it now. Why? To cover something else?

Drugs might explain the change in her daughter, she realized. Panic rooted itself more deeply inside her. Drugs. Not drugs.

But the door was still closed and locked, and she didn't know what to do. She needed to talk to Earl. Earl would know the best way to handle this. Earl would know what to look for. Meg was almost ashamed to realize that she was thirty-four years old, but she had no idea what drugs or drug paraphernalia looked like. She had avoided that whole scene scrupulously in college, and around town here, if people were doing drugs, they weren't doing them when she was around.

Pipes. She'd heard about hash pipes. What would one look like? A regular pipe? Probably not. It was probably something smaller, more easily concealed. Cigarette rolling papers. Now *those* she would recognize. Bags of strange substances. She would recognize those.

She lifted her hand to hammer again and realized it would do no good. Allie was not going to let her in. She needed Earl.

"What's going on?" Vivian asked.

Meg jumped and turned to see that her mother had come upstairs. "I don't know. Allie said she's not hungry, and her door is locked." She tensed, ready for her mother's usual lecture on how it was all her fault for letting the child run wild.

Vivian's mouth opened and her face darkened, as if she was indeed about to say what she always said. But then she surprised her daughter. "Well," she said, "we can pick the lock or we can go downstairs and wait her out."

Her mother's reasoned response was almost as much of a shock to Meg as her daughter's locked door. Having braced herself for an argument, she hardly knew what to say.

"What if she's doing drugs?" The words almost seemed to clog her throat, but they managed to make their way out.

Vivian's habitual frown deepened, but it looked

worried rather than angry this time. "Then we've got another problem to deal with. After she comes out, we'll search her room. In the meantime, leave her be, Meg."

"But...but, Mom...she may have tried to kill herself. What if...?"

Vivian then did something so amazing that Meg's heart stopped. She reached out and hugged her daughter. For a minute Meg was so stunned that she stood stiffly, but then the warmth of being hugged by a mother who hadn't once touched her in fifteen years filled her, and she sagged. Tears burned her eyes and ran down her cheeks. "Mom..."

"It'll be okay, Meg. You did this a couple of times, too, remember? And at just about this age. I thought for sure you were devil-worshiping, remember? All those posters in your room, and the black candles..."

Meg remembered. For a year or so, she'd been into wearing black and being angry over nothing in particular. Rebellion against her parents and everything they stood for. She remembered. It had all seemed so cool. But she had never seriously thought about suicide, the way Allie apparently had. "I wasn't," she said now.

"I know that." Vivian patted her shoulder. "I'll go down and get a screwdriver. We're going to go into that child's room."

Meg nodded and stayed where she was, by the door, feeling as if years and lifetimes stood between her and her daughter. *Allie, Allie, where did I go wrong?*

Vivian returned with the screwdriver and edged Meg out of the way, bending to work it into the small hole. The music was still blasting, so Meg didn't hear the click when the lock opened.

Vivian straightened and shoved the door inward.

Allie was sitting on her bed, her broken leg propped up, her eyes closed. Incense clouded the room with choking jasmine, and the music was deafening. Allie didn't even hear them come in.

Meg hurried across the room, scared that Allie was unconscious, but when she touched her daughter, the girl jumped and sat up. Vivian hit the switch on the stereo, casting blessed silence over the room.

"What are you doing?" Allie demanded. "Why did you come in here? Can't you just leave me alone? All I want is to be left alone! This is *my* room! Get out!"

Meg tried to be reasonable. "Allie, we were worried."

"Worried? Yeah, right. You hate me. I know you hate me. You just won't leave me alone! Get the fuck out of my room!"

Shock silenced Meg. She stood looking at her daughter as if she were a stranger. Allie never used those words. Allie never talked to her this way. This wasn't Allie, her baby, her sweet little girl....

"That," said Vivian, "will be enough, Allison. You don't talk to your mother that way. Ever."

"Why not?" Allie shrieked. "Why not? You're always yelling at her. Why shouldn't I? She hates me. *You* hate me! Everybody hates me. Now leave me alone!"

Meg shook free of her shock. "Nobody hates you, Allie. We love you."

"Yeah, right! You never wanted me to be born!"

Something filled Meg then, something so terrible that she felt as if her entire body were melting, as if her brain were slipping away, far, far away, from a reality that couldn't be happening. As if her entire being were pulling away into a dark little box. As if light-years of distance were filling the gap between herself and her daughter.

She sat down on Allie's chair, feeling as if some other person were controlling her body.

"I'm not leaving," she heard herself say. "I'm going to sit right here until you tell me what's going on."

When Earl got to the Williams house, guilt was riding him like a ten-ton weight. Matt. Allie. He figured he'd fucked up everything royally. But at least he could apologize to Allie, make her understand why he'd gone running off like that when she wanted to talk to him. She would understand.

But he still felt awful about it, because Allie hadn't been talking much to anyone lately. Because when she'd finally reached out to someone, that someone had run off, telling her, "Not right now."

Christ, he took the award for insensitive ass of the year.

Vivian opened the front door of the house to him before he'd even climbed the porch steps. Her expression was concerned, and he felt his heart lurch uncomfortably. "What's wrong?" he asked without preamble.

"Allie. She locked herself in her room and refused to come out. We got in, and she started screaming that everyone hates her and that she should never have been born. Meg's sitting with her, but the child hasn't said a word in nearly an hour now.''

The words lit a fire under Earl. He ran past Vivian and upstairs to Allie's room, where he found Allie sitting on her bed looking furious, with tears streaming down her face, and Meg sitting in the chair nearby looking like a marble statue.

He didn't know whom to speak to first. Allie wouldn't look at him, he noticed. And Meg didn't seem to be aware of him. He felt Vivian hovering behind him, as if she was afraid to cross the threshold. The smell of incense thickened the air and made him wonder if Allie was doing drugs.

Allie first, he decided. Moving cautiously, trying not to seem threatening in any way, he perched on the bed beside the girl. He didn't wait for her to acknowledge him.

''I'm sorry I ran off like that when you wanted to talk,'' he said. ''It's not that I didn't want to talk to you, but I had an emergency.'' He hadn't planned to tell her about Matt, not wanting to add to her problems, but looking at her rigid posture and expression, he decided he'd better. It was the only way he could make her understand that he wasn't just making excuses. ''Matt Dawson is in the hospital. He was beaten up pretty badly.''

''My God.'' The whisper came from Meg.

For a few seconds Allie didn't respond at all. Then, jerkily, she turned her head toward Earl. ''Is he going to be okay?''

''I hope so. He had a fractured skull, a broken arm, some broken ribs and a whole lot of bruises.''

Allie nodded slowly, absorbing the information. "Can I see him?"

"Tomorrow, maybe. I know he'd like that. Now, what did you want to talk to me about?"

"It doesn't matter."

Clammed up again. He wanted to kick himself. "Yes, it does matter. It mattered before I left, so it still matters."

"Nothing matters anymore," Allie said.

"Really? You're sitting here crying. That would seem to indicate that something still matters."

"I'm just mad."

"Mad about what?"

"Everything. *Everything.*"

"That's a lot to be mad about." He was quiet for a few moments, trying to let the girl know he wasn't going to pressure her, trying to let her know he wasn't going to go away again. Then he said the only thing he could think of saying. "We love you, Allie. All of us love you, and we're worried sick about you."

She turned toward him then, her eyes reddened and glaring. "That's a lie! A *lie!* Mom never wanted me at all. I ruined her life! I ruined Dad's life! And now he's dead because of *me!*"

15

Meg stopped breathing. *I ruined her life. I ruined his life.* It was a nightmare revisited, and deep in her heart she knew where those words had come from. Impossible as it had seemed, she knew.

In a sudden gasp she drew air into lungs that felt tight in a chest that seemed to be trying to squeeze her heart into stillness. "Allie…" Her daughter's name came out on a croak. "Allie…"

The girl wouldn't look at her, wouldn't look at any of them.

"Allie…did you hear your dad and me fighting the day he died?" She felt Earl's gaze lock on her, but she was past caring what he thought of her. She was losing her daughter, and she had to take any risk necessary to get her back.

Allie looked at her then, glaring from hot, angry eyes.

"You were at Sandy's…." Meg said almost helplessly, hoping against hope that she was wrong.

"I came home early. I heard you. I heard you…."

"Oh my God!" Meg felt her heart shattering. Everything she had kept hidden inside for the sake of Allie and Earl was laid open now. And it was killing her daughter.

"Allie...Allie, we just had a fight. We both said things we didn't mean. Baby, you're the best thing that ever happened to me. Ever."

"That's easy to say. But I heard you!" Allie was sobbing, and when Earl reached out to touch her, she jerked away. "Dad was saying his whole life would have been different if you hadn't had me. I heard him! And I heard you say you didn't want me, either!"

Meg felt that like a fist in her chest. She gasped for air, struggled for words. "I never... Allie, I never said that. I know I never said that!"

"Maybe not exactly, but that's what you meant!"

Earl reached out again for Allie, and this time the girl curled against his side and buried her face in his shoulder. He held her tightly and looked at Meg. "Maybe," he said softly, "you ought to tell us what you *really* said."

"Oh, God." Meg gulped air, trying to focus on the fight that she'd been trying so desperately to forget for the last eight months. "It was... He was talking about leaving me. Because...because I'd gotten cold, he said. I got angry...he got angry.... I remember yelling at him that he couldn't abandon his daughter, and he said something about how he'd never wanted to be a father in the first place, and I yelled something about how I'd never wanted to get pregnant, either, that I'd wanted to finish school, but he'd..." Her voice broke. She was panting now, torn up inside and wishing she could just die. But she had to keep on to save Allie.

"But I never meant I wasn't glad to have Allie. We weren't even talking about that, Allie. I swear we weren't. I swear it on a stack of Bibles. You were a surprise we hadn't planned on, but we were so *thrilled* to have you. Oh, baby, nothing in my life ever made me as happy as having you. The day you were born was the best day I've ever had...."

Her voice trailed off as gulping sobs overtook her. She fought for control, drawing deep breaths until the tightness in her chest and throat eased enough that she could speak again.

"Your dad felt the same way, Allie. We both loved you. We loved you more than anything in the world. And if we could have done it over again, neither of us would have changed anything except...except the way you were conceived. But we never, *ever* regretted having you...."

Then Allie said something chilling, her voice muffled against Earl's shirt. "You were fighting about *me*. Daddy wouldn't be dead except for me. I should have gone with him in the car."

Dead silence filled the room. Earl looked at Meg. "You'd better leave," he said. "Just get out of here now."

Meg got up stiffly, feeling as if her body belonged to someone else. Slowly she walked from the room, past her mother, whose expression was inscrutable. Downstairs she grabbed her jacket, then went out back to stand on the deck in the cold.

She deserved to die. She had hurt Allie beyond measure, and now she had hurt Earl. She wished she could curl up in a small little ball and die.

* * *

Earl held Allie until the girl stopped crying from exhaustion. When she rested quietly against him, he said, "You know I love you, Allie. I love you as much as if you were really my daughter."

She nodded limply.

"Do you want me to get your mom?"

"No." It was a raspy croak in a voice worn out from weeping.

"What about your grandmother?"

"No. I hate them. They hate me."

"They don't hate you, Allie. Honest to God, they love you."

She sniffled but didn't say anything. So he held her a while longer and wondered what the hell could be done about this.

It boggled his mind, that Bill had been thinking about leaving Meg. He sure hadn't said anything about it to Earl. And he knew how people could say terrible things in anger, things they didn't mean, but how could you explain that to a fourteen-year-old girl who'd had her heart torn out by those angry words? More importantly, how could you make her believe it?

But he had to try, the only way he knew how. "Remember that time when you were eight, and your mom and dad wouldn't let you go on that trip with your friend's family? They said they didn't want you to be so far away from home for so long with people they didn't know well. Remember?"

Allie nodded.

"Anyway, maybe you remember screaming at them that you hated them. You didn't mean that, Allie. But you said it. Because you were mad. But if your parents didn't love you, why would they care who you went on a trip with, or for how long? You need to remember things like that right now, Allie. Because they'll help remind you that your mom and dad always loved you."

He got no response to that, and he suspected she was feeling too bruised and hurt right now to believe what he was saying. And the situation was probably all the worse because Allie had apparently been struggling with this since the day her father died. Eight months of being unable to believe that her parents wanted her, eight months of believing she had caused her father's death, however indirectly.

Christ, this was a mess.

"Another thing you need to know," he said to her now. "You didn't kill your dad. The argument didn't kill your dad. He skidded on snow and ice, and it could have happened to anyone. It just happened to him that time. For no good reason. It was an *accident,* Allie."

Although he didn't fully believe that himself. He could well imagine Bill driving off in a rage, driving too fast, miscalculating that curve in a way he might not have done if he hadn't been angry. But even so, it wasn't anybody's fault. Except possibly Bill's.

What was everybody's fault was the way this child was feeling right now. There were too many goddamn secrets in this house. If Meg had ever just once admitted she'd argued with Bill before his accident, a whole lot of this might have been avoided.

Even now, he felt there were still secrets. Still things that hadn't been admitted. Both Meg and Vivian had hinted at them by seeming to skirt things.

That feeling had been growing on him for some time now.

They weren't yet to the bottom of this viper's nest.

And except for Allie, he probably would have walked away from the whole mess right now.

"You need to come in," Vivian said to Meg. "You're going to catch your death out here."

"Good."

Vivian touched her arm tentatively, and Meg jerked it away.

"I've fucked everything up, Mother," Meg said flatly. "I killed my father, I killed my husband, and I may be killing my daughter. What's the point of coming inside?"

Vivian drew a sharp breath. "It's my fault," she said. "I've been...terrible to you all these years. Blame me."

Meg looked at her mother, trying to feel something decent, but feeling only bitterness. "A little too late for that, don't you think?"

Vivian compressed her lips. "Yes," she said finally. "Maybe it is." Then she turned and went back into the house.

It was all coming apart, Meg thought, staring out into the dark places beneath the trees, hardly noticing the cold wind that was blowing down from the mountain, or the way the sky was fading from blue to indigo. All the threads that she'd been clutching at for years, trying to hold the fabric of her life together, were unraveling so fast she couldn't hope to catch even a few of the loose ends. She couldn't hope to halt the disintegration.

Little by little all the secrets were coming to light. They were tearing Allie apart. And now Earl knew most of it, and he would probably never forgive her. How could he? Bill had died because of their argument, and Allie had been wounded by it. Earl would probably never speak to her again.

So be it. She told herself it didn't matter. But somewhere deep inside she knew that the loss of Earl's friendship was going to be one of the worst blows of her life. And the wound was never going to mend, no more than any of her wounds had mended.

As the evening faded into night and the cold seeped into her bones, she felt herself growing smaller and smaller, until she was just a pinprick full of agony.

Earl came downstairs and found Vivian waiting in the foyer. "Allie's sleeping," he said. "Where's Meg?"

"Standing out on the back deck freezing to death. She won't come in."

"Well, forget it, then," he said, fed up with all the lies, secrets and deceptions. "I've got to go to the hospital to check on Matt, and then I'm going home. Call me if Allie needs me."

Vivian reached out to grip his arm, stopping him. "You're mad at Meg," she said.

"I'm mad at all of you except Allie right now."

Vivian nodded. "Okay. Fair enough. We've all had a share in this mess. But there's something I didn't know before a couple of days ago. Something I didn't want to believe until I thought about it. You need to know, too."

Earl clenched his jaw, not sure he wanted any more

ugly secrets to be told. This whole mess was ugly enough. He'd been telling Meg that she needed to get rid of the secrets for Allie's sake, but he figured he already knew enough for the child's sake. Anything else he didn't need. Anything else would just confirm his distaste for the entire lot of them. Because even as he told Allie that words spoken in anger were rarely true, in his heart of hearts he believed otherwise. Something had happened to cause that level of bitterness between Meg and Bill, and he really, truly, didn't want to know what it was. His memory of Bill was already clouded enough. And his admiration for Meg had just died a brutal death. How could she *ever* have said she hadn't wanted Allie, no matter how angry she had been?

"You need to know," she said insistently. "She told me...Bill raped her. Not with a knife or anything. He overpowered her."

But Earl hardly heard her last words. His mind stuttered to a stop on the word *rape*. He couldn't... wouldn't...absorb that. Without another word, he grabbed his jacket and left the house.

Vivian waited another half hour, but when she saw that Meg was shivering violently, she couldn't stand by another minute. She went upstairs and shook Allie awake.

The girl's eyes fluttered open, at first bright, then darkening as she remembered everything.

Vivian didn't bother to be kind. "You get yourself out of bed right now and come downstairs. You need to help me get your mother inside before she freezes to death."

With each second she woke up more, Allie's pain grew until the tears were threatening to spill again. For a wild instant she wanted to roll over and bury her head in the pillow and tell herself it didn't matter what her mother did anymore. But then she remembered how she felt about her father's death. It didn't matter if her mother loved her, she realized. She had to do the right thing anyway.

It was a mature thought, and it felt almost alien inside her, roiling up mind and heart, but the sheer sense of it reached her.

She pushed herself up, grabbed her crutches and followed Vivian down the stairs.

When she saw her mother's shivering figure standing in the dark on the deck, she felt a surge of bitter love. She looked at her grandmother then, and saw the worry and fear on the woman's face. So the old battle-ax *did* have some feeling besides anger. Allie's response was one of angry gladness that someone other than her was hurting now.

"Boy," she said, not caring if she shocked Vivian, "we are one messed-up family."

Vivian gasped, but didn't lecture her. If she had, Allie was *that* close to hitting her. Right now she was feeling as if all the adults in her life had messed up everything for everyone and had caught her in their pile of crap. She wasn't feeling at all charitable.

"Open the door," she told Vivian. Then she hobbled cautiously onto the snow-covered deck and came to a halt facing her mother. "Get inside now," she told Meg, "or we're both going to freeze to death out here, because I'm not budging until you do."

Meg's blank eyes focused on her. Then, after an

interminable moment, she nodded and turned, going into the house. Allie followed, and Vivian closed the door.

"Both of you sit at the table," Vivian said. "I made some hot cocoa to warm you up."

Meg sat as if she didn't care what she did anymore. Allie wanted to stomp away, as far away as she could get, but something made her do as she was told. Vivian put a mug in front of her, topped with a melting marshmallow. A favorite treat. To Allie, that marshmallow looked like her life, melting into a shapeless puddle.

Meg was shivering violently. Vivian went to get her a blanket and wrapped it around her. Even from across the table, Allie could feel the cold as her mother's frigid body soaked heat out of the air.

"That was a stupid thing to do," Allie told her mother harshly.

Vivian gasped, but Meg didn't even glance at her.

"You know," said Allie, "if you don't do anything else right, you still need to finish raising me. You made me, Mom. Now you have to take care of me until I'm eighteen, whether you like it or not."

Allie could hardly believe the things she was saying. They were coming out of some deep, dark place inside her, a place she'd been trying to keep under lock and key for a long time. Words she had thought she would never speak. But speaking them felt good. Very good.

It would have felt even better if her mother had responded in any way at all. But Meg didn't look at her. She just sat there staring blindly at her cocoa and shivering helplessly.

And Allie started to get scared.

* * *

Earl went by the hospital and found Matt in a semi-private room, so full of painkillers that his responses were muffled monosyllables. He patted the boy's shoulder, told him he would be back tomorrow and headed for the nurses' station.

"If Matt Dawson's parents come in," he said to Wilma Lehman, the charge nurse, "don't let them see him alone. Make sure the door stays open and someone keeps an eye on them."

Wilma, a fiftyish woman with iron-gray hair and a wide mouth, nodded. "You can count on us. We have a pretty good idea what happened to him."

Satisfied he no longer needed to worry about Matt's safety, Earl headed home to worry about a lot of other things. He needed to find a way to get Matt to talk about his dad beating him. Failing that, he needed to find a way to make Matt's mother feel safe enough to point the finger at her husband. But if he was going to protect Matt, he sure as hell needed something more than some bruises and broken bones that the boy said came from a fight.

As a man, he would have loved to walk up to Ben Dawson and tell the creep that if he ever so much as said boo to the boy again, he was going to beat him to a pulp. As a lawman, he couldn't do that. He couldn't do any form of that. And it was enough to drive him nuts.

By the time he got in his front door and was considering whether to thaw a venison steak for dinner, he'd cooled down enough to feel guilty as hell for walking out on Meg and Allie the way he had. But he didn't want to think about that, because in order to think about that, he would have to think about what had made him feel so crazy. He didn't want to think about Bill leaving Meg, or Bill and Meg saying those terrible things in Allie's hearing, however unintentionally. And more, he didn't want to think about what Vivian had said about Bill raping Meg.

His friend wasn't that kind of man. And there was an ugly suspicion taking root at the base of his brain that Meg had made that claim to explain her out-of-wedlock pregnancy to her overly religious parents.

But he hated what that said about Meg.

He pulled the venison steak out of the freezer—his last one, and big enough for two. He tossed it on the counter, weighing whether he wanted to waste that much meat on himself or just settle for something else, like the leftover chicken carcass he'd been picking at on and off since last week. The chicken didn't appeal to him, and when he pulled it out to look at it, he thought it appeared too dry. But there was nothing else in the fridge, and in the pantry there was only a can of minestrone soup.

Sighing, he threw the chicken in the trash and put the steak in the microwave to thaw. Anything was better than going to the market right now.

But thinking about why he hadn't done his usual shopping last week brought him right back around to Meg and Allie. It seemed there was no safe place to tread.

He flipped on the tube and got the evening news, which proved to be neither uplifting nor distracting. He switched instead to some game show, which was at least making cheerful background noises.

He'd never, ever been so sick of the solitude of his life. All of a sudden he couldn't stand his own company. He found himself wishing he would get called out to some accident or crime. Not that that was likely to happen. Unless something major came down, his deputies could usually handle things.

Right about the time he decided he might as well go to the office tonight and deal with the mountain of paperwork that never diminished, no matter how hard he worked at it, there was a knock on the door.

He was almost overjoyed to see Sam Canfield, his friend and deputy, standing there, looking cold and none too happy himself. He'd looked better when they'd been searching the mountain for Allie.

"What's up, Sam?"

"Not a damn thing. I'm rattling around in that house thinking of Vera, and I figured if I didn't get out of there, I was going to wind up howling at the moon like a lonesome coyote."

Vera was Sam's late wife. She'd died eighteen months ago in a skiing accident.

"Come on in," Earl said. "We'll howl together over a venison steak."

"Sounds better than howling alone." But Sam had always been a perceptive man, and as he shed his jacket he asked, "What are you howling about?"

"You don't want to know." Which, when translated, actually meant that Earl didn't want to talk about it. He didn't know how he could. Even if he'd been able to bring himself to speak of the things he'd learned today, doing so would be betraying a confidence. He had no right to tell anyone else what he'd heard.

"Have it your way." Sam followed him into the kitchen and leaned back against the counter as Earl took the venison out of the microwave.

"Plenty for both of us," Earl said. "I hope you're hungry."

"I could get that way in a real hurry. Want me to do anything?"

"I'm just making some instant mashed potatoes and frozen spinach. I think I can manage."

"I don't doubt it." Sam folded his arms. "Something bad happen?"

"Depends on how you want to look at it, I guess." Which was true. Knowing what was troubling Allie was a big plus, one he shouldn't overlook in his disgust and anger. Now that they knew what was at the root of her problem, they could start dealing with it.

But he shouldn't have left. God knew what was happening up there now. Allie might be hysterical. Vivian might be giving them both hell in her inimitable fashion. Meg had looked as if she were ready to have a nervous breakdown.

But he couldn't stomach looking at her now. He couldn't. And that made him feel like a king-sized shit.

"Okay," said Sam. "Have it your way." As if he were indifferent.

Earl knew better. He and Sam had been good friends for years now, and Sam was rarely indifferent. "What do you know about date rape?" he heard himself ask. As soon as he did, he felt a lead bowling ball settle in his stomach.

"Why? Somebody accuse you?"

"Hell, no. I'm speaking theoretically."

"Well, theoretically, it's hard to prove. A lot of times there isn't any obvious injury. He says she was willing, she says he overpowered her. A swearing contest, plain and simple."

"So what do you think about it?"

Sam shifted, unfolding his arms and resting the heels of his palms on the counter to either side. "Think? I think it happens. I think it probably happens more than we realize. I think girls sometimes let it go too far, and then, when they want to stop, guys think it's some kind of game and she doesn't really mean it. Or they think if they push hard enough, she'll realize she really *does* want it. And sometimes I think it's a case of a woman wishing she hadn't done it after the fact. Messy business. Hope I never get another case like that."

"You've had one?"

"When I was a cop in Boulder. Two students. Ugly."

Earl turned to look at him. "What happened?"

"The girl got pretty well taken apart by the defense attorney. By the time he was done, I don't think even *she* was sure what had happened anymore."

"What did you think?"

"I thought he was guilty or I wouldn't have pursued the investigation. But that's what's a bitch about it, Earl. Did he really do it? At what point did it stop being ordinary fooling around and become forceful? All I can say is, when a woman says *no,* that's gotta be it. Period. That's the line you can't cross, even if she doesn't claw his eyes out, or even if he doesn't leave bruises and welts or use a weapon."

Earl nodded. "I guess it has to be."

"Sure it does. There's all kinds of persuasion that amounts to force. Hell, just take a two-hundred-pound guy and put him on top of a woman who's got her panties off and what's she gonna do about it? What if she loves him? Is she gonna scream? Probably not. Is she gonna hit him? Not likely. But if she says no and he doesn't listen, that's it." He shrugged. "Doesn't mean you can prove it in a court of law, though."

"No. But it would be easy to lie about."

"Sure it would. And that's the problem. But I don't think very many women lie about it. At least, not when they get to the stage of actually having to be questioned in detail about what happened. That's when it gets ugly, and if you ask me, most women, if they're lying, are gonna stop right then and there."

"But would she go ahead and marry the man who raped her?"

Sam laughed. "Come on! How many women stay with men who beat them? Why wouldn't one marry a guy who'd date-raped her? She loves him. He says he's sorry, he got carried away, or he blames her for letting him get to the point where he couldn't stop anymore. Why the hell not marry him?"

"That's a point."

Sam went to the fridge and pulled out a bottle of beer, twisting the cap off and downing half of it in one long gulp. "Thank God for booze." He wiped his mouth with the back of his hand. "People are fucked up, Earl. You know that. Christ, how can you be a lawman and not know it?"

Earl shrugged. "Maybe I don't want to believe everybody's fucked up."

"Well, that's okay. There are always exceptions. Like Vera. She was the most un-fucked-up person I've ever met. Except maybe you. But the basic rule is still the same. Ninety-nine percent of us are royally fucked up."

Which was hardly a heartening philosophy, Earl thought as he went back to cooking. But he knew how Sam was on these nights when he was missing Vera as if a part of his soul were lost forever. He got cynical and bitter about life in general and the world at large. Always. And Earl always stayed with him until the mood passed.

It suddenly struck him that maybe he could have done the same for Meg, instead of tearing out of that house as if demons were on his heels. He certainly owed her as much as he owed Sam.

But Meg was different. Meg had meant something to him, something bright and beautiful and good. And discovering she had feet of clay, especially ugly feet of clay, had rocked him as little in his adult life had.

So maybe his life had been too simple until now. Maybe he could have been better prepared for the shock he was feeling. But he at least needed some time to get used to this.

Right now, Sam needed him, and it was almost a relief to turn his attention to a familiar problem. "Vera was one of the special people," he agreed. "What happened?"

"You mean why was I remembering her tonight?" Sam finished the beer and reached into the fridge for another one. Earl got uneasy. His friend rarely drank, let alone heavily. "Well," Sam continued as he twisted the top off the longneck, "nothing happened.

I was just sitting there, minding my own business, watching the game. Not really thinking about anything except that I've seen San Francisco do better. And then I reached out just the way I used to, to take Vera's hand, like she was sitting beside me. And for an instant I was sure she was there." He took a long swallow of beer. "It sounds stupid after a year and a half, but it was a hell of a shock when I reached out and found empty air."

Earl's chest tightened with sympathy. "It doesn't sound stupid."

"Sure it does. After eighteen months you're supposed to be used to the way things are now. Anyway, after I got past the shock, I got to thinking maybe I ought to sell the house. Change venue. Make it so different that I'm not always looking for Vera every time I turn around."

"That might help." Then again, it might not. It might only make Sam more lonely than he was now. Earl had no idea. And the housing market in Whisper Creek was lousy besides. "Not a good time to sell," he said finally.

"It never is around here."

"You could try rearranging things. Changing some of the furniture."

"Yeah. And digging up the flower garden she planted, and sodding over the vegetable plot, and painting the house a different color and..." He trailed off and took more beer, a sip this time. "Shit. Every damn thing in my life reminds me of her."

Earl turned the steak. "Yeah." He couldn't think of anything more useful to say.

"That's not a bad thing, really," Sam said after a

few minutes. "Remembering Vera. It's a good thing. It reminds me how special she was, what we had together. I don't think I ever want to forget that."

"Sure you don't."

"But it would be nice if it didn't hurt so damn much."

"I could give you the one about time healing all wounds."

"Yeah." Sam gave him a wry, sad smile. "I've heard that one so many times I know it by heart."

"I bet you have."

"It's getting harder to believe."

Earl nodded. "I imagine so."

"But by and large it's easier. It's just that occasionally it gets out of hand. Something catches me. But even that's happening less. Anyway, enough of my pissing and moaning. What the hell's eating *you?*"

"Nothing I can talk about."

After a moment Sam said, "Okay. What are we going to do about the Dawson kid?"

"Damned if I know. Everything I think of is so full of holes it don't hold water."

Sam almost grinned. "Ah, life. Ain't it wonderful? Well, if you want to look the other way, I'll take Ben Dawson out behind the woodshed and whale some sense into him."

"I've thought about that. Problem is, *we'd* wind up in jail, and he'd just take it all out on Matt."

"Funny, isn't it, how the slime of the world so rarely get what's coming to them?"

"Oh, they get it sooner or later," Earl said, forking

the steak from the pan to a platter. "Sooner or later. That's what I'm here for."

But later, as he and Sam were watching the game and eating supper off TV trays, he found himself thinking that maybe that wasn't *all* he was here for. Maybe catching the slime wasn't enough.

Maybe sometimes you had to get down in the slime with them and help them out.

16

Earl insisted on driving Sam home, since the deputy had managed to put away the better part of a six-pack by the time the game was over. It was a mercy, Earl supposed, because Sam fell right into bed and was asleep before Earl was out the door. He wasn't really skunk-drunk, just numbed and sleepy.

But as he drove back through the darkened streets of Whisper Creek, Earl found himself noticing how quiet and empty everything was. Not that that was unusual. This was a hardworking town, and most of the stores and businesses still closed between six and nine. By ten, most everyone was tucked into their homes for the night, unless they were working the night shift at the mine.

Ordinarily Earl enjoyed the quiet of the nighttime streets, especially when there was snow on the ground. It filled him with a sense of magic that harkened back to something in his childhood that he had long since forgotten.

Tonight was different somehow. Tonight all he

could feel was the loneliness of the quiet streets, a loneliness that felt like a vast, echoing emptiness.

He knew, of course, that Whisper Creek hadn't changed. Something inside *him* had changed, and what the streets were making him feel was a reflection of that.

He drove around for a while, scanning storefronts, telling himself he was just being a good sheriff, even though he knew perfectly well that he was duplicating the efforts of his deputies.

But he didn't want to go home. Didn't want to sit in the silence and solitude of his existence until it was time to go to bed. Something about what had happened today with Meg and Allie, and tonight with Sam, had left him feeling as if there was a yawning pit in the center of his life.

A yawning pit he'd never noticed before.

Finally he pulled in at the convenience store and went inside to get decaf and a doughnut. The night clerk was familiar to him, a middle-aged guy named Cal Tinker who'd embarked upon a career as a night store manager after an injury had cost him his job at the mine.

When he went to pay, Cal waved away his money. "You know we provide coffee and doughnuts as a courtesy to the police."

"But I'm not on duty."

"Doesn't matter. Having you here is good enough."

"Thanks, Cal."

"One hand washes the other. I feel a whole lot better about working nights knowing you guys are gonna be dropping by often. If the store weren't paying for the coffee and doughnuts, I'd do it myself.''

The store was empty right now, so Earl hung around for a few minutes, eating his doughnut and drinking his coffee. In an hour or so, the place would get busy as the night shift, Monday's first shift, stopped in for coffee to take with them to the job. But right now it was just him, Cal and the quiet town.

''My daughter wants to go to Harvard,'' Cal told him as they stood leaning against opposite sides of the counter.

''Harvard, huh? Good school.''

''Expensive school. I told her she can go if she figures out how to pay for most of it. Her mom and I are both already working, and I told her we weren't going to take second jobs when she could just as well start off at Colorado Mountain College and transfer to Boulder. She got all huffy, said her future depends on it.''

One corner of Earl's mouth lifted. ''So does yours.''

''That's how I'm seeing it. She's smart enough. Maybe she'll get a scholarship. Then we'll talk about Harvard.''

''Sounds fair to me.''

'''Course it is. You're smart, Earl, never having kids. They'll drive you nuts.''

Which dragged Earl's thoughts back to Allie. Maybe he'd never had one of his own, but he had one. Sure enough.

''So anyway,'' Cal continued, oblivious of the direction Earl's thoughts were taking, ''I've got a sixteen-year-old sure her life will be ruined if she doesn't go to Harvard, and I've got a thirteen-year-old whose life is going to be ruined if she doesn't get a date to the school dance next Friday. Now, I ask you, when did thirteen-year-olds start dating?''

"Beats me." Reaching back more than twenty years into his memory, Earl found he couldn't even remember at what exact age he'd discovered an interest in girls. He knew for sure he hadn't had a date until his sophomore year in high school, when he'd finally screwed up the courage to ask Rita Murchison to go to a matinee with him. The one date had been enough, and he hadn't asked another girl out until the following year. These days Rita was the mother of five, married to a miner and working at the local drugstore. "I'm pretty sure I didn't ask a girl out the first time until I was fifteen or so."

"Me neither. I think I was sixteen." Cal shook his head. "That girl's too young to go out with a guy that age, and I can't imagine the boys her age wanting to go to dances with girls. But maybe I'm nuts. Maybe they're growing up faster than they used to."

"Faster than we did, that's for sure. A hundred years ago…"

Cal sighed and nodded. "I'll keep that in mind. A hundred years ago, my girls would have been working or married by now. The thought gives me the creeps."

"Well, at least your oldest wants to go to Harvard. If you're lucky, she won't change her mind because some guy comes on the scene."

Cal brightened. "That's right. Maybe Harvard isn't such a bad thing after all."

"Besides, she won't get a scholarship if her grades

fall because she's fooling around with some guy instead of studying.''

Cal seemed to be feeling considerably better by the time Earl left the store. Earl wished *he* was. Instead, he was thinking about how normal Cal's concerns were. How normal the man's daughters' concerns were.

And how abnormal Allie's concerns were. No fourteen-year-old girl should be thinking about the things she was worrying about. No child should ever have to wonder if her dead father had hated her and whether her mother loved her. The thought of it made his gut twist.

When he got back to his house, he found the light on his answering machine blinking.

''Earl, this is Vivian. I need help with Meg. Can you come?''

He went. Without a second thought. Ignoring the disgust and anger he felt about the situation up there.

He went. Because he needed to.

Vivian answered the door even before he knocked. ''Thank you for coming,'' she said. ''Meg hasn't moved or spoken a word in hours. I can't get her to answer me. Or go to bed. Or anything.''

''Where's Allie?''

''Sitting with her in the kitchen. The poor child is scared to death.''

In the bright light of the fluorescent fixtures, Allie and Meg both looked as white as ghosts. But Allie's eyes were alive, flying instantly to his face, expressing her anguish. Meg didn't move a muscle. Her gaze was fixed on the table in front of her, and it never wavered.

"It's like she's dead," Allie said, her voice rising. "Like she can't hear me."

"She's not dead, Allie." He'd seen too many corpses not to know the difference. What she was was catatonic. Christ. He'd seen people like this before. Sometimes they came out of it eventually. It was as if things had just become too painful to bear, and they pulled away inside themselves for a while. He hoped it wasn't anything worse than that.

"Then what's wrong with her?"

"She's had too much to handle. She's gone into some quiet place inside herself. She'll bc okay." He hoped. Because as bad as things were before, if Meg had a psychotic break right now, they would be worse than he wanted to contemplate.

Allie's eyes were brimming with tears as she looked up at him. "You're sure?"

"As sure as I am that the sun will rise. Don't you need to go to bed? You've got school tomorrow."

She reached out and took his hand. "You won't leave? You'll take care of her?"

"I promise."

The tears spilled over and began to run down her face. "I said terrible things to her, Uncle Earl. Terrible things."

He couldn't imagine that Allie had said anything truly awful. He didn't think she was either old enough or cruel enough to have said anything that could account for Meg's current state. But it was a chance to teach a lesson. "Did you mean what you said?"

Allie shook her head. "Not really."

"So you were angry. People say lots of things they don't mean when they're angry. Now head up to bed. Vivian will tuck you in."

"Of course I will," said Vivian. "Come along, dear."

Which left Earl alone with the silent, frozen Meg. Alone with all his mixed-up feelings.

He sat at the table across from Meg and wondered how to penetrate the walls she'd built around herself. Wondered if she had well and truly snapped after carrying so much secret ugliness around inside her.

Now that he was past his first flush of anger and disgust, he was able to consider Meg's situation a little more sympathetically. Being widowed eight months ago would have been enough trouble for most people. But it had happened right after an argument, and he was willing to bet she felt at least as responsible for Bill's death as Allie did. Maybe more so, because she'd been the one arguing with him. That would have been hard for anyone to live with, and apparently she'd never told a soul about the argument, so she hadn't had anyone to help her deal with her dirty secret.

In addition to the stress caused by her widowhood and her secret, she'd had Vivian's disapproving presence all these months, certainly enough to wear anyone down.

Then there was Allie, running away last weekend and perhaps being suicidal. More stress, topped off with the revelation that Allie had heard the fateful argument. Then there was his reaction, he admitted guiltily. Hardly surprising, when he thought about it, that Meg had withdrawn into herself. It must all seem so insurmountable. Too many problems and no help in sight.

He wasn't even going to factor in the possibility that Bill had indeed raped Meg all those years ago. And he was hoping against hope that Allie hadn't heard *that* accusation in the course of her parents' argument. If she had, wouldn't she have mentioned it?

No, when he thought about it, it was hardly surprising that Meg was sitting across from him looking like a statue. And the problem was still what he was going to do about it.

If he *could* do anything about it.

Sitting there staring at her, he felt all his old feelings of friendship and respect tangling up with his dawning feelings of attraction and maybe something more, and twisting around the ugliness that had been revealed today. He was a storm of mixed emotions, and out of this he was supposed to find some way of helping her deal with her feelings?

He was beginning to feel overwhelmed himself.

He had walked out of here once today in order to avoid saying things he would regret. He wasn't going to walk away now, because he didn't know how to deal with this problem. Instead, he promised himself that if Meg was still staring blankly by morning, he would get her to a doctor and a hospital.

That gave him eight hours to get through to her. He just wished he had some idea how to do it.

He didn't like feeling helpless. His job made him feel that way all too often, but he'd kept his personal life on a steady keel, always taking care to be as much in control as he could. Now he wasn't in control, and he didn't know what to do, and his gut was churning with so many feelings he didn't even want to try to sort them out.

Not knowing what else to do, he started talking. Rambling, really, keeping his voice pitched low and soothingly. He had a feeling it didn't matter what he said, just that he gave her something external to cling to so that she could climb out of the abyss into which she'd fallen.

He started by talking about Matt Dawson. "The kid's really banged up, Meg," he said. "Broken arm, broken ribs, fractured skull, bruises—I could kill his father. But I *can't* do that, because I'm a cop. Have I ever told you what a pain it is to be a cop? Everybody thinks I'm lucky because I get to deal with the world's assholes and lock 'em up. Well, they don't know. They don't know how little I can actually do about shit like this.

"I can't arrest Matt's father unless I get some evidence that he beat the kid. Matt denies it, and nobody's ever seen it happen. The mom's so scared she won't say boo."

He kept rambling, hoping for any sign of response or awareness, however small. He told her about Sam, and about how the deputy had reached out for his dead wife, then realized that might be the wrong topic.

And somehow, some way, he found himself talking about Bill.

"Bill was my friend. But that doesn't mean I think he was perfect. I know better. There were times when I didn't feel too all-fired wonderful about things he thought and said. Now I know this whole damn town thinks he's a hero because of the way he stood up for the union during the strike. And I guess that *does* make him a hero. But that wasn't all of him, and I want you to know that. I know he had a temper. I know he was selfish at times. Sometimes too selfish. I used to get uneasy at the way he'd leave you and Allie home all those weekends when he wanted him and me to go hiking. Sometimes I even used to say no, because I figured you might like him home for a weekend every now and then.''

As he talked, he found himself thinking about Bill in a way he never had before. Realizing that something about Bill had never become a married man or a father. Not that Bill was bad at the roles of husband and dad, but some part of him had always remained a bachelor. A young bachelor. A guy who thought he had a right to take off nearly every other weekend to do what *he* wanted to.

At the time, Earl hadn't really thought about what that might mean. He tended to be an accepting sort of guy who didn't evaluate the lifestyle decisions of other people as long as they weren't breaking the law. He'd always just assumed that both Meg and Bill were happy with the way their marriage was running. Now he wasn't so sure.

If *he'd* been married to Meg, he didn't think he would have wanted to take all those weekends away from her. Sure, from time to time he would still have liked to go camping and hiking. But he would have wanted Meg and Allie to come with him. Bill had seemed to prefer to go without them, although there were weekends when he'd taken Allie with him, or both Allie and Meg. But those were the exceptions rather than the rule.

He'd kind of assumed that Meg and Allie just didn't want to go. That they were content to have Bill go by himself. Now he wondered.

"He should have stayed home more with you and Allie," he heard himself saying. The words came from his heart, but even so, he was surprised to be saying them. "It's my fault, I guess. I shouldn't have been so willing to go off with him on all those trips."

Trips of the kind they'd grown up taking together. Trips that should have become less frequent after Bill married, but never had.

Earl's mouth tasted sour. He didn't like thinking he might have abetted problems in Bill and Meg's marriage. But he supposed he had.

"Anyway," he went on, "he could be too selfish. And some of his opinions kinda had me wondering where he'd left his brain. In some ways, he was still a kid at heart."

Building this house himself, from the ground up, when Meg was trying to care for an infant. Which, now that he thought of it, meant Bill was rarely around to help care for Allie. And Meg was always trying to juggle caring for her daughter and helping to build the house.

At the time, Earl had thought of it as his two friends building a dream. But maybe Bill had been building an escape. Maybe, now that he thought of it, Bill had spent a whole lot of time trying to escape his marriage. Viewed from that angle, it was hardly surprising that Bill had been talking about leaving at the end.

God, it was strange how different things could look if you just put them in a slightly different light.

Which could explain why Meg thought she'd been raped. And why it had taken her so long to believe it herself. Yeah, he could see that.

Meg still wasn't responding to him, so, with a sigh, he got up from his chair and went to take her by the elbow.

"Come on, Meggie," he said gently. "You've got to get to bed."

Much to his relief, she stood up and let him lead her upstairs. When he told her to lie down on the bed, she did so, scooting over to one side and burying her face in the pillow.

She'd given up. The thought panicked him.

Outside in the hallway, he found Vivian. She was standing outside her own bedroom door, her face gaunt.

"Allie's asleep," she said. "How's Meg?"

"The same. She's lying on her bed with her face buried in the pillow."

Vivian nodded slowly, as if she was reluctant to accept the news. "I need a cup of tea. Join me?"

He went with her because there was very little else he could do, but he was determined not to leave yet. Somehow he had to find a way to reach Meg. Maybe Vivian could tell him something useful.

Vivian put the kettle on. He noticed that she didn't use the microwave to boil the water. Stupid thing to notice, but he noticed it anyway. Old habits die hard. And maybe that had something to do with the way Vivian had been treating Meg. Old habits.

When the water boiled, Vivian poured it over tea

bags in mugs and brought the two cups to the table. She didn't ask if he wanted milk or sugar. The sliding glass doors rattled a little as the wind gusted down the mountain. All he could see when he looked at them, though, was the reflection of the kitchen.

"Well," said Vivian, "she can't keep on like this. She's got to come out of it."

"I'm sure she will." Even though he wasn't sure at all.

"She will," Vivian said firmly. "She gets her strength from *me.*"

Interesting comment from a woman he'd thought hated her daughter. "What's with you anyway?" he asked bluntly. "Friday you could barely be civil to her."

She sighed heavily, cupping her hands around her mug. "I've been doing a lot of thinking," she said finally.

"About what?"

"About what I've been doing." She shrugged a heavy shoulder and dunked her tea bag. "Allie's running away was a shock. Then Meg telling me that Bill had raped her." She shook her head and put her face in her hands. "Meg told me I was making things harder on Allie. I got to thinking about that."

"And?"

"And. And. And. When you all were down in Denver, I didn't have anybody to be irritated with but myself. I got pretty irritated, I can tell you. I sat in this big old empty house, and all I could hear was my own voice and all the things I'd been saying. I've always been an irritable woman. It's easier."

"Easier than what?"

Vivian lifted her face from her hands. "Easier than feeling anything else. That's all."

He nodded, understanding. He had a tendency to get angry himself when his feelings were raw.

"Easier than worrying," she said. "Easier than fearing. Easier than grieving. My momma used to be the same way, snapping all the time. Never saw her cry. It's a kind of strength."

"I suppose it is."

"But it isn't healthy," Vivian said. "I figured that out. Maybe it works for me, but it hasn't been helping Allie or Meg." She sighed again, shook her head and pulled out the tea bag, dropping it on a saucer in the middle of the table that held tea bags from earlier. "Back in the old days, on the farm, the weather would turn sour. Not enough rain. Too cold. Grasshoppers. It didn't matter what, but things were going bad. So my momma would get all snappish, and my dad would get all angry, like getting angry at the sky would make any difference. All us kids would tiptoe around so as not to rile them. I figure they were worrying."

"Probably."

"But I'm the same way," Vivian told him. "I've always been the same way. I was worrying about Allie these last few months, so I was snapping at Meg about how she was raising that girl. God forgive me, I've been mad at Meg for fifteen years now because my husband died. 'Tweren't *her* fault. But I blamed her and got mad at her because it was easier than crying."

But Vivian was crying now, one huge tear running down her sagging cheek. "It's my way. But after the last week, I reckon it's poisonous. And maybe it's too late to mend the damage I've done. I don't know. But I *do* know I wasn't being a strong Christian woman. I was being a bad woman, and I was being weak. I figured that out.''

He felt a natural urge to tell her that she wasn't a bad woman, but remembering the emotional wreckage upstairs, he didn't speak the words. ''It's been hard on Meg.''

''I know. I wasn't being fair to her. But I didn't want her to lean. In my family, we don't lean.''

She said this as if it were ample justification, even now that she'd had a change of heart, and Earl found himself feeling sorry for this woman and her crabbed, distorted emotions.

Finally he fell back on the old saw that he reminded himself of from time to time when he'd screwed up. ''You can't change the past, Vivian. All you can do is try to do better from now on.''

Vivian nodded again. ''You're right.''

''And sometimes even the strongest of us need to lean. Meg's had an awful lot to deal with.''

''More than I guessed.''

''Me, too.'' And he still wasn't comfortable with a lot of it. Especially the part about Bill raping Meg. That was a tough nut to swallow, and he was wondering why he should have to swallow it at all. Part of him wanted to pretend he'd never heard it.

''So...'' He hesitated, damning himself, then asked, ''You really think Bill raped Meg?''

Vivian pulled a tissue out of her pocket and dabbed at her eyes. ''It sounds far-fetched. I didn't believe her at first.''

"But now?"

"I was thinking about that, too, on Saturday. There's no way to know for sure, now. But I believe *she* believes it."

And that was probably all that mattered, Earl thought. If Meg felt violated, then she *had* been violated, and no set of facts could change that. But believing her meant being disloyal to his lifelong friend. The choice was bitter.

Vivian spoke. "I know I raised her to think sex outside marriage was a sin. I know when she was in high school she promised me she'd wait until she was married. But who can say for sure? Kids go away to college and get different ideas. But there was something in her eyes when she told me.... I believe her."

And Earl was remembering how much Bill had always hated being thwarted. He'd always just told himself that Bill went for what he wanted, that he was aggressive, but in hindsight, he found he was remembering it slightly differently. Bill always got what he wanted. And sometimes he went too far to get it.

There'd been that time in high school when Bill had wanted to date Debbie Jakstrow. But Debbie had been dating one of the football players. Ted Askew, he seemed to remember. So Bill had planted a rumor about Ted and some other girl, and Debbie had broken up with him.

It had seemed juvenile, even then, and Bill had professed to be ashamed of his own action. But he'd gotten what he wanted. He'd dated Debbie for the rest of the school year.

And there had been other such instances.

Christ, Earl found himself thinking, had he been so totally blind to his friend's failings? Had loyalty caused him to twist the truth around, to ignore what was right under his nose? Maybe. *Maybe.*

Growing up as he had, two steps removed from the gutter, Earl hadn't had many friends. In retrospect, it still seemed a little astonishing that Bill, coming from one of the better families in town, had made a friend out of a kid who came to school in tattered hand-me-downs, and whose parents were the kind of people no one had wanted to know. Something had drawn the two of them together in grade school and had kept them together until Bill's death.

And Earl's judgment had been affected, he supposed. By the honor of being befriended by one of the "better" kids. By the fierce loyalty he had always felt toward anyone who treated him well. What was he going to do? Sacrifice his one true childhood friend because the guy acted like a jerk sometimes? Who didn't act like a jerk at that age, anyway?

But Bill had kept on acting like a jerk in some ways. Ways that Earl had remained firmly blind to. The realization left him with a strong feeling of disgust.

"What do you think about Bill raping her?" Vivian said.

"I'm sitting here thinking it's entirely possible. He always got what he wanted."

Vivian sighed heavily and sipped her tea, sagging so that he feared she was going to become a puddle on the floor. "She hasn't been happy," Vivian said in a faint voice. "She pretended to be, but I could see she wasn't. Not completely. Not for a long time. I just didn't want to see it.''

"Nobody does." But maybe he'd seen it, too. In little ways. God, if he could have gotten his hands on Bill right then, he would have shaken the truth out of him.

Angry, disgusted, annoyed with himself, he stood up and began to pace the kitchen. "Damn it," he said, not caring whether his curse shocked Vivian. "I always thought they had the real thing. But this is making me think. I'm remembering things...."

Too many things. Bill wanting to be away every other weekend. The way the two of them stopped going into Denver together. The way Bill had started stopping off in town for a couple of drinks before he went home from work. The way, little by little, some of the sparkle had left Meg's eyes. And he'd always wondered why they'd never had another kid.

Christ.

Suddenly, in his mind's eye, he remembered the day they'd finished building the house. Allie had been almost two then. Bill had screwed the last screw on the lock for the front door and then had popped the cork on a bottle of champagne. They'd toasted the house.

He could still see Meg and Bill as if they were standing right in front of him even now. Dusty, dirty, tired and laughing. But Bill had been looking up at the house. And Meg had been looking at Bill with something hungry in her eyes. Something painful. Why hadn't he paid attention to it right then?

In retrospect, he would have bet his entire savings

account that Meg had loved Bill, but Bill had never really loved her.

Talk about a punch to the gut.

But that couldn't be true. Because if it were, he couldn't imagine Bill staying married so long. Couldn't imagine him getting married, even though Meg was pregnant. Unless...unless Meg had been something Bill had wanted. Not loved. Just wanted. To possess. Then he could see it.

He could see it all too clearly.

Single women didn't grow on trees in this little town. Bill probably thought he had a prize, and she wasn't worth trading in for bachelorhood. Having someone at home to raise the kid, do the cooking and warm his bed would have suited him. It was easy.

At least until something better came along. Or until the woman wasn't warming his bed as well as she used to. What had Meg said? Something about Bill accusing her of being cold? That would fit.

Bill had wanted Debbie, too, in high school. He'd been prepared to do anything to get her. He'd gotten her and had dated her for six months. Then had dropped her cold. He'd never really cared for Debbie. Even Earl had known that, but it was high school, and emotions were fickle. But Bill had wanted her. And had had her. And had kept her—until she was no longer what he wanted.

Maybe he'd done the same thing with Meg.

Maybe Bill had never been capable of really loving anyone. Even Allie. Dear God, maybe even Allie. Because if he *had* been capable of loving her, how could he have been planning to leave her? How could he have said what he'd said about that child ruining his life? Of course Meg had said something about not wanting to get pregnant, which he could understand in the heat of anger, but nothing about Allie ruining her life. Bill had said that.

Bill would have *meant* that.

Feeling sick to his stomach, Earl stopped in front of the deck doors and pressed his forehead to the icy glass.

"I don't think," he said hoarsely, "that I ever really understood Bill."

"Nobody did," Vivian said. "You only ever saw what he wanted you to see. He was a manipulator. I knew that all along. But as long as he was taking good care of Meg and Allie, I wasn't going to say anything. Meg loved him."

"Yes, she did." He wondered what the hell Bill had wanted from *him*. Damned if he knew.

"But it was all about what *he* wanted," Vivian said. "And Meg was always giving it to him. Men are like that."

"Not *this* man."

"Maybe not," Vivian said, but her tone suggested that she was reserving judgment.

He turned to face her. "Why have you been beating her up these past few months?"

Vivian sagged. "I told you. Habit. Besides, I was angry. Angry that she was grieving for that man. He was never good enough for her. Never."

There had been a time when it had crossed Earl's mind that *no* man was good enough for Meg, including himself. But after today, he wasn't at all sure about that anymore. So what? He wasn't sure about much anymore.

''Where does this get us, Vivian?''

The woman looked at him, her perennially unhappy face unhappier than usual. ''I don't know,'' she said. ''I don't know.''

He didn't know, either. All he knew was that he had to try to find some way to fix this mess. He owed it to Allie, if nothing else.

17

Vivian went up to bed. She didn't ask Earl to leave but instead offered him the spare bedroom. He took that as meaning she didn't want to be alone if either Allie or Meg went critical all of a sudden.

He could understand that. But he resented it a little, too. Resented her leaning on him after the way she had always treated him. On the other hand, he supposed it was a huge leap forward that the woman was asking for help, however tacitly.

A leap forward for *her*. He couldn't see that it was necessarily going to help anyone else out. Even if she had mended her ways, it was going to be a long time before either Allie or Meg accepted that Vivian didn't disapprove of them both.

And Vivian's rehabilitation didn't make a bit of difference to the fact that both Allie and Meg had major problems to deal with. Nor did it change the fact that Meg was lying catatonic in her bedroom.

He went to check on her and found her in exactly the same position, as if she wanted to crawl into her pillow and hide forever. He couldn't blame her for that. Not after what he'd heard and learned today.

There were problems, and there were problems. Some were just aggravating and frustrating and could annoy the hell out of you. And some were so big and insurmountable they seemed to open a gaping pit in your heart and mind, leaving you forever changed. This was in the forever-changed category.

He felt something inside him weakening and softening toward her. The anger and indignation he'd been clinging to were giving way to a deep-seated ache, a hard, unhappy, excruciating ache of concern for her. He didn't want to relax his guard. Didn't want to give in to it. Didn't want to make room for a whole battery of feelings that would only open him to more pain.

He'd had enough pain these past months. He'd grieved for Bill, grieved for Meg's and Allie's loss. At some point or another, he had to stop grieving and get on with life, but instead he was now aching for the fresh pain Meg and Allie had suffered. God, did it never end?

That was when he decided to just give in and let it happen. Bottling things up didn't do a damn bit of good. If he'd learned nothing else today, he'd learned that.

Hiding from it didn't help a bit.

Finally, accepting that it had to get worse before it could get any better, he stretched out beside Meg on the bed and closed his eyes. When she emerged from her numbness, he was going to be here. And he was going to pay the price for all that.

But concealed behind his closed eyelids, hidden in

the privacy of his own mind and heart, he admitted something he'd known all along. He cared far too much for Meg to ever keep his distance. Wherever this mess took her, he was going to be there right beside her.

When he woke up, the bedside light was still on and the house was silent. Meg had moved and was curled up beside him, her arm thrown across his chest, her breath whispering against his cheek. That was probably what had disturbed him, he thought. He wasn't used to sleeping with another person, most especially a person who was curled around him.

His body liked it, though. No question of that. He was as hot, hard and heavy as he'd ever been in his life, and the feeling shamed him a little, because Meg was wounded and hurting, and such reactions had no proper place in this night.

But his body wasn't responding to reason. It *liked* having Meg close, and if he were to be honest, so did his mind, heart and soul. It was as if the gaping emptiness he'd recently discovered in his life had found something to fill itself.

The thought scared him. After what he'd learned, he didn't know if he could trust Meg with feelings like this—never mind whether she would even want them. In fact, he was pretty sure she *wouldn't*. How could she possibly, in the midst of all the turmoil she was currently suffering? She was fragile now, like a cracked crystal vase that might shatter under the least pressure.

And even if she weren't, she had never thought of him as anything but a friend.

That was all he was to her, he reminded himself, closing his eyes and steeling himself against the feelings that were rising in him like a flood tide. Just a friend. The fact that he had always wished he could be something more didn't matter.

That he could admit that to himself now, finally, after all this time, terrified him. Because the lies that he had told himself were comfortable and had concealed the fact that he had felt disloyal to Bill for all those furtive, wistful thoughts that he had banished the instant they occurred to him.

Because he didn't feel disloyal now. Because his impression of Bill had altered so irrevocably over the last twenty-four hours that he was no longer able to feel disloyal.

Unsettled to the very core of his being, he closed his eyes tighter and tried to find the equilibrium that seemed determined to elude him. But he couldn't hide from the feelings rising in his own body, and he couldn't hide from the reality that Meg was no longer his best friend's wife.

All he could do was cling to the fact that what she needed from him was friendship. Period. Nothing more. And that he would be betraying *her* if he tried to be anything more.

And maybe betraying Allie, too.

But his mind refused to focus on Allie right now. Meg was too close, her breath soft and sweet against his cheek, her body warm against his side. Her arm a gentle weight on his chest. It was getting harder and harder to think of anything except the physical ache that was filling him, harder and harder to ignore the throbbing need of his body.

What he needed to do, he told himself, was move. Now. But he couldn't make himself do it, and part of him rationalized it as not wanting to wake her. He definitely didn't want to admit that he was paralyzed by a need so deep that it beggared anything he had ever felt before.

But then she stirred, and he heard her breath catch, and he knew she wasn't asleep anymore.

Now he had no excuse not to move, but he still couldn't make himself pull away. He needed this closeness too much. He needed it as he had never needed anything in his life before.

"Earl?" She barely breathed his name, but he heard so much pain in the single syllable that his throat tightened. All of a sudden he was able to move again, but only toward her, not away from her.

He rolled onto his side until he was facing her and wrapped her tightly in his arms. The feeling was so good that for a few seconds he couldn't speak. "Welcome back," he said huskily.

"How's Allie?"

"Scared to death for you."

"I don't know what happened. It was like I turned into a small point inside myself. I couldn't move, couldn't talk...but I could hear you. I could hear Allie."

"It was just too much to handle. It happens."

"No. I shouldn't have..." But whatever she'd been about to say was swallowed by a sob. The tears came then, an endless flow of them, as if they'd been dammed up for a long, long time and now she couldn't contain them any longer.

He held her while she cried, feeling as if each tear

fell straight into his heart. He had no idea how long she wept, nor did he care. Every sob sounded as if it had been wrenched from deep within her soul, and the sounds that wracked her body pierced his heart.

He murmured reassurance to her, hardly knowing what he said or whether she heard it. There didn't seem to be a whole lot he could do to make it better, though, and any comfort was going to have to come from within her.

Eventually she grew quiet against him, exhausted. An errant sniffle escaped her from time to time, as did a heavy sigh, but the storm had passed. He found himself stroking her hair and thinking that if he had known her secrets all along he probably wouldn't have advised her to act any differently. It was a sobering realization.

"Allie's going to hate me forever," she said presently, her voice muffled and thick.

"I don't think so, Meg. That child loves you and desperately wants to believe you love her. She'll come around."

"God! I can't believe how I've hurt her."

He couldn't deny that. Allie had been wounded terribly by what she had heard, and while Meg might be able to convince her daughter that she had always loved her and wanted her, she wasn't going to be able to erase Bill's words. Nor would anything she could say now mend what Bill had said. Only Bill could have done that, and Bill was gone.

"What do I do, Earl?" Meg asked sadly. "What *can* I do? I know Bill would never have said those things if he'd known Allie might hear them. *I* never would have said them, no matter how angry and hurt I was feeling. But how do I convince Allie of that?''

''I don't know. All you can do is keep on loving her the best you can. Then maybe she'll figure it out herself.''

A shaky sigh escaped Meg. ''I wish I'd cut out my own tongue.''

He'd felt that way a time or two in his life. Like everybody else in the world, he had a temper, and sometimes it got the better of him. Less these past years than when he was younger, but he'd said some things that he still regretted.

''It's too late for that now, Meggie.''

''I know. It's too late. Everything's too late....'' Her voice trailed off, and she pressed her face to his shoulder, as if by sheer pressure she could stop the tears. She said something broken that he couldn't hear.

''What's that?'' he asked. His fingers were burying themselves in her silky hair, and he was thinking that he wouldn't mind holding her like this for the rest of his life.

She tipped her head back and repeated herself in a muffled voice. ''Do you hate me?''

Hate her? Hell, no. He was mad at her, a little, though that was beginning to ease. He was furious at Bill for what he suspected was less than a loving attitude toward Meg. He was pissed at himself for feeling yearnings that were out of place at this time, with this woman. But hate Meg? He couldn't do that. He simply wasn't capable of it.

''No,'' he said. ''I don't hate you. I could never hate you, Meg.''

"But I did awful things...."

"No, you were human. Maybe the hardest part of being a human being is giving ourselves permission to be fallible. You got angry, said some things you regret. You probably regretted them almost as soon as you said them."

"I did. Oh, I *did*. Even before Bill jumped into the car and drove away."

He hesitated, then decided to say it, because he figured she was thinking it, even if she wouldn't admit it. "You didn't kill him, Meg."

She caught her breath, then he felt the hot salt of her tears soaking his shirt again. "Earl, you don't know...."

"I know," he said flatly. "You didn't kill him. The two of you had an argument. That's normal. People have arguments all the time. But *you* didn't jump into a car and drive too fast down a snowy road because you were mad, did you?"

"But—"

He cut her off. "Listen to me, Meg. I've been thinking a lot about Bill today. I was remembering things I'd kind of forgotten. Maybe because I didn't want to face that Bill had warts like everybody else. But the fact is, Bill didn't like to be thwarted. Ever. He always wanted his own way. I figure the things you said burned him up, made him feel he couldn't just walk away from your marriage like it was nothing. He wasn't pissed because you got mad, he was pissed because he couldn't have his own damn way. And it'd be just like him to drive like a bat out of hell because of it. I've seen him do it, Meg. In some ways, he never really grew up."

She shook her head, and he heard her sniffle.

"Listen," he said. "You didn't make Bill get in that car, and you didn't make him drive too fast. He was running away because he couldn't have his way. That's all it was. Acting like a temperamental two-year-old."

The oddest thing happened then. He heard her make a sound like a short, sad laugh, then she tipped her face up. In the lamplight he could see the sheen of tears dampening her cheeks and trembling on her eyelashes.

"What?" he said, feeling confused.

"Just that...it's so true, Earl. He could be just like a spoiled two-year old at times."

He nodded and, almost in spite of himself, gave her a squeeze. It was true about Bill, and for some weird reason, just saying it out loud made him feel better. As if some kind of dirty secret weren't secret anymore. "I loved him, Meg," Earl said. "He was like my brother. But I may as well admit there were things about him I didn't like too much. And too many good people spent too damn much time trying to keep Bill from throwing a temper tantrum. Too much time trying to keep him from getting angry. We all did it. Hell, I watched you tiptoe around him for fifteen years. And I was tiptoeing the same way."

"Was that so wrong?"

"Naw. But it wasn't necessarily good for the rest of us."

"But he wasn't like that all the time."

"No." And it was true. There were plenty of times when you couldn't have asked for a better friend. Times when Bill would just be there for you in ways that made you feel good inside about having such a friend. ''Nobody's all bad, Meg, just like nobody's all good. We loved him, you and me. And I guess he loved us, at least as much as he could.''

''As much as he could.'' She repeated the words softly, then fell silent for a little while. ''You're right,'' she said presently. ''I was feeling like he didn't love me at all, because he wanted to leave me. But maybe...'' She trailed off, leaving the sentence incomplete.

''He loved you as much as he could.'' It wasn't a whole hell of a lot, but Earl felt reasonably confident in making the statement. At least this way Meg could believe that Bill loved her. And Bill sure as hell wasn't going to come back from the grave and tell her otherwise now. Some lies were good lies.

And, now that he thought of it, most of Meg's lies had been told for a good reason. The problem came only when the lies started to eat you alive.

She was growing softer against him, and he wondered if she was falling back to sleep. He supposed he ought to get up off the bed and settle in the armchair. It would be the wise thing to do, for both of them. Neither of them could handle the explosive emotions involved in what might happen if he stayed where he was. And God forbid she should ever wonder if he'd taken advantage of her.

But he still couldn't make himself pull away, and when he felt her hand tighten against his back, holding him closer, he knew that nothing was going to drag him away.

''I wish...'' She whispered the words, let them trail away.

"Wish what?" he asked finally.

"I wish I'd met you first."

His heart stopped. She couldn't mean that. She was just feeling low and emotionally whipped. She couldn't mean that she would rather have been married to him than Bill. He didn't have Bill's class, or his good looks, or his exciting personality. He was a dull man, quiet, uneducated and rough around all his edges. He'd grown up the hard way, and it showed. Meg deserved something better.

When his heart started beating again, it was a slow, heavy beat. As if he knew he was hovering on the edge of something momentous. He found himself squeezing his eyes shut and waiting...waiting....

Then he felt it. A butterfly wing brushed his stubbly chin, so light he almost wasn't sure he'd felt it. Then again. His heart rate accelerated, causing him to draw a long breath. His body grew heavy, and every nerve ending seemed to wake up to the sensation of her against him.

No. No. He couldn't let himself feel these things. It was dangerous. And she didn't mean anything by that kiss on his chin, not a thing except gratitude that he was here and listening to her. She must have felt so alone these past months with no one to talk to, no one to understand all the wounds she was dealing with in addition to the loss of her husband. It was just gratitude.

But then she pressed herself closer, and her hand grew firm against his back, as if she wanted to pull him inside her. He stopped breathing.

"Earl..."

He found breath. Found voice. "No...." he said,

but he didn't sound as if he meant it. "You'll regret this."

"No...."

His heart took a precipitous tumble as he thought she was agreeing with him, and he clenched his teeth against the wild, overwhelming urge to tell her he wanted her, that he would crawl naked over hot coals to once, just once, know what loving her was like.

"No...." she said again. "I need this. I need you. Earl...please..."

If there was a rational answer to that plea, he didn't know what it was. "Meggie..."

"Please," she said again. "I need you.... I'm not cold. But I'm so empty...."

He was lost. He needed her so much himself that there was no way he could deny her need. He just prayed that tomorrow she wouldn't hate him. "Be sure, Meggie," he whispered. "Oh, God, be sure...."

"I'm sure." Her voice caught. "I've needed... you...for a long time...."

How long? he wondered. How long? But he couldn't ask. Wasn't sure he wanted to know. Didn't want to consider possibilities that would have been barred by friendship and marriage. Just wanted to deal with now. Because now was a moment he'd been waiting for since before he was born.

Her breath feathered his chin and cheek, like the brush of the softest down. The sensation filled him with a complexity of feelings so overwhelming that he felt as if he were about to burst, feelings so powerful that for a few moments he felt as if he were nothing *except* feeling.

He rode the eagle's wing, soaring above the clouds, and the strength of the sensation filled his eyes.

"Earl...?" A tentative, questioning sound.

He opened his eyes and looked square into Meg's, saw her fear, saw her beginning to fold up into herself again, as if he had rejected her. He couldn't stand it.

Twisting his head, he brought his mouth to hers, hovered there, just barely touching her lips with his until the exquisite moment of anticipation drew out tight and fine, ready to shatter. Some part of him knew he was never going to forget this moment, was never going to forget the way her mouth felt against his.

Then he kissed her. It was not their first kiss, but it was as thrilling and deeply satisfying as if it had been. These lips, forbidden to him for so long, welcomed him, drew him into a safe, warm place, offered a security that he couldn't believe was illusory.

Her tongue was warm against his, stroking his knowingly, telling him that whatever Bill might have thought of her sexuality, she was as hot as a flare. Her hands kneaded his back, urging him closer, and when he moved in nearer, she rolled onto her back. He threw his leg over her and broke away long enough to look down at her.

Her lips were gently swollen from his kisses, her cheeks flushed and her eyes heavy-lidded with passion. He had never seen a more beautiful sight in his life.

The drive to bury himself in her was growing stronger by the second. But to do that, he had to undress them both, and he was afraid that the mere act of doing that might bring them both to their senses. He hesitated.

Then she reached up, popping the snaps on the front of his denim shirt in one loud ripping sound. He didn't need any more encouragement. But he didn't want to be rough with her. Not at all.

So he unwrapped her as if she were a long-awaited present, taking care with each fastening and fold, as if the gift-wrapping mattered as much as what it contained. Savoring each precious moment. Her sweater slipped away gently, revealing her breasts, cupped in lace and silky tricot. They were fuller than he'd anticipated, and he paused for a moment, admiring the offering.

Then he dipped his head and began to sprinkle kisses all over her, learning the taste and texture of her satiny skin, learning her hills and hollows as if he never wanted to forget an inch of her. And he didn't. He expected that after tonight she might never want to be close to him again, and part of him was sounding wild warnings that he ought to stop now, before he destroyed their friendship forever.

But the Klaxons were dim in his head, lost in the pounding desire that hammered in his blood and rushed in his ears.

Only now, now as he was holding her and undressing her, did he realize how long he'd wanted to do this. How much he had wanted her all along. Crashing into his mind was a memory of all the nights he'd fallen asleep with her image in his mind, all the nights he'd wished Meg's clone would suddenly turn up in his life.

And now the real woman was here.

He rose on his knees, slipping her slacks from her, drawing his fingertips down her legs as he tugged the cloth away. She shivered and whispered his name, and his body became a burning brand, his mind an explosion of white heat. She wanted him right now, and that was all he could think about. Nothing else mattered.

He cast his own clothes aside quickly, then reached for the last scraps of hers, tossing her bra and panties away as if they were wisps of down. She lay naked before him, her arms reaching up for him, her hips pulsing in a gentle rhythm that echoed the pounding in his own body.

"Are you sure?" he asked, his voice thick and raw.

"Yes...yes...."

He could wait no longer. It was as if every cell in his body was responding to a call from every cell in hers. He needed to feel her beneath him, needed her warmth and welcome as he had never needed anything in his entire life.

Her legs parted as he lowered himself over her, and when her thighs clasped his hips, the sensation unleashed a hammering tide of pleasure that filled him to overflowing.

But still he lingered, reluctant to have these moments slip away too fast. He teased the small ripe berry of her nipple with his tongue and teeth, reveling when she moaned in response, when her legs locked across him, trying to draw him closer still.

He was merciless to them both and kept right on teasing her, sucking gently on her breasts until she began to buck impatiently beneath him. Her nails dug into his shoulders, and she was saying his name over and over again.

Until finally he could no longer resist. With one strong thrust, he entered her. For an instant the pleasure was so intense he couldn't move. His eyes squeezed shut, and he held himself still, letting the tide of feelings pour through him. So good. So *good*...

When he opened his eyes, he found her looking at him with a dreamy smile on her face. "Earl," she whispered. "Earl..." As if his name was the answer to every hope she'd ever had.

He had never felt so welcome in his life.

He thrust again and listened to her sharply drawn breath, savored her fingers digging into his shoulders. Then again, until a red haze seemed to fill him and lift him out of himself, to a place where there was nothing but the irresistible quest for culmination.

He lost touch with the earth and found heaven, and she was with him every second of the way. The quivers of her completion caught him and carried him sharply, suddenly to his own. He emptied himself into her.

And felt renewed.

He dozed, and she slept. The quiet night hours slipped slowly away, and he counted them each time he woke, willing them to pass more slowly. Because with morning would come reality.

Allie's problems would become paramount again, and Meg's guilt would reawaken. It might even extend to him. He needed to go to work, although today of all days he didn't want to leave the side of this woman and her daughter.

He dreaded the coming of daylight.

But finally he could evade the world no longer. Rising, he dressed silently and slipped from the room. He needed to go home, shower, shave and change, and get to his office. He would call from there, he decided.

He hesitated over the bed, longing to kiss her one last time, but he didn't want to wake her. After what she had been through, she would probably sleep long into the morning, and he didn't want to deprive her of the healing of sleep.

He heard Allie's alarm clock go off as he passed her door. She would be getting ready to go to school. He slipped quietly down the stairs and out of the house, into the dim early-morning grayness. And then he was gone, leaving miles between him and those he was worried about.

18

When Meg opened her eyes, morning sunlight was filtering gently through the blinds of her bedroom. For a few seconds she felt a depth of contentment she had never before felt in her life.

Then she remembered. She and Earl had made love last night. And while part of her wanted to cling to the wonder of it, to take the memory out and savor it as if it were a priceless gem, the rest of her was appalled at her behavior. How could she have done such a thing when her daughter was so deeply wounded? How could she have taken her own pleasure under such circumstances?

And what about Earl? What must he think of her now, after the wanton way she had asked him to make love with her? That she had even been able to think of such a thing with Allie so hurt?

God, she hated herself. Loathing filled her until her throat burned with it and tears scalded her eyes. What was wrong with her? How could she have been so…so…?

She couldn't even find a word for what she thought

of herself. She just knew she had to be the lowest slime that had ever crawled the face of the earth.

Rolling over, trying to evade the light that was snaking through the blinds, she found her face pressed into the pillow beside her. It smelled of Earl. Faintly. Just enough to pluck at her heart and cause her tears to spill in a heavy cascade.

Earl. He could never be hers. Never. She had no right to even think of such a thing. What had she been thinking last night? How could she have given herself that way, especially since he had been so reluctant? He must be wondering what kind of woman Bill had married. He must be wondering what kind of mother she was for Allie.

She would never be able to face him again. God, she had destroyed the truest friendship she had ever known, and all for a few minutes of...what? Desperate escape? Affirmation? Need?

She wasn't even sure what had driven her to behave so uncharacteristically, and she wasn't at all sure she wanted to know. She was beginning to realize that there were places inside her that were better left in a dark dungeon, far away from the light of day. Her soul, she thought, was an ugly thing.

Finally she forced herself to get up, shower and dress in a sweater and slacks. Vivian would be downstairs, and she dreaded seeing her mother after yesterday. If the woman had hated her for what had happened with Bill and her dad, she was certainly going to hate her more after what had been revealed yesterday.

And Meg couldn't blame her. She deserved every

bit of anger and disgust the world wanted to heap on her.

Vivian was in the kitchen, as usual, but, to Meg's surprise, so was Allie. Vivian said good morning, but it was on Allie that Meg's attention latched.

The girl was sitting at the table, hands wrapped around a mug of hot chocolate, looking very small and very young. But she looked up at her mother with shadowed eyes and asked, "Are you okay?"

Something in Meg's heart ripped. She managed a nod and made her way tentatively to the table, sitting across from her daughter. "Are *you* okay?" she asked Allie uncertainly.

The girl nodded, fixing her gaze on her mug.

Vivian set a mug of coffee in front of Meg and said, "I need to go clean the bathroom. I'll leave you two to talk."

Dimly, Meg was a little surprised at her mother bowing out; that wasn't characteristic of her. But she was also surprisingly uneasy at being left alone with Allie, as if she needed a buffer between herself and Allie's pain. That realization disturbed her. She had never needed or wanted anyone between herself and her daughter before.

"I'm sorry," she said eventually, finding it difficult to summon even those few words. Her mouth felt heavy, as if it was too much effort to speak.

Allie nodded, still staring into her mug. "I didn't go to school today," she offered, stating the obvious.

Meg managed a nod.

"I thought...I thought maybe we needed to talk."

Meg agreed, but wondered how she was going to manage to talk when her lips felt like lead. And she couldn't imagine how she was ever going to make Allie believe that both she and Bill had loved her. Not after what Allie had overheard.

The memory of that argument had been burning bitterly in Meg ever since Bill's death. So much hurt had been inflicted, so many ugly things had been said, and there was no way now to mend any of it. No chance to make it better. And nothing she could ever say would take back Bill's words, words that must be branded on Allie's heart.

And Meg, who had been living with her mother's hatred for so many years, knew exactly what kind of pain Allie had to be feeling.

Allie spoke. "Dad didn't want me, did he?"

Oh, God, what a question. And this whole thing had gone too far for lying now. Allie knew too much. Fighting the weight that seemed to be crushing her, Meg said, "Not originally. But that doesn't mean he didn't want you after you were born, Allie. Sometimes people don't want to get pregnant. It comes as a shock, or at the wrong time. But that doesn't mean they don't change their minds when the baby comes. Your daddy doted on you. He thought the sun rose and set on you." As far as Bill was capable of such feeling, Meg thought with a hot burst of anger and resentment. She knew as well as anyone how little real feeling Bill was capable of. She'd spent her entire marriage feeling like an acquaintance. Feeling distanced.

Last night, with Earl, she hadn't felt distanced. She had felt closer to him than she had ever felt to anyone in her life. What was wrong with that? she wondered. Why should she feel as if that was a betrayal?

Allie lifted her gaze and looked at her mother. "Then why did he say those things about me ruining his life?"

"Because he was angry, sweetie. He was angry at *me*. Not at you. He would never, ever, have said those things if he'd thought you would hear them. He was trying to hurt *me*."

The girl nodded dubiously. "But he must have been feeling them all along, if he said them."

A deep pang pierced Meg's heart, driving back her depression with concern for Allie. "Honey, your dad didn't *have* to marry me. If he really didn't want to be your dad, he could have just walked away. Nobody put a shotgun to his head. He *wanted* you after he got used to the idea of having you. And you didn't ruin his life. He only said that because I was trying to use you as a reason for him not to leave me. I shouldn't have done that, Allie. That was wrong. But that's why he said what he said. To let me know that he wasn't going to stay with me just because of you. But if he'd moved out, he still would have wanted to see you every weekend. He still would have taken you camping like he often did. I'm sure of it, Allie."

"Maybe." The girl's chin quivered, then steadied. "And what about what you said? I kept you from finishing college."

"You didn't keep me from that. I was exaggerating, trying to show him how little he'd really given up because of you. He still did exactly what he was planning to do all along, Allie. He finished school, and he came back here to work in mine management. That was his plan. As for me—I wasn't all that dedicated to finishing college. Not back then. I was an art major. Passable, but not a Picasso. I might have managed a job in commercial art, but I'm just as happy working at the credit union.'' Which wasn't entirely true, but she wasn't going to tell Allie that, because she would be misinterpreted. ''And none of it matters, anyway, because there isn't one thing in the world that I'd trade you for. Not one.''

''Really?'' Allie's expression was painfully hopeful.

''Yes, really. And there isn't one thing I'd do differently if it meant not having you.''

Allie nodded, and Meg thought she saw the tiniest smile lift the corners of the child's mouth. ''It must have hurt you bad when Dad said he was leaving.''

Meg's mouth turned sour as she thought back to that day. ''It did,'' she admitted. But not in the way Allie probably thought. It had hurt her pride. It had made her feel as if she had wasted all those years she had devoted to Bill and their future together. But none of that was like the hurt to her heart and soul when she had thought she might have lost Allie. Those were superficial concerns, though that knowledge was not something she wanted to share with her daughter.

''Why was he leaving?'' Allie asked. ''Did he fall in love with someone else?''

She couldn't lie about that, even though it would have been easier. Not about something like this. ''No. He was just...tired of me. Maybe sick of me would be a better description.''

''Oh, Mom.'' Allie's expression was sad and almost pitying. ''You must have felt so bad.''

''I did. That's why I got so angry.''

"So maybe he was sick of me, too. Maybe it wasn't just you."

It was a kind thing for Allie to say, but Meg couldn't let her believe that for an instant. "He wasn't sick of you, Allie. He never would have gotten sick of you, no matter what. He loved you."

Allie's face crumpled, and large tears began to roll down her cheeks. "I wish I could believe that."

Meg's own depression went up in a puff of smoke, burned by a savage anger at Bill and at herself. Rising, she rounded the table and knelt beside Allie's chair, drawing her daughter into her arms and hugging her tightly.

"It's okay, sweetie," she murmured. "It's okay. I swear Daddy loved you. He always loved you. It was *me* he didn't love. Honest to God, he said those things to hurt *me,* not you."

But Allie's sobs continued to come, and Meg faced the horrible possibility that nothing she could say was going to make Allie feel any better about what Bill had said. The cure for that was going to have to come from somewhere inside her daughter, and it was going to take time.

But she talked anyway, as her knees began to ache on the cold, hard floor, as Allie's tears soaked her sweater, as she stroked her daughter's soft, fine hair.

"I remember the first time your dad saw you, right after you were born," she said. "He just got this huge, silly grin on his face. I think that was the happiest I ever saw him, except maybe when he was playing baseball with you. He just lit up like a neon sign, and all he said was 'Wow!'"

She could tell Allie was listening, trying to hold in her sobs so she wouldn't miss a word.

"The day you took your first step, he called everybody he knew to tell them about it. He was sure you were going to be a dancer, because you were so graceful right away. And what a kick he got out of it when you were two and started writing letters of the alphabet after seeing them on *Sesame Street*. He was the one who got you the Big Bird doll."

"Yeah?" It was a muffled sound, carried on a sniffle.

"Yeah. That was when he decided you were going to be the next Einstein. He could hardly wait for you to grow up enough to start playing T-ball. He used to sit in the middle of the floor and help you put together your wooden puzzles. You remember those, don't you? I've still got them in the closet. He bought you your first Big Wheel tricycle, too, long before I thought you were ready for it. He even had to build blocks onto the pedals and put a pillow behind you so you could reach them. But he was just so tickled when you drove it back and forth out front."

She kept on in that vein, gradually bringing up memories of the recent past so that Allie would see that her dad had loved her right up to the end. When she finally fell silent, she was hoarse and Allie's tears had stopped. The girl was resting gently against her now, all resistance and anger gone.

Meg's knees shrieked at her to get up off the floor, but she was terrified of shattering this tenuous moment of comfort her daughter had found. Finally, though, the pain became too much.

"I've got to get up, sweetie. My knees are killing me."

Allie nodded and drew back. Meg's legs didn't want to obey her at all, but she managed to lever herself upward, grimacing as she did so. "Man! That hurts."

Allie gave her a wavery smile, and Meg pulled out the chair beside her, so they could remain close.

"How do you feel?" she asked Allie. "Did I help at all?"

Allie nodded. "I feel better." It was tentative, but a step in the right direction.

"You know the problem I'm having here, don't you?"

Allie shook her head.

"I'm still so mad at your father I could smack him. I could shake him. But he's not here to yell at, and he's not here to tell you he didn't mean what he said. And that makes me madder than all the rest of it."

A small smile, like a ray of sunshine through a storm cloud, appeared on Allie's face. "I'm kinda mad at him myself."

"I can sure see why."

Allie sighed, a long, not-quite-steady sound. "He didn't mean it."

"No, honey, he *didn't* mean it. He meant it about wanting to leave me, but all of the rest it was just because he was mad at me and wanted to hurt me."

"Did you love him?"

Meg had a feeling she should have been surprised by how far back she had to go in her memory to answer that question. It was a long way back, but she didn't tell Allie that. "Yes, I did. I loved him desperately.'' For a few years. Then his essential indifference had started to take a toll on her. And little by little her feelings had faded, had become something else. Had become familiarity, loyalty, concern for her daughter. But not the romantic kind of love that had first drawn her to Bill. That had caused her to marry him.

"I'm sorry," Allie said. "He hurt you, too."

Meg hesitated, wanting to say something but not sure what. She didn't want Allie's memory of her father to be tainted by such things, but she didn't know how she could erase the basic truth of what had happened. Allie had heard the argument. Allie knew her father had been planning to leave. And when Bill had stormed out of here that day, he had sworn he was never going to come back.

"There's no point thinking about that now," Meg said. "It's best just to remember the good things. They're all that matter now."

"I guess so." After a bit, Allie reached out and linked her hand with her mother's. "When I went up into the mountains?"

"Yes?"

"I was going to kill myself."

Meg drew a sharp breath and looked at her daughter. For a few moments her throat was so tight she couldn't speak. Then she managed to say, "We kind of...thought that might be the case."

"Well, I changed my mind. Matt kind of...well, he sorta helped me see things differently. So I decided not to do it. I really *did* slip and fall, Mom. Honest."

Meg nodded and squeezed her daughter's hand.

"What about now? Do you still feel like killing yourself?"

"No. I just wish I could have talked to Daddy one last time."

That, thought Meg, was one of the saddest things she had ever heard.

Earl's intention to call Meg around ten-thirty or so and see how she was doing went up in smoke. Ben Dawson had finally decided to show up at the hospital and try to see Matt, and he wasn't in any mood to have the nurses telling him no. A couple of male nurses were summoned to hold the fort while Earl was called.

Dawson was drunk, and rip-roaring mad that they were trying to prevent him from seeing his son. When Earl arrived, the man was shouting that they had no right to keep him from his kin and threatening to beat up the two male nurses who were blocking the doorway of Matt's room.

When Dawson's eyes settled on Earl, they grew even hotter. "You!" he said, as if Earl were the source of every ill in his life.

Earl was in no mood to put up with Dawson's crap. "Get away from that door," he said, his voice steely.

"My son is in there! You can't make me leave."

"Your son wouldn't be in there if you didn't beat him. Now get away from that door."

"I never laid a finger on that boy!"

But there was something in the way Dawson's gaze shifted that said he was lying. Earl was hardly surprised.

"You ain't got nothin' on me!"

The argument wasn't improving Earl's mood, especially since he didn't have enough proof to arrest Dawson. All he had was suspicion, and based on that alone, there wasn't a whole lot he could do. "I got a boy who's getting beat up too often," he said to Dawson. "And right now, you're not exactly acting like a model citizen. I could arrest you for assault for threatening the nurses."

"They're keeping me from my boy."

"I told 'em to. You may think you're smart and sneaky, Dawson, but you're dumber than rock salt. This whole damn town knows who's beating Matt. So let me put it to you plain and clear. I better not ever see another mark on that boy. Because if I do, I am going to spend the rest of my life hounding you until I get enough to slam you in jail for the rest of your days."

"If he told you I'm hitting him, he's lying."

"He never said who was hitting him. Damn shame, because if he ever said a word, I'd have you locked up so fast your head would spin. That's all I need, Dawson. One word from Matt. Don't you ever lay another finger on him."

For an instant Earl thought Dawson was going to take a swing at him. But the man changed his mind, choosing instead to be righteously indignant. "The law's not going to tell me how to raise my boy. I only done what's best for him."

Earl's jaw tightened until he had to speak through his teeth. "Putting him in the hospital isn't what's best for him."

"You can't prove nothing. You're still trying to get even for the time I bested you in that fight."

Earl couldn't believe that Dawson was referring to a schoolyard scuffle they'd had nearly thirty years before. "I don't give a damn about that fight," he told the man. "I haven't given a damn about it in at least twenty-five years. What I give a damn about is that boy lying on the bed in the room behind you. I warned you, Dawson. I only warn once."

Matt's father glared balefully around him, then stormed away, threatening to sue the hospital, the sheriff's office and anyone else he could think of. Earl waited a bit to make sure he was gone, then went into the boy's room. Matt was looking pale and uneasy.

"He's gone, Matt. But you might want to think about this. Once you get out of here, I can't protect you anymore, not as long as you don't tell me who's doing this to you. Just think about it."

It would only be a day or so before Matt was out of here, Earl thought as he left the hospital and checked the parking lot to make sure Dawson's beat-up truck was gone. In another day or so, casts notwithstanding, that boy would be prey to his father again. Dawson might even take it out on Matt for what had just happened.

The thought made Earl's gut twist.

By the time he got back to the office, it was past noon. By now Meg must be wondering what had become of him, why he had sneaked out so early and why he hadn't called. After last night, he owed her more than that, and he knew it as well as anyone.

But he was still uneasy, and his hand hesitated over the telephone. He felt guilty about what had happened between them. Not because he didn't want Meg, and not because he hadn't wanted to make love to her, but because she was his best friend's widow. Because he felt he might have taken advantage of her in her emotional state last night.

Even though he had repeatedly asked if she was sure, his conscience was stinging him. She hadn't exactly been in the best state of mind. She'd had some kind of emotional break that had lasted hours, and he had the feeling she'd been clinging to him in desperation more than desire.

He should have been strong enough to stop it. For both their sakes. But he hadn't, and he castigated himself for his weakness, even though there was no escaping that he'd been wanting Meg for years.

That shamed him, too, but the secret was out, and he could no longer hide it from himself. Could no longer pretend that he hadn't been lusting after Meg ever since he'd first set eyes on her. Maybe he hadn't betrayed Bill in fact, but he'd betrayed him countless times in thought.

And that didn't make Earl very proud of himself right now.

But that was the least of it. The most important thing was that he might have wounded Meg last night. That possibility really concerned him, and he didn't know how he was going to square it with himself or her if she was feeling like hell about it now.

She had trusted him, and he'd blown it. No other way to look at it. But he needed to call her right now, to keep her from feeling that he'd used her. Whatever other problems she might have with what had passed between them, considering that Bill was right in the middle of it all, he didn't want her to wonder about *his* motives.

So he picked up the phone at last and dialed, and sweated bullets until she answered.

"Hi, Meg," he said. Oh, God, what a way to start. That husky note in his voice was a dead giveaway how he melted the instant he heard her voice. He'd been able to hide that for a long time, so what the hell was wrong with him today?

"Hi," she said. Guarded. Uncertain. He felt his heart sink.

"I'm sorry I had to leave so early," he said. "I needed to get to work."

"Sure."

Well, that wasn't very encouraging. What now? His mind seemed to have gone utterly blank. There was no way to make casual conversation when he was this worried. Finally he said, "Are you okay?"

"I'm fine."

Nothing more. No softening. No encouragement. He ground his teeth. "Meg...about last night."

"I don't want to discuss it, Earl."

Worse and worse. "Okay. Fine. I'll see you later." He hung up without waiting to hear if she said anything more. Then he sat for a long time, staring out the window, ignoring the paperwork on his desk, thinking about how he had probably betrayed Meg's friendship, and how life was going to be damn empty if Meg wasn't a part of it anymore.

19

Allie was sitting out on the front steps, bundled up in a jacket, watching night fall over the world, when Earl pulled up. He got out of his car and came to sit on the step beside her.

Neither of them said anything for a long time. Allie scooped up some pebbles and tossed them into the carpet of pine needles nearby. The snow was melting away, returning the world to its more usual late September hues.

"Uncle Earl?"

"Yeah, Chipmunk?"

"Did my daddy love me?"

Earl felt his heart ripping in two. Turning, he put his arms around the child whom he loved as if she were his own and drew her head onto his shoulder. "He loved you, Allie. He loved you more than he ever loved anybody. Honest to God."

She nodded against his shoulder, and he was relieved to see she wasn't crying. "That's what Mom said."

"She's right. Your daddy doted on you. You were

the best thing that ever happened to him in his entire life.''

''Okay.'' She gave a long sigh, and he felt her relax the last little bit, until she was a soft, slender reed in his arms. He hugged her a little closer and closed his eyes against a sudden wave of emotion.

''Your mom loves you, too, Allie. More than life. She'd do anything to make you happy. And so would I. Don't you ever, ever doubt that we all love you.''

She sighed again, and her hand curled on his chest. ''Mom was reminding me of all the good times I had with Daddy.''

''There were a lot of them, weren't there? All those times we went camping, and the time the three of us went down to Denver to try out that new arcade.''

''And I beat you both.''

''Miserably. I've never been so embarrassed in my life.''

A little laugh escaped Allie.

''But remember how proud your dad was of you? He was proud of everything you did. Like the time you caught that huge fish.''

''What kind of fish was it?''

''I haven't any idea. I've never seen one like it. But it was an awful lot of fish for a little girl. And you wanted to throw it back, so we did.''

''And remember the mountain lion we saw on the hike that time?''

Indeed he did. The three of them had been traipsing along merrily, enjoying a beautiful summer day in the mountains, when they'd come around a corner and all of a sudden they were looking at a huge, tawny cat sunning itself on a flat rock. They'd frozen, then he and Bill, as one, had tucked Allie behind them. She'd peeked at the cat from between their bodies.

The cat had wakened and looked at them with something akin to disdain before stretching hugely, then wandering off into the woods. Several minutes had passed while Earl and Bill waited for the cat to get comfortably away before they moved again. Allie's eyes had been as big as saucers.

There were a lot of memories like that, and he could see them dancing in Allie's eyes as she sat up and smiled at him. "He didn't mean it."

"No, he didn't mean it. He was just angry."

"I feel bad about Mom, though. He really hurt her. And he wasn't going to take it back."

"You shouldn't worry about that now. I think your mom kind of knew what was happening before he said anything to her. People usually do."

She nodded and looked off into the trees. "It's too bad they didn't get to make up."

"It sure is." He didn't tell her that Bill had never made up with anyone over anything he'd done in his life. She didn't need to know that.

"He was okay, wasn't he? My dad, I mean. He wasn't a bad person."

"Good God, no! A little careless sometimes, but he wasn't a bad person at all. You remember him well enough to know that."

"Sometimes I find it hard to remember him at all."

"How do you mean?"

"I don't know. It's like he's all fuzzy. When I get out pictures, I can remember him better. But...mostly I remember him as a feeling."

"That's probably how most of us remember after a time."

"Do you think he would have driven slower if I'd been in the car with him?"

Earl's heart lurched. "No, sweetie, I don't. And don't blame yourself for that. He wasn't really driving that fast. It was just too fast because of the ice. Ice killed him, Allie. Not you. Not your mom. Not even his own temper. Ice killed him." Not that he really believed that, but he was convinced it wouldn't do anyone any good for Allie to believe otherwise.

A little while later Meg came out of the house, wearing a jacket, and sat on the other side of Allie. None of them said anything for a long time as the light faded from the world.

Earl could feel the sorrow in the air. Not a wrenching grief like they'd all been feeling before, but just a bittersweet sorrow, as if they were saying goodbye to something. It seemed to rise up the valley with the night and slip slowly out from under the trees until it filled the world. He let the feeling wash over him and wondered what it was going to mean. Especially since he still had some major fences to mend around here, judging by his phone call with Meg earlier.

But he couldn't worry about those fences right now. Instead, he let the feeling fill him, let the sense of goodbye run through him.

Things, both good and bad, came and went in life. And there were times, like now, when he would sit and remind himself that what seemed important now would seem insignificant in a year's time. That a year from now he would be worrying about something else and probably wouldn't even remember these moments with Meg and Allie beside him. Wouldn't remember the feeling that he was letting go of something important.

Sometimes thinking that way would soothe him even when the worst was happening. But tonight the thought only made him sadder somehow, as if he never wanted to lose these moments. As if forgetting them would somehow be the worst loss of all.

The door behind them opened, and Vivian poked her head out. "Dinner's ready. I set a place for you, Earl, so don't be thinking about leaving."

Funny, he thought, how he and Vivian had managed to come to an understanding. Little more than a week ago he would have thought they would be enemies until their dying days. He wondered if he would ever know what had changed her mind about him.

Then he wondered if it really mattered.

Meg, he noticed, didn't look at him as she rose to go inside. Allie took his hand, though, dragging him along. Well, he told himself, two out of three wasn't bad. The thought made him smile wryly.

Vivian had cooked a big turkey, and Earl's stomach started rumbling the minute he saw it. "Turkey and stuffing," he said aloud. "I died and wcnt to heaven, right?"

As far as Vivian was concerned, he couldn't have said anything more right. She actually smiled at him. Meg's gaze scraped over him as if she didn't really see him. Allie looked uncertainly at her mother as if she was wondering why Meg was being so distant to Earl.

Great. Another problem for the girl to deal with. Earl had a sudden urge to shake Meg until her teeth rattled. After the last ten days, he couldn't believe that she would do something yet again to upset Allie.

The meal was suitable for a Thanksgiving feast, complete with lighted red tapers in candle holders, and the mood should have been cheerful. Instead, it was almost somber. Allie tried to talk about going back to school the next day. Vivian and Earl encouraged her, but then that petered out. Earl picked up the ball and talked about his workday, eventually coming around to Matt Dawson's father.

Allie's interest perked up considerably. "I want to visit Matt."

Meg responded for the first time. "We'll do that tomorrow after school, if you want."

"He might not still be there," Earl warned them. "Broken bones can go home."

"But what about his dad?" Allie asked. "What if he hurts Matt again?"

"What Matt needs to do," he said, "is tell me who's doing this to him. If he'd just *tell* me, I could get him out of that house and into foster care. But unless he's willing to speak up, there's not a whole lot I can do until someone actually sees it happen. So far all he says is that he's getting in fights with some unnamed persons."

Meg spoke. "But we remove small children from homes when there's no evidence except bruises or broken bones."

"This is different. Matt is old enough to point a finger, and he's pointing it away from his father."

Meg shook her head and looked down at her plate. Between them, the gay red candles wavered and sputtered in a ghostly draft. "It's so sad," she said.

"I'll talk to him," Allie announced. "I'll talk to him just the way he talked to me. Maybe I can make him see how stupid he's being."

Earl spoke. "I wouldn't start out by telling him he's being stupid."

Allie drew herself up. "I know better than that, Uncle Earl."

"Just checking."

She gave him a grin, a familiar expression he hadn't seen in too damn long. Meg caught the look, and for a few seconds a smile flitted over her own face. Then her expression set again, and he saw a reflection of Vivian in her face. The idea that gentle, sweet Meg might become like Vivian saddened his soul.

And from the way Vivian was looking at Meg, Earl got the distinct impression that the woman wanted to talk to her daughter but couldn't, in present company.

So after dinner he offered to do the dishes with Allie's help. Allie, who was still getting around on crutches, looked at him like he was crazy.

"You can help," he said. "You can sit there in that chair and kibitz, okay? Tell me where everything goes."

Vivian took Meg's elbow. "You come with me, young lady," she said sternly. "We need to talk."

Meg looked as if she was about to refuse, but after a moment she shrugged and followed her mother.

"Whew!" Allie said. "I wonder what Mom's in trouble about?"

"Probably nothing. But that's a heck of a way to start a conversation."

Allie giggled. "I always get uptight when somebody calls me young lady. I know I'm in for it."

Earl nodded and started carrying the plates from the table to the counter, scraping them in the trash can as he passed by. "Yup. I used to hate being called young man. Or, worse, Earl Patrick Sanders."

"Oh, yeah! The *whole* name." She said it portentously. "Alexandra Bethany Williams. That's even worse than young lady."

"What I always wondered was, is there some school parents go to so they learn how to say that? Because every parent I ever knew does the same thing."

"Teachers do the young lady, young man thing. Not the whole name."

"Probably because they don't know the whole name. Which is a blessing, I guess, or the whole school would have started calling me Earl Patrick Sanders."

She laughed but looked at him curiously. "Were you in trouble a lot?"

"Let's say I was in trouble more than I should have been."

"Kind of like Matt?"

"Kind of worse than Matt."

"Oooh." She looked both amazed and somehow pleased at this notion of him. Earl hoped he wasn't saying exactly the wrong thing to a young, impressionable mind. "Well, I cleaned up my act eventually. I finally figured out that I was just making things harder on myself."

Allie nodded. "It's never fun to be in trouble."

"Nope. But some kids do it to get attention. Unfortunately, they get the wrong kind of attention. I sure did. So finally I got smart and straightened myself out, and look at me now.''

''Yup. The stodgy sheriff of the county.''

''Stodgy?'' He paused with a plate in each hand. ''I'm not stodgy.''

She giggled, and the sound did his heart good. She, at least, was going to be all right, he thought as he resumed doing the dishes. But kids were wonderfully resilient.

He wasn't so sure about her mother.

Vivian took Meg into the den and told her to sit in the armchair. The moment reminded Meg strongly of all the times in her childhood when one of her parents wanted to have a ''word'' with her. She resented the feeling, but right now she didn't seem to have the will to tell her mother to go stuff it. The last twenty-four hours had taken a serious toll on her, and while she wasn't as completely withdrawn as she had been last night, she was still hiding in some safe little cubbyhole in her own mind. Away from thoughts of Bill and Allie, away from memories of what she had done last night with Earl. Away from the fears of what he must think of her now.

But Vivian's thoughts were on a very different track, and she made that immediately evident. ''We need to talk about the last fifteen years.''

Meg looked up at her, feeling the first inkling of surprise. ''Sure,'' she said sourly. ''We can probably cover the whole time period in about fifteen minutes.''

Vivian put her hands on her broad hips and

frowned down at her. "We're going to talk about me and you, mostly me, and we *can* cover that in fifteen minutes. If that's all you can spare me."

Meg felt the sting of embarrassment. "Sorry," she said, and tried to withdraw back into the safe cubby. But Vivian wasn't going to let her escape feeling.

"I was wrong," the older woman said flatly.

Meg looked up at her, disbelief drawing her out again. "You?"

"Me. I was wrong. I've been wrong about a lot of things, and it's time I owned up to it."

"No, you weren't wrong. Dad had a heart attack because of me. And I wasn't paying enough attention to Allie." Meg's voice caught, then steadied. She refused to give in to the sorrow that kept wanting to clog her throat. Sorrow for omissions, sorrow for actions, sorrow for not being a better person.

"You didn't kill your father," Vivian said. "It was easy for me to blame you, but Earl is right. The shock wouldn't have killed him if he didn't already have a bad heart. It was just…it was just easier to blame you." Vivian sat down suddenly, as if her legs couldn't hold her anymore. "I blame too much, and I blame too easy, and it's time I got around to admitting that some things just happen. It's easier to be mad, Meg. Far easier to be mad than to feel anything else. It's the way I've always been."

Meg nodded, surprised that her mother was showing so much self-awareness. Wondering where all this insight had come from.

"What you told me about Bill…about him forcing himself on you…it got me to thinking. You should have been able to tell me that back then, child. I was stewing around here, wondering why, if it was true, you didn't tell me back then, and I finally figured it out. You knew I'd just get mad at you anyway.''

Meg nodded, noting that her mother's eyes were moist, and felt something fierce rising in her, something very close to angry vindication.

Vivian sighed and pulled a handkerchief out of her apron pocket to dab at her eyes. ''I guess that means I was a bad mother. You were hurt, and you knew I'd get mad at *you*.'' Vivian shook her head.

Something inside Meg fractured, and a trickle of warmth toward her mother began to flow through her. It was the first genuine warmth she'd felt toward the woman in at least fifteen years. ''You weren't always…a bad mother. Not always.''

''I wasn't good enough,'' Vivian said stubbornly. ''You should have been able to come to me when you were hurt. But you couldn't. And I attacked you for things that weren't your fault. Maybe there were times when I did right by you, but I figure there weren't many of them. So…now I need to fix some of what I did wrong. God knows, it's my Christian duty.''

''Fix what?''

''I need to tell you that you didn't kill your father. And that if I'd known Bill had forced himself on you, I never would have let you marry that no-good skunk. I'd have kept you at home and helped you raise Allie myself. And, frankly, I don't know how you managed to stay married to that man for fifteen years. He always treated you like you were of no account.''

''Not always, Mom.'' She had to catch her breath as pain tightened her chest. ''Not always.''

"How would you know? The way I treated you—well, it set you up for that man. Probably even made him look good to you. Far as I can see, he was a good daddy, and he was a good worker at his job, but he wasn't much of a husband to you. Always struck me he thought you were some kind of trophy to show off and then put up on the shelf."

Those words so accurately described how Meg had grown to feel during the course of her marriage that she couldn't speak. She closed her eyes against the pain that threatened to overwhelm her. All these years...all these years. She'd denied it to herself, excused it because Bill had been forced to marry her because of Allie. Had told herself that he really loved her, because if he hadn't, he would have left her. Had well and truly deluded herself into believing she had a perfect marriage.

But now...now she saw it for what it was. A house of cards she had created herself, a delusion she'd insisted on. Bill had been there for Allie, not for her. Had Allie not turned into a surprise delight that even Bill hadn't been prepared for, Bill would have left years ago. And finally even Allie hadn't been enough to make him stay.

Whatever Bill had wanted at his deepest core, she knew she hadn't been it. And in the end she had to admit to herself that Bill hadn't been what she had needed, either. It hadn't been bad. It just hadn't been...wonderful. Not even great.

She had told herself that was the normal course of passion, that it burned hotly for a few months, then settled down. But she'd never felt essential to Bill. And with brutal honesty she now admitted that he'd never been essential to her, either. The whole thing had been a sham.

"Sorry," Vivian said. "I shouldn't be so blunt about your marriage. I know you loved him."

"Did I? I can't remember now...." It was almost a plea.

"You did," Vivian said. "I saw the way you lit up when he came into the room. You loved him. Sorry to say, he never deserved it, but you loved him. He was a shallow man, Meg. I saw it all along, but he was what you wanted, so I kept my mouth shut. Probably the one time in my entire life I was silent when I should have been talking."

Even through her pain, Meg felt a smile tug at the corner of her mouth. She had never guessed Vivian had it in her to keep any opinion to herself. "It's okay," she heard herself saying. "That was one mistake I had to make for myself."

"I suppose." Vivian shook her head. "That's part of the reason I was quiet about it. When a woman has that look in her eye, she's never going to listen to reason. But to get back to my failings..."

"Mom, it's okay. You don't have to do this." She suddenly found it impossible to stand the thought of Vivian humbling herself. As often as she'd been furious with her mother, despite the many criticisms she could have offered, she relied on her mother to be righteous and confident, whether right or wrong.

"No," said Vivian firmly. "I have to say it for the good of my soul, and you need to hear it so you don't spend the rest of your life thinking you disappointed me and broke my heart. The fact is, I've been too hard and too harsh. I excused myself because that was the way I was raised. But then I look at you and see how different you are with Allie, and I realize that I should have learned the lessons of my childhood better. What hurt me as a child certainly hurt you. I should have been a kinder person than my mother.''

That was such a sad thing to say, Meg thought, feeling an urge for the first time in a long time to reach out toward her mother. ''We can make it better now, Mom.''

''Maybe.'' Vivian suddenly looked old and weary. ''I'm getting on, Meg. I'm sixty-five years old. I don't know how good I'm going to be at changing bad habits at this stage. But I'll try. And that brings me to another thing.''

''Yes?''

''What I said about you letting Allie run wild. You're more casual about child-raising than I was. But I don't see that it's doing that girl any real harm. Except for this bad patch we've just been having, she seems healthy, happy and bright, and she's got a good heart. So you couldn't be all that wrong with what you're doing.''

That was a huge admission coming from Vivian, and Meg's heart swelled. ''Thanks, Mom. I've been feeling awful about this whole mess. I wish I'd cut out my tongue before I ever said anything that hurt Allie.''

''You didn't know she was listening. People say things when they get angry. God knows *I* do. And I think the child is beginning to understand that.''

''I hope so.'' She thought of her daughter in the kitchen with Earl. Even here, with the door closed, she could hear the faint sounds of Allie's laughter.

The girl *was* feeling a little better. God willing, Allie would keep on laughing.

"One more thing," Vivian said. "Then I'll let you go. Meg, if you find a chance for happiness, take it. Don't let what happened between you and Bill make you feel so guilty you think you don't deserve to be happy. Because it's high time you were."

Then Vivian was gone, and Meg was left sitting there with her memories, her fears, and even the faint inkling of some hopes she had buried for so long that she could hardly remember them. She had settled for the way things were. She was still settling.

For a long time she had told herself that was a mature attitude. Nothing was perfect. You made the best of what you had. The secret of happiness was being happy with what you had.

All the old aphorisms came back to her, all the little sayings that had guided her throughout much of her adult life. But now she found herself wondering if they were wise statements or merely useful ones. It seemed to her now that settling for what she had had merely left her in a state of stasis, going from one day to the next with little hope and fewer dreams.

Maybe it wasn't enough to be happy with what you had. Maybe human beings needed dreams to aspire to. Otherwise, why not just sit down in front of a TV and let the years slip away?

That was what she had been doing, she realized. After the first few years of her marriage, when she had realized that Bill was never going to love her the way she wanted to be loved, that all her dreams had merely been modified versions of *The Donna Reed Show* and *Father Knows Best,* ideas that hadn't a hope

346   *Rachel Lee*

in hell of ever being realized, she had given up. She had accepted. She had settled.

She had told herself she was happy. But she had never really been happy. So many parts of her had been unfulfilled. And Allie had become her raison d'être, the only thing that brought joy to her every day. Beyond that, she had been living in a flat emotional landscape.

Even the last year had been a desert. Not because of grief as much as because she had not wanted to face how little she had actually lost. Bill's removal from her life hadn't been the devastation she had expected. She'd been laboring under a terrible burden of guilt because of their argument, but she hadn't been laboring under impossible grief.

She had been saddened, yes. She had even missed him. She had wished he hadn't died. But his passing hadn't gutted her heart. It had simply left her a little emptier than she had been all along.

It pained her to admit it. Pained her to realize that she'd lived fifteen years of her life in an incredible state of denial, doing all the right things because it was expected. Not because they satisfied or fulfilled her.

Except for Allie. Always except for Allie. Every bit of love in her had fixed on her daughter. She wondered if Allie had ever sensed that. Maybe part of the girl's problems over the past year had been realizing she was the only thing in her mother's life that really mattered. What a terrible burden for a child.

No wonder Allie had been escaping more and more into the Internet chat rooms. The child needed her own space. She didn't need to feel that her mother depended on her for conversation and entertainment.

But she might well have felt that way. Meg had pretty much abandoned all her friendships since Bill's death—mostly, she admitted now, because she felt guilty that she didn't feel the kind of grief her friends seemed to expect her to feel. Because the pretense of feeling it had exhausted her. Well, it was time to get off her duff and reestablish those friendships. Time to rebuild her own life.

She was in the midst of those thoughts when Allie crutched into the room and sat facing her. "You okay?" her daughter asked.

"Grandma and I were ironing out some of our problems. I'm fine. A lot better."

"Good. I was worried about you."

Meg felt like a slug. Allie shouldn't be worrying about her, not at fourteen. "Sweetie, I'll be fine. I'm always fine. Sometimes I just get a little screwed up in my thinking is all. I'm sorry I scared you."

Allie shrugged. "We're even. I scared you pretty bad, too, didn't I?"

"That's a fact."

Allie nodded. "I kind of think it's been hard on both of us. I thought Dad didn't love me. And you know he didn't love you. It would have been nice if we'd had a chance to talk to him before he died."

"I imagine people feel that way every time someone dies."

"Probably." The girl sighed and settled back in her chair. Meg, moved by an overwhelming surge of love and concern, rose and went to sit on the arm of Allie's chair, where she could stroke her daughter's silky hair and offer the comfort of touch.

"I haven't been the best mother in the past year," Meg said. "I've been too self-absorbed."

"Like we haven't all been?" Allie said with teenage sarcasm. "We've all been acting kind of weird. There was a lot of stuff to deal with."

"And do you think we've dealt with it?"

Allie shrugged. "Some of it, maybe."

Meg realized this was the most adult conversation they'd ever shared, and she found herself savoring the moment, even as she realized that she had somehow overlooked just how much Allie had matured in the last year. "Do you feel better about your dad now?"

"I guess. Both you and Uncle Earl think he really loved me. You would know."

Propelled by concern, Meg slipped off the chair arm and knelt facing her daughter. "I want *you* to know that, Allie. Whatever else was wrong in this house, however stupid your father and I were about some things, there was one thing we did right. We both loved you more than anyone or anything else in our lives."

Allie nodded, and it seemed her eyes weren't as haunted as they had been for the last eight months. "I believe you, Mom. I really do. I'm not worried about it anymore. I got to thinking that it's stupid to let a few things Dad said when he was angry ruin everything else."

"And what about not being with him in the car? Is that still bothering you?"

Allie looked away for a minute. When she returned her gaze to Meg's, her expression was sad. "A little.

Part of me thinks it's really bad that I'm still here, having fun, going on hikes and all the rest of it, when he's dead. But then I think, how stupid can I be? I didn't die. That means I have a right to live.''

"That's a remarkably adult observation," Meg told her. "It's not unusual for people to feel guilty that they're still alive when someone they know has died."

"Do you feel that way?"

"Sometimes. I felt that way when *my* dad died. And I felt that way a little when your father died. Except that, since I had you, I had something good to live for. Not that I've been doing a really great job of it."

"You haven't been so bad." Allie gave her a smile. "It's been a tough year. So I'll talk to the psychologist at school tomorrow, and I'll work all this stuff out the way I need to. But what about you, Mom? Who's going to help you?"

"You know what? I'm doing a whole lot better after this past week."

"Why? I thought I almost killed you with worry."

"You did, sweetie. But you also made me face a lot of things. Getting all this out in the open has made me feel a whole lot better."

Except about Earl. Last night was still burning in her memory, along with embarrassment and humiliation. But Earl was gone when she and Allie emerged from the study, and after Allie went to bed, Meg was alone in a silent, echoing house.

And her heart felt as if it were full of snow.

20

Meg got off work early the next afternoon and picked Allie up at school to take her to the hospital to see Matt Dawson. Matt was due to be released the next morning, but in the meantime he was still in bed and on painkillers.

Meg talked with him for a few minutes, but it made him uncomfortable, so she excused herself and left him alone with Allie. She found a vacant chair in the main lobby where she could wait comfortably and tried to read a magazine.

But all she could think about was Earl. Earl had called her yesterday morning, but she'd been so embarrassed that she'd practically choked when she tried to speak. He'd come over last night to see Allie and had hardly spoken a word to her. But then, she'd hardly spoken a word to him. Since then, he hadn't even tried to call. Not that that was such a long period of time. Sometimes they didn't speak for up to a week.

But that was when they had been just friends. They weren't just friends anymore. Something momentous had happened between them, and she knew *she* wasn't going to be able to return to business as usual.

But it occurred to her that she didn't know what she expected to change. Or how she wanted it to change. Or if she wanted anything to change at all.

And maybe that was at the root of her entire problem.

Allie had an agenda, and she sensed that Matt knew it. He tried not to look at her and kept mumbling things about how he couldn't wait to get out of this shit-hole, and how sick he was of having people hovering over him every minute.

Allie ignored his language, guessing that he was trying to shock her, and refused to be sidetracked. "What are you going to do?" she demanded.

"Do? I already told you what I'm going to do. I'm going to get out of this place."

"I mean what are you going to do about your father?"

"Nothing. I don't have to do anything about my old man."

Allie sighed and walked around the bed to the other side, so she could look into his face. She half expected him to turn away again, but he didn't. "Remember up on the mountain?" she asked.

"What about it?"

"You said you wouldn't kill yourself because you weren't going to give anybody the satisfaction."

"So?"

"Well, you talked me out of killing myself."

"Great." He didn't sound especially thrilled about that, but she saw something different in his gaze. As

if it really mattered to him. That gave her the courage
to face him with her hands on her hips and say
sternly, "So you lied to me."

"I never lied to you."

"Yes, you did, Matt Dawson. You said you
wouldn't kill yourself because you didn't want to give
anyone the satisfaction."

"I'm not gonna kill myself!"

"I don't know what else you call what you're doing. Your dad just keeps beating you up worse and
worse. What do you think is going to happen when
you get out of here? Especially after Uncle Earl
wouldn't let your dad see you."

For a few moments Matt looked wildly angry, and
Allie had to resist the urge to step back.

"Stop it!" he said hotly.

"No, I won't stop it. You're committing suicide,
Matt. This time he put you in the hospital. Next time
he might kill you. And what good is that going to do
anybody? Your dad'll go to prison for the rest of his
life. You'll be dead. And your mom…"

"Leave my mother out of it."

"No. Why should I? She ought to be protecting
you. If your dad goes to jail for killing you, she probably will, too."

"She doesn't have anything to do with it."

"Yes, she does!"

"Get out of here!"

"No."

He closed his eyes and turned his head away, shutting her out. But Allie had gone so far already that
she wasn't prepared to walk out. Instead, she pulled
a chair close to the bed and sat, waiting. After a long

time, he seemed to grow calm again, but he still wouldn't look at her.

"Just tell me one thing, Matt," Allie said finally. "Why are you letting him do this to you?"

It was a while before he looked at her, and when he did, his gaze was haunted and pained. "So he doesn't do it to my mother."

Allie caught her breath and felt her heart beginning to hammer. She couldn't imagine such a situation, and it appalled her. And scared her. Maybe the things her dad had said to her mother weren't that bad after all. She didn't know why, but the thought of Matt's dad hitting him didn't shock her as much as the idea that Matt was getting beaten up to protect his mother.

And worse, she couldn't understand why Matt suddenly looked so ashamed, as if *he* had done something wrong. He didn't have anything to apologize for. But she *did* understand something else.

"Your dad can't hit either of you if he's in jail. And if you tell Sheriff Sanders that he did this to you, he'll be in jail a long time." Allie hoped that was true. She didn't have any idea how long you went to jail for beating somebody up. But it had to be a long time, at least long enough for Matt to finish growing up in one piece. "Your mom would be safe, too, Matt."

"He won't do anything."

"Who? The sheriff? Yes, he will. You don't know how bad he wants to put your dad in jail for hitting you."

Matt didn't answer. But he closed his eyes again.

"Tell him, Matt. Just tell him. Then, when you get out of here tomorrow, your dad won't be waiting to smash your head in with a baseball bat. He won't be able to touch you."

He hunched his shoulders, as if trying to escape what she was saying, then winced as he jolted some bruised or broken part of his body.

"Look at you!" Allie said desperately, her voice rising. "Just look at you, Matt! Nobody has a right to do that to you. Nobody! He needs to be in jail."

There was a silence so long that Allie fancied she could hear every single crack in her heart growing deeper. Matt had helped her when she needed it, and she couldn't stand the thought of not being able to help him. Especially since she really liked him.

"Matt?" She spoke tentatively, despairingly, as a lone tear ran down her cheek. "Matt. Please."

He opened his eyes, saw the tear on her cheek, and something in his face changed. He stared at her. Then, at long last, he said, "Okay. I'll tell the sheriff."

Allie didn't wait for him to change his mind. She jumped up from her chair, clapping her hands with relief. "I'll get my mom to call him right now."

"Allie, wait...."

"No, I'm not going to wait, and you're not going to change your mind. I'm getting Uncle Earl right now." Then she leaned over the bed, and dropped a shy kiss on his bruised cheek. "It'll get better now, you'll see. Nobody's ever going to hurt you again."

Then she grabbed her crutches and hurried from the room and hunted up her mother. Meg looked up with concern as she heard Allie's swift approach. She dropped her magazine at once and stood up. "Allie, what's wrong? You're crying."

"It's okay, Mom. Mom, you gotta call Uncle Earl

right now. Matt's going to tell him who beat him up. And, Mom?''

"Yes?''

"Mom, I love you to pieces." Balancing on one leg, Allie threw her arms around Meg, holding her so tightly that Meg could feel her ribs creak. But, oh, God, it felt so good.

"I love you, too, sweetie.''

Allie smiled up at her. "Everything's gonna be okay, Mom. I promise. Call Uncle Earl while I keep Matt company. I don't want him to change his mind.''

Meg watched her daughter crutch away down the hall to Matt's room, feeling as if a whirlwind had just blown through her life, sweeping away a year's worth of cobwebs. *Mom, I love you to pieces. Everything's gonna be okay.* And for some reason, Meg believed her.

Grabbing her purse, she went to call Earl.

The call from Meg made Earl's heart leap. Maybe she had forgiven him for not being there when she woke up yesterday. But as soon as she started talking, his heart started to sink. Then he realized he was being a jackass, because what she was saying was some of the best news he'd heard in a while.

"Matt wants to talk to me?" he repeated, hoping he hadn't misunderstood what she said Allie had said.

"That's right. Allie says he wants to tell you who beat him up.''

"I'll be right there.''

On the way out the front door, he grabbed Sam, who was just coming on duty. "You're coming with me. I want two of us to hear this.''

Sam, who was looking a little hangdog this afternoon, followed him.

Something had happened to the weather since lunchtime. The instant Earl stepped outside, the cold air punched him like a fist. "Damn!" he said to Sam, and hurried to zip his jacket. "Who opened the north gate?"

"Cold, isn't it? You ask me, we're in for one hell of a winter. I can see it now. Three hundred inches of snow instead of two hundred."

"If it keeps on like this, it'll be too cold to snow." But he was exaggerating, and he knew it. One thing for sure, though, it was early in the year for this.

"So what's up?" Sam asked after they climbed into his car and pulled away from the building.

"Meg called. It seems Matt Dawson's ready to say who's been beating him up."

"Well, yee-hah! It's about damn time."

"I'm just hoping he doesn't change his mind before we get there. And that's why I want you there. If both of us hear him say it, he'll have a hard time backing down later."

"You think he'd do that? I mean, he's refused to say who it was for a long time now. If he's decided to talk, he must have given it a lot of thought."

"Or not. But I do know I gotta get Dawson off the streets before that kid gets out of the hospital."

"That shouldn't be too hard. I saw him going into the saloon not five minutes ago. He's probably flush, since today's payday at the hardware store where his wife works."

"Yeah, probably."

"Yeah, I figure he'll be drinking for the next couple of hours."

They pulled into the hospital parking lot, and Earl spared a second to admire the view. The hospital was on a hill, and from the lot it was possible to see most of the valley and small hills where Whisper Creek nestled. In the late-afternoon light, everything looked golden. And cold, he remembered as the wind snaked into the collar of his coat. Then he realized he had paused because he was reluctant to see Meg. Stupid.

He strode into the hospital with Sam beside him, ignoring the looks from people who wondered why two cops were here. He didn't bother to enlighten them.

He saw Meg first. She was sitting in the waiting room and stood up the instant she saw him. "Allie's still with Matt," she said almost apologetically, as if she expected him to be annoyed that she was still here. "She's afraid he might change his mind."

"Great. That's why we hurried. And that's why we're both here. Makes it harder for him to change his mind later."

Meg nodded.

And Earl fought a totally inappropriate urge to reach out, take her into his arms and ask her if she was going to keep him in misery for the rest of his days. To ask her if she was okay. If he could do anything to make her life better. Hell, he was going nuts. His thoughts weren't following any kind of logical path at all. He forced himself to look away.

"Let's go, Sam."

Leaving Meg behind in the waiting room was, incredibly enough, one of the most difficult things he'd ever done. And that was a sure sign he'd lost his ever-loving mind.

Matt looked sullen when he saw Earl and Sam, but Allie's face lit up like Christmas. "Uncle Earl!" She greeted him with a warm hug. He considered making her wait outside, then decided the boy was less likely to back down from what he'd said if Allie was right there.

"How you doing, Matt?" he asked.

"Fine."

"You look like you went nine rounds with Mike Tyson, son. It's gotta be hurting."

Matt shrugged.

Earl stifled a sigh and waited while Sam balanced his clipboard on the bedside table and took out a pen. "Okay," he said. "Allie's mom says you want to make a statement about who beat you up."

Matt's eyes drifted to Allie, as if he was reconsidering. Allie stepped forward. "Tell him, Matt. Nobody can help you if you don't tell. Anyway, he already knows. He just needs a witness, right, Uncle Earl?"

"That's right. You won't be saying anything I don't already know. I just need *you* to say it, son."

"What happens then?"

"I go pick up your father and put him in a cell. And if I have a single word to say about it, the man won't ever see the light of day again until you're safely grown up and moved away."

"And my mom?"

"Nothing will happen to your mom. Although if she's got an ounce of brains, she'll move away before your dad gets out of prison."

Matt nodded slowly, then looked at Allie.

"All you have to do," she said, "is tell the truth."

Earl felt touched, hearing her say that, because it was something he'd said to her more than once as she was growing up. *All you have to do is tell the truth.* Maybe it was high time he started practicing what he preached.

Matt drew a deep breath, gave a slight shake of his head, then said, "Okay. Okay. My dad beats me up. He gets drunk and mean and wants to hit somebody, and I'm there. And I guess I always give him an excuse for it. Like when I was gone up the mountain with Allie overnight. He got really pissed at me for not being home."

"That's no excuse to do that to you." Earl glanced at Sam, who was writing industriously on the report form. "How many times has he done this to you?"

Matt shook his head. "I don't know. On and off since I was twelve."

"Once a week?"

"I guess. Yeah, pretty much. Pretty much every time Mom gets paid. Sometimes it's not so bad."

"This time was the worst?" Obviously, but he wanted the kid to talk about it, to give them as much as he could.

"It's the first time he ever hit me with a baseball bat. Usually it's his fists."

"Do you fight back?"

Matt shook his head and suddenly looked closer to nine or ten than sixteen. "What's the point?" he asked. "It just makes him madder."

"What about running away?"

"No." Matt looked away and swallowed hard. "No. He'd just beat my mother."

Earl questioned him for a while longer, dragging out details that could be confirmed by other people, people who remembered the boy's bruises and could tie them to his testimony. Nearly an hour later, he felt he had enough.

"That's it, Matt." He leaned over and touched the boy's shoulder. "Chances are good your dad'll cop a plea and you won't have to testify against him. And tomorrow, when you get out of here...?"

Matt nodded and looked questioningly at him.

"You're coming home with me, okay?"

For the first time in days Matt smiled. Earl had the uncomfortable feeling that he was the target of some hero worship. Well, that would wear off quick enough once the kid was living with him.

Putting his arm around Allie's shoulder, he took her back out to Meg. Sam, with a finely tuned instinct that Earl had always appreciated, hung back.

"You should be proud of Allie, Meg," Earl told her. "She convinced Matt to tell us what's going on."

"I *am* proud of her," Meg said warmly, avoiding his gaze and turning instead to her daughter. "I'm *always* proud of her." Allie beamed. "But what happens to Matt now?"

"Uncle Earl's taking him home with him."

Now, at last, Meg's gaze met his. "You are?"

He couldn't tell if she was impressed or doubtful. He hoped she was impressed. "I sure am. That boy doesn't need to be thrown on strangers right now."

Meg nodded. "You're a good man, Earl Sanders." He felt his chest swell, but before he could do more than smile, she had turned back to Allie. "We need to get home for dinner, honey."

Allie didn't have her mother's qualms. "You come, too, Uncle Earl. Please?"

There'd been a time when Earl wouldn't have hesitated. But now he did, looking at Meg. If she didn't want him...

"Yes," she said, glancing quickly his way. "Come, too, Earl. Vivian's making a big pot of spaghetti and marinara."

"Can't pass that up," he said, when what he really meant was he couldn't pass up an evening with Allie and Meg. "But I have to go make an arrest first." An arrest that would give him a great deal of pleasure.

He and Sam didn't have any trouble finding Dawson. The man was still sitting at the bar in the saloon, knocking back boilermakers. His eyes were reddened and bleary, and amazingly enough, he didn't get obstreperous. Earl had been expecting a fight. Hell, he'd actually been hoping for it. He wouldn't have minded an excuse to land a few well-placed punches on this cretin.

Maybe Dawson sensed that. Whatever the reason, he didn't say a word as they handcuffed him, read him his rights and transported him to jail for booking. He didn't even mutter any threats.

After he and Sam had seen Dawson safely locked up, they went outside. Sam was getting ready to start his patrol, and Earl was planning to go up to the Williams place and deal with the last remaining problem in his life: Meg.

"Hell," said Sam, "that was a disappointment. I

was sure that old souse was going to kick up a fuss. I was hoping I'd be able to charge him with battery on a law enforcement officer.''

In spite of himself, Earl grinned. ''Yeah. Me, too. Probably just as well. I might not have been able to stop myself if he'd provoked me.''

''Yeah, there is that.'' Sam rocked back on his heels and looked up at the fading sky. ''More snow's coming. I can feel it. We'll be dusted again before dawn. See you tomorrow, Earl.''

'''Night, Sam.''

They walked their separate ways to their cars. Earl watched Sam drive off toward the south of town, then climbed into his own car and started it. But he didn't move for several minutes. Instead, he sat thinking about just what he thought he was going to accomplish with Meg tonight. Break through her icy reserve, maybe? Get to the root of what was bothering her? Get her to forgive him?

But maybe the more important question was what did *he* hope to gain? It was a question he asked himself rarely, because most of his life he hadn't felt entitled to much. Oh, what he could work for and pay for, yes, he was entitled to that. But he'd never once gone for the brass ring.

Not even becoming sheriff had struck him that way. He'd run after the old sheriff retired, and with the man's endorsement, which had made him a shoo-in. He hadn't thought of it as going for something beyond his grasp.

He'd learned at a very early age the disappointment of exceeding his reach. And while he was often the first to encourage others to pursue their dreams, he was himself guilty of conservatism in such matters. He generally adjusted his goals and desires to fit what he felt he was capable of and entitled to.

Which, now that he thought about it, made him a chickenshit.

He would have laughed, except that, for some reason, his heart was beginning to pound uncomfortably. He was on the brink of committing himself to a course that might well be disastrous, and that wasn't his usual style.

He thought about Meg and found himself adjusting his desires to his perception of what was possible. Make up with her, go back to their comfortable friendship. That would at least ensure that they would always remain friends. And they could, he was sure, get past what had happened between them the other night, especially since neither of them seemed to really want to remember it. Meg would probably be thrilled to act as if it had never happened.

But was that what he *really* wanted? He asked himself that question with a great deal of trepidation, because he wasn't sure he really wanted to hear the answer. He wasn't accustomed to examining what his desires would be if there were no obstacles to restrain him. It was a lifelong process to pare things down until they were reasonable.

But this was too important. He felt it in his gut and in his heart. He needed to know what it was that he would ask for if there was nothing at all to stand in his way. Because this time he knew he wasn't going to be able to content himself with half measures.

So he looked the question dead in the eye. He

asked himself, "If I could have anything I wanted, anything at all, what would it be?"

The answer came to him silently, an overwhelming hunger in his heart. He looked at it, and now that he was facing it, he knew exactly what it was going to cost him to lose it.

This was one brass ring where it had to be all or nothing. And nothing, this time, looked like a bottomless pit in hell.

But he couldn't hide from it any longer. He had looked at it, faced it, recognized it.

His mind made up, his heart beating uncomfortably, he released the brake and headed for the Williams house. Nothing would ever again be the same.

21

Dinner actually went quite well. Vivian was glad enough to see him, Allie chattered like a chipmunk all the way through the meal, and even Meg relaxed enough to join the conversation and smile.

Which only made it a lot harder for Earl to bring up the things he most wanted to bring up. He didn't want to rock Meg's boat, to bring that pinched look back to her face. He wanted her to keep smiling and talking.

It was a damn good excuse not to do anything difficult.

And he was almost chicken enough to seize it. He waffled all the way through dinner, then was perfectly willing to let Allie be an excuse not to drag Meg away for a private conversation.

But he wasn't a man to avoid doing the difficult thing for long. This was one of the times in his life when he had to bite the bullet, and he knew it. He was just biding his time for the right moment.

And when Allie and Vivian went upstairs, there was no excuse to postpone any longer.

Meg looked at him, as if surprised he wasn't leaving. Well, of course. Since Bill's death, he'd always left when Allie went to bed. Except the other night. The dangerous night. The night she clearly wanted to forget.

But he sat there stubbornly, trying to find the words to broach the issue that was smoldering between them. Trying to find a way to open a topic that terrified him.

He cleared his throat. "Uh... Vivian has sure had a turnaround." He wanted to kick himself. *Vivian.* Yup, bring up the woman's mother. Great entrée to a personal conversation about him and Meg.

"Yes." Meg relaxed a little, as if she was relieved at the direction he'd taken. Man, that was encouraging, to know she was afraid he was going to say what he had every intention of saying. When he got around to it. "She says she's been rethinking her actions."

"From what she told me, that woman had a hard childhood."

"She did. Her dad was a very poor man, a farmer. Just enough land to starve on, he used to say. When she married my father, things got better. He had better land, a bigger farm. It was still a lot of hard work, but not the kind of situation where one bad year could make you go hungry. We did without when things got tight, but we never went hungry."

"That's good. I did some going hungry in my life."

Her face softened, and for an instant he thought she was going to reach out for him. Then she said, "I know you did, Earl. You had a terrible childhood."

He shook his head. "No worse than a lot of kids. But I can understand how those things can affect us."

"Have they affected you?"

"Sure they have."

"How?"

The question he'd had to answer for himself tonight. The answer he didn't really want to give her. But he felt obligated to. Especially considering what he wanted from her. "I tend to lower my sights."

"Lower them? But, Earl, you're the sheriff. That's an elected position. Most people wouldn't have the guts to even try for it."

"I probably wouldn't have myself, if old Bob Sweet hadn't insisted on endorsing me. I won that election because of him."

"But you won the last one because of yourself."

"Maybe."

She frowned, looking at him as if she wasn't happy with what she was hearing. "What else have you lowered your sights on?"

"Oh, lots of things." He tried to shrug it off. "So...are you feeling any better about the past week or so? About Allie and everything?"

She nodded, giving him a look that said she didn't intend to forget what he'd said, or the question he hadn't answered. "We talked about it. The really sad thing is that she's decided she feels sorry for *me* because Bill didn't love *me*."

"Hell." The thought pierced him, too. Not because of Allie, but because of Meg. She deserved a whole lot more than that. She deserved someone to love her better than Bill had. And in the pit of his stomach, he felt a flicker of anger against his old friend. He felt as if the layers of misguided loyalty were burning away, making him see the real toll of Bill's superficiality.

But something else remained, and it made him speak now. "Bill wasn't all bad, Meg."

"No. Nobody is. He had plenty of good points."

"He just wasn't...capable of real depth of feeling. Looking back at it now, I think we stayed friends all these years because I admired him so much."

She nodded. "Probably. He liked to be admired. It was probably one of the strongest impulses he had. Which is why he wasn't a bad person. He needed approval. And my failing was that I stopped giving it to him."

"Why did you do that?"

"Because...you're going to think I'm nuts...but I realized a few years ago that something that happened between us before we got married was...bad. That it wasn't my fault."

"The rape, you mean."

She gasped, and stared at him. "I never told you!"

"Your mother did. What he did was wrong. I can understand that realizing that would have affected your feelings. It sure as hell affected mine. About him, I mean. Because when I was thinking about it, I realized that he *was* capable of that. That Bill was always willing to take what he wanted, and a little resistance was meaningless to him. He took it as a challenge. So, I was thinking about that, and thinking about some of the things he did in high school, and I realized that you were telling the truth. You didn't make it up."

Air escaped her, as if she'd been holding her breath for a long time. "Sometimes I'm not sure I didn't."

He resisted the impulse to go to her and hold her, knowing that it was not yet the right time. But, oh, how he wanted to wrap her in his arms and hold her tight. "You didn't."

"How can you know? You weren't there."

"I know because I know Bill. Sadly enough, it sounds just like him."

She nodded slowly, then rose and walked away from him, finally coming to stand before a bookcase. She stood staring at the books, as if the titles fascinated her. But he noticed that she wrapped her arms around herself as though she were freezing. He also couldn't help noticing her slender lines, the delicate curve of her neck and back, and her gently rounded hips. Things he'd been refusing to notice for years were jumping up to grab his attention right now. At exactly the wrong time.

"Even so," she said finally. "Even so, I shouldn't have let it affect my feelings for him. Damn it, Earl, we'd been married for ten years and I had no serious complaints. None at all. How could I have let that memory poison everything?"

"Maybe because things weren't all that good to begin with. Maybe you weren't as happy as you kept telling yourself."

"I wasn't," she admitted, her voice muffled. "But I told myself that that was the way it was for everyone. That nobody has a perfect marriage."

"I don't suppose anyone does. But there's perfect, and then there's cold. And no matter how guilty I feel about saying it, in a lot of ways, Bill was a cold fish.

He never let anybody ever really get to the heart of him. Except Allie.''

"Except Allie," she agreed. "Well, I'm ashamed to admit it, but I haven't really been grieving a whole lot, either. I've been feeling guilty, but I haven't been grieving. I got over that pretty fast. It's terrible, Earl, but I don't miss Bill. I haven't missed him in months.''

"And you feel guilty about that?"

"Yes, I do. He was my *husband*.''

He stopped himself from shrugging. "Meggie," he said as gently as he could, "I don't think that makes any difference. Whatever happened between you and Bill in the past, all this says is that by the time he died, you weren't in love with him anymore. And that's not a crime. How could it possibly be a crime? Except that we're taught love is forever.''

"Isn't it?" The question was almost bitter.

"No, it's not. Love is something two people have to work at. And if somebody stops working at it, it dies. Or maybe, if one person doesn't feel it, the other person eventually stops feeling it, too. But you didn't do anything wrong. *Feelings* aren't wrong. It's what we do with them that counts.''

"Meaning?"

"Meaning you didn't do anything bad because of the way you felt, Meggie. Not one thing. Believe me, there's no law that says you have to miss Bill a certain way, or for a certain amount of time.''

"Yeah." Slowly, she turned and looked at him. "Then why do I feel like I cheated with you?"

The words hit him like a blow to the gut. Because he'd been wrestling with the same feelings. Because he'd been secretly hoping against hope that Meg wouldn't feel that way. But she did. And the pit of his stomach sank as if it were filled with lead. "I felt the same way," he said finally. "For a while."

"What changed your mind?"

"The simple fact that things have changed, Meg. Bill is gone. He's no longer your husband. You're a single woman now, and that means whatever you and I choose to do has nothing to do with Bill any longer."

She nodded thoughtfully, but he couldn't tell what she was thinking, or whether she believed him. What did it matter, anyway? Logical arguments had little influence over emotions. If she felt she had cheated, she had cheated.

"You're right," she said after a few minutes. "I know you're right. And if you'd been anyone else in the world, I don't think I'd have felt that way."

So his friendship with Bill was standing between them. For the first and only time in his life, he found himself wishing he'd never met Bill Williams. Wishing he didn't have a history with Bill to stick in Meg's craw.

"It feels," she said, "almost incestuous."

Oh, God! His stomach turned over.

"And that's stupid," she continued. "Really stupid. Just because you were Bill's friend..."

"I was *your* friend, too, Meg."

"Yes, you were. All these years I counted on that fact. More, I think, than I counted on the fact that Bill was my husband. In retrospect, I think I always sensed that he wasn't really tied to me, that he was just biding his time."

She closed her eyes, then looked straight at him, a stare that seemed to pierce his soul. "The thing is, Earl, I'm feeling guilty because at least a thousand times in the last fifteen years, I wished I'd met you instead of Bill."

He couldn't breathe. His diaphragm froze in mid-breath, leaving him feeling as winded as if he'd just been punched. He knew he needed to say something, but he was locked between one breath and the next.

"It sounds awful, doesn't it?" she said, plunging ahead as if she wanted to make sure he understood just how awful she really was. "It *was* awful. The thought would flit across my mind and I'd brush it away, the way you brush away a fly, wondering where it came from. Well, I can't pretend it wasn't there any longer. And I can't pretend I don't know where it came from. Maybe the truth is that I was cheating on him all along."

But he didn't see it that way at all. Dragging in air at last, he rose and faced her. "No. Thoughts like that aren't cheating. Thoughts like that come about because we're not happy. Because something essential is missing. And to tell you the God's honest truth, I spent most of the last fifteen years wishing I'd met you first, too."

He watched her pale, then saw the rush of color to her cheeks. He was going about this all wrong, he thought, and he was going to be lucky if she ever spoke to him again. But it was too late to turn back now.

She didn't say anything for so long that he began to fear she was seeking a gentle way to tell him to get lost. He floundered around in his own mind to find something he could say, but instead he found himself considering the abysmal fact that he, who was rarely at a loss, was at a total loss now. Because he cared so much.

She spoke. "Do you think we were awful to feel that way?"

He shook his head, grateful that she'd given him something to focus on. "No. I think what we felt was perfectly natural. It happened. But we didn't act on it. We remained loyal to Bill, so there's nothing to apologize for."

"I guess so."

"Meggie, feelings catch us unawares. They rise up out of nowhere before we even know they're coming. They're not inherently wrong. They're only wrong if we feed them. Nurture them. Encourage them. And neither of us did that. We had these fleeting feelings that we put away as soon as we had them."

"I certainly did. I was ashamed for even thinking it."

"You see?"

"But what now, Earl? What now?"

His hands clenched, and he felt suddenly awkward, too big, too rough, too much the country bumpkin. He didn't have any smooth words or flowery phrases. All he had was what was in his heart.

"What now?" he said. "Well, that depends on you, I guess. Because if I could have anything at all in the whole world, it would be you."

Her eyes widened, and her hand flew to her throat. "Me?"

"You." It was out now, and now that it was out in the open, it didn't seem like a dirty little secret anymore. It seemed like something so beautiful it made him ache. It was so beautiful, in fact, that his fear seemed to be evaporating. "I love you, Meggie. I'm not sure when I started loving you this way, but I know I love you now more than life. I'd do anything for you. Anything at all. All I want in life is to be with you and try to make you happy."

He held his breath, waiting for her answer, expecting her to tell him that he'd misunderstood her, that while she was glad to have him as a friend, she could never consider him as a husband. He was absolutely sure she had to want so much more than a small-town sheriff with bad roots.

But it seemed to him that a little smile had come to her lips, just a hint of it, and something seemed to be leaping to life in her eyes. He wanted to reach out and grab her close, but he sensed, in some indefinable way, that it would not be the right thing to do at this moment. That she had to come to him of her own accord.

"Do you really mean that?" she asked.

"I never meant anything more in my life. I'd marry you in a heartbeat, and I think Allie would be happy if I did, too. I'm sorry Bill died, Meg. I truly am. But he did, and you and I are alive now, and we have a right to live and be happy. Just give me a chance to make you happy, Meggie. Please."

She stepped toward him, a tentative step; then she took another one, more boldly. "Ask me, please," she said quietly. "Bill never asked me."

His heart leaped to the sky, and jubilation filled him. "Meggie, I love you with my whole heart. Will you marry me?"

The smile broke on her face, widening, then crumbling as her eyes filled with tears. "Yes, Earl," she said. "I will be thrilled to marry you."

Enough was enough. He picked her up off her feet and whirled her around in sheer joy, and when she laughed, he felt his heart leap yet again.

"You're sure?" he said more than once. "Meggie, are you really sure? You can handle being married to a cop? And then there's Matt. I was thinking about fostering him. But if you can't handle that—"

She laid a finger over his mouth, silencing him. "The only thing I can't handle, Earl Sanders, is life without you. Everything else will take care of itself."

He held her close to his heart then, for a long time, drinking in the comfort and joy of being so close to her, drinking in the warmth with which she filled his heart.

A little while later they went upstairs to wake Allie and ask her what she thought. The girl leaped off the bed, as best she could with a cast, and hugged them both, squealing for joy.

Meg looked down at her daughter, searching Allie's face carefully. She wanted to be absolutely certain that she wasn't overlooking something important because she was so swept away by her own feelings. She didn't want to repeat her mistakes of the past year.

"Are you sure, honey?" she asked her daughter. "You don't feel...left out or anything?"

Allie shook her head vigorously. "I was afraid for a little while that I might lose you, but not anymore. I know you love me."

Meg's heart swelled, and she hugged Allie until her arms ached.

Then Allie promptly announced she was going on-line to tell all her friends.

Vivian accepted the news with grace and even a small smile. "Can't say I couldn't tell which way the wind was blowing," she said. "Well, I guess you won't be needing me anymore."

Meg and Earl exchanged glances. Then Meg said, "Of course I need you, Mom. I'll always need you. But are you sure you want to help take care of so many people?"

"So many? Who don't I know about?"

"Matt Dawson," Earl said. "I'm thinking about fostering him."

"Hmmph. Well, he's no trouble at all. Does my heart good to see a boy eat like that."

"Then you'll stay?" Earl said.

Vivian cocked an eyebrow at him. "Pretty generous offer from a man I said some nasty things to."

"I've forgotten them, Vivian. Besides, I've been called worse in my day. We'll just pretend it never happened."

Later, Meg and Earl curled up together in bed, not making love yet—that would come later—but reveling in their closeness. And Meg confided something that made Earl feel like the luckiest man on earth.

"I've never been this happy, ever," she said, nestling her head on his shoulder. "Never, except the night Allie was born."

That put him in pretty good company, he thought as he watched the September snow falling outside the window. Pretty good company indeed.

RACHEL LEE

MIRA